DON'T *Regret Me*

A *Bridge City Beats* NOVEL

STEPHANIE LOUISE

For my friends who became family.

Contents

I

Zack

May 1996

"Don't fucking do it, man." Adam belched and set his beer on the desk, the scents of malted hops and salty bar peanuts escaping his lips. "You'll regret it."

The opening band's wailing guitars and thudding drumbeats vibrated the back-office walls of Escape, an ancient but awesome dive bar in Southeast Portland. Zack had slipped the manager a hundred bucks to let him use the phone, but Adam tracked him down like a spiky-haired bloodhound before he could go through with the call.

"Fuck off, Adam!" Zack held the receiver in a death grip while his best friend tried to pry it from his hand, almost knocking over the beer. "Go back to dry-humping your girlfriend on the dance floor."

Tired of the struggle, Zack socked him in the stomach to get him to back off. It wasn't hard enough to hurt much, just to steal his breath and make him understand how determined Zack was to make that call—the one he'd started dialing a thousand times. He always stopped before pressing the last number—a seven—though it felt anything but lucky.

Pressing it meant rejection.

Again.

Adam's breath left in a rush as he clutched his stomach. "Fine, dickhead!" he wheezed. "Have at it! What are you going to say? Hey, Mandy, I've had seven beers, and I'm a thousand miles away. Wanna fuck?"

Zack's fist ached to throw another punch, but that made him laugh. "What, no good? Seems like a panty-dropper to me."

Adam had a point, the fucker. What would Zack say if he had the balls to press that final seven, and she picked up?

I just need to hear your voice.

I still think about you every day.

Adam's expression softened, but his grip on the phone didn't budge. "Trust me, you don't want to do this. Nothing's changed, and she made it clear she's never leaving Denver. You gonna move there? How when we're writing and recording all the time in Portland? We're about to sign a new contract, for fuck's sake. Push through the beer haze and *think* about it."

Zack had done all he could to *not* think about the impossibility of a relationship with her in the seventeen months since the breakup.

It wouldn't work.

It couldn't work.

Nothing would change that. But it was harder to remember the reasons with his brain soaked in beer and his heart still bleeding for the only woman he'd ever loved.

Yeah, *loved*. Zack "One-Night-Only" Maine fell in love. Hard. They'd only had seven perfect days together, but time didn't mean shit. How many couples were together for decades and couldn't stand each other?

He'd never been in love before Mandy Reid crashed into his life. But he knew what it was when, on the night she broke his heart, he seriously considered doing the unthinkable—leaving his band and moving to the base of the Rocky Mountains for her.

"Sleep on it," Adam said, tugging on the receiver. This time, it slipped easily from Zack's fingers as the fight drained from him. "If you still want to call her when you're sober, do it. I think it'll just hurt more, but maybe your last conversation didn't give you the closure you need. Regardless, drunk-dialing's not the way to go."

He didn't want closure. He wanted her.

Zack's eyes stung with tears of defeat as he sank into the chair behind the desk. "I really fucking miss her." He never cried, not even when his grandfather died. This loss hit so much harder because the person he missed was still living and breathing but just as impossible to reach.

An image of her waving goodbye through the back window of a cab flashed in his mind—her sad, red-rimmed eyes locked on his as the car pulled away.

The memory still hurt like a fresh wound, the pain relentless and raw as the first tears slid to his chin. Sure, the beer was partly to blame for the rare show of emotion, but mostly, it was the hollow, aching pit in his chest.

"I know, brother." Adam clapped his shoulder. "But you have to let her go. It's been long enough. You can start by fucking her out of your brain. That blonde in the Sex Pistols shirt was good to go. I can't join you, but I'll be your wingman."

Zack scoffed as he wiped his damp cheeks, still shocked as hell that Adam—the dude who'd once banged twins on the roof of the Hollywood Palladium while high on mushrooms—had turned monogamous and boring.

Okay, not *boring*. He was still always up for a good time; he just kept his dick in his pants unless Kyla was around. Then his dick was in her. *A lot*. And they sure as hell weren't quiet about it.

Zack had plenty of filthy memories of the night the three of them shared seven months ago—his dick between his best friend's lips, Kyla's virgin ass gripping his cock... It was one for the books. But for Zack, it was a history book. He'd be up for another threesome if they asked, but he knew they wouldn't risk shit getting complicated.

When had sex gone from a fun, harmless hobby to something so serious and sacred?

Of course, he knew damn well if he had Mandy back, he wouldn't want to share her either. Imagining the unworthy dickheads she'd probably been with since their breakup made his hands clench.

"Thinking about hitting me again?" Adam put up his fists. "I'll hit you back this time, asshole."

"Why can't I just get over her?" Zack swiped the beer and drained it, hoping it would shut off the crushing pain in his chest. He had no luck with the first seven, but maybe number eight would do the trick.

But if he could drink or fuck her out of his brain, she would've been out a long time ago.

"Because she made you feel things you'd never felt before. Like Kyla did to me. If she ditched me now, I'd be a miserable mess, too." Adam took the empty bottle from Zack's hand and tossed it into the trash. "But you can't keep doing this. How many times this month have I had to drag your hungover ass out of bed to rehearse for the tour? You've always been a bit off the rails, but it's getting worse. Even your playing's suffering. Is it just missing Mandy or something else?"

"My bedroom's right down the hall from yours, Adam. Maybe I'm always exhausted because you and Kyla keep me up half the fucking night with your sex noises and weird techno boning soundtrack." He took a cigarette from a pack on the desk and lit it, taking a long, slow drag to savor the burn before exhaling a thick cloud.

"Cut the bullshit." Adam nudged his arm, sending a jagged trail of smoke toward the cheap paneled ceiling. "Tell me what's wrong."

The truth was, Zack was sick and tired. Sick of falling asleep in empty beds that reeked of cheap perfume and stale cigarette smoke. Tired of settling for a few hours of shallow naked fun after Mandy opened his eyes to what sex could be when there were feelings involved beyond lust.

Since he was fifteen, playing backyard parties with his friends for beer money, girls had been all over him like honey on toast. He ate up the attention, taking full advantage of the many perks of being a young, hot musician and, eventually, a rich and famous rockstar. If you only get one life, you might as well live it up while you can, right?

He spent thirteen wild years living it up, believing he was happy as he fucked his way around the world. Between gigs, sex was a pleasant escape that pushed any ugly, lonely feelings far into the background. Those women were only interested in the *idea* of him, not the real deal, which was fair since he was only interested in getting off and getting out.

After Mandy, that wasn't enough anymore.

And when Adam announced last month that he was moving out of the house the guys had shared for four years to move in with Kyla, it was a reminder that everyone's lives were going forward while Zack was stuck, clinging to the past. If he didn't find a way to move on, he'd be all alone in a half-empty mansion with nothing but regrets and his spinning, fucked-up thoughts. The image was so tragic he could puke.

He looked up at his friend. Adam's expression was etched with concern—his brows pinched together as he frowned—but, as always, free of judgment. More importantly, he looked ready to listen. It helped that his usual distraction was in the other room, probably still taking shots of peach schnapps and sweating off her makeup on the dance floor.

Their lead singer, Tyler, was easy to talk to, but now he had a wife, a kid, and no time for Zack's problems. It was impossible not to mourn the simpler days when the three of them hung out all the time, and all that mattered was music.

Uncomfortable with the growing distance between him and his partnered-up bandmates, Zack had kept his selfish, inconvenient emotions locked tight.

Now, he was ready to talk.

"I feel so fucking alone."

Saying the words made him feel relieved and pathetic all at once. Despite having the best friends in the world and an army of loyal fans, he'd struggled most of his life with an emptiness nothing would fill. At least, nothing that lasted longer than an orgasm or lingered after the booze wore off. His connection with Mandy offered the first reprieve that didn't begin and end with sex or substances.

"Now that Ty's married and you're with Kyla," he continued, "I'm the third or fifth wheel every goddamn time we go out." He put a hand up before Adam could interrupt. "I know I sound like a dick. I'm glad you guys are happy, but it kills me that I'll probably never have that again."

Watching his two best friends fall in love constantly reminded him of what he was missing. He'd give anything to have it back. The problem was that he had no clue how to make it happen. Even if he felt a spark with someone else someday, how could he open himself up again, knowing how much it hurt when it crashed and burned?

"Bullshit. Of course, you can. Getting wasted on a Wednesday night and hiding in the back-office of a club feeling sorry for yourself isn't the way." Adam pointed at the door. "Ms. Perfect might be shaking her ass on that dance floor right now, but you're too blitzed to notice her."

"I've tried. I talk to them, laugh at their stupid jokes, and all I can think is that they aren't *her*."

He also had to wonder about their intentions. Did they want to swipe the cash from his wallet when his pants were on the floor and he left to take a piss? Were they hoping to get favors from him to boost their career? Did they want to fuck him to sell a dirty story to the tabloids?

Since Tomorrow Mourning's debut album was swept up in the early ripples of the grunge wave five years ago and exploded, he'd experienced all the above and plenty of other sketchy bullshit that prevented him from trusting people outside his circle of friends.

Mandy had been the only exception. She was always around musicians and wasn't dazzled by platinum records and Billboard charts. She wanted to know about his family, his favorite movies, and what he dreamed about. And made him comfortable enough to let down the armor of his ego and be himself.

"This is why you need to stick to whiskey," Adam said. "When you start thinking about that girl, beer sends you into a fucking doom spiral."

"I don't want to think about her at all!" Zack's shouting drowned out the drum solo rattling the office window. "I drank so much so I can fucking forget."

Adam breathed a heavy sigh, his blurry form perched on the edge of the desk with his arms crossed. "Let's figure this out. What does Mandy have that the other women you meet don't?"

Zack scoffed. "Everything. She has her shit together. She's smart and had big plans for her life that probably shoved her even further out of my league.

And she didn't give two fucks about my status or money." He never thought a woman would accept him, flaws and all, but Mandy made it clear she wanted the real man, not the tabloid myth. And he trusted her, something that wasn't easy to come by in his world. "On top of that, she's hotter than a goddamn volcano in July. I'll never get another shot with someone like her."

"Maybe if you got *your* shit together, you could." Adam kicked Zack's boot with the tip of his shoe, snagging his attention before it drifted down another twist of hopelessness in the beer doom spiral. "If you think someone like Mandy's out of your league, change into the guy who isn't."

Zack scrubbed a hand over his face as he let out a bitter laugh. "How the hell am I supposed to do that? Go to Charm School and get a brain transplant?"

He was a nice enough guy but could be crass, moody, and impulsive—qualities not everyone found appealing.

"No, smart ass. Start by cutting out the live fast, die young bullshit. Quit drinking so damn much and avoid women who want you for the wrong reasons. If I can do it, you sure as hell can."

Again, Adam was right. Even through the beer haze, Zack knew things had to change. *He* had to change. He'd be thirty in two years, and it was getting harder to slap on a fake smile and pretend the wild, reckless life he'd been living for over a decade was still enough to make him happy. Even before Mandy, it was wearing thin.

He couldn't do it anymore.

"Mandy was cool as hell," Adam said. "I'm not denying that. But do you honestly think she'd want you to still be miserable after all this time? Or would she want you to move on?"

Zack already knew the answer to that. One of the last things she said to him was that she hoped he'd never forget her, but he had to let her go. She told him to find someone who'd give him everything she couldn't from a thousand miles away. And she thanked him for disrupting the tidy, buttoned-up life she thought made her happy, showing her what else was possible if she were brave enough to claim it.

What she didn't say was that she loved him, too. He swore he saw it in her eyes, felt it in the way she touched him, but when he said it right before she climbed into that cab on the best and worst day of his life, she didn't say it back.

Whether that was a blessing or a curse, he still didn't know.

"We're about to fly to Europe for six weeks." Adam squeezed his shoulder and gave it a little shake. "We'll get to hang with all our friends, play massive shows, and see epic shit. Think of all there is to look forward to instead of looking backward."

Zack exhaled a long, steady stream of smoke. "Sure, I'll get right on that."

"You fucking love Italy." Adam grabbed the cigarette, took a hit, and passed it back. "We had a blast the last time we toured there. In between shows, you can drown your sorrows in pasta, wine, and hot European chicks with sexy accents. You might meet someone you like even more."

Zack huffed a humorless laugh as he ashed the cigarette into the potted plant beside the filing cabinet. "Like that could ever fucking happen."

Regardless of how impossible that seemed, he needed to stop torturing himself with memories of the past. He'd never be capable of anything beyond a one-night stand if he didn't. And if the tour suffered or they lost their seven-figure, three-album contract because he couldn't get his head in the game, he'd disappoint his bandmates, their fans, and everyone else who was counting on him.

Enough was enough.

For their sake and his sanity, he had to grow up and move on.

But how?

He nodded along to the beat of the Tool cover being played in the other room as he thought. When the idea struck, he began opening drawers in the desk, rifling through their contents—mostly invoices and filing folders.

"What the hell are you doing?" Adam took the cigarette and crushed it into the plant's dirt before Zack accidentally lit the room on fire.

Mandy swore by lists to declutter her mind or put a tough task into smaller, more manageable steps. Right now, he needed to do both.

When he found a notebook and pen, he wrote *Shit to Change* at the top of a blank sheet in big, bold letters. He sensed Adam reading over his shoulder but didn't care. After fourteen years of friendship, there were no secrets between them.

What were the biggest things holding him back from having something real? That was easy. His dad told him all the time.

1. Stop fucking groupies, barflies, and other women who don't give a shit about me.

2. Don't drink so fucking much.

"If number three is to stop cursing, you've already beefed it." Adam smirked at Zack's death glare. "Sorry. Seriously, this is a good idea. Keep going."

3. Stop being a selfish asshole.

That one he heard in his mother's voice as he wrote it, minus the cursing. It was something she hammered into his brain every time he was late to holiday dinners, forgot someone's birthday, or dropped a wad of cash on something ridiculous. The last time he bought a new car, she told him he could've saved thirty-six starving kids instead as if she'd just done the math in his driveway.

Zack's fingers froze, the muscles protesting the most difficult one, but it had to be done. The only alternative was to accept being alone and miserable, drowning his sorrows in temporary pleasures that only made things worse.

He touched the pen's tip to the paper and wrote.

4. Get over Mandy.

Staring at the words made his eyes burn again, tears and alcohol blurring the letters together. Committing the task to paper made it feel more definite and final. Zack could be a lazy, procrastinating shit, but when he set his mind to something, he made it happen. It was how he went from the fifteen-year-old stoner punk buying his first bass for fifty bucks at a swap meet to touring the world and playing to audiences the size of small cities.

It wouldn't be easy, but he'd get through every item on the list.

As the cold, hollow ache returned, every cell in his body screamed for relief. He grabbed the bottle of whiskey poking out from beneath a pile of paperwork in the open desk drawer and took a long, burning swig.

"What the fuck are you doing?" Adam smacked his arm, spilling a few drops on his leather jacket.

"You're the one who said to stick to whiskey." Zack grinned around the mouth of the bottle as he took another drink.

He'd work on making all the changes he'd laid out—starting tomorrow.

Zack tore the paper from the notebook and shoved it into his pocket. He stood on unsteady feet and staggered sideways before Adam grabbed his arm, keeping him upright. "Let's go find that blonde."

2

Mandy

The petals on the bouquet of irises on Mandy's desk were turning brown and wilting, but she wasn't ready to toss them. They were a thirty-second birthday gift from Ted, her boss for the last thirteen years. He'd owned Rollin' Rockies for two decades before she came along, and everything Mandy knew about running a rock club and dealing with rowdy, eccentric musicians, she'd learned from him—a mentor and second father of sorts.

It certainly wasn't the pay that kept her around. Ted's energy and her love of music made living in a tiny bungalow and driving an old beater worthwhile.

She grabbed a pen, scanning her trusty checklist for the following night. Three bands were scheduled, and the headliner was an up-and-coming indie group from Olympia, recently featured in *Spin*. They'd requested two cases of Rainier beer backstage, a meatless food spread, and only blue lights to be used during their set.

Some bands were super high maintenance and took advantage of the club's generosity, but luckily, tomorrow's requests were pretty basic and easy to fulfill. She'd already handled the beer and food and spoken with the club's lighting guy. The show had sold-out in two days, so she'd also scheduled a few extra bartenders, servers, and bouncers to handle the enormous crowd. With an upper level of seats and the expansive floor space below, the club's capacity was fifteen hundred. Sold-out shows would be chaos if understaffed.

With every detail on her list checked, it was time to go home.

There was a soft knock on her office door even though it was open wide, as always. Mandy lifted her gaze from the list to a twenty-something guy with neon green hair grazing his shoulders and a pierced lip.

"Ash!" She smiled and waved him in. "You were amazing last night." She realized it'd been a long time since she'd used those words to refer to something other than a musical performance.

Ash was the lead singer of the previous night's headliner, Crunching Gravel. It wasn't the best band name she'd ever heard, but it was certainly not the worst. That title goes to The Cherry Pops, a punk trio of barely legal girls in lingerie. Ted, being the decent man he is, requested that they put on actual clothing to avoid a riot.

"Thanks, Mandy." One side of his mouth tipped up as he sank into the chair across from hers, the large oak desk between them. "We appreciate the gig. Tough to get booked at big clubs these days unless you're a Nirvana clone."

She laughed. "Sad but true. Grunge is having a moment for good reason, but we aim to book more diverse talent."

"That's why I'm here." He dragged his fingers through his shaggy green locks. "My buddy's band, Toxic Shade, could use some exposure, and I was hoping you'd check them out. They're what would happen if you stuck The Clash, Soundgarden, and a shit ton of weed in a blender."

"That paints quite an image." Mandy grinned as she leaned back in her chair, her interest piqued. "Got a demo?"

He dug into his pocket and slapped a cassette on her desk. "They're fucking killing it. They just need stage time. And a manager."

The last three words echoed in her brain. Countless bands who deserved a shot at the big leagues came through the club, but getting representation was tough. They aren't interested if you don't have connections or look and sound like whatever trend was raking in cash.

Getting into band management was her biggest dream because she wanted to help those underdogs succeed. She'd give it a shot if she didn't need the security of a steady paycheck so desperately. For now, it was too risky.

"I'm happy to give it a listen." She slid open the top drawer of her desk and set the cassette inside. Ash's eyebrows jumped as his gaze snagged on something in the drawer.

"Holy shit." He leaned forward. "Is that a backstage pass from a Tomorrow Mourning show?"

She should've tossed it ages ago, but she liked having proof that she wasn't always the dull, stuffy rule-follower. The pass reminded her she possessed a wild side, even if it'd been forced back into dormancy. And, of course, it reminded her of Zack.

As her fingers grazed the plastic over his face in the band photo, memories she tried hard to forget rushed in—sipping champagne beside him in a private jet, the irresistible spark of mischief in his eyes as he dared her to stage-dive, the warmth of his leather jacket draped over her shoulders.

"Yeah." Mandy shut the drawer as her heart clenched in her chest, hoping he'd drop it. "I have to get home, but I'll listen to the tape first thing tomorrow and get back to you."

"Can I see the pass? They're one of my top three of all time. Did you meet the guys?"

She sighed, opening the drawer and taking out the laminate. "Yeah. It was a long time ago."

Not long enough.

Her other exes were purged from her heart and mind a few weeks after a breakup. Not Zack. He was different in every conceivable way, leaving an indelible mark she couldn't shake. His vibrant, up-for-anything spirit was infectious, and when she was by his side, she'd never felt so young and alive. No one had ever made her laugh so hard or overwhelmed her with pleasure so completely that her overactive mind went gloriously blank.

Getting to know him during their week together was like opening a pile of tiny presents one by one, feeling herself falling for him a little further with every discovery.

Until the last day blew it all to shit.

Part of her hoped she'd one day wake up and magically be over him. A bigger part never wanted to let him go.

Ash took the pass, examining every detail with wide eyes. "This was from the 'Stumble' tour. Fuck, you're lucky. What were they like?"

Mandy fiddled with the corner of the latest copy of *Rolling Stone* magazine that sat on her desk. "Tyler's pretty serious but kind. He's good at keeping the other guys in line. Extremely talented, of course. And a chain-smoker." She read he'd had a baby with the lead guitarist for Killing Daisies, so hopefully, he kicked the habit for his daughter. "Adam's as wild as the tabloids claim and has a great sense of humor. He taps his feet like he always has a drum beat in his head."

"And Zack?"

She sat back in her chair, crossing her arms over her chest. "Zack is…" It wasn't an easy sentence to complete. Like Adam, Zack was as wild as the tabloids made him seem, but there was so much more to him than that. "One of a kind. Smarter than he gives himself credit for. Sweeter than he gives himself credit for, too. And funny, protective. He's the guy you'd want on your side in a fight or manning the stereo at your party."

Zack was always confident and unapologetically himself—two more qualities she admired and envied.

And missed like crazy.

Unfortunately, some of his less admirable qualities made any sort of relationship impossible.

"Damn, I'm jealous. If I ever met them, I'd lose my shit." Ash's teeth clicked against his silver lip ring as he talked. "Anyway, thanks again. Let me know what you think of the tape." He handed back the pass, pushed off his chair, and waved as he left.

Male voices chatting and laughing echoed in the hallway before her boss, Ted, appeared in her doorway.

"Nice young man." Ted smiled, but it trembled at the edges. "Can we talk?"

Mandy gestured to the chair Ash had vacated. "Of course."

He closed the door. He *never* closed her door. The back of her neck tingled as he settled into the seat with a heavy sigh.

"We go way back, my friend." His brittle smile disappeared. "I don't know how I ever ran this club before you came along. You've become an essential part of this old place. It's heart and soul. I mean that."

Her head cocked. "I appreciate the praise, but... What's wrong?"

He sighed again, heavier this time. "Times are tough, kiddo. Between the backstage renovations and Ella's medical bills, I tapped out my savings and retirement fund. So, I made a few investments, hoping to boost them back up. They failed, and it's put me in a bad spot."

"Oh, no." She frowned as his shoulders drooped and fine lines crinkled around his eyes. He was so upbeat most of the time that it always threw her when he was in distress. Even after his wife Ella's MS diagnosis, he stayed positive, finding the best doctors and sharing frequent treatment updates with an optimistic grin. "Will you be okay?"

He shrugged. "I will now. That's why I'm here. As you know, the plan was for my son to buy the club after I retired, but he can't afford to take it over now, and I need the cash. I got an offer to sell a while back and turned it down. When he upped his offer, I couldn't pass it up."

"You're..." Mandy struggled to swallow as her throat constricted. "Selling the club?"

"It's already sold. I should've told you sooner, but you have enough stress, and I wanted to make sure the deal wouldn't fall through."

"Ted, this place means everything to you."

He waved a dismissive hand, but his glassy eyes reflected the anguish of his decision.

What did this mean for her? Was she out of a job? She couldn't let her mind shuffle through all the terrible things that would happen if that were the case.

One consequence stubbornly poked through anyway–*I'll lose my house.*

"It used to," he said. "My passion for it's just not there anymore. I'm almost sixty-three and tired. Most new music sounds like noise to me, and the bands deserve better than I can give them now."

"But..." Her mind raced in a million directions, none of them good. "What if they tear it down? Or strip it and turn it into a Kmart or something? Or even worse, a damn country bar." She shuddered at the thought. "Denver needs this club to keep the rock scene alive."

While the Pacific Northwest was the incubator for the grunge and Riot Grrl movements, Denver's diverse scene included folk, indie-pop, and some of the most powerful, innovative voices in punk and alternative rock. Mandy loved it all, but loud, raw rock and roll would always have her heart, and she was proud to work somewhere that celebrated it. The city and its artists couldn't lose that stage.

A genuine smile tugged at his lips but didn't reach his eyes. "Denver needs *you* to keep the scene alive. You live and breathe music, always have. Helping bands find and grow their fanbase is your passion, and you're incredible at it. Never let anything rob you of that fire."

She swiveled side-to-side in her chair as her knee bounced. "What will you do?"

Ted chuckled, his eyes brightening. "Play with my grandkids, read more books, plant a garden. Don't you worry about me." He pulled a folded paper from his pocket and slid it across the desk before letting go.

Mandy picked it up, unfolded it, gasped, and slapped it back down. "No. I can't accept this."

She slid the check back in front of him with shaking, hesitant hands. Was it a severance? Ten thousand dollars would pay a lot of bills, but then what? It wasn't enough to live on if she gave band management a try and failed. She'd done the math and needed at least five times that much to take the risk.

She had a college degree, but that didn't mean her career opportunities would be endless. The harsh reality was that music majors often ended up in dead-end minimum-wage jobs on the outskirts of the industry. Or something that made a bit more but didn't involve music at all, which would almost be worse. When that money ran out, she'd be scrambling to find work that would cover a mortgage and all her other expenses.

He slid the check back to her. "It's not what you think. The new owner wants to keep you on. I made sure of it."

That was somewhat of a relief, but she wouldn't feel truly secure until she got to know the new owner and received the same reassurance from him.

"When Ella got sick," he continued, "you picked up my slack before I could even ask, taking on much more than I should've allowed. Consider this the well-earned bonus I was never able to give you." He tapped the check with his fingertip. "You deserve this and so much more. Take it."

The idea of coming to work and not seeing Ted's smiling face made tears prick her eyes. She slid the check into her purse and stood, moving around her desk and pulling him into a bear hug.

"Thank you." She blinked back the tears threatening to spill and squeezed him tight. "I'll miss you. And don't think I won't pop by your house to harass you and Ella now and then."

He let her go with a warm grin. "I'm counting on it. I'm sure her baking skills have something to do with it, but I know you kinda like me, too."

Mandy laughed, swiping a knuckle beneath her lashes. "That woman does make a mean lemon lavender bundt cake."

The door swung open. A tall, broad-shouldered man in a suit stood in her doorway. His dirty blond hair was slicked-back and stiffened with gel, like weathered straw in a hay bale. His expression was flat, and his sharp gaze locked on Mandy in a way that made her instantly uncomfortable.

"Can I help you?" she asked, stunned that someone would enter her office without permission.

The man thrust his hand out. "James Sutter. Mandy Reid, yes?"

"Yes." Her brows furrowed, and she looked to Ted for an explanation.

He cleared his throat. "I apologize. I was about to tell Mandy you were here and introduce you two. Just didn't get the chance yet." He turned to her. "James is the new owner of the club. I hope you'll get along as well as we always have."

"I'm sure we will," James said with an odd lilt to his voice that she wasn't sure how to interpret.

Ted touched her shoulder. "Mandy keeps this place going. She's great with the talent and puts out fires like a champ."

She knew he meant she was great at handling challenging, unexpected situations, but once, she'd done it literally. On a packed Saturday night, the lead singer of a hardcore punk band squirted lighter fluid on his camo cargo pants while onstage, and his bassist lit them on fire. Mandy made a beeline for the nearest fire extinguisher and aimed it at the fire while the flaming idiot screamed into a microphone. She appreciated theatrics and creative expression, but arson was a hard limit. She stopped the show and spent ten minutes yelling at them backstage for endangering everyone in the club. It also earned them a lifetime ban.

While accepting of all shades of weird, she ran a tight ship.

Mandy smiled at her new boss, knowing how essential it was to make a good first impression. She watched as his gaze flicked to her chest and back up again. It was blink-and-you'd-miss-it fast, but she caught it. Her first impression of him wasn't so great between that and barging into her office.

Mr. Sutter's eyebrow lifted. "From what I've heard from you and others in the industry, she has quite a reputation as a hard worker. I hope my approach to running things won't clash with hers."

That last bit worried her. Ted's management style was pretty hands-off, and he trusted her to get things done without micromanaging. Hopefully, Mr. Sutter would do the same.

Ted rubbed his hands together, a nervous glint in his eye. "Well, we have paperwork to finish, and I need to get home to my better half." He hugged Mandy again. "See you around, kiddo."

She squeezed him hard before letting go. "Definitely. Take care of yourself, Teddy Bear."

His smile grew at that. She'd given him the nickname years ago, and after a while, everyone on the staff used it, too. He was a kind, generous man with a big heart, and she hated to see him go. He was such a vital, ever-present part of the place that his leaving seemed too impossible to be real. She could've prepared herself for the change if she'd known this day was coming.

Again, Ted's eyes glossed with tears as he walked out of her office, maybe for the last time.

A hug goodbye wasn't enough. If the new owner didn't object, she'd give Ted a proper sendoff with a massive retirement party, filling the venue with everyone who loved him. Countless rockstars making millions owed their careers to his tireless dedication to promoting talent. His connections with local reps and producers ran deep, and when he believed in you, he made sure your music reached the right ears.

There was so much about him she'd miss.

Mr. Sutter turned to her from the doorway. "Carve out an hour tomorrow after lunch to discuss operations moving forward. My office isn't ready yet, so we'll meet here."

Mandy already had a packed schedule, but she'd make it work. What choice did she have? "Looking forward to it." She watched her new boss's back as he followed Ted down the hallway.

Tomorrow, she'd do her best to get to know the man replacing someone irreplaceable.

It had to go well because if she lost this job, she might as well give up on her dream of managing bands someday. Even worse, the safe, secure life she'd worked hard to build would completely fall apart.

3

Zack

The phone rang beside Zack's head, and he groaned in protest before answering. "What?"

"That's how you answer the phone, Zachary?"

He sat up in bed, leaning against the black padded headboard. "Hey, Dad. Sorry. Just woke up."

"It's one in the afternoon, son."

"Late night. What's up?"

"*What's up* is that you need to bring your mother back some of those amaretto cookies you got her the last time you were in Rome."

Zack rubbed his eyes and let out a big yawn. "Why isn't she asking me?"

"Because apparently you... spent some time with the daughter of a friend of hers last night. A friend from *bible study*, Zachary. There were photos of the two of you necking at some bar, and your mother found them on the web this morning."

It had to be the blonde in the Sex Pistols shirt. She didn't seem very pious when she was swallowing his cock in a coat closet.

"Shit." Zack winced. "Sorry, Dad. About the cursing and the photos. Haven't been myself lately."

"Really? Seems par for the course to me."

Zack laughed, shrugging a shoulder. "Fair enough."

"Look. You're an adult, and while I'm incredibly proud of your success, I understand that you're faced with... unique temptations in your line of work. Although we don't agree with many of your choices regarding those temptations, I try not to judge them. You know that. But when it affects your mother—"

"Got it. Don't be stupid in public." He knew he also had to stop being stupid in private, mostly for his own sake.

It took a lot to earn his mom's approval, so Zack had stopped trying years ago. The last time she smiled about something he'd done was when he paid off their mortgage. She usually just scowled in disappointment at his leather jacket, ripped jeans, and "sinful indulgences."

"I'd appreciate it. Why haven't you felt like yourself?"

As a minister, his dad had counseled people with problems for over twenty years, including Zack. Might as well add his advice to Adam's from the night before.

"Remember Mandy?"

Silence. "Of course. I wish I'd had the chance to meet her, but from what you've said, she's a wonderful woman. Have you become reacquainted?" The hope brightening his tone was about to be crushed.

"I wish." Zack slid a cigarette from his pack on the nightstand and lit it. "I need to let her go for good, but I don't know how."

"Why not reach out and try again?"

Now that he was sober, he knew how stupid that would be.

When Mandy returned to Denver after their week together, she ignored his calls and messages for eight days before finally picking up. The conversation lasted three hours. She said she'd shut him out because she thought a clean break would be easier.

But she answered that day because she missed him. They reminisced about their time together, talked about their families, and she even played him a few songs on her keyboard. It gave him hope that they'd make it work.

They talked nearly every night for two more months before she said she couldn't do it anymore. A long-distance relationship wasn't enough for her, so they needed to move on.

He had no right to disrupt her life now when he still wasn't the man she deserved. And reaching out last night after chugging enough beer to drown an alley cat wouldn't have inspired her to give up her job and life in Denver to move to Portland for him. It might've even earned him a restraining order.

"Because the distance between Portland and Denver hasn't changed, and neither have I. Not yet, at least. I want to kick old habits so I'm not alone the rest of my life, but I don't know how to do that either."

"If I tell you to pray for guidance, would you listen?"

Zack hit his cigarette, releasing the smoke in a huffed laugh. "What else you got?"

His dad grumbled into the receiver. "Reflect on what you'd like to change, and decide to do it for yourself, no one else. Examine ways to alter your routines and lifestyle to encourage those changes. If you want to drink less, stop going to bars. If you want to stop engaging in meaningless sexual encounters, stop putting yourself in situations where you're drunk, lonely, and surrounded by beautiful women."

"So, become a monk?"

"Zachary." His dad's tone said his patience was wearing thin.

"Sorry." He took another drag of his cigarette and crushed the glowing ember into an ashtray. "Why am I still hung up on her after all this time? How do I change *that*?"

"Start by not drowning your feelings in sex and alcohol. You still feel strongly for her because she showed you what's possible if you put your life in order. And no, that doesn't mean becoming a monk. It means proving to yourself and the next woman you care about that you can be faithful, relied on, and trusted. That you can put others before yourself."

"What if I don't have it in me?" He'd stayed faithful to Mandy for a week but hadn't been tested long-term. How could he predict his feelings after being with the same person for months or years?

"Listen, son." His tone was gentler this time. "Do you remember when you were twelve, and your mother caught that terrible flu in the summer? She was bedridden for two weeks. While I was working, you made her soup, did laundry, and kept the house clean so she could rest. Instead of running around with friends, riding bikes, and enjoying the sunshine, you put your mother's needs before your own and never complained. When you love someone, you have it in you to step up. When the right woman comes along, you will be the man I know you can be."

Zack appreciated the confidence, especially since his own had checked out lately. His dad always believed in him no matter what shit he pulled as a kid and beyond.

"Thanks, Dad."

"You're welcome. Quit those cigarettes, okay? And don't forget your mother's cookies. Give her a few days to fume before you call and apologize for embarrassing her."

"You got it. Anything else mom wants she won't ask me for?"

"Yes. Grandchildren."

Zack laughed, the sound rough from the smoke. "So just the cookies then, got it. I'm going to guzzle a gallon of coffee now. Keep it real, Pops." He laughed harder at his dad's mumbled prayer for patience before hanging up.

The brutal hangover made his head throb as he slid out of bed.

"Fucking beer," he groaned.

He hit the bathroom and felt a few notches better than dogshit after a shower. As he walked out, he caught the scent of coffee in the air. After pulling on a pair of black sweatpants, he headed to the kitchen for a caffeine fix.

"Morning, sunshine," Adam said with an obnoxious, taunting smirk. His spiked hair was dyed electric blue.

"Fuck off. You look like Sonic the Hedgehog."

Adam laughed as he pointed at a pan on the stove. "Kyla dyed it. And she made coffee and eggs because she's a fucking angel."

She walked into the kitchen wearing a pair of boxers and Adam's favorite Iggy Pop T-shirt. "And you earned it by fucking like the devil." She smacked Adam's ass cheek, and he shot her a dirty grin that said she'd be getting more before she drove home to Corvallis.

Zack rolled his eyes, grateful he was too irritated to get turned on by her comment. He liked Kyla, and she was great for Adam, but hanging around his best friend and the chick they'd shared in what was supposed to be a typical, temporary fling wasn't easy. Her presence was a constant reminder of how much simpler things were when everyone parted ways at the end of a dirty night and how different things had become.

Before Kyla came along, Zack and Adam were always like perverted versions of Thing One and Thing Two, causing trouble and shamelessly indulging in the perks of their job. Booze, women, music—lather, rinse, fucking repeat. Now, the distance between him and his partner in crime intensified the feeling of something missing in his life.

There was an added layer of shittiness on top of it all because Zack couldn't have the woman he wanted in his kitchen, making coffee and wearing his clothes.

Zack grabbed a fork and stabbed it into a bright yellow chunk of scrambled egg in the pan. "Thanks for last night, man."

"What did he do?" Kyla handed Zack a clean plate as a not-so-subtle hint to eat like a human being.

He took the plate, returned it to the cabinet, and kept eating from the pan. It was an asshole move, but he paid half the rent, so he'd do whatever the hell he wanted.

"Dick." Adam smacked Zack's bare shoulder so hard it stung. He turned to Kyla. "I stopped him from drunk-dialing Mandy."

Adam pulled the same plate from the cabinet and pushed it into Zack's chest. *Fine.* Adam paid the other half of the rent, and she was kind enough to cook, so he'd play nice. Zack picked up the pan and poured half the eggs on his plate before digging in.

"Sorry, Zack." Kyla's bottom lip puffed out in a pout, and she offered him a steaming mug of coffee. "It'll get easier, I promise."

He scoffed, taking the coffee. "Fucking *when*? I'm sick of this shit." He lifted the mug in thanks and took a long sip that burned his tongue, but he didn't care.

"What club does she work at again?" Kyla asked. "I know you said it once, and it had a cute name."

"Rollin' Rockies." Zack stuffed another forkful of eggs into his mouth and chased it with a slug of coffee, the hangover lifting. He hoped she was out and managing bands as planned, but she might still be saving up to follow her dream. "And we don't use the word 'cute' in this house."

Adam wrapped his arms around her from behind. "Don't censor my girl. She doesn't like rules." He planted a kiss on Kyla's neck as she grinned.

It was too early, and Zack was too hungover to deal with their touchy-feely bullshit. It would get worse when she moved back to Portland next month. She'd be staying with the guys until their lease was up in September, then moving with Adam into a smaller rental house across town. Zack still hadn't decided whether to renew the lease alone or downsize.

After the last bite of eggs, he set his plate in the sink. He plunked an ice cube in his mug, swirled it around, and downed the rest of the coffee before setting it on the counter and wiping his mouth. "Later, horndogs."

"Where are you going?" Adam asked.

Zack knew he should go for a run, shower, and get a few hours of practice in. "Back to bed." The urge to wallow alone for a while won out.

He locked his bedroom door, flopped backward onto the black bedspread, and stared at his bedroom ceiling. Feeling low and apparently masochistic, he closed his eyes. Like he'd done a million times, he let his mind drift to the day he met Mandy.

4

Zack

The calluses on Zack's fingertips stung as he came down from the adrenaline high of Tomorrow Mourning's headlining set at Denver's McNichols Arena. They rarely toured around the holidays, but their manager, Sophia, booked them for a local radio station's winter festival with a paycheck too big to pass up. The next day, they'd head to slightly warmer Dallas for two shows before a New Year's Eve gig in Phoenix.

Tyler wanted a post-show beer away from the chaos, and a roadie insisted they check out Rollin' Rockies, the oldest rock club in the city. Zack was glad he did—the place's vibe was chill and electric at the same time.

The stage was empty, but Alice in Chains blared through the speakers while people sat at tables, booths, and bar side, drinking and shooting the shit. A Christmas tree sparkled in the corner, and tiny white lights dotted the walls. Smoke hovered in a dense, swirling cloud below the ceiling, giving the place the distinct aroma of sweat, spilled beer, and ashtray. The guys played a lot of venues like this when they were coming up, so the whiff of nostalgia added an extra layer of kickass to the place.

Tyler, hiding his signature dark hair and brooding eyes beneath a ball cap, slipped a cute blonde waitress fifty bucks to give them the most private table possible. She led the trio to a booth in a back corner and took their order—three bottles of whatever beer was cold and local. Once the drinks were on the table,

Zack tossed back half of his in a few deep swallows. Every nerve ending in his body was riding the post-show buzz, and if he were going to sleep that night, he'd need a little help.

Tyler pointed the mouth of his bottle at Zack. "You fucking killed it tonight, my friend. And I liked that sick three-sixty jump off your amp. The crowd ate it up."

Zack shrugged. "If Flea can bounce around and show off with his bass, so can I."

Adam scratched the stubble on his chin. "Just don't come out naked with your dick in a sock, and we're good."

"Speaking of naked…" Zack scanned the room. After the show, he'd hung out with the road crew and hadn't hooked up with anyone. He could use a pressure release in the form of a soft, warm female body. "I bet these Colorado girls might like a break from the flannel and knit hat-wearing douchebags."

Tyler laughed, shaking his head. "Have at it. Amy will throw a shit fit if I don't call her from the hotel by three, so make it fast."

Adam looked around before focusing on a table by the bar, letting out a low whistle. "Targets spotted." He tipped his chin toward a table of four twenty-something women laughing and drinking pink liquid in martini glasses. They were making eyes at the band and whispering to each other as they stared without even attempting to be subtle.

Game on.

"Let's do it." Zack finished his beer. "Two for each of us while Ty gets a date with his right hand. But first, I gotta piss." He left the table in search of a bathroom.

A sign led him to the end of a long hallway, and once he finished, he headed back toward the table. As he rounded a corner, he collided with another body, and whatever they were holding crashed to the ground and scattered all around them.

"Fuck!" The music mostly smothered Zack's shouted curse. "I'm sorry."

His gaze slid from the two dozen or so CD cases on the ground to the face of a woman so beautiful that he gasped. Fucking *gasped*. Like he'd seen a unicorn or opened his door to find Mick Jagger on his front porch.

Long, chestnut hair streaked with gold flowed over her shoulders in waves. The hallway light was too dim to make out the color of her eyes, but he didn't miss their head-to-toe sweep of his form as she stood close enough to touch. Her clothes were casual but cool—blue jeans and a bulky black sweater that exposed nothing but a teasing hint of collarbone. He usually didn't go for women covered in so much fabric, but on her, it made him even more interested in what was hiding beneath.

"It's fine," she said, her hands shaky and her chest rising and falling with quick, shallow breaths. Either the collision flustered her, or it was him. Zack hoped it was him. "I shouldn't have tried to carry them all at once. I just hope nothing's broken."

She kneeled and started picking up the cases. Once he recovered from the fantasy-triggering sight of this goddess sinking to her knees, he helped with the rest, inspecting them for damage as he made a stack in the crook of his arm.

"No cracks on these." He stood up. "Where do you want them?"

"Oh. Um..." She bit her plump bottom lip. He smiled at how adorable it was while trying not to give off creeper vibes by staring at her mouth. "My office. Do you mind?"

"Lead the way." He followed her down the hallway past the bathrooms. She unlocked a door, entered, and held it open for Zack. As he passed her, he caught the scents of lemon and vanilla.

She was gorgeous and smelled like fucking dessert—it couldn't get much better than that.

"Thanks," she said, setting her stack on the desk. As she took his pile, the tips of her fingers grazed the backs of his, lingering for a beat.

The unexpected contact quickened his pulse. "No sweat."

He looked around the office while she double-checked the CDs for damage. A few houseplants hung by the window. A photo of her with an older couple—possibly her parents—hung on the wall, and beside it was a calendar with a picture of the Roman Colosseum.

"Ever been to Italy?" he asked.

She turned from the CDs to face him, leaning back against the desk. There was enough light in the room to see that her eyes were hazel and flecked with a deep shade of forest green. "I wish. Haven't traveled much. You?"

He smiled, relieved she hadn't recognized him. It was nice pretending to be normal sometimes. "Yeah, I've been all over. Aside from the mind-blowing pizza and cool old buildings, you're not missing much."

At that, she barked a laugh. "Cool old buildings? Not a history buff, I take it?"

"I just said that to make you feel better." He shrugged. "Italy's fucking rad."

"Honesty's always better. Even when it stings."

"Tell that to Prince Charles." Zack was glad he wasn't famous enough for his sex life to make the nightly news.

Her shoulders lifted as she laughed. "Touché. Also, what an idiot! Diana's perfect."

As he continued his visual sweep of her space, his gaze snagged on the mile-long list on her desk with *To Do* in neat black letters at the top. "What's your job here? You're important enough to have an office, so it must be something big."

"Officially, I'm a promoter, but I do lots of extra stuff to ensure everything runs smoothly. More of a manager, really."

"Do you like it here?"

She nodded, the edges of her mouth lifting. "I love this place, but I want to manage bands someday. That's the dream."

"It's a big one. You want to work at a management company or start your own?"

"Start my own. I want to be the boss, choosing the artists I work with and focusing on them instead of impressing a CEO. I almost have enough saved to take that leap. Next year's my goal."

Her ambition was impressive. Too many people settled into easy, comfortable lives instead of chasing what they really wanted.

"I hope you get there. The industry needs more reps who aren't greedy assholes who only care about trends and profit."

Her eyebrow arched. "What makes you think I'm not a greedy asshole?"

"Trust me, I've met enough as a musician to sniff them out."

"Must come in handy in your world." She crossed her arms over her chest. "I have a finely-tuned BS detector that serves me well in mine."

"Good thing I don't plan to shovel any in your direction."

She let out a sweet, unrestrained laugh that made him grin. Whatever nervousness she had in the hallway was gone. This was her space, and she was comfortable here. More importantly, she was becoming comfortable with him.

Now, Zack was the nervous one, something that only happened when he saw a music legend he idolized or had to have blood drawn. Hell, he didn't even get stage fright anymore. But for some reason, being in a small room with this girl made his heart race and his palms sweat.

"I'm Zack."

"I know who you are."

His eyebrows jumped. "Oh, yeah?"

"Music's my obsession. That, and Cameron Crowe movies. And chocolate. I freaking *love* chocolate." She tucked a strand of hair behind her ear. Her fingernails were short and unpolished. She wasn't wearing makeup, either. He was used to women looking like they'd spent hours in front of a mirror, but she didn't need it. "I apologize if you want me star-struck and weak-kneed, but I'm around past, present, and future rockstars all the time. I'm immune to your glow."

That made him laugh. He had an ego the size of Pikes Peak, but it wouldn't be shattered if she didn't fall at his feet. In fact, he liked that she wasn't still talking to him just because he was rich and famous. It was a nice change.

"You're really beautiful." The words tumbled out, and when he said it, her cheeks flushed pink. So, she was immune to his status but not his flirting.

"I bet when you walk out of here, you'll pull that same line on the pink martini girls you were checking out at table six."

"I forgot they existed after crashing into you." His head jerked back when he realized what she'd said. "Wait. You were watching me?"

One side of her mouth tipped up. "Don't make it sound creepy. I noticed you."

Zack was no stranger to being stared at by pretty women, but being noticed by her was different. Special. "What's your name?"

Her eyes narrowed a bit, skittering over his face before her lips parted. "Mandy."

"Let me buy you a drink, Mandy."

Her lips quirked into a coy little smile, and she went quiet as she considered his invitation. The suspense had him more on edge than a Hitchcock flick.

"I can't. I'm working until three."

So, they were both obsessed with music and had jobs with crazy hours. He wondered what else they had in common and wanted more time to find out. "Then I'll buy you breakfast."

Her smile grew. "I know what that means." Her tone took on a husky edge that made his cock stir in his jeans.

Taking a chance, he stepped closer. The tips of his steel-toe boots touched the tips of her spotless blue Vans. Her gaze landed on the point of contact, and the neckline of her sweater slipped an inch.

"Tell me." His fingertips twitched with the urge to trace the line of her collarbone. It wasn't a body part he'd ever paid much attention to, let alone found sexy. But he swore it was whispering his name, begging to be touched.

Finally, her eyes met his. "Breakfast means sex."

The word *sex* from her lips was like taking a quick hit of a drug.

He wanted more. "I don't know what Denny's you go to, sweetheart, but mine just has bacon, eggs, and French toast."

She laughed, raising a brow. "I know how this goes. If we have breakfast together after we've both had long nights, a bed will sound really nice. You'll invite me back to your hotel or ask how close my apartment is. Then, you'll kiss me, and... you know the rest."

Fuck. Talk about a cliffhanger. He wanted to hear more of whatever filthy story was playing out in that pretty head of hers. Better yet, he wanted a starring role while it played out for real.

"What if I kissed you now?" Zack leaned closer, watching her pupils expand and throat jump on a hard swallow. "Then can breakfast just mean breakfast?"

"No." Her attention dropped to his mouth, and when he wet his bottom lip with a quick drag of his tongue, her eyes tracked the movement. "With a mouth like yours, breakfast could never just mean breakfast."

A knock at the door broke the delicious tension crackling in the air.

"Yeah?" Mandy called out, her raspy voice leaving no doubt she felt it, too. She cleared her throat as the door opened.

A guy with bleached spikes and a punchable face stuck his head into the room.

"Sorry, Mandy, but the drummer for the headliner's arguing with the sound guy. You're better at shutting this shit down."

She heaved a sigh. "I'll take care of it. Thanks, Kev."

The thought of her getting between two angry men made Zack uneasy.

"Want help? I'm tougher than I look."

She laughed, probably because he looked plenty tough with his black leather jacket, tattoos, and skull-crusher boots. "Thanks, but so am I."

He didn't doubt that. She was small but not delicate. He guessed she was around five-seven, and she was slender but blessed with grabbable curves in his favorite places. Her thighs looked strong and toned through her jeans, and it wouldn't surprise him if she was a runner or took kickboxing lessons.

She swept her hair over one shoulder, exposing her neck. He wanted to swirl his tongue over her pulse point and sink his teeth into that tender, sensitive flesh. "Sometimes big, scary rockstars just need a hug and a lollipop."

It was Zack's turn to laugh. "You're not wrong."

She moved to the door, and he followed closely behind, checking out *her* behind—nice and strong there, too.

With her hand on the knob, she stopped, glancing at him over her shoulder. "As fun as it would be, I don't do casual flings. Thanks for the help with the CDs, but this is where we say goodbye."

Damn.

"Okay." He was disappointed but wouldn't push after a clear rejection.

Exhaustion from the show was setting in anyway, and he was ready to find his bandmates and bail. He was no longer interested in the table of basic chicks drinking pink martinis, knowing that if he took any of them back to his hotel, he'd be wishing they were half as cool and beautiful as Mandy.

If he couldn't have gold, he wasn't settling for plain old rocks.

"It was nice crashing into you, Mandy."

She hesitated before opening the door as if she'd changed her mind. With the faintest shake of her head, she turned the knob. He stayed a few steps behind as they walked the hallway toward the music and life of the club. Shouted male voices broke through the din, and she flew backward. He caught her by the arms before she hit the ground.

"You okay?" Zack set her back on her feet.

She nodded, but her hands trembled. The asshole who bumped into her was screaming at a long-haired guy whose hands were raised in surrender, clearly not wanting things to get physical. The aggressor was taller than Zack but not as built. Sweat drenched his white tank top and glistened on his shaved head, all the skin from his neck to his wrists covered in ink.

Zack caught the guy off guard, pinning his chest to the wall and gripping his elbows so he couldn't throw a decent punch. "What the *fuck* is your problem? You could've hurt her!"

The guy kicked at his shins and struggled against his hold, but it was useless. Veins bulged beneath the freak's eyes as he fought to break loose.

"Chill the fuck out, psycho!" Zack sensed Tyler and Adam at his sides before he saw them.

"You good?" Tyler asked. He wasn't one to join a fight blindly, but he was always ready to jump into a friend's corner.

Zack gave a nod. "I got it."

Mandy waved over someone across the room, and two massive guys with "Security" printed across their shirts rushed over. Zack let the angry asshole go, and the men dragged him away.

Zack turned to find Mandy clutching the fabric of her sweater over her chest, her hands still shaking. The flash of fear in her eyes made him wish he'd kneed the crazy fucker in the balls when he had the chance.

"Hey." He approached her slowly and touched her shoulder. "Are you okay?"

Her wide, glassy eyes met his, and he couldn't look away.

While waiting for a response, he took a deep breath to calm himself. His system was already charged with post-show adrenaline, and the encounter with the testosterone monster had it surging fresh and hot in his blood.

And there was her.

As they stood there, the strange, crackling energy between them returned—like the air right before a thunderstorm. He was used to the pull of lust and physical attraction, but this was something different, deeper.

She straightened her rumpled sweater and stood tall as if shaking off the ordeal and slipping back into boss mode. "Meet me outside the front door at three. French toast is on the menu, but I'm not. Got it?"

Zack grinned at her unexpected and welcome change of heart.

She said yes.

They'd only talked for about fifteen minutes, and it wasn't enough. He'd pin a hundred assholes to a wall to spend more time with her.

His grin widened as the same easy smile she wore during their chat in her office returned. "See you at three.

⟡

After devouring heaping plates of food and endless cups of coffee, Zack held the door open for Mandy as they exited the Moonlight Café. They'd talked nonstop between bites of crispy, greasy bacon and syrup-drizzled French toast. They chatted about bands they loved and exotic places they wanted to visit. She told him more about her job at the club, and he shared stories from his life on the road.

When he talked, she really listened, asking questions like she cared about the answers. He was used to women losing interest whenever he spoke about anything real and not asking about his life offstage because they didn't care. They didn't want the real person, just the fantasy.

Mandy was so easy to talk to and laugh with that he could've sat across from her all day, drinking coffee and getting to know each other. If only they weren't both exhausted from the long night.

When they stepped outside, the air was frigid, their breaths coming out in swirling white puffs and clouds. He pulled his jacket closed at the front while she zipped up hers. The sky was still dark, but the orange glow on the horizon said that sunrise was on its way.

"So, what's so great about Colorado?" he asked as they strolled along the empty sidewalk.

"Everything. The mountains, the wildlife, the nightlife. You won't find better hiking trails anywhere else."

"You've obviously never been to Oregon." He nudged her arm with his elbow, itching for contact. Their knees had bumped under the table several times, but it wasn't enough. With her, he wanted more of everything. "We've got all that and beaches."

"And rain. Lots of rain."

"Hey, don't say it like it's a bad thing, lady. I fucking love the rain. I'd never live anywhere else."

"Same for me. My parents are here, the club. Life is good."

"No boyfriend?" He probably should've asked earlier, but she didn't seem like the type to go out with a strange guy at three a.m. if she had someone.

"Nope. I date a little, but my hours make it tough for people with nine-to-fives. I'm heading out when they're getting home. You?"

"No, no boyfriend." He flashed a grin as she shoved his shoulder. "I don't date. Casual shit's enough for me."

"Oh, to be young, hot, and famous."

Zack reached out and took her hand into his. When he looked over, pink colored her cheeks as she smiled. He didn't hold hands. What was the point? But he liked seeing his effect on her. And he wanted to touch her, and that was the best he could do on a public street. Not that it'd ever stopped him before, but he could tell she also wasn't the type to let him maul her where anyone could watch.

"At least you're two out of three," he said. They walked in comfortable silence for a few more blocks. It was a damn shame their time would expire when his tour moved on to Dallas in the afternoon. He wondered why she agreed to a date, knowing their time was short. He turned to her as they waited for the light at a crosswalk. "Why did you say yes to coming out with me?"

"Honestly…" Mandy's teeth sank into her bottom lip as if she were deciding how much to reveal. "Since turning thirty, I've been reflecting on my life so far and realized that I haven't had nearly enough fun. I was pretty sheltered growing up. Church every Sunday, twelve years of Catholic school. I'd never even seen an R-rated movie until twelfth grade. When I moved out, I focused on college and work, avoiding trouble but also avoiding fun to a pathetic degree. Old habits die hard, I guess. Anyway, I decided I need to say yes more."

"Minister's son." He raised his hand. "I know all about sheltered."

Her jaw fell open. "*You* were raised by a minister? Talk about rebelling. What does he think about your lifestyle?"

"He's proud of my success and mostly keeps the hell and damnation lectures to himself." Zack knew he was lucky to have a dad whose unconditional love overrode any judgments about his son's choices.

"And your mom?"

His mom was a different story. There was unconditional love, but she wasn't shy about her harsh opinions.

"She's proud in her own way, but we butt heads a lot."

"Because you're a dirty heathen like me?"

He laughed. "That's part of it. It started when I was ten and quit church. My dad wasn't happy, but eventually, he respected my choice. She wouldn't let it go. It embarrassed her. And the head minister's son rejecting their teachings was unacceptable, so the other leaders gave my parents shit. When she came home, she passed the shit onto me."

A rift grew as her disapproval and Zack's stubbornness led to daily arguments.

On top of that, the friends he grew up with cut him off like a diseased limb because their parents worried his heathenism was contagious. Zack had always had a rebellious streak, but constantly feeling like a disappointing outcast sent it soaring.

He stole cigarettes from gas stations and lit firecrackers in the school bathroom. Metal and punk blasted in his bedroom because the angry lyrics and music made him feel understood and less alone. That feeling inspired him to ditch his childhood dream of being a pilot for the dream of being in a band.

Meeting Adam and Tyler when he was fourteen changed everything. They were fellow misfits who liked the same bands and hated the same fake bullshit—a match made in hell. During freshman year, when he announced to his parents that he was starting a hard rock band with his new friends, he thought his mom's head would explode.

"That's so unfair," Mandy said. "Religion should be a choice, not forced on anyone. Why did you stop going?"

"My best friend died in a car accident."

She stopped walking again and turned to him, the edges of her mouth curling down. "I'm so sorry."

"It was a long time ago." He shrugged, the old wound tightening his chest as they started walking again. "After the funeral, I asked my dad why God let it happen. He said, 'God works in mysterious ways, and it's not our place to question.'"

"Ugh. I've heard that one. Frustratingly dismissive, isn't it?"

"Yep. Instead of shutting me up, I asked a million other questions. Things like, 'Why does God care if I say *fuck* but lets kids starve to death?'"

"Fair question." Her shoulder bumped his. "You were a pretty smart ten-year-old."

"I was a smart-mouthed little prick."

"Some things never change." She bumped his shoulder again. "Kidding."

Zack laughed at her teasing jab. "You're not wrong." His mind circled back to what she said earlier about not having enough fun. "You work in a rowdy rock club. How do you not have fun every day?"

The stoplight lit up, and they crossed the street, still hand-in-hand.

"You know as well as I do that even if you love your job, it's still work. And I have to keep a distance from the wild stuff so people know who's in charge. I can't toss back shots or stage-dive when I'm on the clock. I can't share a joint with the talent, toss panties onstage, or wear anything unprofessional."

"That's your idea of fun?" he asked, imagining her doing all those things at one of his shows. A guy could dream.

She chuckled, her eyes drifting to the pale yellow sky as snowflakes started to fall. "Not very creative, I know. But I watch that stuff happen all the time, and the people doing it seem to enjoy themselves."

It was a tragedy that she worked in a place where she watched people have fun but never let herself jump in—like working at the best buffet in the world and being forced to eat nothing but salad. This woman deserved to taste it all.

He released her hand and hooked an arm around her shoulders, a thrilling rush of ideas zipping around his brain. "We can work with that."

Her steps halted. "What do you mean?"

"I mean, you have three days off. You said it at the café. You're coming with me to Dallas."

"Uh, no, I'm not." She scoffed, shooting him a look like he'd lost his damn mind. Since he was offering more than a one-night stand with someone for the first time in his life, there was a good chance he had.

"You want to say no to three days of music and *fun*? You know, the thing you just said you don't have enough of. And this isn't ride-at-Disneyland fun. This is *rockstar* fun. Private jets, limos, free food and booze, and you'll get a backstage pass to see one of the biggest bands on the planet. And the best, if you ask me."

Her eyes narrowed, studying him. "I've known you for three hours, Zack. I'm supposed to trust you with my safety and well-being for three *days*?"

"We're not Motley Crue, screwing girls with whiskey bottles." He curled a knuckle beneath her chin. She said she had a good bullshit detector, so hopefully, she saw the truth in his eyes. "You'll be safe with me, I promise. You have my permission to kickbox me in the balls if I get out of line."

He held his breath as she considered his offer. Bringing her would make the upcoming shows a different experience, but not in a bad way. He wanted to hear more about her club and to see her on the side of the stage as he played. He could go a few days without his usual debauchery to ensure she had a great time.

"This is crazy," she said.

"Absolutely. But you want to say yes, don't you?" He tucked a loose strand of hair behind her ear, letting his thumb slide across the smooth skin of her cheek.

"What about the rest of your band? They wouldn't mind if you invited some random chick to tag along?"

"Nope. We can bring anyone we want. I think they'd like you." It wouldn't be the first time he'd brought a woman along, but it would be the first time it wasn't just about sex. Even if things didn't go there, he'd be happy just talking and getting to know her better.

"Where would I sleep?"

"That's up to you. I'm sure you know my vote, but you can have your own room if you want."

"What if you get tired of me, hook up with someone else, and I'm stranded in Texas? How would I get home?"

"I won't even look at anyone else. You have my word." He stroked her cheek again before tucking his hand in his pocket. "And since after Dallas, the private jet will take us to Phoenix, I can't fly back with you. But you can keep the ticket in your bag as soon as I set up your flight home."

"You have an answer for everything, don't you?" She closed her eyes, her head shaking. "I can't believe I'm even considering this."

Her eyes opened, a slow smile stretching across her face.

"Yes." She said it so softly that it was nearly drowned out by the sounds of cars rushing by as the town woke up.

Zack grinned at the victory. "Yes."

He looked forward to checking everything off her "fun list" and then some, ensuring she returned home safely with a head full of unforgettable memories.

"I won't tell my parents until I get back because they'd freak," she said. "But I'll tell my boss. Ted will slice you up Krueger-style if anything happens to me."

He laughed. "I like him already. Where do you live? I'll get you home so you can pack."

Mandy pointed to the window above their heads. "Want to come up?"

Not wanting to seem too eager, he waited a few beats before answering. "Abso-fucking-lutely."

She smiled and took his hand, leading him through the gate of her complex and up the stairs to her small studio apartment.

Inside, it smelled like a garden—lemons, herbs, and flowers. The pale blue walls made the lacy white curtains over the windows look like clouds. She had more photos of herself with her parents on the walls and a few with bands taken at the club. In all of them, she was sexy but dressed like a librarian or schoolteacher—covered from neck to ankles. Like in her office, several potted plants were on the windowsills and in small frog-shaped pots on the kitchen counter. A charcoal gray blanket covered her bed in the corner, with several fluffy pillows resting against the dark wood headboard. Beside it was a shelf filled with books organized by size.

"Nice place."

She set her purse on the counter. "Says the guy who probably lives in a mansion."

He did. Two years ago, he and Adam signed the lease for a gated five-bedroom house in Portland's posh Southwest Hills. The massive garage housed their music gear and workout equipment, and the backyard was perfect for parties and summer BBQs.

"Want something to drink?"

Zack sat on the edge of her bed. "No, thanks." Exhaustion from the long night made his eyelids heavy despite all the coffee at the café, but he wasn't ready to stop talking to her yet. "Do you play?" He pointed to the large keyboard set up beneath the window.

"Not much anymore. Growing up, I played piano and violin, then I was corrupted by rock music and never looked back."

"Corrupting's my favorite part of the job." He held two crooked fingers above his head like horns as she laughed. "So, how did a Catholic schoolgirl who played classical get into devil music?"

Despite him turning down her offer of a drink, Mandy filled a glass with water and set it on the nightstand beside him. "In eleventh grade, my boyfriend was an upstanding church boy with perfect grades, so my parents approved and would let him take me out. His older brother was in a Fugazi cover band. He snuck us into a show downtown, and we stood right in front of the stage."

Her lips curved up like the memory was fresh in her mind. "For the entire two hours, I was mesmerized. It was everything—the angry music blaring from the speakers, the passion in their faces as they played, the energy in the room... Like a strange magic had taken over. When I looked around, everyone else in the crowd seemed to feel it, too. The experience connected us, and I'd never felt such a sense of belonging. I was hooked and determined to be in that world someday."

Mandy toed off her shoes and slid them under the bed as she continued. "After graduation, I got a job at Rollin' Rockies, tearing tickets, checking IDs, and stamping hands. Drove my parents crazy, but I was long overdue for some sort of rebellion, and it was still better than the stuff my loser brother was up to. I went to college and got straight A's, so they eventually stopped bitching about my job. Of course, they started again when it became clear I was staying there instead of becoming the concert pianist princess they wanted me to be."

He knew he'd sensed a naughty little rebel hiding beneath her clean-cut exterior. And it was incredibly hot that the same loud, angry music he loved and played had set it loose. Being a fellow musician put another point in her corner.

Although their time was short, he was excited to have three days to learn more about what made her tick.

"I'm rambling." Her nose wrinkled. "And probably boring the hell out of you."

"Not even a little. I like hearing about your life. If you were boring, I wouldn't be sitting here." He picked up a well-worn copy of *Fear and Loathing in Las Vegas* from her nightstand, a tasseled bookmark poking out of the top. "What's this about?"

She grinned as she closed the curtains, darkening the room, but there was enough light to make out her features. "It's about people having more fun than me. Notice a theme?" She chuckled. "The main characters buck societal norms and chase a good time without shame or fear. Reading it lets me live vicariously through them without getting arrested or risking an overdose."

Zack set the book back on the nightstand. "I mostly read horror and thrillers, but I'll have to check it out sometime." He pointed to the massive framed poster above her bed. "You're an art fan?"

She followed his line of sight. "A class in college got me into Post-Impressionism. That's Van Gogh's *Sunflowers*, my favorite."

"It's pretty." As he stared at the print, a wave of bone-deep exhaustion made his chin drift to his chest. He shook himself awake.

"You look beat." She took his face in her hands. Her soft, warm skin was so soothing, his eyes closed. "I'm right there with you. I'll admit, I had naughty intentions when I invited you up, but—" A yawn cut off the rest of her sentence.

Fuck. Nothing like being cockblocked by exhaustion. They'd have three days together, so why rush it? It felt right to make this experience different from what he was used to.

"I can go back to my hotel," he said, giving her the out.

She shook her head. "I want you to stay."

Those five words changed his life.

Despite how things ended up, not returning to his hotel that day was the best decision Zack had ever made. Still, the memory of holding Mandy as she slept made the hollow ache in his chest unbearable.

He'd give every cent he had to return to that night when everything was new and perfect.

Before reality busted in and fucked it all up.

5

Mandy

Mandy ate five bites of her turkey sandwich in the club's break room before pushing it aside. Her stomach was in knots about the impending meeting with her new boss.

It had to go well. Their first encounter included him barging into her office without knocking and stealing a pervy glance at her chest. Still, she'd brush those details aside and give him a chance to make a better impression.

"How's it goin', Mandy?" Robby, the club's sound engineer for a decade, grabbed a mug and filled it with coffee. His head-to-toe black clothes and jet-black hair down his back made him look more metal than rock, but he was a master behind a soundboard, regardless of genre.

"Great," she said, smiling as she touched her churning stomach.

She preferred to keep a cheerful, brave face at work to encourage high morale and project confidence, even when she felt anything but. She was tough when a situation called for it but believed honey got more people on your side than vinegar. It was one of the few lessons from her childhood that she agreed with. She also stuck with her mom's habit of washing dishes right after dinner and her dad's insistence never to neglect dental check-ups or oil changes. Their beliefs that purity is a girl's most precious asset and that being gay is a sin were among the many that she'd tossed in the garbage heap where they belonged.

"The crew missed you last night." He raised his mug. "Why don't you ever come out with us?"

"Sadly, I'm not as young and free as the rest of you." She knew thirty-two was far from old, but she had responsibilities outside work that none of them understood. Responsibilities that didn't allow for a few rounds of shots at the dive bar up the street with her rowdy coworkers. "I'm excited about tonight's line-up. I'll pop into soundcheck after my meeting with James to grab a sneak peek."

Robby's shoulders stiffened. "You have a meeting with him? What about, if you don't mind me asking?"

"Going over a few things to help him settle in. Why?"

His eyes darted to the doorway and back to her. "He asked me a shitload of questions about what I do around here. Did the same to the bartenders. Gave us all a weird vibe."

"Weird, how?"

"Like he wants to change how we do things." He lowered the volume of his voice. "Honestly, he seems like a stuck-up prick."

Loud footsteps approached. James Sutter appeared in the doorway with a yellow legal pad and a stack of invoices in the crook of his arm.

His gaze slid to Mandy. "Ready for that meeting?"

She glanced at the clock. Although she had twenty minutes left of her break, she was more interested in getting this meeting over with than continuing to pick at her sandwich.

"Of course." She secured the plastic wrap around her food and stuck it in the fridge. On the way out, she tapped Robby's elbow. "See you at soundcheck."

She followed her new boss to her office, sitting behind her desk while he took the chair across from hers.

"Let's get down to business." He slapped his stack of papers onto her desk and leafed through them. "First off, I've looked at the books, and we're hemorrhaging money on useless details. Backstage food and beverage costs are exorbitant. The sound engineer is vastly overpaid. Drink prices are ridiculously low compared to venues of similar capacity in the city." A disdainful puff of air escaped his lips. "No wonder your old boss had to sell."

Mandy cracked her knuckles, a habit she only did when irritated. Maybe she subconsciously hoped it would irritate the person irritating her. "The talent is why people come to the club, so backstage, they deserve more than the typical deli tray and generic booze other venues serve. Being treated well also keeps them coming back. The sound engineer, Robby, has over a decade of experience, and we're lucky he hasn't moved on to arenas. The generous pay keeps him here, and he more than earns it with his skills. Drink prices are low because we get loyalty discounts from vendors that we pass onto the patrons, who are typically under forty and broke. Being able to afford to drink here keeps them coming back."

He sat quietly, watching her. "The era of spoiling musicians with top-shelf liquor and a free buffet is over. They'll play here because the pickings are slim in Denver. This is the biggest club in the city, and they know execs come here scouting for talent."

Mandy bit her tongue so hard she tasted copper. This man knew nothing about the place he'd bought. Even worse, he didn't seem interested in learning its true value.

"Patrons will keep coming," he continued, "as long as you book bands that get asses in the seats. The weird sound guy's out. It's not rocket science. I'll find someone willing to work for less. As for the bar..." His fingertip stabbed the invoice at the top of his stack. "Our liquor discount should mean greater profit margins, not cheaper drinks to court a bunch of sweaty, burger-flipping punks."

Heat flooded her chest. She took a long, slow breath and exhaled through her nose as her anger flared. She loved the bands who played there. And the sweaty punks who helped make the club the city's destination for a guaranteed killer Saturday night. Who the hell did this guy think he was disparaging people he'd never met?

"Are you a music fan, Mr. Sutter?"

"James is fine. And while my tastes are irrelevant, I enjoy blues and jazz. I'm a fan of money, Mrs. Reid." His gaze shot to her left hand and back to her face. "Pardon me. *Miss* Reid."

His error about her marital status was the least obnoxious thing about him. He should apologize for coming into a place where creativity sparked and thrived and trying to rob it of that magic.

He might change his mind once he spent some time watching the club in action, but she could tell he was the spoiled, stubborn type who changed his own tire more often than he changed his mind. If that were the case, hopefully, he'd decide that he could make more profits with less hassle somewhere that catered to stuck-up, entitled assholes like him—like a country club or Mercedes dealership.

She nodded slowly, trying to keep her expression neutral instead of letting it convey how badly she wanted to strangle him with her phone cord. "Of course, profits are important. They keep the lights on and the staff paid. But you should understand the vital role that Rollin' Rockies plays in not only the Denver community but the entire state and beyond. Bands get discovered here and take off. It's a safe place for the misunderstood to feel like they belong. The club—"

"Mandy." He leaned forward, bracing his forearms on his knees. "It's cute that you have romantic notions of what happens under this roof. But I own bars and restaurants all over the city, and I don't need *you* telling me how to run my business."

Cute?! What an asshole! His condescending words and tone made her skin prickle.

"If you can't fall in line," he said, rising from his chair. "I'll find someone who can."

The weight of his threat punched her in the stomach. She couldn't lose this job, but the thought of working alongside this dickhead day in and day out made her want to scream.

"There won't be a problem, Mr. Sutter." She wasn't ready to be on a first-name basis with this jerk, even though he'd taken the liberty without her permission. He seemed like the type to do that with lots of things, and she made a mental note not to be caught alone with him whenever she could avoid it. "I look forward to working with you."

She bit back the words she wanted to say. Things like *Screw you!* and *How does it feel to be an enormous prick?*

When he was out the door, she shut and locked it behind him, leaning her back against the wood while trying not to vomit or cry. How long would she be able to hold her tongue while the place and people she cared about were under attack?

I'm going to lose my job.

She'd never had to worry about that, taking for granted that she always had a reliable income. It was why she felt secure enough to leave her old apartment and take on a mortgage. Without a paycheck. she'd be screwed.

I'll lose my house.

The financial implications were the most obvious, but there were countless other reasons why leaving this job would be devastating. This place was like her second home. Her office had always been a safe space to focus and recharge. In those walls, she'd passed tissues to coworkers dealing with painful break-ups and played mediator during band disputes.

It was where Zack first told her she was beautiful and asked her out after helping to pick up her dropped CDs. She imagined him standing by her desk, their shoes touching as his effortless magnetism drew her in.

That room and the club surrounding it were special to her for a million reasons, and in a few minutes, James Sutter blew that security to pieces.

She sank to the floor as mourning took hold—for the bright, beautiful past with Ted at the helm and the future that now looked bleak and gray.

If James Sutter had his way, greed would smother the club's spirit. Profits would become more important than helping local talent flourish—art sacrificed on the altar of the almighty dollar.

She didn't want any part of that but couldn't quit without a backup plan.

"Time to figure out a Plan B," she muttered, trying not to freak out but failing miserably. Her throat tightened as if trapped in a fist, making it hard to breathe.

Tomorrow, she'd start looking for another job. In the meantime, she'd keep her chin up and mouth shut. No matter what James Sutter tossed at her next, she'd deal with it.

Because there were far worse things than having to answer to a dickhead.

6

Mandy

The new audio engineer that Mr. Sutter—Mandy still refused to call him James—hired looked fresh out of high school. The braces added to the effect, as did his bewildered look as he struggled to figure out a piece of the club's equipment five minutes before the first band went on.

She watched from backstage through a crack in the curtains, hoping he'd succeed but also hoping he failed to teach her new boss a lesson.

She got a headache just thinking about explaining the change to the regular bands with a rapport with Robby and faith in his skills. No one's testier than a musician whose guitar cut out mid-performance or got the nails-on-a-chalkboard squeal of feedback while they played.

In the two weeks since James Sutter bought the club, he'd also increased drink prices and printed new menus to reflect the inflated costs. As she stood backstage with the night's opening act, she watched him breathe down the bartenders' necks to ensure they weren't pouring too heavily. At the same time, he sipped his third glass of twenty-year-old bourbon.

A real piece of work, this one.

Unfortunately, her job hunt wasn't going well. She'd given resumes to every major club in town before trying the smaller ones. No one was hiring. The office jobs in the want ads all required computer skills she didn't have. Unless she wanted to make minimum wage waiting tables in a skimpy uniform, she was stuck witnessing James's antics and their effects on the club for the foreseeable future.

The house lights went out, and the room erupted in applause and excited shrieks.

Mandy turned to the band. "Okay, guys. That's your cue. Have a great show!"

The performers took turns hitting the stage. When they were all in their places and the music started, she headed for her office. After hours of running through her usual checklist to set up for a successful night, she needed to get off her feet and have a few minutes of peace. On the way, she grabbed a cranberry and tonic from the bar. She never drank alcohol on work nights, but she could pretend.

The music's volume faded as she walked the long hallway. As soon as her door closed, she sank into her desk chair, and all the air whooshed from her lungs. She toed off her ankle boots and set her stocking-covered feet on her file cabinet, settling in.

Craving a little comfort food, she opened her desk in search of dark chocolate almonds, and instead, her fingers landed on the tape Ash gave her from his friend's band. With the recent upheaval at the club, she'd forgotten all about it. She rolled on her chair's wheels to the stereo in the corner, slipped the cassette in the tape deck, and pressed play.

The intro began with gentle, hypnotic guitar chords before evolving into something heavy and urgent. The drums thudded hard, the bass lines were solid and inventive, and the vocals were captivating and unique.

Ash was right—the power of the singer's voice reminded her of Chris Cornell, while the punk sound backing him up was *London Calling* era Clash. There were no weak links—every member held their own.

As the tape played on, it became clearer with every song that these guys could make it with the right representation.

She'd give anything to be the person to do that.

Unfortunately, a band starting out wouldn't earn much, at least not at first. Any commission she'd get the first few years likely wouldn't pay her water bill. But she knew a few reps who might be interested in taking them on—people already established with offices, years of experience, and fancy business cards. She'd already called them all to see if they had any job openings she was qualified for, which was a dead end, too. But they might help these guys.

There were countless times over the years when she'd recognized that unmistakable, undefinable quality in an up-and-coming artist that set them apart. Every time, she did her best to steer them toward local reps while wishing like hell that she could be the one helping them reach their full potential. That sting of disappointment never got easier to bear.

If things had gone as planned, she'd probably have an office and fancy business cards by now, courting clients and ushering them to success. She had to hold on to hope that someday, she'd get there. And after dealing with her new boss, she was even more excited by the notion of becoming her own.

As she relaxed, the phone rang. She turned off the tape and rolled back to her desk.

The chair creaked as she leaned forward and put the call on speaker. "Hello?"

There was a beat of silence on the other line. "Uh, hi. Is this Mandy?" The voice filling her office was feminine and unfamiliar.

"Yes, who's this?" She sipped her drink.

"My name is Kyla. You don't know me, but if you're the right Mandy, you know my boyfriend, Adam Hyatt."

Mandy almost choked on her mocktail. "You're with *Adam*?" Aside from MTV and the brief conversation with Ash two weeks ago, she hadn't heard the name in months. "The same Adam who got arrested last year for stealing a 'Beaver Boulevard' road sign?"

The sign stealing wouldn't have made headlines or been jail-worthy if he weren't famous and smoking a joint while he did it.

The woman, Kyla, snickered. "I could've done without that reminder, but yes. That Adam. He's changed a lot."

"Sorry." Mandy set down her glass and sat straighter, wanting to know the reason for the call to get it over with. No point waking up old ghosts. "What's this about?"

"Zack's going through some tough stuff right now."

Hearing *his* name was like a fist squeezing her heart.

Then, the memories flooded in—both terrific and terrible—but she shook her head to clear them. She couldn't go there with a club full of people down the hall. Hell, she didn't want to go there at all, but she needed to know what was wrong.

"What do you mean? Is he okay?"

"Sort of." Kyla paused. "I have a few questions that might help him. Would that be okay?"

"Questions?" Mandy set her feet on the carpet, a frown pulling at her lips. "About what?"

"I realize how weird this is. He doesn't know I'm doing this, and neither does Adam. But even the first night I met Zack, you were clearly a sore spot for him. His feelings for you never went away, and I wonder if they're all one-sided or if maybe—"

"Look," Mandy snapped, rubbing the tender center of her chest. The spot tightened and burned every time she thought about Zack, even after all the time that'd passed. "I can't do this. I've moved on, and he needs to do the same."

The lie twisted in her gut.

"Oh." Kyla was quiet again. "Sorry I bothered you with this. I'll let you go."

"No, wait." Mandy pinched the bridge of her nose, taking a deep breath. The woman seemed nice enough and didn't deserve to have Mandy's discomfort with the topic taken out on her. "Zack's a great guy. My feelings for him are... complicated."

That was one word for it. With him, she'd done something she swore she'd never do again—love someone she couldn't trust. And he hadn't changed his reckless ways when it mattered most, so regardless of how she felt, he left her no choice.

She had to give him up.

Kyla made a low humming sound as if working through the admission. "I know he can be an immature dickhead, but when he talks about you, he lights up. Then, the light goes out. It's like his heart breaks all over again. He's wanted to call you, but I think he's afraid to disrupt your life. If there's a chance it can work between you, I think you should try."

"No." Mandy wiped a tear from the corner of her eye.

He broke my heart first.

"We don't make sense together," she continued. "The distance sucks, and our lives are too different. I couldn't sit around hoping he'd grow up and be ready for—" She stopped, her lips pressed tightly. "Something more serious and stable."

That, and she couldn't erase the image of some random blonde groupie in a miniskirt sitting in his lap with her hands all over him. If Zack couldn't resist the temptation of other women for a week, she'd never be able to trust him long-term. Trust was everything.

But even if other women weren't an issue, he drank too much and partied too hard. She'd seen what that lifestyle did to her brother. She wasn't about to waste years of her life watching another person she loved self-destruct or trying and failing to fix him, too.

"He wants to change that," Kyla said. "I hope I'm not being disloyal to him by saying this, but I think seeing his best friends fall in love made him realize more than ever what he's lost."

Mandy pressed harder on her chest, fresh tears stinging her eyes.

He wasn't the only one who'd lost something.

"I still care about him, too. Always will. I wish things were different, but—" A sharp knock at her office door cut her off. "One second, okay?" She slipped her shoes back on and called out, "Come in."

The door swung wide, and James Sutter entered her office, clinging to the doorknob as if he needed it for balance. So, besides being a prick, he was a drunk.

Perfect.

He shut the door behind him and dropped into the empty seat across from her.

"I enjoyed watching you work tonight," he said, a distinct slur to his words.

"Okay." She wasn't sure how else to respond. "Full house tonight, so plenty to do." *Other than drink and boss people around.*

The scent of expensive liquor wafted over as he shifted in his chair. "I enjoyed watching you, period." His eyes drifted to the front of her dress. Even though not a hint of cleavage showed, she felt exposed. "I've caught you looking at me, too."

She couldn't hold back her scoff as she crossed her arms over her chest. The call with Kyla was still on speaker, but it stayed silent. She probably figured Mandy was busy and hung up.

"You're mistaken, Mr. Sutter." She picked up her drink and took a sip, trying to look casual while alarm bells screamed in her head. From working at the club, she'd seen what shitty men were capable of, especially under the influence of alcohol. While keeping her eyes on him, she slid open her top drawer. A sharp pair of scissors sat on a pile of notepads. "I'm here to work. That's all."

His pupils flared as his eyes shamelessly raked down her body again. "I know how badly you need this job. Your old boss gave me the impression that you're struggling to make ends meet. I have some... side jobs you can do for extra cash."

Mandy bolted from her seat and flung open the door, her heartbeat thudding in her chest. "Get the hell out of my office before I call a bouncer in here to boot your ass out of your own club."

The bastard chuckled, the sound gruff and devoid of humor as he stood on unsteady feet and staggered to the door. "You're no fun." He traced her jawline with his fingertip, and she slapped his hand away. "Let me know when you change your mind."

She slammed the door behind him and locked it before collapsing into her chair, huffing like she'd run a sprint. Adrenaline raced through her blood, the edges of her vision going cloudy. She didn't know whether she was more pissed or terrified, but both were definitely on board.

"Mandy, are you okay?"

The voice startled her before she picked up the receiver and held it to her ear. "I thought you'd hung up."

"Not a chance. I know a dangerous dickhead when I hear one, and I wanted to make sure you were safe. I would've called 9-1-1 if he tried anything."

Mandy didn't have many people watching out for her these days and appreciated the gesture. "Thanks, but I'm fine. That's my new boss. Lucky me, right?"

Kyla was quiet so long that Mandy again wondered if she'd hung up. "You should find something else."

Mandy chugged half of her drink to cure her dry mouth from the shock of the encounter. "Trust me, I've tried. Unfortunately, all the clubs in town are fully staffed, and I don't know of any bands looking for a manager with zero experience who'd make me the commission I'd need to get by." She drained the rest of her glass. "Sorry. I don't usually unload my problems onto strangers. Not when I'm sober, at least."

Kyla snickered. "I'm happy to listen. My days consist of trying not to get bitten by animals, so it's nice to be handed someone else's problems for a change."

"Zookeeper, dog catcher, or vet?"

"Door number three," Kyla said with a light, melodic laugh. They hadn't talked long, but Mandy liked her already. Zack was lucky to have friends who cared enough to help him, even if it was pointless. "Anyway, if you think there's a chance for you and Zack, call him. He'd love to hear from you."

The Tomorrow Mourning laminate stared from the open desk drawer. She slid a fingertip over his photo, wishing she had more than photographs and impossible dreams to hold on to.

"Thanks for calling, Kyla." Mandy shut her eyes to staunch the flood of memories, but his face was all she saw. "Hug him for me, okay?"

They ended the call, and she left her office, scanning every inch of the club for her asshole boss. Fortunately, he was nowhere to be seen, so she ordered another cranberry and tonic at the bar. This time, with a splash of vodka.

Her pulse still raced, and her knees wobbled as the adrenaline rush faded. Her mind raced, too, flying in all directions and refusing to settle.

I'm in danger.

I have to get out without losing everything I've worked for.

Zack is still heartbroken.

She tried slapping on her "boss mode" mask, but it wouldn't stick—her frown kept returning, her shoulders tense and high. So much had happened in the last fifteen minutes that she struggled to process everything.

As the opening band played their closing song, she waded through the crowd to get backstage and tell them what a great job they did, even though she'd missed most of their set. They were talented, and Mandy enjoyed nothing more than live music, but she'd had other things on her mind all night. Now, she had an indecent proposal from that sleazebag and thoughts of Zack on top of the heap.

One thing Kyla said echoed through her mind—*It's like his heart breaks all over again.*

Despite his mistakes that ended their relationship, she didn't want him to hurt. She thought he'd moved on. If the countless photos of him with beautiful women taken at awards shows and exotic locales were anything to go by, he had.

But from what he'd shared about his childhood, he'd faced a lot of rejection for being true to himself and forging his own path. It was clear he used sex to self-medicate—a temporary respite from the loneliness they had in common. What if that's also how he buried the pain from their breakup? She had plenty to distract herself from it all hours of the day, but maybe in between shows, he didn't.

Was it possible that all this time, he'd been missing her as much as she missed him? She still thought about him every day, clinging to memories of the most intense and exhilarating week of her life.

With Zack's handsome, scruffy face fresh in her mind, she thought about the day they met.

Mandy had broken all her rules with him—*don't let a man I just met into my home, never share personal details with a stranger, no sex talk until at least date three.* The biggest one came right out of the gate—*never sleep with a man on the first date.* The few guys she dated before him made it easy to stick to, but like with so many things, Zack was different.

It wasn't just his panty-dropping good looks that had her stripped and ravenous hours after meeting him. It was his passion for life and music. And his genuine desire to get to know her even though their time was short. He was the polar opposite of dull and uptight, a guy who knew how to have a good time but also appreciated moments with her that were slow, quiet, and sweet.

And in those first hours together, she was hooked.

Hell, she still was. But now it was clear—they were doomed from the start.

7

Mandy

Late December 1994

After that first meeting at the club, Mandy brought Zack to her apartment. He looked out of place in her cozy haven of pastel walls, overstuffed bookshelves, and houseplants, but she couldn't imagine him anywhere else.

He poked around her space a bit, asking questions with a curious grin and paying attention to the answers despite being dead on his feet. Like he wanted to soak up every detail, making each second count of their limited time together.

When the exhaustion won over, he sat on her bed, his beautiful moss-green eyes at half-mast. He asked if she wanted him to return to his hotel. The answer was easy.

"I'll be right back," she said, eager to freshen up. It'd been a while since someone she was attracted to had asked her out, plunging her into a frustrating sex drought. It'd been over six months, so there was a decent chance she'd attack him despite her exhaustion.

Behind her closed bathroom door, she quickly brushed her teeth, washed her face, and changed into her usual bedtime attire of sweatpants and a baggy Mudhoney T-shirt while one of the biggest, hottest rockstars in the world sat on her bed. She also put on clean, black lace underwear—much sexier than the basic pink cotton she'd been wearing all day.

She had a thing for musicians, but that was a bonus. She liked Zack. He was considerate and funny, and so far, she hadn't bored him to death, which was a plus.

He'd asked why she said yes to going away with him. She'd answered truthfully but with the condensed version. Really, there were two reasons, and both could be traced back to her thirtieth birthday.

When Mandy blew out the candles on her cake, she wished for an adventure bigger than she'd ever had. Okay, that didn't set the bar high, but his offer to join his band in Dallas fit the bill perfectly. Going so far outside her comfort zone with a group of strangers was scary, but it was also thrilling to have a chance to enter a wild world few people ever get to see. She'd witnessed plenty of outrageous things at the club, but being backstage with a major rock band would be another level. And she wouldn't just have to watch people indulge in their desires from the sidelines—she could take a big bite of the forbidden fruit and lick her lips clean.

It would be the opposite of the stifling box she'd been raised in. She'd grown up under the thumb of parents who'd instilled the fear of God in her so deeply that she felt guilty even *dreaming* about sex. She went to church every Sunday, where old, self-righteous men told her how to live her life and to shut down "impure thoughts" if she didn't want to fry in eternity. And she went to Catholic school five days a week for twelve years, where an army of nuns hammered it in even further, making her so ashamed of her desires she learned to keep them locked up tight.

Even though she no longer believed in a bearded sky daddy, the fear, shame, and guilt stuck. On her birthday, she vowed to shed those final remnants from childhood that she carried like a suffocating weight around her neck. She was sick of being a prisoner to archaic ideals about what women should and shouldn't do with their own damn bodies. She was done settling for dull-to-mediocre sex in dull-to-mediocre relationships. Time to experiment, to figure out what she liked and didn't.

There's nothing like a milestone birthday to remind her that the clock was ticking, and it would be a tragedy to fall in love someday and settle down without exploring her sexuality.

When Mandy spotted Zack at the club, she froze before ducking into the shadow of the massive DJ booth. The man was like Henry Rollins and James Dean, all wrapped up in a sexy black leather package. She couldn't look away. All her life, she'd been trained to want a clean-cut, straight-edge, church-going guy with strong morals, but apparently, her vagina didn't get the memo.

As she watched him talking and laughing with his bandmates, desire bloomed low in her belly, her thighs clenching with a sudden, primal need for friction. She'd *never* felt a surge of desire so intense. Not even the first time she saw Keanu shirtless in *Point Break*, but that was still a close second.

While pretending to stare at her notebook, her eyes narrowed in on Zack's mouth as he licked a stray drop of beer from his lip. His confident swagger and that beautiful, worship-worthy mouth made one thing abundantly clear:

If she were going to sin, with him, it would be worth it.

Of course, she chickened out when he shot a flirty grin at the tipsy women at table six. Then, it wasn't hard to talk herself out of the crazy fantasy, and she got back to work, collecting the stacks of promo CDs from the DJ booth and carrying them to her office.

Then came the crash.

He apologized and helped her pick up the mess without hesitation. Was there an actual *gentleman* hiding beneath that rough veneer? In her office, he was fun to flirt with and clearly interested.

As they talked, something sparked between them that felt like more than simple attraction or even lust. The way he looked at her made her feel warm and wanted. She intended to chase that feeling all the way to her bedroom.

Then Kevin interrupted, breaking the spell and allowing the overthinking to kick in.

Zack's a stranger.

He could be dangerous.

What if he pressures you to do things you don't want to?

With all the *what-ifs* buzzing in her brain, the dull, responsible buzzkill Mandy took the reins and shot him down. The safe, smart thing to do was to go home and ride her vibrator until every battery in her apartment was toast. In her fantasies, he couldn't hurt or disappoint her. That would have to be enough.

But again, everything changed in a blink. When he caught her before she fell and slammed the aggro guy into the wall for knocking into her... That was all it took. She was a sucker for protective men. And witnessing how quickly he shifted from full of rage for the asshole to tender and sweet with her clinched it.

The spark grew while they talked for hours like old friends catching up. But their looming expiration date kept things simple while making it easier to be open and honest. What was the harm in showing her true, unfiltered self to someone she'd never see again?

She was aware of his playboy reputation, and it was clear he'd love to get into her pants, but this seemed like more for him, too. A guy like Zack didn't need to make big promises or crazy invitations to get laid. And he didn't need to bother getting to know someone he'd never see again. He just had to aim one of his sexy smiles in a girl's direction, and panties would drop.

Mandy dropped her dirty clothes—boring pink panties included—into the hamper beside the shower before grabbing a spare toothbrush from her medicine cabinet. She took one last look in the mirror and kicked herself for not owning lingerie. It'd always seemed like a pointless waste of money, but if she walked out in a skimpy, lacy number, seeing the look on his face would've been worth every cent. Instead, she resembled someone about to scrub an oven or paint the kitchen.

When she left the bathroom, Zack was still fully clothed and passed out on top of the blankets. The sight made her grin—if his fans could see their hero now.

"Hey. Big bad rockstar." She leaned over him, brushing her knuckles along his rough, stubbled jawline. He hummed in his throat but didn't budge. She crouched to unlace his boots and slipped them off, setting them beside the bed.

"I got you a toothbrush. And sleeping in jeans sucks, so it's cool if you want to sleep in boxers."

His hands slid from the blanket to the fly of his jeans. She swallowed hard, watching him unbutton his pants before he sat up and pushed them off his legs and onto the floor. His sleepy eyes slid to hers.

"Looking at me like that's gonna get you in trouble," he said, his voice gravelly from sleep, "no matter how fucking tired I am."

Her heart hammered as she fought the urge to sink to her knees at his feet. She didn't even enjoy blowjobs much, but suddenly, the thought of his hard dick in her mouth while that low, sexy voice urged her on made her want to give it another shot.

He slipped his shirt over his head, and the sight didn't make it any easier to stop staring. Several black-line tattoos covered his chest and biceps—a bass guitar, his band's logo, a stunning raven with spread wings. His taut muscles flexed and rippled beneath the artwork as he tossed his shirt to the floor. When he stood, their bodies were inches apart. He took the toothbrush and disappeared behind the bathroom door.

Mandy caught her breath as she filled a glass with water at the kitchen tap. The man's presence was disarming, the scent of his sweat and musky cologne thick in the cramped space. She drained the glass and set it on the counter.

When she heard the telltale squeak of her shower turning on, she was glad she'd done a load of towels before work and set clean ones on the rack. A few minutes later, he exited the bathroom in his boxers, a thick cloud of steam in his wake as he shook out his damp hair.

He pulled back the sheets and slid under the covers. She hesitated for a moment before climbing in beside him. He hooked an arm around her waist and dragged her closer, her back pressed against his chest. His skin was hot from the shower, and he smelled like her pomegranate body wash, but there was a hint of something darker, sexier layered beneath that was distinctly him.

Maybe it was strange to be pressed against a half-naked guy she hadn't even kissed, but it felt good. And she felt safe with him. The hardness poking into her lower back said it felt good for him too.

"Good night, gorgeous." He breathed the words into her neck as he nuzzled against her skin.

She glanced at her bedside clock and bit back a laugh. Their idea of "good night" came at six in the morning. Finding someone else whose sleep schedule mirrored a vampire's was rare.

The last guy she dated was getting ready for work as she went to bed, leaving no opportunities to be wrapped in strong arms as she drifted off to sleep. She planned to savor the safe, warm feeling along with whatever new experiences came her way over the next three days.

⸻◆⸻

Mandy awoke to her bare arm being stroked with fingertips that felt rough, but the touch was gentle. She was lying on her back, and when she opened her eyes, Zack was watching her. His cheek rested on her pillow, and their faces were nearly touching.

"Good morning," she croaked. She was too groggy to worry about morning breath or eye crusties.

"Sorry." His fingers stopped moving, and she kicked herself for saying something. "I didn't mean to wake you up."

"Don't stop, and you're forgiven. It felt nice."

He flashed a sexy, crooked smile, the touch resuming. "You're pretty when you sleep. Peaceful. I don't get much peaceful these days."

She propped her head up on her hand. "Groupies don't look peaceful when they sleep?"

"I don't know. I always sleep alone."

The admission surprised her. It was easy to imagine him starting his days with one or several women in his bed. No judgment thought. She admired people who freely chased pleasure without shame or apology and hoped to become one someday.

"Afraid your snoring will turn them off?"

He gasped with mock outrage. "You whimper in your sleep like a scared little kitten. I discovered a new turn-*on*."

Mandy grabbed a pillow, knocking the side of his head while they laughed. "I do not!" As she settled back on her side, his soft gaze warmed her from the inside. She felt beautiful and desirable, even in sweatpants and an old T-shirt.

"Actually..." Zack toyed with the ends of her hair before brushing them along her cheek. It tickled, igniting goosebumps on her skin. "I'm hoping to find a turn-*off*. If you stay perfect, I might accidentally fall for you before our time's up."

The way her pulse kicked up at his words and touch said it was a risk for her, too. The realization surprised her. Since her high school sweetheart broke her heart in a not-so-sweet way—by screwing her best friend at a prom afterparty—she didn't get carried away with men. Sadly, it wasn't hard to do. The guys she dated often seemed to put on an act, trying to appear cooler or kinder than they were.

She valued real, and even after such a short time together, she could tell Zack was fearlessly, unapologetically himself. It was a damn shame he lived so far away.

"We can't have that," she said.

He shook his head, their lips brushing with a featherlight touch that made her forget to breathe. She tipped forward when he started pulling back, boldly chasing him for more, and pressed her mouth to his. Her tongue parted his lips, and a rumbling groan broke in his chest. His sturdy arms wrapped around her, dragging her on top of him.

His impressive erection slipped out of his boxers and settled between their bodies, the warm, silky head pressed against the skin below her belly button. Aching to feel it a few inches south, she moved further up his body, lining up their hips and grinding against him.

"Fucking hell," he mumbled against her lips. "Is that a yes?"

"You didn't ask a question."

Zack flipped them both over, her on her back, and pinned her wrists above her head. "My cock asked you loud and clear if it could slip inside that tight heat between your legs." He pumped his hips, sliding the underside of his shaft along the seam of her pussy through her clothes. A soft moan escaped her lips as she squirmed beneath him. She was already wet from the kissing, and now her panties were on their way to soaked. "The way you're grinding against it like a cat in heat feels like a yes."

"Stop comparing me to cats."

They both laughed, their noses brushing.

"And yes," she said. "It's most definitely a yes."

Zack released her wrists and gripped the hem of her T-shirt with one hand while the other slipped beneath it, teasing the sensitive skin at the waistband of her sweatpants. Again, she wished she'd worn something a little sexier than her lazy Sunday clothes, but he didn't seem to mind. They'd be on the floor soon anyway.

"You're so fucking beautiful." He lifted the hem of her shirt to below her breasts, stroking the skin of her belly before his touch drifted lower. "Just so you know, I get tested every month and always wear condoms. Totally clean."

"Good to know, and I'm clean too." She grabbed his wrist, stopping him. "I have a confession to make first."

"Mmm..." The deep, sexy sound rumbled in his chest as he quirked a brow. "Are we role-playing naughty priest and dirty little sinner?"

She grinned, her cheeks heating. "Maybe later. But seriously... When I first saw you, I thought you were hot, and, well, I wanted to use you for a one-night stand. If you were interested, of course." She slapped a hand over her eyes but peeked out through her fingers to gauge his reaction. "Saying it out loud makes me sound like a weird stalker asshole."

He blinked. "You wanted to use me? For sex?"

She nodded, her hand still over her eyes as mortification made a bonfire of her face. "Kind of. Yeah." Her hand slipped to her side, and she met his gaze. "I'm sorry. That's not how I feel anymore. I mean, I still want to sex you up all over this place, but I like you."

He kissed her shoulder, her skin muffling his hysterical laughter. She didn't think anything she'd said was *that* funny. "I like you too, dirty little sinner. And feel free to use me all over this place."

Their smiles collided in a kiss that quickly turned ravenous.

This was happening. She was going to have sex with Zachary Maine. Before blowing out those birthday candles and promising to say yes to adventure and pleasure, she wouldn't have let him touch her like this. Hell, she wouldn't even have kissed him. She would've denied herself the thrilling experience to avoid eternal damnation and ending up on the business end of a fiery pitchfork.

She didn't believe in those transparent, misogynistic scare tactics anymore, but their barbed hooks were in deep. There was a twinge of hesitation over what they were about to do.

She didn't even know his middle name and was letting him inside her body?

What seemed hot and exciting seconds ago suddenly felt irresponsible and reckless. Her first one-night stand had somehow become three. Everything was moving so fast.

What the ever-loving hell am I thinking?

She broke the kiss. "I've never done this before," she blurted.

Zack's hand stilled on her hip. "Are you a... virgin?"

"No. Although, considering the quantity and quality of sex I've had, I might as well be." She traced the lines of a tattoo on his bicep that said *loyalty*. It was a quality she valued highly. He must, too, if he'd shed blood to permanently etch the word into his skin. "I meant that I never bring strangers home. It's embarrassing, but I've only been with three guys—my high school boyfriend, a guy I dated in college, and someone I met at the club. Sex didn't come until we'd known each other for months."

"I don't want to be a stranger to you." His sweet words and hot exhales on her belly made her head swim, but the hesitation didn't budge. "Ask me anything." His eyebrows jumped like he'd surprised himself. "Saying that to a woman is something *I've* never done before."

She smiled, feeling special that he was willing to open up to her and grateful he wasn't being pushy. "What makes you happy besides music and your work?"

"I expected you to ask my favorite color or movie or whatever, but okay." He tapped his scruffy chin as he considered the question. "Rainy days. Sitting around a firepit with my friends, passing a joint around the circle." Zack smiled as if imagining his friends made him happy. She witnessed how quickly Tyler and Adam jumped to his side at the club, and she admired and envied those tight bonds. Aside from Ted, it'd been ages since someone she completely trusted had her back. "What about you? Same question."

"Waterfalls, ducklings, autumn leaves, and good books."

He chuckled, amusement sparkling in his eyes. "Ducklings, huh? They are pretty fucking cute. Even though I hate that word."

"The cutest." She ran her fingers through his hair, the strands soft against her skin. The gentle touch made his eyes flutter closed before finding her again. Watching him react to her was addictive and quite the ego boost. "Favorite song."

"I'll tell you, but you can't laugh."

She grinned at his unique ability to look serious and playful simultaneously. "Ooh, I'm intrigued. Spill it."

"'You Give Love a Bad Name.'"

Her jaw dropped at the admission. "Seriously? Bon Jovi? I love that song, too, but I'd *never* guess you did."

"Don't put me in a box, lady. I'm an enigma." His low chuckle shook their bodies as she rolled her eyes. "And the bass line's sick. Yours?"

"INXS. 'Need You Tonight.'"

Zack burst out laughing, and she smacked his arm.

"Hey! What the hell?"

"I didn't promise not to laugh." He laughed harder as she playfully smacked him again.

"For your information, it's one of the sexiest songs ever written. Every woman wants to feel desired like that. To make a man sweat."

"Well, you're definitely sweat-worthy, sweetheart." His thumb swept over her bottom lip, and the noise in her head that'd caused her hesitation quieted. "It is a cool track. I met Michael Hutchence once in New York, and he's as chill and humble as he seems in interviews. Nothing fake about that dude."

She could tell he wasn't name-dropping to show off like many of the heavy hitters that came through the club. So far, Zack was unique in ways that made her happy to have him in her bed.

The next question came to her quickly. "Tell me something you've never told anyone before."

He let out a slow whistle. "Kicked it up a notch. Okay." He fiddled with the drawstring on her sweatpants, wrapping it around his finger. "I love my life. I do. All of it. But..."

His expression shifted, the light from seconds before fading out. As much as she wanted to know what had caused it, she didn't want him to feel sad or uncomfortable.

Mandy pressed a kiss to the center of his forehead. "You don't have to answer if you don't want to."

His gaze trailed back to hers. "I can count on one hand the people I trust a hundred percent. I'm lucky to have my friends and my band, but at the end of the night, alone in my room... I get stuck in my head. I think about all the stupid shit I've done, trying to figure out why I do it and how to stop. I end up feeling like something's missing and get really fucking lonely."

She stroked his cheek with her fingertips, her heart cracking at this glimpse into the pain buried beneath his tough, playful veneer. "Some*thing* is missing, or some*one*?"

His eyes remained latched to hers. "Someone, I guess. But how can I trust people's intentions? Even some members of my family hound me for money. They don't call on my birthday or ask how I'm doing. They just use me like a fucking ATM. It would be worse if I actually *dated* women. How do I know I'm not being worked by a gold digger? I'd rather be lonely than played like a fool and sucked dry."

Her lips turned down at the tragedy of it. "I'm so sorry, Zack. That's awful. Regular people have trust issues, too, but you're right. There are women who'd use you for selfish reasons. But I'm sure plenty would appreciate the real you."

He shrugged like he didn't buy it. "Your turn. Tell me something you've never told anyone."

Her lips twisted as she thought about the question. She wanted to say the first thing that popped into her head but was unsure how deep to go. He'd been honest and open, so she'd reciprocate.

"I'm really lonely too. Mostly because of my own messed-up trust issues."

When she didn't say more, he nudged her elbow. "Want to tell me about it?"

They weren't stories she shared easily. While she didn't want to kill the mood with her messy past, she wanted to be as bravely open as he'd been.

"I was close with my older brother, Nathan, growing up. We'd make massive Lego cities on the kitchen table and build stick forts in the backyard. We'd make goofy faces at each other during church to make each other laugh, which drove our parents crazy."

She chuckled at the memories before her smile faltered. "He started partying hard junior year. When he shifted from beer and pot to cocaine and pills, I didn't recognize him anymore. When he wasn't angry and irrational, he was moody and depressed. My parents shipped him off to rehab a few times, but it never stuck. I returned from school one day to find my violin and CD collection gone. My mom's jewelry, too. He'd stolen from his own family to feed his habit."

The pressure to be the good, easy daughter became greater than ever. Mandy kept her room spotless and her problems to herself to avoid giving her parents more to worry about. She learned to set aside her needs and accept the leftover scraps of their attention. Even after living on her own for a decade, she still often accepted less than she needed from the people in her life.

"Damn," Zack said, his head shaking. "What an asshole. Where is he now?"

"In prison for cocaine possession and intent to distribute. He got six years. I've visited a few times, but even sober, he's not the guy I used to know. Watching my parents go from denial to trying to pray away his addiction to pouring all their energy into trying to fix him taught me that you can't force someone to change if they aren't ready. And that once trust is broken, it's almost impossible to get it back."

"Shit." He stroked her face, his gaze soft with sympathy. "I'm so sorry."

Her brother's problems and their lingering effects had become taboo subjects in her family. It was a relief to talk about it. While they were on the topic, she might as well share the other major root of her trust issues.

"Also, my high school boyfriend and former best friend got married last year. The two people I told all my secrets to and trusted most in the world were hooking up behind my back for months before I walked in on them screwing in a bathroom at a party."

His eyes blew wide. "Holy shit. That's fucked."

"To make it worse, all our friends knew and didn't tell me. Then ditched me after the breakup. I hate that I miss them sometimes, but I'd rather be lonely than have people in my life who hurt me."

Zack's jaw ticked, his stubble grazing her chin as he shook his head. "You don't deserve to be lonely." His hand slipped into hers, their fingers entwined. "Those people were worthless fucking dickheads who didn't deserve you. And I know I'm a stranger, but I'd *never* hurt you. Or pressure you to do something you aren't ready for. If you've changed your mind about sex, I'm happy just to hang out together until it's time to get on the plane."

She smiled. "Thank you." She felt lighter after sharing things she usually kept inside, and those words meant more than he could ever know. "I haven't changed my mind. I want this. I want *you*."

His lips moved to her neck, pressing a trail of slow, tender kisses on her skin. As his fingertips skated up her ribcage, she was suddenly self-conscious about her right boob being slightly bigger than the left. And the tiny scar on her thigh from crashing her bike when she was ten. What if he found her disappointing once her clothes came off?

"Zack?"

"Hmm?" His questioning hum tickled the crook of her neck.

"Why me?" She inwardly cringed at the tremble of insecurity in her tone.

He lifted his head to look her in the eye. "Why not you?"

"I think I'm pretty, but you go out with tens, hell, elevens. I'm maybe a—"

He touched her lips. "Nope. I don't know how you were going to finish that, but I can tell I don't want to hear it." His hand trailed down her hip, his palm sliding along the outside of her thigh. "You're fucking gorgeous and don't even know it. That means your exes were useless fuckwads for not making damn sure they told you and showed you every second they were lucky enough to be with you." His eyebrows drew together as he studied her face, which must have given away how much she appreciated hearing that. "Why me? You said it was for sex, but you shot me down at first, so it wasn't just that. You could easily have gone home with someone else."

She held his gaze, the invisible tether that connected them growing stronger by the second. "No one else defended me or made sure I was okay when that guy pushed me. No one else looked at me like you did."

"Like what?"

"Like you didn't just see the plain, invisible worker bee who doesn't know how to have fun. My coworkers jokingly call me 'Mom' and 'Fun Police' because I'm the buzzkill who enforces rules and cleans up messes. They like and respect me, but they think I'm boring. And mostly, they're right. I've said no enough in my life. I knew I'd regret it if I didn't say yes."

His head tilted, something like disbelief in his eyes. "There is *nothing* boring about you, Mandy. It's hot that you're a tough, responsible boss-lady. And I promise to make you glad you said yes."

She lifted her head off the pillow to press a soft kiss to his lips. "You already have."

"And if things go further and I do something you don't want, you say no, and it stops. You hold all the power here. Understand?"

No one had ever said those words to her, and it was exactly what she needed to hear. Even more importantly, she saw the laid-bare sincerity in his eyes.

"Zack?"

"Yeah?"

"You don't feel like a stranger anymore." As he watched, she slipped her shirt over her head and tossed it to the floor.

Lust blazed in his eyes, his pupils widening as his appreciative gaze raked over her bare skin. "Can I kiss you again?"

Instead of answering with words, she slipped a hand behind his neck and pulled his lips to hers. The kiss started tender, but the heat between them built to an inferno. His hand slid to her breast, his rough palm cupping her flesh.

He broke the kiss, pulling back an inch. "Since the second I saw you, I was itching to touch underneath all those layers."

"Then take them off," she whispered against his lips.

He smiled, peppering kisses and gentle nips along her jawline. "Can I ask one last question first?"

She stifled a groan. "I'd hoped we'd moved on from talking, but go for it."

"What do you fantasize about?" The kisses stopped, his gaze trained on her face. "When you close your eyes and touch yourself, what do you think about?"

Her cheeks heated, filthy thoughts flooding her mind.

"There," he said with an amused grin, pointing at her face. "What made you blush like that? What were you thinking?"

She took a deep breath to help settle her racing pulse. "After a few cocktails, my coworker Emily often goes on about how great her boyfriend is at... certain things. I've tried what she talks about, but I don't get the hype."

"What does she talk about?"

"Well..." She averted her gaze, staring at the ceiling. "Oral."

When she looked at him, a slow smile spread across his lips. "Okay. Go on."

"I don't mind giving a few instructions to help a guy out. A little to the left or whatever. But I've always had to dictate every single step for it to feel good. Then, I'm worried I'm taking too long and they're bored, so I fake it to get it over with. I wonder if they were terrible at it or if I don't like it."

"And you want someone who knows what they're doing to help you figure that out?"

She nodded, back to avoiding eye contact while she internally died from embarrassment.

"And you're wondering if I'm good at it?"

Again, she nodded.

"Mandy, look at me." His wicked grin remained firmly in place, growing wider as she watched him. "Want to judge that for yourself?"

She could only nod weakly, the image of his mouth on her blanking her mind. The heat in her cheeks flared. "Unless it's not something you like."

He let out a dark, rumbling chuckle that stoked the fire building between her legs. "Baby, I can't think of anything I'd rather do than make you come on my tongue." His dirty and convincing reassurance fanned the flames even higher.

"Don't get hurt if I don't."

That sexy, mischievous grin returned like he craved the challenge. "Impossible. I'll stay between those thighs all goddamn day if that's what it takes. Is that all you were thinking about when you blushed?"

She shook her head, wetting her lips as the filthy thoughts returned.

"Tell me," he whispered against the skin between her breasts before pressing a kiss to the spot.

Mandy knew she could say anything, and he wouldn't judge her. The realization was strangely comforting.

"I boss people around for a living. So, I like the idea of letting someone take control." The heat returned to her cheeks as the corner of his mouth curled up. "And not being treated like some fragile, precious thing. I've never trusted anyone enough or felt brave enough to ask for that."

"You want it rough?" His tone dropped an octave, spiked with something dark and a little frightening that made her shiver.

"Yes." She was finally using the word in all the ways she wanted to. He made it easy to claim the things she'd always talked herself out of.

"If you decide you trust me and want that..." Zack's strong fingers raked through her hair, tugging at the roots enough to make her scalp tingle. The bite of pain was like a teasing whisper of what this notoriously experienced man could unleash. "I can do rough."

The words, paired with the raw hunger in his eyes, made her pussy clench, eager to stretch around his girth as he filled her. "Maybe we'll get there, but I want our first time to be slow and easy. Is that okay?"

"Anything you want is okay. Don't fake *anything* with me. Ever. Understand?" When she nodded, he captured her lips in a kiss so potent and consuming that her kitchen could've exploded, and she'd be oblivious.

She sensed she wouldn't have to fake anything with Zack. And already, she respected his raw, genuine nature enough never to try.

The memory of what came next made her sweat. Their first time was perfect. It was also the first time she was too lost in pleasure to worry about her physical imperfections, the fate of her soul, or her inexperience.

If Mandy weren't at work, she would've slipped her hand down her pants to relieve the pulsing ache between her legs. From their first time to their last, Zack had bedroom skills that left her with a craving nothing else could satisfy.

Even outside the bedroom, their connection was electric and addictive. Seventy-two hours wasn't enough. So, she'd called Ted from Dallas to ask to use vacation time to turn three days into seven. When she wasn't deterred by his fatherly lecture of concern, he said yes, and they were off to Phoenix.

She discovered more about what turned her on in that week than she'd ever imagined possible. The fleeting nature of their time together made it easier to let her inhibitions fall, to feel instead of overthinking.

That trip was also when she discovered how much he disliked kids. They stopped for lunch with his bandmates before their flight, and the toddler at the table across from them kept grabbing chunks of soggy pancake and stuffing them into her wet, sticky face. When the little girl spit out a mouthful of orange juice, Mandy thought he'd puke.

He said he *never* wanted to be a dad and listed at least a dozen solid reasons for his decision. Back then, she wasn't sure she wanted kids either, and since their one-week-only arrangement ensured this relationship would be brief and casual, it didn't matter anyway.

Until it did.

That was one of the many reasons she hadn't told Zack about their son.

8

Zack

When Zack opened his front door, Kyla threw her arms around him and squeezed. It wasn't the first time their bodies were pressed together, but in the seven months she'd been with Adam, she hadn't made a habit of giving Zack random hugs.

"What the fuck was that for? Where's Adam?"

She shook with laughter against his chest before letting him go. "Nice to see you too, Grumpy Puss. You're stuck with just me right now. He's doing a photo shoot for *Modern Drummer*."

She'd be grumpy, too, if she were sexually frustrated and running on two broken hours of sleep. He'd tossed and turned all night, drenched in sweat, tormented by memories of Mandy. Since committing to letting her go two weeks ago, it felt like his body and mind constantly protested the decision. His heart was pretty pissed-off, too, aching like some heavyweight meathead had used it for a punching bag.

As an added kick in the nuts, he hadn't had a drink or smoked weed in two weeks, so he'd experienced every bit of the misery, intense and raw.

"Sorry, princess." Zack scrubbed his hands over his face, exhaustion making his eyes burn. "Late night."

"Shocker." Her nose wrinkled. "You need a shower."

"Is that how you talk to a man in his own home?" He waved her inside and shut the door. "Your manners are shit, lady."

In truth, he appreciated her bluntness. His best friend deserved a girlfriend who wasn't fake or shy about her opinions.

The second Adam met Kyla at a pastry table before Tyler's wedding, he was hooked on the sweet little veterinarian with long, dark hair and a smart mouth that got impressively dirty during their threesome.

As Zack got to know her, he understood the other reasons his friend was so drawn to her. Her intelligence challenged Adam. Their sex wasn't the only thing they did loudly—their couch conversations about everything from biology to art to the meaning of life were also deep, passionate, and lasted for hours. She treated him like a normal guy instead of being awed by his star power.

While Zack missed their wild, carefree days and often found her chipper presence annoying, he was glad Adam found happiness with a worthy partner.

Zack's feet dragged as he went to the living room and collapsed into a black leather recliner across from the massive TV. Zoning out with a shitty movie or some *Jerry Springer* might help get his mind off things. It's hard to be too sad about your life when people were brawling over finding out their parents were cousins.

Kyla followed and sat on the matching black leather sofa beside it. "I called Mandy."

His stomach lurched as his dry, scratchy eyes bulged out of his skull. "You fucking w*hat*?"

"I know, I know, I probably shouldn't have."

"Probably?" He gripped the armrests like he planned to rip them from the frame. "Why the hell would you do that?"

"I thought about how you tried calling her. Adam said there have been other times he's pried a phone from your hands before you could call her wasted and sad. I thought maybe if we talked, woman-to-woman, I could find out if she still has feelings for you or if we all need to work harder to help you get over her."

He shoved off his chair and paced the living room. "It's not your goddamn business, Kyla!"

She flinched, her face crumpling. "I'm sorry."

The hurt in her expression made him feel like an asshole. She shouldn't have done it, but her intentions were good. The night of the threesome, she asked about past relationships, and of course, he talked about Mandy. Kyla knew from the start how much he wanted a second chance.

He flopped beside her on the couch with a worn-out sigh. "No, I'm fucking sorry. I shouldn't yell at you for trying to help my pathetic ass." He swallowed past the lump in his throat and braced himself. "What did she say?"

Kyla set a gentle hand on his knee. "That her feelings for you are complicated. She cares about you, always will, and wishes things were different. And to give you a hug for her. Which I did, even though you smell like a gym sock."

A question burned on his tongue, but he feared the answer. Might as well yank off the fucking bandage while he was already miserable. "Is she with someone?"

"I don't know. I'm sorry." She pulled her hand away, and the corners of her mouth fell. "Zack, there's something else."

"What?"

"She has a new boss, and he's a fucking creep. I overheard him hitting on her, offering money for 'side jobs' because she's struggling." Kyla shuddered.

"Are you fucking kidding me?" His hands curled into fists as rage heated his blood. There was a lot of awful to unpack in those sentences, but first, he wanted to kill her fucking boss. Once he found out the shithead's name, he'd start shopping for a shovel.

"It was terrible. I stayed on the line to make sure she was okay."

Thoughts of murder shuffled to the side as his brain snagged on something else. "What do you mean she's struggling?"

Kyla shrugged. "Sounds like her pay isn't great, but it's too risky to go for what she wants."

"What does she want?" Of course, Zack wished it was him with every cell in his tattooed body, but he knew he wasn't that lucky. Whatever it was, he'd move the Rocky fucking Mountains to make it happen because she couldn't stay at the club. When Kyla took too long to answer, he wanted to scream. "For fuck's sake, Kyla, spit it out!"

"To manage bands. Cool, right? But she needs the steady paycheck too badly to go for it."

She had that dream when they met. He'd hoped she'd chased it by now, but the fact that money held her back pissed him off. What happened to her savings? Would it be weird to mail her an anonymous box of cash?

"I feel like a jerk for breaking chick code," she said, "but I understand what Mandy means to you, and you deserve to know."

"Thanks," Zack muttered, feeling like he'd taken a two-by-four to the gut.

She nudged his knee. "It might be a dumb idea, but Adam said Fury Fuel's manager needs an assistant for the tour's first leg. He asked if my sister was interested because she got laid off, but she hates traveling. Maybe Mandy can take it?"

His head reared back as what she'd said sank in. "Seriously?"

Shane Marx, an industry heavy hitter, repped Fury Fuel. If Mandy had trouble transitioning to management, a position like that could get her foot in the door. More importantly, it would get her away from the dangerous fucking shithead at the club.

"It's a step down from her current gig," she continued, "but the pay's insane, and she'd learn a lot from him. It could be a stepping stone, like my internship at the animal hospital. I learned a ton assisting the head vet."

Zack's battered heart backflipped in his chest as the full scope of the possibilities struck. The position would bring more than a career boost for Mandy. Fury Fuel opened for the first three weeks of Tomorrow Mourning's co-headlining tour with Killing Daisies. He'd see her backstage and whenever the bands mingled between gigs if she got that job.

Instead of forcing himself to work out how to let her go, he'd have a second chance to prove he could be the man she deserved. If he succeeded, they could figure out the distance issue together.

If he failed, would it kill him to see her every day, only to say goodbye again when the tour ended? Abso-fucking-lutely. But having her back in his life, even temporarily, would be worth it. Ensuring she was safe and building a better life for herself would be worth it.

And if it didn't work a second time, he might get the closure he needed to move on.

When Kyla left, Zack sank into his couch, his brain shifting into overdrive.

Since his breakup with Mandy, he'd found comfort in knowing she was in the city she loved and happy with her job at the club.

But that was no longer the case.

She deserved a better life than the one she was stuck in. She deserved to see the world and have all her biggest dreams come true. Aside from flying to Colorado, tossing her over his shoulder like a goddamn caveman, and dragging her to Portland, what could he do? Shameless sinners like him weren't built to be anyone's savior.

He couldn't even save himself from the misery that set into his bones every time he thought about how she smelled like vanilla and lemons or how her voice sounded as beautiful and soothing as the music they both lived for.

What he could do was pull strings.

There was power in what he did for a living, and it was time to use it for more than inspiring pretty girls to scream in the front row.

He picked up the phone, hitting speed dial for his band's manager, Sophia Cruz. Her secretary answered, transferring the call to Sophia's office.

If this worked, he'd have to lie to Mandy. She was too proud to accept help and would never accept the opportunity otherwise. There was a chance she still wouldn't, but he had to try.

"What can I do for you, Zack?" Sophia asked, her tone upbeat.

"I need a phone number. And a favor."

9

Mandy

After successfully dodging her boss for a week, Mandy was disappointed and on edge to find him watching her from the other side of the empty club. He'd been spending more time at his other businesses, giving everyone a welcome break.

She didn't know when he'd arrived or what he'd been up to but didn't care. As usual, she and the rest of the crew handled everything fine without him. All he ever seemed to do was sign checks, drink top-shelf bourbon, and bitch about profits not meeting his projections.

Maybe he was as terrible at math as he was at being a decent human being.

It wasn't an event night, so she'd been at the club since nine in the morning, preparing for the busy weekend ahead. She could finally tackle the last task on her list—a chat with the lighting guy. It'd been a long day, and she wanted to get home.

When her eyes briefly met Mr. Sutter's, he leaned an elbow against the cherry wood bar, a slimy grin tugging at his lips.

Her skin prickled as she returned her attention to the new, cheaper lighting guy he'd hired. The tech was the only other straggler because he took forever to set up his equipment for the next day. His eyes glazed over as she explained the Saturday headliner's special requests—no green lights, no strobes, and focus red beams on each performer whenever the smoke machine's triggered. Simple stuff, but his face blanked with a look that said he was stoned, in way over his head, or both.

"Mandy." Mr. Sutter's voice instantly made her shoulders stiffen and skin crawl. At least he sounded sober this time. "A word."

She thought of a few she'd like to say as she walked in his direction, stopping a few feet away. It didn't feel far enough. The unspoken threat he posed hovered between them like a toxic fog, mingling with his nauseating stench of expensive cigars and arrogance.

"Yes?" she asked, unable to keep the dip of impatience from her tone. She was exhausted, and her feet hurt. How someone with so much money did so little while she hustled and scrimped drove her mad.

"Open mic nights are back on the schedule. I told you to cancel them."

She bit back an exasperated sigh. It was the only time she'd gone behind his back, but she felt compelled to take a stand for something so important to the community.

"I was going to talk to you about that. Phone calls flooded in from patrons and performers, begging us to bring it back. Performers count on that initial exposure and the opportunity to hone their set. Patrons enjoy that glimpse into burgeoning local talent, excited to see the next big band or songwriter before they explode."

The words rushed out because organizing open mics was her first passion project when she came to work for Ted. He loved the idea and encouraged her at every step. The event had been a mainstay on the club's calendar for over a decade, and the Denver music community needed that outlet.

"How about we make a deal?" His head tilted, but his cold, creepy gaze remained on her face. "You get to keep your open mics, and I get to take you to dinner."

Mandy bit the inside of her cheek, willing her hands to resist the urge to punch that smarmy smirk off his face. "Thanks, but no. I have to get home." As she turned to walk back toward her office, his hand seized her elbow, squeezing until she jerked it back, freeing herself from his grip. "Don't *ever* touch me again."

He stepped forward, his looming presence smothering. The club was too quiet. She looked around to find that the lighting guy was gone, and they were the only ones left.

"Or what?" Mr. Sutter's lips twitched.

"Or I'll report you for harassment."

He barked a laugh that was as joyless as him, the sound echoing in the empty room. "To whom? There's no one above me." He arched a challenging brow. "And you're stuck being under me."

She wanted to throw up all over his shiny leather shoes, which probably cost more than her car. Her purse and keys were in her office. The look in his eyes and the darkness descending on the windows sent a jolt of fear shuddering up her spine.

"I'm leaving," she said, her voice shaky.

On wobbly knees, she rushed to her office, swiped her purse from the bottom drawer of her desk, and made a beeline for the club's front door. She felt his intense gaze on her back as she picked up speed, a flood of adrenaline putting her senses on high alert.

The slow, measured footsteps of the predator behind her tapped closer, but she didn't look back.

"Get home safely, Mandy."

Inside her car, she locked the doors, and her lungs emptied with a loud, shuddering rush of breath. Her hands shook as they thrust the key into the ignition, and she took off with squealing tires, putting distance between her and the place that no longer felt like a second home.

He'd stolen that from her.

And he'd steal more if she didn't get out.

She'd spent the last few weeks circling want ads, making calls, and filling out applications. She scheduled a few interviews on her days off, but each one would be a pay cut. The ten thousand dollars from Ted wouldn't last long, and she'd already dipped into it to replace her busted water heater.

She was already tight with her money, but she'd live on ramen and use dollar-store shampoo if it meant getting away from *him*.

She parked beside her mother's car in the driveway of the small but cozy bungalow—the last safe space she had besides her parents' house. Even there, she couldn't fully be herself and relax.

After turning off her engine, she took a minute to catch her breath and wipe the terror off her face so her mom wouldn't worry. She didn't need to know that her daughter's once simple, structured life was spiraling out of control.

Mandy wished she could call Zack.

He was a great listener and made her feel safe. Kyla said he'd tried calling Mandy because he still had feelings for her, but what if it was more than that? He'd said once that she made him feel safe, too. Or maybe he just wanted to hear her voice. How many times had she replayed his TV and radio interviews because she ached to hear his? That rolling, sexy baritone always calmed her while inspiring a rush of fluttering warmth low in her belly and deep in her chest.

But calling him would reopen old wounds for both of them—she wasn't prepared to do that.

Apparently, nothing in her life could be simple anymore.

She didn't even have close friends to talk to and help her sort through the mess. Ted would feel awful knowing she was in danger because he'd sold the club to that shithead. Friends she made in college either moved away after graduation or got wrapped up in their careers and drifted apart. Over the years, the list of people she could confide in had dwindled to nearly zero, making her feel even more lost and pathetic.

And lonely. Deeply fucking lonely.

She got out, unlocked her front door, and listened.

Quiet.

Her mother had talents Mandy wished she'd inherited. The gentle sounds of her mother singing a lullaby helped to soothe the empty spaces of her heart.

She walked to the last door on the right, opening it slowly before tiptoeing inside. Her mom smiled, but her eyes looked tired. The small bundle in her arms was fast asleep, pale skin glowing under the tiny moon-shaped nightlight above the crib. Mandy leaned over and kissed her son's soft, sweet-smelling forehead before taking him and holding him to her chest.

"Thanks, Mom," she whispered.

Mandy felt a comforting pat on the shoulder as her mom left the bedroom.

Her shifts at the club didn't start until late afternoon on Friday through Sunday, allowing her to be with little Phoenix for most of his waking hours. For that, she was grateful. On Wednesdays and Thursdays, she was off by five and got to put him to bed. Her mom watched him while Mandy worked, and together, they kept him on a consistent routine. It had its challenges, but her mom adored her grandson and was happy to help. Childcare costs were ridiculous, so Mandy was grateful for that, too.

She swayed side-to-side beneath the glowing stars on the ceiling, the weight of his tiny body pressing into her chest. As she held him, the stresses of her day melted away. The struggles of being a single mother were many, but the quiet moments reminded her why it was all worth it. There was nothing she wouldn't do to make sure her son had a roof over his head.

Fortunately, breastmilk was free, and she pumped twice at work and fed him throughout the day when she was home. It was great for her budget when that was all he needed, but at almost eight months old, he was also on solid foods and occasionally formula, so their grocery bills grew as quickly as he was.

If she had to take a pay cut somewhere else, she could get a second job. Or sell her eggs. Evidently, they were strong and made adorable offspring. Of course, Phoenix didn't look like her, aside from the chestnut locks that gently curled at the ends. He looked like his father, breaking her heart a little every time she looked at that innocent little face.

She kissed his soft cheek. "Good night, Little Bug," she whispered, inhaling his sweet, familiar scent as she set him into his crib.

The sheet covering the mattress featured Winnie the Pooh and all his friends from the Hundred Acre Wood—her favorite books as a child. One perk to getting a day job would be reading those stories to him before bed every night. And she might get more than the five hours of sleep she typically ran on.

Of course, if she couldn't find a day job, she'd be stuck.

As the terrible end to her workday replayed in her mind, she cursed that she'd have to go back tomorrow and take whatever else her boss and his sick urges dished out. Before grabbing her arm tonight, he'd only used words to intimidate her.

After that escalation, what was next?

As much as she never wanted to return, she had to stick it out until she found something that would give Phoenix the best possible life. Since the second that line on the pregnancy test turned blue, what she wanted no longer mattered—his needs came first.

Always.

Her stomach growled, and she tiptoed out of the nursery, heading for the kitchen. The two slices of mushroom and garlic pizza from a few nights ago were calling her name.

When she opened the refrigerator, half of its contents—including the leftover pizza—were missing. They'd been replaced with prepackaged salads, celery sticks, and cut-up melons. She mumbled a curse. Only one person had the means, motive, and opportunity to toss all that food—her diet-obsessed mother.

Mandy wasn't in the mood to argue, so she grabbed an apple off the counter and took a bite. She'd raid the snack stash in the pantry later.

She left the kitchen to find her mom folding tiny onesies on the living room couch. "I'll do that, Mom. Leave it."

Her mom set the clean laundry down, frowning as she took in Mandy's expression. "You look beat, honey. Get some sleep. I'll finish this before I go."

Mandy sat on the couch, resting her head on her mom's sturdy shoulder, which smelled like baby powder and home. "Thanks for everything."

"Any luck finding a new job?"

Mandy lifted her head and grabbed a soft green blanket from the pile, folding it in her lap and setting it on the cushion beside her. She hadn't clued her mother into her career woes to spare her the stress and disappointment, so the question caught her off guard.

"What do you mean?"

"I saw the jobs circled in the want ads." Her mom picked up the green blanket, refolded it into a neater square, and set it back on the couch. "It's about time. They've never paid you what you're worth."

Mandy nodded, agreeing and feeling even more defeated. Ted was an amazing boss and always made her feel valued, but after expenses, he never had enough to pay the employees as much as he wanted to.

But she'd happily take a boss who treated everyone with respect and was generous in every way he could afford to be over a coldhearted jerk like his successor.

"I'll find something better," Mandy said, trying to convince them both. "I have a few interviews this week."

"If you need some money, your father and I can—"

"No. But thanks." Mandy needed to solve her own problems. All the free babysitting was more than enough. "But I appreciate it."

"Not to sound like a broken record, but you can always go after Phoenix's father for child support. He's certainly good for it."

Mandy let out a sigh, edged with irritation. She was tired of this conversation. They'd been having it since her belly swelled to where it was impossible not to tell her parents about the surprise grandchild on the way. She was used to hiding truths about herself, afraid to disappoint them. More than that, she didn't want to see the judgment in their eyes.

When the doctor confirmed that the white plastic stick she peed on told the truth, she could almost hear the collective voices of her holier-than-thou relatives, all praying for the poor, unwed mother who made her living hanging around drunk degenerates and rock musicians. And drunk, degenerate rock musicians.

As predicted, her parents were furious. Since her announcement, her father had struggled to look her in the eye, and they hardly spoke. She was supposed to be the child who made them proud by becoming a concert pianist, marrying a perfect, clean-cut man and devoting her life to raising a flock of perfect little churchgoers. In their eyes, she'd failed on all fronts.

Since Phoenix was born, they'd urged her to sue for child support, but that would mean telling the man who never wanted to be a father that she'd made him one behind his back. Sure, it took two to tango, and they'd done plenty of that in their brief time together, but they didn't plan for the condom to break. She'd made the choice to have their son and never regretted it for a second.

"I can't, Mom. Please don't go there. It's been a long day."

Her mom folded the last onesie and added it to the finished pile. "Look, I don't want *that man* around my grandson any more than you do. But you deserve a lighter financial burden, so you don't have to work yourself into the ground."

Mandy rubbed her temples with deep circles, the first pangs of a headache throbbing beneath her skin. The situation wasn't so black-and-white. And like many things in her life, she constantly second-guessed her decisions. Her parents did the same in stereo: *Why don't you sell the house and move in with us? Why don't you get a respectable job? Why don't you go after the father of your child—who doesn't even know he's a father—for child support?*

Her biggest question to herself: *Why haven't you told him yet?*

It got louder with every month and milestone that passed. Zack would never see the first time his son crawled or smiled. He didn't get to hold him after he was born. Mandy stole those moments from him. She felt guilty about that, knowing how devastated she'd be if the tables were turned.

But she told herself the absence was a gift. Zack could go on living the wild, untethered life he loved. And her son wouldn't have a father who was never around or, even worse, a bad influence if he ever decided to pop in to say hi while reeking of beer and cigarettes with a pretty groupie under his arm.

But no matter how hard she tried to convince herself that they were all better off as things were, she knew deep down that keeping Phoenix a secret was a mistake. The fear that her son would have to suffer the consequences of her silence grew stronger every day.

"I'll figure it out," Mandy said. "Please don't worry about us."

Her mom's eyes rolled. "Impossible. I want the best for both of you." She stood and bent over to kiss the top of Mandy's head. "Get some sleep, honey. And think about what I said about child support."

Mandy nodded. "Thanks, Mom."

Once her mom was out the door, she locked up, shuffled to her bedroom, and kicked off her shoes. She flopped onto her bed, staring at the framed sonogram photo on the wall.

Everything changed that day.

It was six weeks after she and Zack parted ways in Phoenix. Before the appointment, she'd thought of all the reasons having a baby was a terrible idea—she lived in a tiny shoebox apartment, was finally about to chase her managing dream, and valued her freedom and independence too much to give them up.

But once she heard that fluttering heartbeat, their mistake didn't feel like a mistake anymore. They planted that tiny, wiggly bean the night she fell in love for the first time.

Plus, as her doctor so kindly reminded her, Mandy was thirty, and her fertility window would narrow in the next few years. It might be her only chance to be a mother.

When she returned from the appointment, she dialed Zack's number while clutching the sonogram, prepared to tell him the news. She planned to assure him he only had to be as involved as he wanted, no pressure.

He answered the phone, completely trashed. Alcohol, weed, or both slurred his voice, and he struggled to string together a coherent sentence. Music blared in the background, and she heard at least a dozen people laughing and talking. She couldn't tell him something so life-changing when she wasn't even sure he'd remember the conversation.

Through web searches over the next few weeks, she watched for signs he was ready to change and could handle the news that he'd be a father—they never came. Instead, he was getting in fights, smoking pot with fans after shows, and she'd seen a very unflattering shot of him exiting a strip club clutching a half-empty whiskey bottle while Adam held him upright. During one of their calls, Zack claimed he'd given up sleeping around, but a tabloid photo of him on a beach with some woman in a bikini said otherwise.

She still couldn't trust him as a partner, and their son deserved a father who wouldn't view him as a burden or mistake. A father who was a positive role model, capable of giving Phoenix love and guidance as he grew up. When it was clear that Zack couldn't be that person for their son, she called him one last time and broke off contact.

It was devastating.

Mandy never meant to fall for him. She never imagined it would be possible to feel such a strong connection after such a short time, but it was undeniable—he was the love of her life.

But since having them both was impossible, she had to choose.

She chose Phoenix.

All the money she'd saved to manage went to diapers, pediatrician bills, baby clothes, and a mortgage to invest in their future. She clung tightly to the memories of what she had with Zack, mourning the loss of how he made her feel seen, special, and beautiful.

She wished things were different, but at least she had Phoenix—the best parts of both of them in one sweet, adorable little package.

It was easier for everyone this way. Zack's life would remain unchanged, her parents wouldn't worry about his influence on their grandson, and as long as Mandy solved her job issue soon, Phoenix would keep his peaceful, secure life and predictable routines.

At least, it was easier for everyone but her.

But again, that didn't matter. All that mattered was Phoenix.

10

Zack

The tip of the joint smoldered in an ashtray beside the phone, the skunky scent thick in the air as Zack dialed and waited. He'd cut way back on smoking weed, but if he didn't take the edge off, he was going to lose his shit. At least it was natural and wouldn't send him doom-spiraling. Or pickle his liver.

This phone call needed to go well. Too much was riding on it, and the anticipation made his palms sweat. The two hits he'd taken settled his nerves a little, but his knee still bounced like mad under his kitchen table.

There was a click on the other line followed by a cheerful "Hello."

"Hi. Is this Ted?"

"Yes, may I ask who's calling, please?"

"This is Zack Maine. I'm—"

"I know who you are." His sharp tone made it clear Mandy hadn't only shared flattering details. "What can I do for you, young man?"

"I'm worried about Mandy."

"What?" Ted sounded startled, making it obvious how much he cared for her. *Good.* That was essential for the plan to work. "Why? What's happened?"

"The guy who took over for you at the club is a fucking scumbag." Zack picked up the joint and took a long drag as his blood heated, a thin trail of grayish smoke rising from the ember. "Even if he weren't, she deserves a bigger life. A better one."

Ted muttered a curse. "I had my concerns about James, and I've heard stories from my former staff that he's fired. I wouldn't have sold to him if I'd thought he was dangerous, but my son couldn't afford to take over, and my hands were tied. Is she okay?"

"For now. But she needs to get out of there." Smoke drifted from Zack's lips as he spoke. "She's always wanted to manage bands, and she should be doing that instead of making shit pay and working for an asshole."

"Yes, I know. I've always encouraged her, but she'd never let me call in favors to give her a boost. She's a proud, independent woman who wants to earn it on her own. She finally had enough saved and planned to pursue it, but then..." He trailed off before clearing his throat. "Not my story to tell. What do you need from me? I'll do anything for Mandy."

"We have that in common, Ted." Zack smiled, grateful for the ally. He wondered what happened to her savings, but if things worked out as planned, he could ask her himself. "She'd never let me help either, but now, I feel like there's no choice."

Ted made a skeptical rumbling sound in his throat. "I'm listening."

"I need you to lie to her a little." Zack set the joint back in the ashtray. "My band's touring Europe this summer. Shane Marx manages our opener for the first leg, and he's looking for an assistant to shadow him. Running errands, handling band drama, that kind of shit. It's temporary, but she'd learn a ton while making connections on the road. And it's enough money to quit the club and go after what she really wants."

"Oh, my. You've thought this through, son."

"I have. But it'll only work if no one tells her I did this. There's an interview and probably lots of competition for the spot, so she'll still have to earn the job on her own. But you and I both know she'll knock them fucking dead."

"I agree. With all of it. Though, I question your motives."

That was fair. The plan wasn't completely unselfish, but Zack would do it even if he couldn't be near her again.

"I won't lie, seeing her would be a huge fucking cherry on top, but I'm doing this for her. Even if she avoids me the entire three weeks, I'd be happy knowing she's safe and closer to living her dream."

"Three weeks? That's how long she'd be away?"

"Yeah, July eighth to twenty-seventh. It'll be London, Rome, and Paris. We have two shows in each city, a few other gigs nearby, signing events and press in between, and she'll have plenty of downtime to explore and play tourist."

"Wow." Ted let out a deep chuckle. "She'd love that. Where do I come in?"

"You have to be the one to tell her about the opportunity. You can say you heard about it from one of your connections and give her the number. Hopefully, she's so ready to move on she'll swallow her pride and accept the help."

He took another pull of the joint as he waited for a response, the tip glowing red as tiny gray ashes drifted onto his lap.

"I hate to set her up for the shock without warning, but since it's for the greater good... I'll do it."

"Awesome." Zack grinned, the strong marijuana and good news making him feel lighter after a few heavy, brutal weeks. "Thank you. Grab a pen, and I'll give you the number she needs."

After he rattled off the contact information for Shane Marx's secretary and shared all the details he knew, the line went quiet.

"Everything okay?"

Ted cleared his throat. "I probably shouldn't be telling you this, but..."

Zack sat up straighter. "Yeah?"

"Mandy still cares for you, son. When she told me she was going on tour with you for three days, I thought she was out of her mind. But when she called to ask for another four days off, I heard in her voice how smitten she was. That woman's like a daughter to me, and I want to see her happy. She's one of the most selfless, kindhearted people I've ever known, and she deserves to settle down with someone who loves and appreciates her. Someone who'll stick around for the tough stuff and savor the best moments at her side."

"I agree. Completely."

"Good. Having said that, I'm familiar with your reputation. I'm not judging because I've made my share of mistakes. But if you're not the settling-down type, let her go for good. If you can be the partner we both know she deserves... then I wish you luck."

Zack smiled, relieved to hear those words from someone so close to her. He would keep working to become the partner she deserved, no matter what it took. "Thank you, Ted."

"But if you hurt her, no one will ever find your body."

After thanking Ted again for his help and ending the call, Zack allowed himself a selfish moment of pure fucking glee. He'd had plenty of practice at being selfish, so it wasn't hard.

He didn't enjoy playing god with her life, but after what Kyla said, he couldn't sit back while Mandy worked with someone who could hurt her. If it weren't for the upcoming band interviews and preparations for the European tour, he'd already be in Denver, putting that fucker in the hospital or worse. That day would come, but first things first.

The plan could work.

She wouldn't be able to turn down that amount of money, and her biggest dream would come true—two birds, one big ass stone.

If only he could be there to see her light up when she found out. At least Ted got to deliver the news. He deserved that honor for his role in this and for putting Zack's mind at ease about a few other things.

Mandy's still single.

The worry that she shared her life and bed with some unworthy douchebag was finally squashed. And since Ted and Kyla both said she still cared about him, he might have a real shot at getting her back.

They could even overcome their biggest hurdle—distance—if she took the job. By quitting the club, she wouldn't be tied to Denver. She might be open to moving to Portland if she could go anywhere. If she wouldn't move, he'd fly to see her every chance he had.

Unfortunately, the excitement and relief didn't last long. A fresh wave of anxiety rippled through his gut as a harsh realization struck.

If she took the job, this wasn't just his second chance—it was probably his last.

If she went on the tour, he'd have three weeks to prove he was ready to settle down and that they could make a relationship work.

A glance at the clock said he needed to get his ass in gear and get ready for the rehearsal at Tyler's. He showered and threw on jeans and a black T-shirt before heading over.

The vibe was weird at Tyler and Charlotte's since their kid was born—either eerily quiet and tense or noisy, stinky chaos. Fortunately, fatherhood hadn't changed his friend into a dull drone, too exhausted to write new songs while covered in baby puke. He was the same old Ty, just busier and harder to drag out to hang with over beers.

Charlotte answered the door in sweatpants and a massive Pearl Jam T-shirt, her dark hair piled on her head in a messy ball. She was still drop-dead fucking gorgeous, but motherhood had the girl looking overdue for a trip to the salon.

"Make a fucking sound," she whispered in a hiss, "and I'll kill you where you stand."

"Uh, okay."

She stepped aside, holding the door for him before shutting it with a soft click. "Ty's in the studio," she whispered.

He would've thought she'd cracked if there weren't a baby in the house that must be sleeping. He tiptoed to the studio to avoid her wrath.

Tyler sat on the couch, petting their beagle, Roxy. Zack flinched when she barked, but the room was soundproof—probably why the dog was joining them.

"Hey, man," Tyler waved him over. He looked tired, too, his eyes red and underlined by dark pits. "Grab a beer. Adam's late. He went skateboarding with Amber's brother and twisted his ankle. Three weeks before Europe! I'll fucking strangle that idiot if he can't play today."

"Shit. Is he okay?"

Tyler shrugged. "Amber took him to Urgent Care. We'll see."

Adam had to be okay before the tour. At least it wasn't his wrist, but he needed his legs and ankles strong to work the kick drum and hi-hat.

Still avoiding alcohol and the dumb shit he did under its influence, Zack grabbed a Coke and sank into one of the black leather recliners across from the couch.

Tyler set down his beer. "Adam said you tried calling Mandy again. You okay?"

Zack shrugged, trying to look unaffected even though Tyler always saw through his bullshit. "I did something. Maybe brilliant, maybe really fucking stupid."

Tyler rubbed the five o'clock shadow darkening half his face. "If you think it might be really fucking stupid, that doesn't bode well. Let's hear it."

Charlotte walked in, holding the baby. Tyler's expression shifted from concern over Zack's confession to glowing with joy. How a stinky little creature who couldn't even talk made his friend smile like that was beyond him.

"Hey, little girl." Tyler got up, took the baby, and kissed her tiny bald head. Well, not *bald*. There was dark fluff on top, the same shade as Tyler's, but not much of it. She looked like both of them mashed together, which made sense because... science, but it was still weird.

"Sorry to bug you guys," Charlotte said, "but I need to pee and wash my face. If I put her down, she'll start screaming again."

"You could never bug me." Tyler kissed her forehead. "Do whatever you need to do. We're at a standstill until Adam hobbles his ass in here."

She frowned with a wince. "Yeah, Amber said the swelling's bad. Poor guy."

She walked out, and Tyler swayed while the baby grabbed his finger and tried pulling it to her mouth. They loved their kid, but Zack didn't understand the hype. They had zero free time, hardly slept, and had nothing to show for it but endless screaming, crying, and shitty diapers.

"Want to hold her?" Tyler asked.

Zack bit back the *fuck no* that almost came out on reflex. "Nah, I'm good."

"So, what were you going to say before they came in?"

Zack sipped his soda before explaining his plan to get Mandy the assistant gig and away from her asshole boss. As Tyler listened, his usual look of disapproval set in—the deepening crease between his eyebrows, the grimace making the sides of his mouth droop. They'd been close since ninth grade, and since Zack was a master of mistakes, he'd seen that face a lot.

"Damn," Tyler said, his head shaking. "I know your heart's in the right place, but you can't mess with her life like that."

"I'm supposed to let that fuckwad hurt her?" Just thinking about her creeper boss made him see red. "You know as well as I do, guys like that don't stop at words."

"I get that, but what if she finds out? She'll know she got the gig because you threw your status at her problem instead of earning the opportunity for herself."

"Oh, she fucking earned it. You've talked to musicians who've played her club. She does much more for those bands than most promoters and would go above and beyond for Shane. And I told Sophia to make it clear to Shane to keep my role in this quiet, but if Mandy finds out, hopefully, my good intentions will earn her forgiveness."

"Okay, let's be real." Tyler raised a dark and dubious eyebrow. "You're also doing this because you want her back. But seventeen months is a long time. I hate to say it, but she could be married for all you know."

"She's not. Her old boss said she's single and still has feelings for me. Even if she didn't... I want her to be safe and not struggling to get by. But of fucking course, I want her back. If it's my last chance, I'm taking it."

"I get it. Lord knows I did crazy shit to get Charlotte back after we split. And if Mandy's the reason you aren't the hungover mess you've been lately, I'm all for it."

Zack held up his Coke. "When have you ever seen me choose a fucking *soda* over a beer? I'll toss back a few occasionally, but I'm done with blackouts and hangovers. I'm working on ditching cigarettes, too. I want to be better for her than I was."

"Good." A smile tugged at the edge of his mouth. "Then throw kerosene on that bitch and let it rip."

Zack laughed, appreciating that his friend remembered his advice from when Tyler was afraid to pursue Charlotte. Hopefully, Zack's approach to chasing the spark between him and Mandy worked out just as well.

The baby made unhappy, squeaky noises, and Tyler returned to swaying, adding a little bounce.

"Shh..." He rubbed her back. "I've got you, baby girl."

"Is that fun?" Zack asked, still baffled. "I don't get it."

Tyler laughed, shaking his head like Zack was the moron instead of the guy who didn't pull out in time. "I love it. I love her. Some parts suck, sure, but I wouldn't change it."

"Whatever. Seems like a lot of work for no reward."

Again, Tyler gaped like Zack had said something absurd like *French fries are gross* or *I hate blow jobs.*

"The reward is having someone to love unconditionally who loves you back. And Charlotte and I are closer than ever. I get that it's not for everyone. Matty and Amber don't want kids either, and while I'm bummed I'll never be an uncle, I respect his choice. Fatherhood isn't something you should do unless you're ready to sacrifice your needs for someone else's."

With that, Zack was even more sold on never going down that road. He was a selfish bastard, and although he was working on changing that, he'd never want to sacrifice his freedom. If he wanted to stay out all night, he did. If he wanted to fly to Mexico for a week of margaritas and surfing, he did. That condoms weren't foolproof always made him nervous, and if he could stomach the idea of someone slicing open his balls, he'd be first in line for a vasectomy.

He knew a relationship would require compromise and was open to change, but that was different from giving up his freedom. Hopefully, if things worked out, Mandy would join him on the spontaneous adventures that recharged him between tours.

Charlotte returned, looking a little more human. She'd pulled her hair back in a ponytail, and her face shined like she'd slapped lotion on it. The baby let out a crackly, high-pitched wail, and Zack slammed his hands over his ears.

Tyler's eyes darted to Charlotte's shirt. "Oh, shit, baby, your..."

He pointed to her chest, and Zack followed his line of sight. Two dark, wet circles spread over Charlotte's tits.

She slapped her hands over them, her eyes wide before she burst out laughing. "Zack, turn around."

Tyler laughed, too, as Zack turned his head, unsure whether to be grossed out or turned on.

"Are your tits broken or something?"

They laughed harder.

"It happens when the baby cries like that," she explained. "She's hungry."

In his periphery, Zack saw her take the baby and lift one side of her shirt. Thankfully, the wailing stopped.

"Now that I've sufficiently mortified Zack," Charlotte said, "we'll leave you guys to it."

When the door clicked shut, he spun back around. "Dude."

Tyler put a hand up. "Whatever you're about to say, think about whether it'll get your ass kicked. That was a normal human thing. Charlotte's body makes food, and it's fucking cool and beautiful, and if you say some ignorant shit, you'll fucking regret it."

Zack stayed quiet and sipped his Coke.

The door opened, and Adam limped into the studio on crutches. Fucking *crutches*! A flesh-colored strap wrapped around his ankle, but the swelling underneath was obvious.

"Are you goddamn kidding me?" Tyler set down his bottle with a thump. "Is it broken?"

"Sprained." Adam limped to the other recliner. "Sorry, guys. But you should've seen that wicked kickflip."

"It's not fucking funny, asshole!" Tyler's face turned crimson. "I'm more concerned about your kick *drum*. And if you can't play for the tour, I'll *kick* your ass."

"It's my left, so I can hit the kick drum. And I'll get a second hi-hat until I'm healed. The doctor said about two weeks."

"*Two weeks*?!" Tyler's shouting made him flinch. "We leave for Europe in three."

His blowup was understandable, but he shouldn't make Adam feel worse. They were all dealing with the pressure of the tour and the new contract, and obviously, it was getting to him.

"Ty, chill the fuck out," Zack said. "He didn't do it on purpose. Adam knows the songs backward and forward. He'll be ready."

Tyler shoved an angry finger in his face. "Don't make me look like the asshole when this fucker's risking injury on a goddamn skateboard right before the tour. If we fuck this up, we lose the contract. With how you two spend, you'll be back to slinging pizzas at Napoli before the end of the year." He faced Adam. "Gonna go skydiving next? Or take up ice hockey?"

He shook his head. "You're lucky I'm doped up on painkillers, dickhead. I'm sorry. It was stupid. We won't lose the contract because Zack's right. I'll be ready. I heal fast, and my girlfriend's a doctor."

"Yeah, for sick puppies," Zack said. "You're definitely one of those." He'd hoped to lighten the tense mood, but judging by their even more pissed-off faces, he'd failed.

Adam's eyes rolled. "She knows ways to speed up healing, fucknose. Let's play."

In the thirteen years since the band began in a humid Eastside garage that reeked of motor oil and marijuana, they'd been through their share of challenges together and always found a way past them. Most of the time, they didn't even need words.

Tyler and Zack joined in as the walls buzzed with the steady rhythm of Adam's drums. Soon, they were all sweating with blissed-out grins, any lingering tension obliterated.

They all knew that no matter what obstacle life hurled at them next, it would be okay. Because, as it always did when times were tough, the music would get them through it.

11

Mandy

Mandy took a sip of coffee and winced. It was cold. Of course. She couldn't remember the last time she'd enjoyed an entire hot cup of coffee at her house. Too many other things demanded her attention, like the tiny little human clinging to her shirt like a spider monkey.

Phoenix woke up screaming at four in the morning with the telltale white bump of a new tooth poking through his gums. It took an hour, a dose of baby Tylenol, fifteen lullabies, and three frozen washcloths to soothe him. To make the day even more fun, her neighbor's dog crapped on her porch and her toaster stopped working. If her car had a breakdown, she'd probably join it.

She held Phoenix close as she left the couch and stuck the mug in the microwave. After punching in the cooking time and hitting start, someone knocked on her front door.

"Who could that be?"

Phoenix responded by drooling on her shoulder.

Through the peephole, Ted stood on her porch. A broad smile bloomed on her face as she opened the door. The day was looking up.

"Ted! Get your retired behind in here and give us a hug."

"It's so good to see you both." He wrapped his arms around them. "Can I hold him?"

"Of course. My arm could use the break. Can I get you some coffee, tea, slightly burned banana bread?" She was a decent cook, but her baking skills were lacking.

"No, thanks. I'm fine." Ted made goofy faces at Phoenix, earning a sweet little laugh.

She'd never get tired of that sound.

Ted sat on the couch, bouncing Phoenix on his knee as they laughed together. He was a natural, and his grandkids were lucky.

"How's life?" Mandy settled beside them. "And Ella?"

"Everything's great." His smile deflated, making her do something she'd never done before—question his honesty. "I have something to talk to you about, but I'm not sure what you'll think."

Her mind went to his money troubles and Ella's health issues. She couldn't help with either, but he might need a sympathetic ear. "What's up?"

"I heard about a job opportunity you might be interested in. Shane Marx needs a touring assistant for three weeks. I'm not sure if you're familiar with his work, but he's a prominent rep." He laughed again as chubby baby fingers grabbed his cheeks and squeezed.

Her eyes widened at the name. "Prominent is right. His roster's impressive, to say the least. And he has a reputation for being amazing to work with."

"And he's probably amazing to work *for*. You'd learn a lot, and the position pays very well. Significantly more than you make at the club."

"How much more?"

When Ted said the number, Mandy blinked. Her ears must be defective.

"I'm sorry, what?"

She gasped when he repeated the same impossible number, catching Phoenix's attention. That was more than she made in three months. She gave her son a reassuring smile, and he returned to squishing Ted's cheeks.

"They'd pay me that much for three weeks?"

Ted's grin peeked out from between ten tiny fingers. "No, kiddo. That's per week. This is the big leagues."

Her hand clamped over her mouth as her mind raced. Combined with what she had left of the ten thousand from Ted, if she tightened her budget a little more, it would be enough to stay afloat while giving managing a shot.

She could call the band Ash gave her the demo for and put all her time and energy into getting them exposure and landing a record deal. She'd mostly make her own hours, ensuring she had more time with her son.

The thought of finally chasing the dream she'd set aside made her heart race. It was too good to be true. There had to be a downside.

"What's the catch?"

He patted Phoenix's back while her son's wide, moss-green eyes watched her. "The travel, for one. You'd have to be away from this little guy. And the position's temporary, of course. Still, it's an excellent opportunity to get your foot in the door, make connections, and make sure it's what you want to do."

Her head was spinning. Could she do this?

Opportunities this grand didn't come around every day. The timing was so perfect that if she believed in fate, she'd suspect it'd had a hand in it.

She touched Phoenix's chin, earning a gummy smile. It would be hard to leave him for so long. But what if she passed it up, and James Jerkwad Sutter canned her for rejecting his advances? She'd be out of a job with no safety net. And she'd regret not trying, left to imagine what might've been if she'd been braver.

"You said travel's required. Where's the tour?"

The wrinkles framing Ted's mouth lifted as he smiled. "Europe. London, Paris, and Rome. I know you've always wanted to go. This would be on someone else's dime while you make money for yourself and this little one's future. Med school isn't cheap."

Mandy tickled her son's chin. "Will you be a doctor, Nixy?" He giggled before jamming his fist into his mouth. "Europe would be amazing. I have a passport but never used it."

She got it three years ago when her mom invited her on a two-week trip to Paris. Mandy was ecstatic about going overseas. She learned basic French phrases and bought a stack of guidebooks. A month before the trip, her brother was arrested with half a kilo of cocaine in his trunk. Her mom canceled everything to attend court dates and visit him in jail. Mandy stuffed the passport into a drawer, and it'd been gathering dust ever since.

"It sounds like an amazing opportunity," she said, "but I can't leave Phoenix for three weeks."

"You know your mom would love to watch him." He was probably right. Her mom never turned down an opportunity to spend time with her grandson. And despite her distaste for the music industry, once she heard the salary, she'd likely say yes without hesitation. "Ella and I can babysit to give her breaks and help spoil him rotten."

"That's sweet of you, Ted. But I've never been away from him for a day, let alone three weeks. Plus, his first birthday's coming up, and I can't miss that."

"He'd miss you, but I promise he'll be fine. Babies are resilient. And you'd be back almost two months before his birthday."

Phoenix yanked off his left sock and tossed it onto the floor. He hated socks and loved throwing things. Those quirks drove her crazy when she was trying to get out the door or had just cleaned a mess only to find a new one. But she tried to cherish even the minor annoyances of motherhood, knowing someday she'd miss finding tiny baby socks on her carpet and teething rings under the couch.

"Socks are for wearing," she said, slipping it back on his little foot, "not throwing."

She'd miss everything about him if she did this. And there were important milestones that could happen while she was gone. What if he said his first word or took his first steps, and she wasn't there to witness it? Did the benefits of this job outweigh the risk of missing out on moments she'd never get back?

"I know it's not my business, but..." Ted's eyes stayed on Phoenix. "Have you thought any more about reaching out to his father? A first birthday's a big deal."

She gnawed her bottom lip, surprised and uncomfortable by the topic shift. Ted hadn't asked about Zack in months. Then, it was only to ask if she was over him yet before frowning at the honest but unfortunate answer.

"Why are you asking me that?"

"My son has brought so much joy to my life," he said. "I know things are complicated, and Zack isn't perfect, but people can change."

He knew about Zack's tendency to overindulge and that he didn't want kids. Complicated was right—neither issue could be easily overcome.

"Sometimes," Ted continued, "a little motivation can help." His head tipped toward Phoenix.

Was that possible? She'd changed to be better for her son—exercising more, reading about child development, taking infant classes when she was pregnant, eating more vegetables. But she was never as anti-baby as he was. Of course, that might've changed now that his bandmate Tyler had a child.

"I know how much you care about us, and I appreciate the advice. When it feels right, I'll tell him." Anxiety prickled her skin at the thought of coming clean to Zack. But when the time was right, she'd do it for Phoenix. "Thanks, Ted. For offering to help Mom with Phoenix and bringing me this opportunity. I have some thinking to do."

"Think about it, but don't take too long." He pulled a piece of paper from his pocket and set it in her hand. "I've heard things at the club aren't great with James around. I'm sorry I put you in that position. If he runs it into the ground, it'll break our hearts, but it's out of our hands. Time to move on to better things."

Mandy unfolded the paper to find a phone number. "I probably won't get it. There must be hundreds of people dying to work for Shane Marx."

He shrugged, a mischievous glint in his eye she didn't understand. "Call. Knock him dead in the interview. I believe in you, kiddo." He stood up. "Ella and I have a salsa dancing lesson, so I'll see you two later."

She took Phoenix, chuckling at the mental image. "Salsa?"

He grinned, lifting a shoulder. "She's been begging me for years, and my answer was always 'not now, but maybe someday.'" His smile slipped as he held her gaze. "One thing her illness has taught me is that if you keep waiting for someday... it may never come. I know that one day, dancing with my wife won't be possible. So, while I can, I do it for her." He tapped the paper in Mandy's hand. "Do this for yourself. And your son. Stop waiting for 'someday' and chase your dreams *now*."

After their goodbyes, she went to the kitchen to retrieve her coffee from the microwave. She took a tepid sip, and her nose wrinkled.

"Well, Nixy." She put it back in the microwave for another spin. It would be bitter and nasty, but better than nothing. "Guess Mommy isn't meant to have coffee that doesn't taste like dookie."

She glanced at the phone number in her hand, then the wall clock. He'd take his nap in fifteen minutes. She could call the number, potentially setting their lives on an exciting new track. When the microwave beeped, she pulled out the mug, leaned away from the baby's grabby hands, and took a sip. It tasted better than she'd expected and was as hot as she liked.

When life was overwhelming, those little pleasures made all the difference. And they were reminders that her happiness mattered, too. She grabbed a Big Bird magnet off the fridge and stuck the number beneath it before Phoenix tried to eat the paper.

Her body buzzed with excitement over the possibilities as she nursed and rocked her son. She owed Ted a few dozen un-burned cookies to thank him for bringing her the opportunity. She hadn't even thought to ask what band it was for, but if Shane Marx was in charge, they were massive or about to blow up. Before Phoenix came along, she was better at keeping up with industry news, but her priorities had shifted.

When he was asleep, she moved him to the crib and shut the door. She grabbed the phone number off the fridge, went to her room, and called her mom.

"Mandy? Everything okay?" Her parents recently got caller ID, and the fact that Mandy rarely called in the early afternoon must've concerned her.

"Yeah, Mom. I have a big favor to ask. Ted dropped by and told me about an amazing job opportunity."

"Really? Doing what?"

Mandy gave her the details, including the timeline. She held her breath, waiting for a response.

"You'll be in Paris part of the time?"

"I don't know when, but yeah. I'll give you all the specifics if I get hired."

"You know that I wish you'd consider finding something that doesn't involve *those types* of people, but that money would make a nice nest egg for you and Phoenix while you look for something permanent. Of course, I'll do it."

Mandy exhaled a long sigh of relief. "You're amazing. Do you think Dad will mind?"

"You know your father. I'll do all the messy stuff while they play with toy cars and watch cartoons. It'll be fine."

"Thank you so much. I owe you... well, a lot. Why did you ask about Paris?"

"You got me thinking. We had to cancel our trip when your brother got in trouble. I've always wanted to see France, and your father hates traveling. What if I brought Phoenix while you're there? On my dime, of course. We could get him an expedited passport. We'd stay out of your hair when you're working, but we could explore together on your time off."

Mandy turned the idea over in her head. Her mother was a lot to handle in large doses with her stubbornness, hovering, and blunt opinions, but it would mean not missing Phoenix for so long. If their presence didn't affect her work, it shouldn't be a problem. Besides, she'd love having familiar faces around so far from home.

"That sounds fun, but do you want to spend ten hours on a plane with a baby?"

"I traveled with you and Nathan to New York all the time to visit my parents when you were little. And you know how easy Phoenix is. If he has snacks, books, teethers, and a few little toys, he's happy."

"True. Unless he's cutting a tooth, then all bets are off."

"Nothing I can't handle. And he can sleep in my hotel room while we're there since you'll get in so late from the concerts."

Oh, my god. This could really work!

"Okay, but don't get your hopes up. I'm sure plenty of people are clamoring for the position, so I probably won't get it." Mandy tried not to get her own hopes up, but the more she thought about it, the more excited she was. "But if I do, we might be eating croissants beside the Eiffel Tower in a few weeks."

"That sounds wonderful, honey. Let me know how it goes, and kiss that baby for me."

After hanging up, she pulled the slip of paper from her pocket, took a deep breath, and made the call. The friendly receptionist set up a phone interview the next day at noon.

When Mandy ended the call, excitement fluttered through her. Unlike her parents, she was a dirty heathen, but she said a silent prayer anyway that this worked out.

After years of struggling to get ahead, she'd love to have a dream come true.

Speaking of dreams...

She'd thought about Zack a lot since their breakup but couldn't keep him out of her mind since Kyla's call, even when she slept. It was bittersweet to be immersed in an alternate reality where he was close enough to touch. Waking up and breaking the spell made her bed feel colder and emptier than usual, triggering a deep, clinging loneliness she couldn't shake.

As she'd done countless times when she missed his handsome, stubbled face and wanted to relive those precious memories in the only way possible, she opened her nightstand drawer. She pulled out the stack of photographs he'd given her on their last day together.

He'd asked a tour photographer to sneak candid shots of her doing all the crazy things she said she'd witnessed at the club but hadn't tried—stage-diving, tossing panties onstage, sharing a joint with a band after a show, dressing in something risqué, and tossing back shots without a care in the world.

Sometimes, their time together felt like a fever dream—a colorful illusion she'd conjured up after years of denying and inhibiting her desires. But those photos were proof she could break out of her shell and shut off the voices in her head that told her to behave and play by the rules.

The last photos in the stack showed the two of them caught in moments she'd thought were private, but now, she was glad they'd been captured.

After flipping through the photos, she set all but one back into the drawer. It was her favorite—a shot of her and Zack underneath an awning outside the arena in Dallas. Rain poured around them in shimmering sheets, and they'd gotten soaked running from the tour bus. Her hands tangled in his damp hair as he kissed her, their chests pressed together as if their bodies had merged. She could still feel his heart pounding against hers as their drenched clothes clung to their skin.

Minutes later, they locked themselves in the band's dressing room and peeled off their wet clothes before he dropped to his knees and buried his face between her legs.

The memory of the two orgasms that followed made her shiver.

Zack was, without question, the best lover she'd ever had. Not that she had many—only four—but she knew that even if it'd been a hundred, she'd say the same. He knew how to hold her, touch her, fuck her in ways that blew her goddamn mind into confetti. The memories made her skin flush with heat, a surge of desire coiling low in her belly.

Since work, mom duties, and financial stress usually cluttered her brain, it'd been a while since she pleasured herself. With the baby asleep and nowhere to be for a few hours, Mandy let herself sink into some of the filthy memories Zack had given her.

She set the photo on top of the stack and took out a bottle of lube from the drawer, setting it beside her on the bed before sliding her panties off. When she flipped up her skirt, the cool air from the vent above her bed raised goosebumps on her thighs. She dipped two fingers between her legs, discovering she didn't need the lube.

Just thinking about Zack's skills had her slick and ready.

She wished she could call him. To hear his demanding, lust-darkened rasp as she touched herself.

Rub your clit for me, baby.

Suck your fingers and taste yourself.

She closed her eyes, focusing hard on the memory of his deep, sexy commands in her ear. She imagined it was his fingers circling her clit before slipping inside and rubbing at her G-spot. Her lips parted, and she moaned for him, her toes curling against the sheets.

She imagined his tongue plunging deep, lapping up her wetness as if he were starving for it—like he'd done their first time together. She'd been skeptical that men could enjoy giving as much as receiving, but he had her convinced. Neither of them faked a damn thing.

Her strokes quickened, her climax within reach and building. Words he'd spoken in last night's dream echoed in her mind.

That's it, baby. Come for me.

Her breath hitched as the tingling heat bloomed and spread through her core before one last stroke of her clit tipped her over the edge. Her free hand fisted the bedspread as her back arched and her hips rocked. All the muscles in her body tensed and gradually released like a receding wave. She slipped her fingers back inside her slick, warm pussy, and her inner walls pulsed around her fingers with the aftershocks of a glorious and long overdue orgasm.

She breathed a deep exhale, melting into the mattress as she came down from the endorphin rush. When she opened her eyes, the room felt even emptier. Zack's presence felt so real that she was certain he'd be there in the flesh when she opened her eyes. No such luck.

But it was better this way.

In her imagination, he wasn't frowning at the stretch marks she didn't have when they met. He didn't care that pregnancy had made the skin of her belly loose or that her pussy wasn't as tight after pushing an eight-pound baby through it. Of course, she wasn't certain about that last one. It felt the same with her fingers, but maybe she was wrong. She hadn't been with anyone since Zack, so no one had confirmed her suspicion.

It was one of the many lovely insecurities that came with the most wonderful thing that ever happened to her.

Still, she wouldn't trade Phoenix for a perfect body and didn't want anyone who couldn't accept this new, imperfect version of her. Even though she struggled to accept it herself.

She'd seen the women who hang around rockstars, and while Dream Zack was enthralled with every inch of her, Real Zack would probably run far and fast. And back into the arms of someone hotter, younger, and with a lot less baggage.

12

Mandy

As Mandy held the phone to her ear, the awareness that Shane Marx was on the other end of the line was surreal. Even the man's deep, steady timbre as he greeted her oozed power and influence, which made sense since he had plenty of both.

"It's wonderful to speak with you, Miss Reid. I'm familiar with Rollin' Rockies, and from what I understand, you're largely responsible for the club's contribution to the thriving local scene. I'm impressed."

She smiled with pride at the recognition, guessing that tidbit was Ted's doing. "It was a team effort, but I'm passionate about supporting the connection between musicians and their audience." Her job was so much more than that, but she stuck to details that would make her seem the best fit for the position.

They chatted about music and industry trends. When prompted, she laid out her duties and responsibilities at the club, explaining that while she was sad to leave it behind, she was ready to embrace greater challenges. It wasn't untrue, but it seemed wise to leave out that she was afraid of her asshole boss.

"I appreciate your enthusiasm," Shane said. "The job consists of being my go-between with the band and more mundane tasks like running errands, taking notes at meetings and soundchecks, and making phone calls. My regular assistant has fallen ill, so traveling's out for this tour."

"Sorry to hear that. What band are you working for?" She hoped it was a group she liked. It would enhance the experience, but she'd still do her best even if she thought they were talentless hacks.

"I've gotten ahead of myself," he said with a chuckle. "Fury Fuel. They're opening for a co-headlining tour."

Mandy grinned, familiar with the female-fronted hard rock trio. "I love their sound. Their songwriting evolved a lot with the second album. It reminds me of the Pixies' *Surfer Rosa*, with more of a hardcore edge. I can see why you wanted to work with them."

"Wow." His tone conveyed that he was pleased with her response. *Thank god.* She was relieved by how well things were going. "That's an excellent description. And I agree."

"Who are they touring with?"

"Killing Daisies."

She nodded slowly, processing that. "Great."

She was a huge fan, but the lead guitarist, Charlotte Hall, was married to the lead singer of Zack's band. Was there a chance he'd visit his friends on tour?

"And Tomorrow Mourning."

Mandy's stomach dropped to her feet, and she swore she heard a record scratch. "I'm sorry... What?"

"Tomorrow Mourning is the co-headliner. Are you a fan?"

Her fingers strangled the phone as she struggled to breathe past the sudden tightness in her throat. Her mind blanked, forgetting his question. She panicked, knowing she'd been quiet for too long.

What did he ask me?!

This was too important to flub over personal issues. She opened her mouth—she had to say something, but nothing would come.

"Is there a problem?" he asked.

Yes, there was a problem! Several, in fact. She fought to find the right words and the calm, confident tone the situation required, but inside, she was *screaming*.

One nagging thought was the loudest: *Did Zack set this up?*

Of course, Ted didn't know him, and Ted told her about the job. The timing of this opportunity and Kyla's call was suspicious, but it was possible it was all coincidental. Right?

"Of course not," she said finally, with what she hoped sounded like confidence. "It's an incredible opportunity, and I appreciate you considering me for the position."

"I'm glad you feel that way because it's yours."

Oh, my god. Oh, my god.

She wasn't expecting it to be so easy.

"Thank you so much, Mr. Marx!" Would it be inappropriate to excuse herself to throw up into a trashcan? "I'll work very hard for you and the band."

"I'm sure you will. My secretary will take your address to FedEx the contract, details about your flight and hotel accommodations, and tax forms. If you have no more questions for me, I'll see you at Heathrow."

She had plenty of questions, but none that he could answer.

What will I say to Zack when I see him?

Will I have to watch women fall all over him while trying to focus on work?

Then, a question hit that made throwing up in a trashcan even more of a possibility—*What will I do when Mom brings Phoenix to Paris?*

"No more questions," she said, clutching her stomach as her pulse kicked up. "I'm excited to work with you, Mr. Marx. Thanks again."

After rattling off her contact information to his secretary, Mandy floated through the rest of her day in a numb haze.

She got the job.

She could tell James Jerkwad Sutter to shove it.

There'd be planning and packing ahead and a huge decision to make, but first, she wanted to spend as much time as possible with Phoenix before she left.

Saying goodbye to him would be the hardest thing she'd ever done.

Missing him would be tough, but she was determined to make the most of the opportunity. Exploring London, Rome, and Paris could be the adventure of a lifetime. She'd observe and learn from one of the world's top talent reps.

Hopefully, any complications that arose from doing all of that in Zack's orbit wouldn't spoil the experience or jeopardize her job.

I'm going to see Zack.

This trip could be her best opportunity to tell him about Phoenix and give him the chance to meet their son. Maybe the universe conspired to make their paths cross because finding out he was a father was what he needed to stop living recklessly. As Ted said, Phoenix might offer Zack the motivation to change.

She knew damn well that was nothing but a fantasy. More likely, he'd hate Mandy for throwing the unwanted wrench into his carefree life.

If she told him on this trip, it would be the second hardest thing she'd ever done.

But that was far from the only complication. What would happen if her mom ran into Zack during the trip? They were both strong, stubborn, and blunt with their opinions. A clash of their personalities might jeopardize any chance of him accepting Phoenix in his life.

When her mom arrived to babysit, Mandy said she hadn't heard if she got the job. She wasn't ready for a barrage of questions and even less ready to share that Zack would be on the tour. That conversation would be long and likely dramatic, and it needed to wait until she'd fully wrapped her mind around it.

Besides, she was eager to get to the club and tell her shithead boss she quit. Like so much in her life, it was bittersweet but necessary. The club wasn't the same under his "leadership," and she deserved better.

Now, she would get it.

I got the job.

A surge of confidence, relief, and pride rushed in, and it felt right to celebrate her fresh start by dressing up a bit. She put on a flowy black dress that fell above her knees and her favorite silver leaf earrings. She kept her hair down, letting it hang in loose waves over her shoulders.

After a quick pumping session, she stuck the fresh breastmilk bag into the fridge and set a few jars of baby food on the counter before heading off.

On the drive, it occurred to her she'd have to stop nursing before her trip. She'd planned to go for a year, but the distance would make it impossible. Tears flooded her vision at the thought of losing that sweet bonding time with her son.

It would be tough for both of them, but it was a sacrifice made for the greater good.

Blinking back the tears, Mandy reassured herself there'd be plenty of other ways to build and cherish their connection over the years. And she made a mental note to put extra sprinkles on his birthday sundae to assuage some of the mom guilt.

Hell, she might even buy him a puppy.

In the parking lot of Rollin' Rockies, James Jerkwad Sutter's obnoxious, spotless silver BMW sat alone, and she pulled into the spot beside it. She grabbed an empty box from her backseat and popped her trunk. With a surge of pettiness, she dragged her key along the side of his pretty car, leaving a foot-long scratch on the driver's side door. There weren't any cameras in the lot. He'd suspect her, but good luck proving it.

Maybe there was still some rebel in her after all.

She unlocked the club's front door before sauntering in with her head high and shoulders squared, ready for a verbal sparring match if it came to that. Hopefully, it didn't escalate beyond words, so she wouldn't need the fresh can of pepper spray in her purse, though it would be satisfying to watch that bastard choke and cry.

Also in her purse was a voice recorder to capture whatever he said in case she needed it. There was no telling how low he might stoop without witnesses.

He sat alone at the bar with a glass of dark liquid in front of him—at two in the afternoon. His head swiveled toward her as he clutched his glass.

He let out a low whistle. "Don't you look pretty today? What's the occasion? Taking me up on that dinner?"

Mandy tossed her head back as she laughed. "Hell no. The occasion's bittersweet. Bitter because I love this club, and sweet because I hate you. I quit."

She strolled to her office and began stuffing her belongings into the box—the photo of her parents, the Italy wall calendar, the Troll doll with green hair that

Ash had given her as a thank-you for booking his band when other clubs had turned them down.

Heavy, echoing steps grew louder until James's stupid red face glared from the doorway. "The hell you are."

She added the Tomorrow Mourning laminate to the pile of mementos. "Watch me, motherfucker." She rarely cursed, so it sounded strange to her ears, but no other word fit. She didn't judge people who used foul language as easily as they breathed, but it was one of the by-products of her strict, religious upbringing she'd never fully shed. "I've taken more than enough of your bullshit, and I'm done."

He slapped his hands on her desk as she placed her favorite plant at the top of the box. "You *cannot* leave without notice. I'll tell every club in town not to hire you because you left me in the lurch and you're a shitty employee. And a shitty mother. You're about to make your kid homeless because you can't handle a little flirting?"

She stopped packing the items on her desk, clutching the edge of a picture frame. In the photo, she held Phoenix in the hospital's NICU after he was born. It triggered the memory of how helpless and guilt-ridden she felt as she held his weak little body, convinced his severe jaundice and the fluid in his lungs were somehow her fault. Was it the three sips of coffee she had that morning? Were the late work nights to blame? Was she on her feet too much?

It was easy to doubt herself in that moment of extreme vulnerability, but now, Mandy knew she was a good mother. And she wasn't surprised he'd punched low like the pathetic worm he was.

"*A little flirting?* You basically asked if I'd take money for sex. You've repeatedly asked me out, even though I've always said no. And since the day we met, you've stared at my chest more than my face."

A corner of his mouth lifted. "You liked it. All of it. I can tell you were flattered. I'm sure it's been a while since someone's given you attention." He leaned over the desk, his hands still planted on the wood. "Not many guys would want to fuck a pussy that's probably loose and mangled from pushing a kid through it."

She laughed despite the sting of his words, thinking about the running tape recorder in her purse that captured the bastard's true colors. "Wow. You sure know how to sweet-talk a girl." She put the last of her things in the box and hugged it to her chest. "This club and everyone who loves it deserves better than you. I hope someday it goes back into the hands of someone who appreciates it for more than a cash cow."

She took two steps toward the door, her heart pounding against her ribs as she fought to keep her face neutral. He blocked the doorway, his hands gripping the frame.

"Move," she demanded, but she couldn't keep the slight quiver from her voice.

As he stared, she noticed the thin red veins in the whites of his eyes. This close, she smelled whatever liquor he'd been drinking, making her hands sweat.

"I only tried to fuck you," he said, "because I pity you. You're on the wrong side of thirty, probably have stretch marks all over the body that I bet was hot and tight before you shit out that kid."

Her fingernails dug into the cardboard, her muscles frozen as he continued.

"If you couldn't even keep the man dumb enough to dump his load inside you, you won't be able to keep anyone. Those tiny wrinkles around your eyes and mouth will only get deeper, making you unfuckable and unlovable until you die alone."

Tears clouded her vision, but she refused to let him see her break. He'd dug inside her mind and latched onto some of her deepest fears and insecurities. Instead of crumbling, she set the box back on her desk and fought fire with fire.

"I won't die alone, but you will. I know what love is, but I'd bet everything in my bank account that you don't and never will. You only care about shallow, shiny, temporary things that don't matter. So, you'll rot inside your perfect house, convinced all the women who shoot you down are intimidated by how powerful you are when really, they see what a cruel, narcissistic hunk of shit you are like I do." She pulled the pepper spray from her purse, removed the lid, and aimed the nozzle at his face. "Now, get the fuck out of my way before I use this."

He hesitated before stepping aside. She grabbed the box and walked through the club for the last time. Her heart was heavy at saying goodbye to a place with so many wonderful memories, but it was time.

She was headed for bigger, better things.

Mandy vowed never to allow someone to treat her like she was beneath them again. And to one day be successful enough to show the James fucking Sutters of the world that underestimating her was a huge mistake.

13

Zack

*S**he took the job.*

Zack didn't know whether to scream with joy or run out of his house to dance in the goddamn street. Ted called to say their plan had worked and that Mandy was thrilled. Zack imagined her bright, beautiful smile when she got the news. Ted also said she was nervous about seeing Zack again but didn't elaborate, probably out of loyalty to her.

Nervous was understandable, and he felt it, too. Even worse, his lack of patience would make the next two and a half weeks pure torture. But at least at the end, they'd be breathing the same air.

He pulled his list of things to change from his pocket and grabbed a pen from the kitchen counter. With a broad smile, he scratched through the final, obviously impossible task on the list with deep lines of black ink and replaced it with a new goal.

1. ~~Stop fucking groupies, barflies, and other women who don't give a shit about me.~~

2. ~~Don't drink so fucking much.~~

3. Stop being a selfish asshole.

4. ~~Get over Mandy.~~

4. Prove to Mandy that we can make it work.

Seeing those words on paper was an instant relief, the burning knot of tension between his shoulders unfurling. No more torturing himself day and night by trying to let her go. Now, he could focus on doing the opposite.

Of course, the nerves and *what-ifs* didn't take long to creep in.

What if she avoids me?

What if she finds out I pulled strings to get her the interview?

What if we try again, and again, it falls apart?

He stuck the list back into his pocket and headed for the fridge. A six-pack of his favorite beer sat at the front, but he shoved it aside and grabbed a can of ginger ale—something he used to think was only good as a mixer.

Breaking old habits hadn't been easy. He was well aware of how effectively a few beers would turn down the cranked volume of his brain. But leaning on temporary sources of relief would bring the same shitty results, and he was ready for something better.

Along with fewer headaches and better sleep, avoiding alcohol had another unexpected but uncomfortable side effect. With a clear head, he recognized past mistakes that'd probably helped scare Mandy off.

He'd been drinking before their last few phone calls, leaving some details of their conversation blurry. What if she'd been trying to find a reason to stay in his life, and in return, she got slurred words and drunken nonsense? He'd thrown away those precious chances to connect. Considering what she'd been through with her brother made it so much fucking worse and unforgivable.

Recognizing his carelessness made him even more determined never to lose control again. She deserved a better version of him, and so did he and everyone else in his life.

As for the second item on the list, he'd been celibate for a record-setting twenty nights in a row, avoiding bars and clubs full of temptations that were not so tempting anymore. The thought of touching another woman or having a stranger's hands on him turned his stomach. No empty, shallow sex could ever compare to what he had with Mandy, and he'd do anything it took to experience that again. His fatigued right wrist paid the price, but it felt good taking steps to move beyond the reckless but adorable party animal.

Aside from helping Adam climb up and down their stairs with his busted ankle and writing a fat check for his dad's soup kitchen fundraiser, there hadn't been many opportunities to work on the "Don't Be a Selfish Asshole" goal. He'd been looking for ways to prove he could put someone else's needs before his own like his father believed he could.

One idea had been poking at his brain that might be brilliant or royally backfire. Regardless, the wheels were in motion.

Before their flight to Dallas, Mandy started shaking as they approached the airport gates. She'd never been on a plane, and she was petrified. He held her hand as they boarded and helped distract and calm her during the flight.

He hated the thought of her anxious and alone on the long flight to London, especially if she was stuck in the cramped, bullshit business class seats they'd likely booked for her.

Why not take another step to make her life a little sweeter?

As he thought about seeing her for the first time in a year and a half, his limbs buzzed with excess energy. He grabbed his bass and got a few hours of practice in, but it did nothing to burn it off. Even lifting weights and running five miles on his treadmill didn't touch it. When every muscle in his body ached with fatigue, he took a long shower, hoping the cool water might help.

No such luck.

Zack almost never got anxious. Not giving a fuck was his trademark. Letting stressful shit roll off his back, his default mode. But *everything* was different when it came to Mandy.

When he started falling for her during their week together, he hardly recognized himself—opening doors for her, taking her out to dinner, buying flowers. He even held her damn hand. He'd always thought it was a useless way to touch someone, but with her, he craved the contact. It was a way to connect and savor her soft, warm skin no matter where they were.

Craving junk food, he set down the ginger ale and raided the kitchen cupboards. He tore into a bag of salt and vinegar potato chips, and as he dug in, the metallic clink of a key jiggling in the lock was followed by the creak of door hinges.

"A little help?" Adam yelled.

"Your panties get twisted again?" Zack tossed the chips on the coffee table and wiped his salty hands on his jeans. When he got to Adam, his left crutch was stuck in the looped shoelace of his black-and-white Converse.

Zack snickered as he bent over to pull the crutch loose. "Better than your dick getting caught in your zipper. And if you ever do, I'm not helping you."

Adam hobbled to the couch and fell onto the cushion backward with a heavy exhale. "Fuck these fucking things!" He shoved the crutches to the ground with a crash, scowling at Zack's expression. "Glad you're amused, dickhead." He grabbed the bag of chips and shoved a handful into his mouth.

"That's not why I'm smiling." Zack sat beside him, eagerly anticipating his reaction. "Mandy's coming on the tour."

Adam almost choked on his chips, his eyes bugging out. "Are you fucking serious? Because of Kyla's phone call?"

"That started it, yeah. She took the job as Shane's assistant, so she'll be on the first leg."

Three weeks to prove he wasn't an immature fuck-up anymore. That he could be a reliable partner worth relocating her life for. It was a task the size of Mount Hood, but he wanted her badly enough to pull it off.

If it didn't work, he'd have no choice but to let her go for good.

"Not to be a buzzkill," Adam said, "but she'll be there to work. You can't mess with her head and make her lose focus when people are counting on her and she's counting on the cash. Plus, our band's future is riding on this tour. We need you focused so these shows go off without issue, and we can sign that contract."

"Obviously. But this is my last chance to prove to her that we belong together. After work hours, it's on."

Adam grabbed a chopstick from last night's takeout off the coffee table and stuck it underneath his ankle brace, scratching an itch. "I hope it works, man. But you can't let it take you down again if it doesn't. It was fucking scary how broken you were when she called it quits. Don't give her that much power again."

Zack crooked an eyebrow. "So, if Kyla told you to fuck off, you'd be cool?"

"Hell no." He chucked the chopstick into the kitchen, and it landed a foot from the trashcan. "You'd have to drag my ass out of bed and pry the whiskey bottle from my hand."

Zack remembered Adam and Tyler doing that for him—a lot. Adam was right about how important it was to keep his head on straight regardless of how things turned out. He couldn't risk their careers over relationship drama.

He nudged Adam's knee. "I'm not flying to London with you and Ty."

Adam's forehead wrinkled as he plopped his injured ankle on the coffee table. "Why the hell not?"

"Because I'm flying to Denver to go over with her. You remember how scared she was to fly."

Adam let out a slow whistle, tucking his hands behind his head. "Damn, dude. I can't decide if that's super stalker-ish or really fucking sweet."

"Definitely both. I just hope she doesn't freak when she sees me."

That morning, he called their band's manager, Sophia, to ask another favor. Her connections could make magic happen with almost anything, so he asked her to upgrade Mandy's ticket to First Class. And to book him the seat beside hers. The more he thought about it, the more stalker-ish it seemed, but if this was his last shot, he wasn't wasting it with half-measures.

"I have to admit," Adam said, "I was skeptical as hell when you made that list of shit you need to change, but you're doing it. It's nice to see you fall asleep instead of passing out, and I don't miss finding random naked chicks poking around our house at two in the morning, trying to find their underwear."

Zack laughed and grabbed a handful of chips, the bag crinkling as the sharp vinegar tang hit his nose. "You're welcome."

"If she's willing to give it another go, I think you have a decent shot. Although the distance issue is still fucked."

"I've got more money and free time than I know what to do with when we aren't touring. I'll fly there whenever we don't have band shit. I would've before, but she cut things off before I could."

Zack thought about how hopeless he'd felt when making the list in his pocket. So much had changed in three weeks, and he was looking forward to what lay ahead.

There was still a chance she'd want nothing to do with him, but what if the spark was still there? What if she still wanted him and would help find a way to make it work?

The anxiety from earlier eased. In its place was something he'd struggled to find for a long time but was finally within reach—hope.

14

Mandy

Mandy tossed the diaper bag into her trunk and buckled Phoenix into his car seat. Telling her mom that Zack would be on the tour was better handled in person, and she couldn't put it off any longer. Her dad was at work, so at least she wouldn't get the inevitable criticisms in stereo.

She'd known for three days and had already signed the contract, but it hadn't fully sunk in that she'd see Zack again. As if that weren't enough of a shock, according to the travel documents, he'd be staying at the same hotel. All three bands and their staff would have the same accommodations in every city to simplify tour logistics, but for her, nothing about this trip would be simple.

Her stomach twisted on the drive, but Phoenix's babbling and cute little legs jumping along to the Tomorrow Mourning album she put on helped distract her. She often played Zack's band when they were in the car together—a small, risk-free way to have him in their lives. Like his mom, Phoenix loved bopping along to their signature, raw blend of hard rock and punk. And like his dad, Phoenix had a natural sense of rhythm and loved making noise. At a red light, she watched in the rearview as two chubby hands clapped together before slapping the sides of his car seat.

"I love this song, too," she said with a grin. "If you feel like saying your first word in front of grandma today, don't make it one of the curse words, okay?" She imagined the horrified look on her mother's face right before her skull exploded.

When the light changed and Mandy focused back on the road, her worries returned. Her mom already agreed to the massive favor of babysitting while Mandy was in Europe, but what if she rescinded her offer because of her aversion to Zack?

He'd never had the chance to meet her parents, but his career and reputation were enough strikes to earn their disapproval. Knocking up their unmarried daughter didn't help. To make matters worse, she'd made the mistake of confiding in her mother about seeing him with another woman backstage, further sealing it.

After parking in the driveway, she grabbed the diaper bag and took Phoenix from his seat. The front door swung open before she could knock.

"If it isn't my two favorite people in the world!" Her mom beamed as she took the baby. "What a nice surprise."

Considering the news, it was more like an ambush. If she'd called ahead, her mom might've heard something off in her tone and wouldn't have let it drop until Mandy spilled her guts.

"I got the job," she blurted.

Her mom squealed and held the baby tighter. "Oh, honey, that's wonderful!" She pulled Mandy inside with a one-armed hug.

"Thanks again for saying yes to watching him." Mandy shut the door and followed her mom into the kitchen. It smelled like freshly brewed coffee and cinnamon—a comforting combination that helped soothe her frazzled nerves.

"Of course." Her mom set Phoenix into the highchair at the table, buckling him in. "You need the money, and the travel will do you good. I'm happy to help in any way to get you out of that ridiculous place so you can look for a normal job during daylight hours."

Mandy poured herself a cup of coffee at the counter and sat beside Phoenix. If she explained her plans to use the assistant job as a springboard to manage on her own, it would invite yet another tedious lecture about why it was a terrible idea.

From a young age, she learned that defending her choices was a waste of energy because her parents were always certain they knew best. Dealing with their constant disapproval was exhausting, so, as usual, she kept her thoughts inside and her mouth shut.

Phoenix slapped the tray with his palm, snagging her attention. When she decided to be a parent, she knew she'd raise her child differently. To never make him feel like he had to hide anything out of fear of judgment or ridicule. If he was happy, she was happy. She leaned over and pressed a kiss to his cheek.

"Did you apply for his passport?" Her mom plucked a banana from the fruit bowl, peeled it, and chopped it into tiny chunks on a cutting board.

"Yeah, it'll be ready next week. And I signed a contract for the job, so even if something goes wrong with the tour, I'm guaranteed the salary. Unless I violate the terms, of course." She'd grinned like a fool when she signed on that dotted line. Security meant everything to her, especially since Phoenix came along.

"Great, honey. I'll book our flight and hotel tonight. Hopefully, rooms are still available where you're staying, so it'll be easier to get together on your time off."

"Okay." Mandy nodded, hoping her mom would be on a different floor than Zack to avoid surprise run-ins. "But I learned some details about the job that we need to discuss. You should sit."

Her mom's brows furrowed as she slid the banana pieces from the cutting board onto the highchair tray with the side of her hand. "New details? Will you be gone longer than three weeks?"

Mandy shook her head, pulling out the chair beside her. "Please sit."

Her mom wiped her hands on a kitchen towel, setting it in her lap before taking the seat. "What is it?" A large wooden crucifix hung on the wall above her head, giving Mandy the feeling of another set of eyes poised to condemn her choices.

She sipped her coffee, stalling for one more peaceful, precious second before ripping off the bandage. "Zack will be on the tour."

Her mom's eyelids fluttered with a series of rapid blinks. "Excuse me?" A frown deepened the wrinkles framing her mouth.

"The guy I'm working for manages the opener for Zack's band. I swear I didn't know when I first heard about the job."

Her mom's eyeballs ping-ponged around the room like she was solving a geometry problem in her head. More likely, she was connecting dots and imagining all the reasons this was a catastrophically terrible idea.

Finally, her gaze landed on Mandy. "So, when I bring Phoenix to Paris…"

"Zack will be there. Yes."

Her frown lines became canyons, her cheeks reddening. "You can't do this. He obviously orchestrated this to sink his hooks into you again."

Of course, the idea had occurred to Mandy, too, but she hoped it wasn't true. She'd told him how she felt about people gaining an unfair advantage because of who they knew. When they were still in touch over the phone, he'd offered to tap some connections to get her a managing internship, and she'd refused.

When she succeeded—despite the delay caused by her surprise baby, she still believed it was *when* not *if*—she needed to know she'd earned it. If he'd set up this job, that sort of manipulation and betrayal would be unforgivable. Zack would never do that.

"Ted told me about the job. They don't know each other. It's just a weird, small-world coincidence."

"Regardless, you *cannot* risk that man seeing you with Phoenix and getting crazy ideas. Going after him for child support is one thing, but your son doesn't need a drunken loser fighting for custody or whatever else he'd try to pull."

Interesting, coming from someone whose own son is a drunken loser. Mandy bit back the true but unhelpful retort.

"He overdoes it sometimes, but he's not a loser. Just because you don't agree with the little you know about him doesn't mean he's a bad person. He's talented, smart, loyal, protective, and he works incredibly hard. He's more successful than anyone else I've dated and would drop anything to help someone he cares about."

"Don't try telling me he's loyal when he couldn't go a week without growing bored with you and grabbing a shinier toy. And smart? I've seen the tabloid photos of him red-eyed and barely upright with yet another shiny toy on his arm. A real prize, that one."

She didn't know her mom kept tabs on him, but it wasn't surprising. It made sense that she'd want to size up Phoenix's father the only way possible. It'd be nice if it were to look for positive traits, but knowing her mom, it was more of a "know thy enemy" thing.

"He's so much more than that. I shouldn't have told you about the girl, but even though it stung, he didn't really do anything wrong. He was single and free to do as he pleased."

Since he'd promised not to even *look* at anyone else during their time together, it wasn't exactly the truth, but she didn't want her parents to hate Zack. It would hurt Phoenix if they badmouthed his father when he was old enough to understand.

Her mom's eyebrow arched. "Do you think you'll believe it if you say it enough? He invited you off on that crazy escapade, you inexplicably developed feelings for him, and he couldn't show you the respect of keeping his zipper up for a full week? He's disgusting. You deserve better."

"Mom..."

"You can't be around him for three weeks, no matter how much money you'd make. Though I'd *love* to give him a piece of my mind." Her eyes narrowed, her lips tipping further downward. "You'd be better off working for your father and moving in here."

"No!" Mandy snapped before taking a deep breath and forcing her voice back to calm. She didn't know if she was more horrified by the idea of having her impossible-to-please accountant father as a boss, having everything she did and ate scrutinized if she lived with them, or having her mother face off with Zack. "I already signed the contract. And I've made another decision you won't like."

Phoenix smashed a chunk of banana in his fist, pale yellow goo squishing out between his fingers as he babbled at the mess. She'd done a lot of thinking in the last three days. She decided that, while Zack wasn't perfect, Phoenix deserved the chance to have his father's best qualities in his life. She'd do everything in her power to make it happen.

If she and Zack started over as friends, hopefully, he'd be able to handle her confession and be open to meeting their son.

Her mouth went dry, and she swigged her coffee while her mom continued scowling, waiting for the next bomb to drop.

Mandy set down her mug. "I'm going to tell him about Phoenix. And give Zack a chance to meet him in Paris."

"You're *what*?!"

She ignored her mother's red-faced glare and continued. "I'll spend the first week catching up and trying to build a friendship. Then, the second week, when the time is right... I'll tell him everything. He'll have some time to process it before you arrive."

It still wouldn't be easy, but she was more confident with a plan to stick to.

Her mom threw up her hands. "I guess you've already made up your mind. And when I see him, he'll get a piece of mine."

"No. Phoenix deserves a chance to know his father. It might ruin that if you lay into him, so be civil for your grandson. And me. Please." She reached across the table and took her mom's hand into hers. "I appreciate everything you've done for us. Now, I need to do this for him." Her chin tipped to Phoenix. "If you won't watch him under the circumstances, I'll find someone else. And if this changes your mind about Paris, I'll still tell Zack and set up another opportunity for them to meet. I've put it off long enough."

Phoenix stuffed a fistful of mashed banana into his mouth and grinned. Even stressed, Mandy couldn't help but smile back.

"Don't be ridiculous." Her mom sighed, wiping Phoenix's sticky cheeks with the kitchen towel in her lap. "If you're going to be stubborn and take this job, I'll still watch him. And when I bring him to Paris, I'll do my best to be cordial with *that man*. On one condition."

Mandy was about to sip her coffee but set down the mug to give her full attention. "What condition?"

"Go on a date with Steven from church before you leave."

Mandy rolled her eyes with a groan, sick to death of hearing about this "Steven from church" golden boy. "Please tell me you're kidding."

"He's wonderful, honey. Handsome, successful, well educated. And he wears a suit to work instead of ripped jeans and a leather jacket."

Even the mention of Zack's leather jacket made Mandy's heart flutter on cue. Despite the time, issues, and distance that separated them, he still affected her.

But no matter how tempting it might be to give in to those feelings, she'd stay strong. As planned, she'd focus on work and building a friendship that would make it easier to come clean about Phoenix.

Her mom continued, "The only strike against him is he's divorced, but his mother tells me the ex-wife was a nightmare. Poor man."

A failed relationship didn't bother Mandy when she'd had a few. The biggest strike against him was that he wasn't the man she really wanted. Since changing that was impossible with the barriers between them, perhaps it was time to give someone else a try. If she liked Steven, it might make it easier to keep her attention on her work and off Zack.

Besides, finding a backup babysitter she trusted and was willing to watch Phoenix for that long would be impossible, so she was out of options. She couldn't keep the job without her mom's help. If that meant she needed to chat about the stock market over appetizers with this Steven guy, so be it.

"Fine. One date." Mandy stood, pulled Phoenix out of his highchair, and washed his hands in the sink. "But if I don't like him, you need to let it drop and stop trying to set me up with your friends' sons."

"Deal." Her mother's self-satisfied grin grated her nerves, but at least the Zack conversation was behind them. For now.

Mandy returned to the chair with Phoenix in her lap. "Thanks for always taking such great care of him, Mom."

Their mother-daughter relationship wasn't perfect, but she was thankful for the bond her mother and son shared. Since he was born, the two women had been a team, ensuring he had stability and unconditional love.

"I'm happy to do it." Her mom got up, grabbed a piece of paper from the counter, and passed it to Mandy. "Here's Steven's number. Wear that pretty red dress you wore to the Christmas party at Aunt Jan's. It hides your tummy. And give him a real chance, okay?"

She nodded before kissing the silky brown hair on top of her son's head. Her mom had good intentions, but Mandy felt as if she were being pimped out.

And although it made no sense, she felt like she was betraying Zack.

Regardless, if she and Steven turned out to be as compatible as her mother claimed, she'd pursue it.

"I will," Mandy assured her. "I promise."

———◆◇◆———

After a glass of cranberry and tonic and a few bites of spinach artichoke tapenade, Mandy found herself bored to tears. Steven was as handsome and successful as her mother claimed, with his perfectly trimmed dark blond hair, piercing blue eyes, and perfect teeth. She knew the successful part was true because he'd talked nonstop about his job as a stockbroker for a major investment bank since they'd arrived. Another clue was that he picked her up in a shiny ruby-red Mercedes that looked fresh off the lot. He'd probably gape in horror at the ancient Honda in her garage with a backseat littered with Cheerios crumbs and cast-off baby socks.

"Your mother mentioned that you work in a music venue," he said before taking another bite of French bread smeared with tapenade. "What's that like?"

Her stomach did an unhappy twist. A month ago, that question would've elicited a smile and animated descriptions of her day-to-day activities at the club. Now, she suppressed a grimace.

"It can be exciting, especially when a band's playing that I enjoy. It's a lot of work ensuring shows go off with no one throwing beer bottles or tantrums. Or setting fires."

Was she subconsciously trying to scare off Mr. Perfect in his three-piece suit? Probably. But if he couldn't stomach sitting across from a woman who made a living surrounded by punks and drunks, they could get this over with before dessert.

His eyebrows jumped. "Wow. You must be tough to deal with all of that. Of course, you're a mother, so I don't doubt you're tough." He winked. "My daughter keeps me on my toes too."

Mandy's gaze flicked to him as she sipped her drink. She set down her glass. "Daughter? My mom didn't tell me that."

"She might not know. I leave Sierra in the church's daycare during services. She can be a handful, and to be honest, I treasure the break." He chuckled, the sound low, deep, and, she had to admit, kind of sexy.

"I can relate. How old is she?"

"She turned four last May. Your mom said your son's eight months. Any big plans for his first birthday?"

She smiled, pleased to shift to a more fun subject than stocks and mutual funds. "I'm taking him to the zoo, then Iggy's for ice cream."

He raised his half-full pint glass of stout, the faint scents of coffee and chocolate wafting over. "Good ol' Iggy's. My daughter asked me once if we could move there. She packed her Barbie backpack and everything. Hard to beat their Super Bowl Sundae."

The chocolate syrup and cherry-topped concoction was her favorite, too. "The first time I gave Phoenix ice cream, he shuddered from the cold, then tried to pry the pint from my hands to stick his face into it. Big fan."

They laughed together, and as they talked more about their strongest common link—their children—Mandy warmed up to him. Not romantically, but aside from Ted and Ella, she didn't have friends with kids, so it was nice commiserating with someone else in the under-five trenches.

He said he wanted at least two more once he found the right partner. She also liked the idea of someday giving Phoenix a sibling or two—yet another reason a relationship with Zack would never work. Even if he could get on board with accepting one kid, there's no way he'd want more.

Steven was the kind of guy she *should* end up with—one who'd help with algebra homework and volunteer to coach his kid's soccer team. Someone who wasn't traveling the world for weeks at a time with gorgeous women falling at his feet at every stop.

While the idea of never being with Zack again made her want to lock herself in a bathroom stall and weep, she knew she should give Steven a real chance for her son and herself.

"I'm taking Sierra to Bear Ridge Park tomorrow," he said. "Would you and Phoenix like to join us?"

She took Phoenix to a weekly playgroup, and although she struggled to relate to the moms swapping recipes and complaining about their husbands, he loved socializing with other kids. It would be good for him to make a new friend.

"Best swings in the city." She tossed back the last sip of her drink. "We're in."

After dessert, coffee, and more polite conversation, Steven drove her home, opened her car door, and walked her to her porch. He did everything right, but there was no thrilling pull to be closer to him. Still, when he leaned in and pressed a soft kiss to her lips, she let him. If that was what moving on looked like, she had to try.

But there were no butterflies or sparks. No overwhelming urge to grab his shirt in her fists, drag him closer, and devour his mouth. And when he pulled back, there was no dark, intoxicating flash of hunger in his eyes.

After knowing what all of that felt like, she realized she wasn't willing to settle for less.

There was one thing the date made abundantly clear—if this was moving on, she still wasn't ready. So, as she'd done countless nights before, she fell asleep wishing that, somehow, she wouldn't have to.

15

Zack

Tyler and Zack were warming up in Tyler's studio when Adam burst in—without crutches.

They stopped playing.

"My ankle's back in business, motherfuckers!" He thrust out his foot and made wide circles with the joint. "Told you I'd be ready for the tour."

"Great." Tyler tweaked one of his tuning knobs and plucked the string until he was satisfied with the sound. "Now get your ass behind those drums and warm up. Sandra will be here in ten."

On the co-headlining tour, they'd play a cover at each show featuring a different member of Killing Daisies. On one, Amber would take over the drums, another had Charlotte doing backing vocals and joining them on guitar, and Sandra would do a duet with Tyler on a cover of Cheap Trick's "Surrender." She was coming over to rehearse it again before the tour kicked off.

"Yes, Daddy." Adam laughed at Tyler's raised middle finger.

Halfway through the next song, Sandra strolled in with her head bobbing to the beat. Her bubblegum pink T-shirt said *Punk's not dead, but you will be if you touch me*. Zack laughed at its accuracy. The badass, smartass frontwoman was friendly and chill with people she trusted, but she'd destroy anyone who fucked with her or her friends. And she didn't take any shit from anyone. He respected that.

She grabbed a guitar off the wall and tied her mop of curly red hair into a ponytail that reached the center of her back. When the song ended, she clapped.

"Sounding good, boys." Her slender fingers flew across her fretboard as she played the wailing opening riff of "Foxy Lady." She flashed a taunting grin. "Ready to sound even better?"

Zack shook his head with a smile. "Show off."

Her eyebrow arched. "Of all the egos in the room, mine's definitely the smallest. I've got the biggest dick, though."

"The one in your nightstand doesn't count, sweetheart," Adam quipped.

"Your mom wasn't complaining last night," she tossed back.

Everyone laughed, even grumpy, sleep-deprived Tyler. It was impossible not to love Sandra.

"Sorry I'm late coming in," she said. "The baby just woke up, and I couldn't resist squishing those chubby cheeks. Then, she had a code brown, and I bailed. Auntie Sandra has her limits. And a weak gag reflex."

"Good thing you're a lesbian," Zack said, adjusting his strings.

Sandra bent forward as she let out a deep belly laugh. "Nice one." They shared a fist bump.

"Okay, enough screwing around," Tyler said in his most stern dad voice. He'd always had one, but it got more potent after becoming an actual dad. It was easy to imagine him using it someday to tell his kid to stop pulling the dog's tail or climbing the bookshelf. "This song has to be flawless in eight days. Adam, count us in."

The reminder of the tour countdown had Zack's stomach doing somersaults. Since he didn't get stage fright or performance anxiety, it was undoubtedly from worrying about how things would go with Mandy.

The first run-through was great, but he hit a few sour notes, the unshakable nerves throwing him off his game. He still wasn't drinking, but he should've smoked a joint to take the edge off. Tyler shot concerned looks every time Zack fucked-up, but they played through. Adam got the same look when he flubbed a few hits on his hi-hat.

Mostly, they were all equals in the band, but if there was a leader, it was Tyler. He was more mature and focused, especially when the stakes were as high as they were. He also wrote most of the songs and all the lyrics, so he took it personally when Zack and Adam slacked off or wasted time.

Sandra brought her A game, as always. Zack had been to several Killing Daisies shows, and her stage presence hypnotized crowds. Those impressive pipes could take her from screaming with rage to crooning a gentle ballad capable of crushing the heart of even the coldest bastard in the arena. With "Surrender," she added a throaty growl to her verses that challenged Tyler to kick his performance up a notch. His crooked half-smile said he loved being pushed to work harder, dig deeper.

After four run-throughs, every forehead in the room glistened despite the vents pumping chilled air into the space. They took a quick break, and Sandra grabbed a bottle of water from the fridge in the lounge area of the studio. She held the frosty plastic against her cheek before taking a few slugs.

"You guys sound great." She aimed a wry smile at Zack. "Mostly."

"Yeah, I'm the weak link. Break out the tar and feathers."

She capped her water. "I forgot them at home, but I have confetti and a warm Pepsi in my trunk."

Adam chuckled at their banter, earning a glare from Tyler.

"I don't know why you're laughing," Tyler said. "That injury you swore wouldn't be an issue is a fucking issue."

Sandra shrugged. "Amber can take over for the songs he can't handle."

Adam's eyes rolled to the ceiling. "It's healed but still weak from being wrapped so long. I need to show it who's boss, and I'll be practicing for the next eight days until my hands bleed, okay? I won't let anyone down."

Sandra walked behind the drum kit to pat his shoulder. "I'm just fucking with you. We all know you'll be ready, but you know how Ty is."

Tyler's head cocked, a curtain of dark hair covering one eye. "How am I, Sandra?"

"Tough but loveable. The standards that got you guys famous are higher than Cheech and Chong, so you expect everyone who plays with you to have the same standards and work ethic."

Tyler nodded, a grin of appreciation lighting his expression.

"And sometimes," she added, "you're kind of a dick."

Zack and Adam laughed while Tyler scowled, but the edges of his mouth twitched with a held-back smile.

"Same to you, lady," Tyler said. "Now, let's nail it this time and move on to something different. Zack had the idea of giving 'Need You Tonight' a shot, and I think it'll sound badass as a duet with Sandra's range."

She nodded as she sipped her water. "You have me agreeing with Zack. What's this world come to?" She strapped on her guitar. "Let's do it."

Zack didn't tell Tyler why he'd suggested the song—it was Mandy's favorite. He wanted to reach her through music, their strongest common link. Along with booking the seat beside her on the flight to London, it was another gesture to show her what she meant to him.

Sandra attacked the song like the pro she was, adding her signature punk flair to a track that was solid new wave pop. This time, Zack didn't miss a note. Neither did Adam. It was, hands down, the best they'd sounded since picking up their instruments and getting to work.

Charlotte's smiling face appeared in the glass separating the lounge area from the recording area/rehearsal space. When they finished, Tyler waved her in.

"INXS?" she asked. Anna Jude lay in the crook of her arm, her eyes half-closed. "Really? I never would've thought you guys would want to cover them, but it sounded amazing. Especially Sandra."

Sandra grinned and high-fived her. "Haha, motherfuckers. Bow to the queen."

Zack set down his bass and faced her, bending at the waist with his arms flailing forward. "All hail, Queen Sandra. I'm happy to kiss your ass because if Ty ever loses his voice, we're stealing you."

Charlotte scoffed. "The fuck you are."

"Hey." Tyler walked over, taking the baby. "Watch the language around my kid, pottymouth."

Her eyebrow arched. "You weren't complaining about my mouth this morning." She kissed him, his laughter muffled by her lips.

"Keep it in your pants, breeders." Zack tossed a pick at the back of Tyler's head. "One little screamer on tour is enough."

"And again," Sandra said, "I'm left agreeing with Zack. Is it a full moon or something?"

Tyler swayed with the baby as he walked to Sandra. "Look how offended she is by your anti-baby rhetoric."

She looked at Anna Jude, and Zack watched as a beaming grin stretched her face.

Traitor.

"That tiny nose and chubby cheeks get me every time." She planted a kiss on the baby's forehead. "I need to get her a shirt to match mine."

Charlotte snorted. "Yes, please. Ty already got her a Floyd onesie and a tiny green army jacket like his. You'll shit yourself when you see it."

"Are we done?" Zack asked. "It feels pointless to stand around talking about baby bullshit."

"Watch it." Tyler shot a warning glare. "And yeah, we're done. Charlotte and I have that interview with *Spin* in an hour. Anything you guys want me to mention or keep out?"

Zack thought about that. "Talk up the opener, and don't say shit about Adam's ankle. We've been able to hide it from Sophia, and we don't need her worrying about it." Besides their manager, they didn't need the crew stressing, either. Everyone involved in the tour needed to feel confident that the shows would go off without issues since their jobs and futures depended on it.

"Agreed," Tyler said. "It'll mostly be questions about juggling parenthood and our bands. The headline will be something stupid like 'Rocking the Stage and the Cradle' or some shit. But it's *Spin*, and all tour publicity helps, so it was an easy yes."

Adam pointed a drumstick at Charlotte. "Did Kyla tell you she's joining us in Paris?"

Her ecstatic shriek made Tyler smile. "No! That's so fucking cool! I hoped she could get away from work long enough to catch a show or two." She poked Adam's arm. "I have to admit, I worried you'd shred my cousin's heart, but you're great together. I'm happy for you both."

Zack was happy for him, too. And for Tyler. Now that Mandy was coming on the tour, he held on to the hope that he'd be next in line to be blissfully coupled up, but there were no guarantees. Knowing it was likely his last shot with her added more pressure to the already heaping pile.

He couldn't shake the fear that he'd buckle underneath the weight of it, disappointing everyone, especially himself.

He sighed, anxiety burning in the pit of his stomach. "If we're done playing, I'm out."

"I'll walk with you," Charlotte said.

He couldn't keep the surprise and confusion off his face. They were pretty close, but Tyler was their link. Zack never hung out with her alone and had no clue what this was about.

They left the studio, and she walked beside Zack down the hallway. "Kyla told me she called Mandy."

Of course. They were cousins and tight, so it made sense. There weren't many secrets in their group that stayed secrets for long. In some ways, it was nice. If everyone knew what struggles their friends were dealing with, it was easier to help or be understanding if they acted like an asshole. In this case, both applied.

"Not surprised."

"I know it might be weird for you to talk to Kyla about that stuff after you guys..." She trailed off, probably still weirded out that her cousin spent four hours in a hotel room with Zack and Adam, getting fucked six ways to Sunday. "If you ever need a woman's perspective, call me. I know we've never really—"

"I'm scared, Charlotte." His steps halted. His head spun with thoughts, some dark, and he needed to get them out. "Kyla said Mandy still cares about me, but what if she's still done with me? I'll catch it in her eyes the second I see her. And

I'm scared she'll hurt me again. Or that I'll hurt her. If she gives me another chance, I might fuck it up. She's smart, independent, and strong—what if I can't make a woman like her happy for longer than a few days?" His pulse thudded in his neck, his chest going tight.

Charlotte offered a sympathetic frown before hugging him. He sighed, relaxing in the comforting hold.

"Of course, you're scared." She let him go, leading him into the kitchen. "Sit." She pointed to a dining chair, and he obeyed without one of his usual smartass remarks—another sign he was in way over his head.

She set up the coffeemaker, and the rich, dark scent soon filled the air. He would've preferred a beer or a shot of whiskey, but even his dumbass knew that would send things in the wrong direction.

"What if setting this job up for her was a huge mistake?" he asked. "If Mandy finds out, she'll be furious. Like fucking everything else, I didn't think it through."

She set a steaming mug and a sugar bowl in front of him. "You took a huge risk to help her. There's a chance this will blow up in your face, but your intentions are good. If she finds out you're behind it, that might count for a lot. I wish I knew her to predict better how she'd react, but if she's amazing enough that you'd consider leaving the band to be with her, she must be incredible."

His eyes widened. "You know about that?"

She shrugged like it was no big deal, but they both knew it was a *huge* fucking deal. "Ty told me. Don't be pissed. He was trying to explain what she meant to you."

"I didn't even think Ty knew about that." He shoveled three heaping teaspoons of sugar into his coffee and stirred it in.

"Adam told him. You say a lot of crazy shit when you're drunk, which should tell you something."

Zack didn't keep many secrets from his bandmates but wished that was one. He didn't need them worrying he'd ditch them if Mandy made him choose between her and them. But he knew she never would.

In the end, she took the choice away.

"What do I say the first time I see her?" he asked. "Hey, what's up? You're still so fucking beautiful it feels like my chest is caving in?"

Charlotte's lips curled up, and she set a hand over her heart. "That might be the sweetest thing I've ever heard you say about a woman. You do have it bad."

"I fucking love her, Charlotte. I never thought I had it in me to fall in love with someone, but I felt it and chased it. Then I lost it." He took a long slug of coffee, the sugary rush of heat trailing down his throat. "It'll be torture to be close without touching her. To see her laughing and smiling with the crew when all I want is to take her back to my room and make up for every goddamn second we've missed."

"Oh, Zack." Tears gathered on Charlotte's lashes as her smile grew. "I want that for you. Be patient with her. Don't rush things and risk scaring her off."

He tapped a jittery beat with his fingernail on the mug's handle. "I've been trying to change. I've cut out booze and sex for almost a month, but I know I'll fuck-up again. Even if those changes stick, she still deserves better than I can give her. Why would she want someone who's just a wiseass and fuck-up? What if giving her seven perfect days is all I'm capable of? Maybe it's good that the distance gave us a reason to stop because otherwise, there would've been time for my true colors to bleed through and chase her away. That would've hurt worse than thinking it was just inconvenient fucking geography."

"Stop." She touched the back of his hand. "You can be a goofy dickhead, but I've seen firsthand that you're so much more than that. Like when you dropped everything to go change Sandra's tire in the pouring rain. Or when you brought me and Ty dinner the day after I had Anna Jude because hospital food sucks. I saw the tears in your eyes at my wedding because you were so happy for us." She squeezed his hand before sitting back in her seat. "You've always had it in you to love people and treat them well."

He gave a weak shrug, appreciating that she saw the good in him but not fully seeing it in himself. Despite the confidence he projected, it'd always been a struggle. Since he was a kid, his mom, teachers, and even friends' parents made it clear he wasn't good enough. He was too loud, too opinionated, too crass. He asked too many questions and wasn't shy about calling people out for being fake or critical. Since he refused to conform, he had to accept that the disapproving scowls, whispers behind his back, and rejection came with it. He had to accept that people who couldn't see past his rough, brash exterior would always cling to his worst qualities and underestimate him.

But that acceptance came at a price. Over the years, he began to believe that, on some level, they were right.

Aside from his dad, his bandmates and the family they built together were the first people to make him feel like he truly belonged.

"Thanks, Charlotte."

"And I'll do anything I can to help. Hopefully, Mandy will let us drag her away for some girl time after work to get to know her better. Maybe in Paris when Kyla's there, so they can meet in person. She's been worried since that call. She wanted to reach through the phone and strangle her shithead boss."

Zack's hand clenched around his mug, aching to make that fucker pay for treating her that way. But he was grateful Charlotte and Kyla were in his corner. Sandra and Amber always had his back, too. He hadn't had close female friends before they came along, and because of them, he'd come to appreciate women on a different level. One where clothing was required, and sometimes, you had to share your feelings and shit.

Tyler came in with the baby. "Everything okay?" The backs of his knuckles caressed Charlotte's cheek as she smiled.

She nodded, leaning into the touch. The hollow pit in Zack's chest ached, remembering how Mandy's soft skin felt beneath his fingertips. How her body responded like she wanted him as badly as he wanted her. No one else had ever bothered to look past his crass, immature veneer straight to his core, and he'd been certain no one would. She made him feel accepted and, although she never said the word, loved. He craved that feeling like a junkie craves their next fix.

"We're just conspiring to take all your cash and run away together," Zack said.

Tyler and Charlotte laughed, the sound slicing through the sad vibes.

"Keep dreaming, fuckwad." Tyler shoved his shoulder. The baby squirmed, and he made shushing sounds as he gently bounced and swayed. He moved his lips to her ear. "Daddy's got you, baby girl. I don't have boobs, but I'm still pretty awesome."

Charlotte grinned. "Yes, you are. Want me to take her?"

He shook his head, still swaying. "Nope. Practice is over, so it's my turn. Go for a run, lock yourself in the studio with a guitar, whatever you want."

She got up and kissed him. "You're the best, you know that? I'll see if Sandra wants to grab lunch, and I'll bring you back something. There's milk in the fridge if this little one gets hungry."

"Thanks, love." Tyler kissed her again and took her empty seat as she disappeared down the hallway.

"How do you guys make it look so goddamn easy?" Zack asked.

"It's not always easy. When we've had two hours of sleep, and we're snapping at each other, it sucks. But there's enough love and connection to get through anything. After everything we've already been through..." His eyes went distant, and the swaying stopped. "When Amy and Rafael had a gun to our heads, I begged them to kill me and let her go because I couldn't imagine a world without Charlotte in it. And she shot them without hesitation to keep me and my brother safe. There's no bigger test than that. We know exactly what we mean to each other."

Zack would take a bullet for Mandy but couldn't say she'd do it for him. He knew her feelings were still there, but it was impossible to tell how deeply they ran. They had limits; otherwise, she would've given the long-distance relationship more of a chance before calling it quits. They could've kept talking every night, and he would've flown to see her whenever possible. She could've flown to visit him and hang with his friends. She might've been willing to move to Portland if they'd had more time. The city was full of rock clubs that'd be lucky to have her.

Tyler's voice interrupted his thoughts. "That 'for better or worse' line is true. You have to be willing to take the morning breath, PMS rages, and annoying habits, along with the good stuff. Lucky for us, it's mostly good stuff."

Zack thought about what he'd said to Mandy the day they met: *If you stay perfect, I might accidentally fall for you before our time is up.*

He was in her bed, drunk on her scent and warmth, high on the way she listened to him and smiled at him like he mattered. They didn't have time to see all of each other's flaws, though she'd seen more of Zack's than he'd like. He caught her unhappy glance at the pile of dirty clothes on the floor of his suite. His temper got the best of him when some drunk asshole grabbed her hip at an afterparty, and she held him back from beating the shit out of the guy. And she rarely cursed or drank, while he did plenty of both.

His lifestyle didn't seem to bother her, and it was obvious she had a hell of a lot of fun with him. But maybe when the excitement wore off, it was too much for her. Or she might've seen some other deal-breaker and wanted to spare his feelings.

"Thanks, Ty." Zack got up and set his mug in the sink.

"I didn't have much time to get to know Mandy, but I saw how she looked at you."

Zack turned, locking eyes with his friend.

"She loved you. Whether she said it or not, she did. And she brought out a side of you I'd never seen. Like her presence made you want to be a better man." Tyler's head dipped, and he kissed the baby's cheek. "Trust me, I can relate. It took a lot of digging inside myself and clearing out the old garbage to feel worthy of Charlotte. And every day, I work to be the best husband and father I can be. Keep working on yourself for the next eight days so you're ready if Mandy wants to try again. Cutting back on the booze is a great start, but you still look exhausted. The tour pressure's getting to me, too, but don't let it mess you up. Take better care of yourself, and don't even *think* about other women."

Getting enough sleep was challenging with so much on his mind, but that last one would be easy—he only wanted her.

"Thanks, brother." Zack gave Tyler a one-armed bro-hug, avoiding the baby on his arm.

"She won't bite. No teeth."

Zack chuckled. "Pretty sure I'm allergic to anyone under the age of eighteen. Too much stinking and whining."

"I've known you since high school, and trust me, you've done your share of both." Tyler stood, lifting the baby closer to Zack. "You need to get used to my daughter because she's part of our lives now, like it or not."

Zack looked at the baby, who was staring up at him with wide eyes and raised fists like a raver in a mosh pit. Okay, she looked sort of cute, even though he hated that word. The way Tyler said that made him feel like an asshole. He wasn't a fan of kids, but this one was family. They weren't linked by blood but by bonds just as strong.

"Later, little baby dude." Zack lightly touched his fist to Anna Jude's and looked at Tyler. "There. Happy now?"

Tyler laughed, the baby jiggling in his arms with the movement. "I guess it's a start."

16

Mandy

Passport? Check.

Packed suitcase? Check.

Backpack with snacks and books for the flight? Check.

Thinking about getting on an airplane made Mandy want to swipe one of her mom's Valiums. She hadn't flown since her Zack adventure, and he helped keep her panic at bay. This time, she was on her own. Hopefully, the books, crossword puzzles, and other distractions she'd packed kept her from screaming in terror or throwing up on her seatmate.

Running on three hours of broken sleep wouldn't make it easier. Of course, the post-panic attack exhaustion could be a blessing. It might be the only way she'd sleep on the plane to avoid looking like a wrecked zombie when greeting her new boss at the airport.

Despite dreading the flight, she was grateful for the ten hours to clear her head and prepare for the inevitable moment she'd encounter Zack.

What would she say? Would they shake hands? Hug? Imagining their bodies pressed together made her cheeks hot. It'd been a while since she'd had a man's arms around her, so it was wise to stick to a platonic handshake. She didn't want him or her touch-starved body getting the wrong idea.

"That's everything." With Phoenix on her hip, she tossed her packing list on the coffee table.

She'd stacked his things around her luggage, ready for her parents' house. Fortunately, they already had a crib, diapers, and toys because they babysat so much.

More accurately, her mom babysat while her dad was at work or staring at the TV clutching a Coors, taking occasional breaks to play with Phoenix until it wasn't fun anymore. It was the same when Mandy was growing up, and like then, her mom handled all the messy and tough stuff. He had no interest in domestic duties and got no resistance for ignoring them.

Observing her parents' dynamic shaped her expectations for a partner. Aside from being intelligent, hard-working, and successful like her father, that partner would be *nothing* like him. She wanted an equal, someone to tackle life's challenges by her side instead of sitting in the background. Someone she could count on to care about her needs and Phoenix's instead of always prioritizing their own.

Fortunately, her mom always put Phoenix first. She often said that despite not approving of the circumstances that brought him into the world, he was the brightest spot in her life. And he lit up whenever he saw her, their sweet connection undeniable. That helped assuage some of the guilt and lingering hesitation about leaving for so long.

"Well, Nixy." Her heart sank, their goodbye creeping closer. "Time to go." Her voice wobbled as tears welled in her eyes. She wouldn't see him for two weeks—fourteen days of not being able to hold him or kiss him goodnight.

She sank to the floor, setting his wiggly little body on the backs of her raised knees to face her. "Do you have any idea how much I love you?" She sniffed, her throat going dry. "I've tried to make the best decisions for our life, but I've made some mistakes."

With her hands cradling his face, she tipped forward and kissed his tiny nose. He kicked his legs with a wide smile before squishing her cheeks.

"I'm going to see your daddy, Phoenix." The first tear slipped to her chin. "And hopefully, he'll want to meet you. I'm sorry you don't know him yet. He's a good man, but sometimes... that isn't easy to see. I wanted to protect you from his wild life, but avoiding tough things isn't always right."

He squirmed in her hold, and she pulled his chest to hers, holding him close and breathing in his sweet baby scent.

"When I tell him, some things might change for us. Or nothing will. I promise, no matter what, I'll give you the best life I can." She kissed the top of his soft, fuzzy head and stroked the back of his neck. He relaxed against her, his breathing slowing as he drifted off to sleep.

In quiet moments like this, he gave her as much comfort as she gave him. She'd miss that precious bond and everything else about her son as she took this leap that might spark a new beginning. It could lead to giving him everything he'd ever need—a bigger house, more time with his mom, and, someday, college.

She set him in his crib and loaded the trunk. She double-checked her lists, unplugged appliances, and locked all the windows before feeling as ready as she ever would.

While Phoenix slept on the drive, her eyes flicked to his reflection in the rearview. She'd miss his babbling when they watched birds outside their window every morning, the sound of his laugh. The scent of his lavender soap after a bath and how he grew heavier when he fell asleep in her arms, his warm breath tickling her neck.

Knowing he'd miss her too made the entire endeavor feel like a mistake. She didn't want him crying for her in the middle of the night or wondering when or if she was coming back. But parents often travel for work, and she remembered what Ted said—kids are resilient.

Phoenix would be okay.

She batted at fresh tears as she pulled into her parents' driveway. Her mom came out and took him from his car seat while Mandy moved his things into the house. With the task complete, she released a shaky breath.

Her mom's warm hand patted her shoulder. "He'll be fine, honey. And so will you."

Mandy sniffed. "Thanks, Mom." She took Phoenix into her arms, peppering tearful kisses all over his face. "Bye, Little Bug. I love you so much." Her voice cracked with emotion, and she passed him back.

It was time.

As she drove to the airport, she sobbed without restraint, the front of her shirt soaked with tears. She could smell Phoenix on her clothes and planned to fold her shirt tightly and never wash it on her trip. It would be a connection to him that might make the lonely nights a little easier to bear.

The woman at the check-in counter didn't seem phased by Mandy's blotchy cheeks and red eyes, likely because she dealt with broken-hearted travelers every day—people who'd just said goodbye to loved ones seconds before handing over their passports.

"It's your lucky day," the woman said with a sympathetic smile. "You've been upgraded to First Class."

"Really?" Mandy looked down at her damp T-shirt, faded jeans, and the fraying cuff of her gray cardigan, suddenly feeling like a slob. She smoothed a few wrinkles in her shirt and took the boarding pass. "Thank you."

Her heart thudded against her ribs as she shuffled along the gangway and onto the plane, taking her seat next to the window. The one beside it was empty, and if it didn't stay that way, hopefully, she wouldn't be stuck with someone who talked too much or had nasty body odor. A polite, quiet introvert who'd recently showered would be ideal.

She had a lot of thinking to do and a work schedule to memorize, but she also planned to give herself enough relaxing recharge time to prepare for everything that lay ahead. First, she'd have to cope with the fear of broken landing gear and birds flying into engines.

To help settle her nerves, she unzipped her backpack and took out her ancient, weathered copy of *Fear and Loathing in Las Vegas*. She'd read it a hundred times since high school, and the predictability and cadence of Thompson's writing brought her comfort. She'd need it now that she was inside the massive steel death trap.

Her fingers trembled as she turned the pages. She had to re-read the same lines, her mind too crowded with images of doom to focus on the words.

When she reached the end of chapter one, a pair of heavy black boots stopped at the seat beside hers. A shiver ran through her, and it was hard to lift her gaze. When she did, her eyes rounded as a gasp escaped her lips.

It was impossible.

Was she hallucinating from lack of sleep?

Mandy's heart stuttered in her chest as the surreal vision smiled down at her.

His hair was a little longer and dyed a rich shade of dark brown, a few loose strands drifting over his forehead. When they met, it was lighter and spiked. Maybe this was his natural shade since it suited him perfectly. The dark color made his already intense green eyes so much more vivid. Something like anguish shimmered in their depths as they remained latched to hers. She was too stunned even to begin wondering why. First, she wanted to know why he was there.

"Zack," she breathed, unable to keep the disbelief from her tone.

Her gaze broke from his as she drank in the sight of him. He wore a gray Hendrix T-shirt, black jeans that hugged his muscled thighs, and the same leather jacket that starred in her dreams. She could still feel its weight on her shoulders as the warmth of his skin seeped into her bones.

She shoved those thoughts aside.

No.

This is a business trip and an opportunity to tell him about Phoenix. Nothing else.

He will never be yours.

Zack stuffed a black backpack beneath the seat beside her and sat down. The backs of their hands pressed together on the shared armrest, the contact spiking her already racing pulse.

"Hey, Mandy." One side of his mouth lifted, but the distress in his eyes didn't budge. "Been a long time."

"What..." She cleared her throat, sitting up straighter and clutching her book to break the contact. His presence was more disorienting than she remembered, scrambling her senses as they each raced to take him in—the scent of leather, smoke, and cologne, the lingering whisper of his skin against hers, his obscenely beautiful mouth, and those intense green eyes that burned right through her protective layers as if everything she tried to hide was suddenly exposed. "What are you doing here?"

"Sophia told me you'd be on the tour. I remember how scared you get when you fly, and I didn't want you to be alone."

His words caught her off guard. He'd woken up at the crack of dawn and flown a thousand miles to help her stay calm?

"You came all the way from Portland? For me?"

"Is it okay that I'm here?"

Her chin wobbled, and she trapped her bottom lip between her teeth.

Get it together, Mandy.

She couldn't help it. Her emotions were raw from saying goodbye to Phoenix, coupled with the shock of seeing Zack, and it'd been a while since a man had done something nice for her. He must've asked Shane Marx's people for her flight info, upgraded her ticket, and, knowing Zack, worked some rock-star magic to get the seat beside hers. She wondered if someone at the airline ended up with backstage passes and autographs.

"Yeah," she said. "Just surprised. I haven't flown since coming home from Phoenix after we…" She shook her head, clearing away memories of another agonizing goodbye. "Anyway, yeah, still a nervous flier."

She knew she sounded like an idiot. It was impossible to think straight with him so close, managing to look more tempting than ever. She was supposed to have at least a day before running into him and wasn't prepared.

"I brought snacks to share," he said, "and an extra Walkman, some tapes, and a copy of the book in your lap because I remember you liked it."

"Wow. That's sweet." She peeked over her headrest, scanning the other faces in First Class. "Where are Tyler and Adam?"

"Flying private. They'll be in London before us."

This still felt impossible. She'd spend the next ten hours beside Zachary Maine—the first and only man she'd ever loved. The father of her son.

"You smell good," he said. "Kind of sweet."

That scent was Phoenix. He was all over her clothes, making her heart ache with every inhale. Knowing Zack was breathing in the scent of their son made her dizzy, and she had to close her eyes.

"Hey." His warm, callused fingertips settled on her wrist, her eyes popping wide. "You okay?"

She opened her mouth, but no words came. She couldn't tell him now. When she told him about Phoenix, it wouldn't be while hundreds of other passengers were strapped into their seats, having to witness his head exploding. He might start shouting. He might faint, and the flight attendants would scramble to find a doctor on board. Or he'd sit silently for the remainder of the flight, hating her.

Or even worse, regretting her.

She nodded. "Yeah, just nervous. And excited."

"You should be excited. And proud. Working for Shane Marx is a big deal. You'll learn a lot shadowing him." His head tilted. "If you want, I'm sure Sophia would be happy to give you advice. She started from nothing, and now, she can buy ten of these planes."

Sophia Cruz was a legend. Mandy would give her left arm to sit with someone of her caliber and pick her brain. Their paths didn't cross during her week with the band, but now a meeting was guaranteed.

"I believe it. Her talent roster's impressive, present company included."

"Obviously."

She grinned with an eye roll at his (mostly) feigned arrogance. "I read her *Entertainment Weekly* interview last month and was blown away by how down-to-earth she seemed. It's refreshing when success doesn't go to someone's head." She nudged his elbow, and he laughed at the teasing dig.

"Soph's as real as they come and passionate about the music above everything else, like you are. Nothing makes her happier than seeing us succeed, and she's worked her ass off for it. I'd be happy to introduce you."

"I'd love to meet her, but I'll approach her on my own. When I feel brave enough."

She also hoped to chat with Killing Daisies' manager, Eliza Marsh. Like Sophia, she'd climbed the ranks of the male-dominated field before starting her own firm, which represented some of the decade's biggest rock and pop acts.

"I figured. If you change your mind and want the intro, let me know. I'll make it happen."

She was touched but not surprised by another display of his thoughtfulness. During their week together, she discovered it was one of his best features, along with his sense of humor and laid-back vibe, which were already helping to put her at ease.

"Thanks, Zack."

The flight attendant gave the safety instructions, and Mandy reminded herself to breathe. She could've done without hearing the words: *In the event of an emergency landing.*

"Is there anything to drink on this plane?" she muttered.

"Of course," he said. "What do you want?"

"Champagne." It was early, and champagne sounded light and fitting for the start of a new adventure into unknown, slightly terrifying territory.

He touched a button above their heads, and a second later, a flight attendant appeared.

"Hello, Mr. Maine, Ms. Reid." This woman knew their names? First Class was fancy. "What can I get you?"

"Champagne, please." Zack held up two fingers. "Two glasses."

He thanked her with a kind smile when she returned with the drinks.

From Mandy's years at the club, she'd learned that you could tell a lot about a person by how they treated service workers. On their first date, he'd been polite to the waitress at the café and tipped her generously. He'd said please to this flight attendant like it was automatic, not forced for Mandy's benefit—more points in his corner.

It was a relief to discover he wasn't the selfish, arrogant brat the tabloids made him out to be, and she was glad to see that hadn't changed.

"This is weird." She downed her champagne, the bubbles tickling her nose. "Déjà vu."

Their first adventure began with pre-flight champagne, sitting as they were then—with her next to the window and him beside her.

But so much would be different this time. They weren't hours new to each other. There were wounds and secrets now, hovering in the six inches of space between them like a noxious cloud.

Despite that, she wasn't uncomfortable. His carefree nature was infectious. His wild, fun-loving side was, too. They were some of the many things that made her fall for him.

He was the first to beckon the over-cautious good girl out to play. The one who introduced her to a fun, spontaneous side of herself that returned to hiding after that positive pregnancy test. Since then, she's been too preoccupied with work and motherhood to relax and have fun.

That playful energy radiated from the man beside her, calling to her like a sexy, leather-clad beacon.

"I know what you mean," he said. "I wish we could replay our entire time together. That first night in your apartment, Dallas, Phoenix. Everything but the end."

She wouldn't take back her choices, but she'd give anything to replay that time, too. And she had countless times in her head since they parted ways.

With the déjà vu so strong, this almost felt like a restart. The idea sent a tingling thrill up her spine, but that wasn't how life worked. There were no do-overs. No erasing the pain you cause the people you care about. No taking back your mistakes or magically forgiving theirs.

The flash of sadness in his expression suggested he felt it, too—that no matter what happened next, there was no fixing the past.

The engines kicked on, rumbling and whining through the plane, offering a welcome but terrifying interruption. Mandy's eyes screwed shut, one hand strangling the stem of her glass and the other gripping the shared armrest so tightly the vinyl squeaked.

It's safer than driving. It's safer than driving. She repeated the mantra, hoping its logic would seep into her brain and crowd out the panic.

"Why is it so loud?" she asked. "I don't remember it being so loud."

"It's all normal. Here."

She chanced a peek as he poured his champagne into her empty glass.

"Just breathe and drink," he said. "Separately. Although there are worse ways to go than drowning in champagne."

"Yeah, like plunging into a mountain."

"Nope. Kick that out of your head." His knee nudged hers. "Remember when we got stoned in that Dallas alley with Adam and Ty?"

A smile tugged at her lips. "When I couldn't stop giggling at your bodyguard's eighties porn mustache?"

"Yep. Good ol' Pornstache Paul." Zack laughed as his rough, calloused fingertips pried her rigid claw from the armrest. "You were so relaxed, your arms were floppy. Take deep breaths and try to get there."

As their hands intertwined like puzzle pieces clicking together, her eyes opened and found his. This time, the flutter in her belly had nothing to do with nerves.

"Not trying to get fresh," he said. "Just trying to help ground you. If you don't want—"

She replied by squeezing his hand and offering a tight smile of gratitude. As the takeoff approached, she needed something positive to focus on, and his comforting touch certainly qualified.

"What's new in your world, Mr. Rockstar?" She needed a distraction but was interested. Really, she wanted to know if he was happy. Maybe even a bit more settled. It would take longer than a ten-hour flight to figure that out.

He shot her a warm grin like he appreciated the question. "Ty married Charlotte, and they had a kid, but you probably saw that in the papers or whatever."

She had, and the couple always looked happy in the photos. She couldn't help wondering what Zack was like around their baby. Did he still despise kids, or was it easier to warm up to a child tied to someone he loved? He continued before she could formulate a question that didn't sound weird or suspicious.

"Adam's with Charlotte's cousin, Kyla, but you already know that, too."

Mandy wasn't ready to dive into the avalanche of heavy topics that discussing Kyla's phone call would trigger, so she stayed quiet. He didn't say more, so he wasn't ready, either. With perfect timing, the flight attendant refilled their glasses. Before moving on, she set a napkin and a chocolate chip cookie on their trays.

"We're excited for Europe and to work on new songs when we get back." He bit into his cookie and chased it with champagne. A tiny dot of chocolate remained on his bottom lip. As if she wasn't having a hard enough time not staring at his mouth. The tip of his tongue darted out, and the dot disappeared. "The album's selling like mad, and the reviews I've bothered to read are great."

Last she'd read, their latest album was almost double platinum—no easy feat only a year after release. They'd amassed a rabid and loyal fanbase that clearly appreciated their sound evolving from hard rock with a healthy dash of punk to incorporating elements of metal and hardcore balanced by heart-wrenching ballads. Even Tyler's lyrics had deepened, and the beautiful sentiments in some of the new songs brought tears to her eyes.

Zack's pride in his band and their accomplishments were well deserved.

"Cheers to that." She clinked her glass against his. "So that covers your favorite people and work, but what about you? What's going on in your life?" She broke off a piece of cookie, surprised to find it warm, the chocolate gooey and delicious. Was there an actual *oven* on the airplane?

His eyes slid to his half-empty glass. "Still single, still stupid. Not much to tell."

Witnessing his legendary air of confidence slip made her frown. Hoping to repay some of the comfort he'd given her, she let her thumb glide over his wrist.

"You're not stupid, Zack. Impulsive and reckless? Sure. But not stupid."

A grin pulled at the edge of his mouth, and their eyes met as he relaxed against the back of his seat. Without warning, the plane lurched and started rolling forward.

She gasped. "Oh, god!"

Their lives were now in the pilot's hands—a stranger who might have a psychotic break, heart attack, or decide to take a few shots of Jack Daniels in the claustrophobic bathroom, and there was nothing she could do about it. That feeling of complete vulnerability and loss of control made her heart jump to her throat, her stomach rioting with a sudden wave of nausea. On reflex, her eyes clamped shut again as she tried to block out the horrifying thoughts and ignore the cranked-up roar of the engine.

"Hey." Zack gently pinched her chin. "Look at me."

When she did, she was struck by the incredibly inconvenient but overwhelming urge to kiss him. It'd been so long, and she remembered how incredible he was with his mouth. She couldn't think of a better distraction. Or one more inappropriate.

What was it about this man that made all her logic and rules fly out the window?

Mandy's gaze dipped to his mouth, and when she looked into his eyes again, they'd darkened with unmistakable lust.

"You can," he whispered, his breath sweet from the chocolate, her favorite indulgence. He probably tasted like it, too.

"I can what?" Her own lust made her voice sound husky and drugged. It made sense because his presence was more intoxicating than the glass of champagne she clutched in her fist like a lifeline.

The corners of his mouth slowly curled up in a smug, knowing grin that said his confidence was back in full force. "I know what you want. I can see it all over your face." He leaned against their shared armrest, encroaching on her personal space. He stopped his advance close enough for her to feel his warm exhales on her cheeks.

Even after their separation, she couldn't hide from him—a frustrating fact that was also comforting. No one ever questioned her fake smiles or forced cheer when she was stressed. And clearly, he'd caught the desire she struggled to tamp down. Her thoughts might as well be on a fifty-foot billboard written in neon.

Still, she couldn't forget that plenty of other women had been on the receiving end of that effortless charm. Did they feel as drawn in by his natural magnetic pull?

"You're still so good at what you do," Mandy said. A glance at the aisle window told her they were already in the clouds. She'd been so sucked into his sexy vortex she hadn't noticed.

Zack's eyebrows furrowed, and he retreated into his seat, pulling his hand back. "What's that supposed to mean?"

She scrubbed a hand over her face, trying to get a hold of her hormones. If she'd known she'd be sitting beside him for ten hours, she would've masturbated herself into a coma, staunching her libido so his powers weren't so frustratingly effective.

"It means I've seen countless photos of you with different girls." Thinking about those photos made her want to hit something. She'd stare at them, torturing herself, picking apart every detail of the women's perfect faces and figures, wondering what he ever saw in her. And feeling crushed at how quickly he'd replaced her. "You're still a player. That's fine if it's what makes you happy, but you can't pull that shit with me."

"Pull what *shit*?" He seemed offended, but she was being honest.

"Your bad boy charms. That panty-dropping smile, the sexy dark clothes, the way your eyes go smoky as they rake down my body. Even the way you freaking smell is alluring. There's no way you don't know, and I don't buy it for a second that it's all accidental."

He barked a humorless laugh. "I've got news for you, sweetheart. I don't dress for anyone but me. Yeah, I like to flirt, and I'm great at it, but it doesn't mean I'm being fake to get into your pants. I've *never* been fake with you." He shook his head like he resented having to defend himself. "If I looked at you in a way that made you uncomfortable, I'm sorry. I haven't seen you in a long time, and you're..."

"I'm what?"

"You're even more beautiful than I remembered."

Warmth bloomed low in her belly at the unexpected compliment. She didn't need outside approval for anything, but she was still a red-blooded woman, and it felt good to be seen that way.

The feeling evaporated when her hand grazed the love handle at her side. He'd think otherwise if he could see what was beneath her frumpy, old clothes now.

He frowned, squinting his eyes. "And no, that's not just a line, so don't you dare doubt I'm being honest with you."

She hadn't meant to offend him or question his sincerity. She blamed her mother's influence—always making her question a man's words and motives because they want to rob you of your virtue or whatever.

"Zack, I'm sorry." *About everything.* "It's been a while since I've been with someone, and I think holding your hand and letting you comfort me sent mixed messages to my brain."

One side of his mouth curled up. "You said my clothes are sexy."

"Stop."

"And you like the way I smell."

"Quit it." She tried to keep a straight face, but a burst of laughter broke through.

"*Alluring,* you said."

She rolled her eyes as he laughed. Zack *was* alluring. But he wasn't hers and never would be. He couldn't give up his panty-chasing ways when it mattered, and she wouldn't let her heart get broken again. But if they forged a friendship, she hoped he'd be willing to let Phoenix into his life.

"So," he said, digging into his backpack, "what's so great about Hunter S. Thompson?" He pulled out his copy of *Fear and Loathing* and thumbed through it. "The drawings are cool."

"They're by his friend, Ralph Steadman. They are cool. But you know what's even cooler?" She grinned as he watched her, waiting. "The words."

Zack chuckled as she bumped his shoulder with hers. "I'm about to find out. Grab yours, and we'll read together, yeah? It's a long flight."

She nodded, grateful for a decidedly friendly activity that would allow her to catch her breath. "I'd like that."

"That is," he said, "if you can resist my smoky eyes and irresistible allure."

She smacked his arm with her book as he laughed, the sound a soothing balm for the anxiety that was now a manageable hum.

But she'd stumbled on a new problem—not giving in to the urges he inspired would be harder than she thought.

After she flipped to the first page, he lifted her hand to his face. She watched as he slowly grazed his smooth, tempting lips back and forth along her knuckles.

"And if you can resist the urge to kiss me," he said, every word edged with a wicked, taunting dare. The lust reigniting in his eyes made her bite back a whimper, her mouth going full Sahara. "Because I saw on your face how badly you wanted it."

Fuuuck.

She crossed her legs, hoping the hint of friction would ease some of the needy ache he'd stirred between them. Her poker face was dogshit. Spending the last year and a half replaying naughty memories of him in her spank bank didn't help. If she'd allowed a few other ridiculously hot celebrities into her fantasies once in a while, she might've been less feral sitting beside this one.

Thanks for nothing, Keanu.

It would be unfair to lead him on, so she'd have to try harder to hide her attraction.

"Zack," she said, fighting the temptation to confirm his observation by climbing onto his lap and devouring his mouth. It hadn't even been fifteen minutes since takeoff, and already, she struggled to keep her head on straight and body parts to herself. "Read the damn book."

And stop reading me like one.

His low, mischievous chuckle echoed in her ears, and she forced herself to focus on the page. She had a feeling he'd like the book and appreciated that he'd brought it. Like it was a way to connect with her.

About ten minutes passed before his fingertip stabbed a page.

"Wow." He sat straighter. "Maybe it meant something. Maybe not, in the long run, but no explanation, no mix of words or music or memories can touch that sense of knowing that you were there and alive in that corner of time and the world. Whatever it meant."

She grinned. "Cool, right?"

His eyes remained on the paperback. He wasn't reading it from cover to cover, just skimming through it. A few minutes later, he laughed.

"Never do anything the person standing in front of you can't understand," he read, nodding in appreciation of Thompson's humor.

Mandy closed her book. "Did you get me the job?"

She hadn't expected to blurt it out right then but needed to put it to rest. The question had nagged her since Ted told her about the position. If he said yes, she'd be livid. No one had the right to manipulate her life like that. It wouldn't just throw a wrench in her friendship plans—it would end them altogether. She'd be cordial, for Phoenix's sake, but that would be it.

"What?" His expression was flat and frustratingly inscrutable. "Of course not. Why would you ask that?"

"Because Adam's girlfriend called me, overheard my new boss being an inappropriate creep, and suddenly... poof! Job offer making enough cash to quit and pursue my dream falls into my lap."

He angled his body to face her as much as the seat would allow. "I'm sure you got that job because you're a hard worker with a great reputation in the industry. You practically ran that club and supported the local music scene and beyond by keeping it alive. Who told you about the job?"

"My old boss, Ted."

"There you go. I remember you saying his connections ran deep, so he must've heard about it and talked you up to Shane. You earned that job, Mandy."

She nodded, grabbing a bag of pretzels from her bag and biting one with a loud crunch. "Okay." It still seemed like a wild coincidence, but she'd let it drop. She held out the bag, and he took a few.

"Back to Kyla's call..." He bit a pretzel in half, chasing it with a swig of champagne. "She shouldn't have done that, but her heart was in the right place. From what she told you and the fact that I'm sitting here, it's no secret how I still feel about you."

"Zack..." This conversation was inevitable, but that wasn't the time or place to have it. "I'm exhausted. Can we please save this discussion for when we aren't stuck in a metal death trap with a bunch of strangers thousands of feet above the Midwest?"

He nodded with a slight frown, looking disappointed, but his unclenching jaw suggested he might also be relieved. "Sure."

She let out a long yawn and handed him the bag of pretzels. She wasn't lying about the exhaustion—with the day's stress and excitement winding down, the lack of sleep had caught up to her.

The gentle hum of the engine made her eyelids heavy, and she nodded off toward his shoulder. Since resting her head there would be inappropriate, she leaned against the hard plastic wall beside the window and closed her eyes.

17

Zack

With Mandy's breathing slow and even, Zack set the pretzels on his tray to avoid waking her with his crunching.

Now, he could look at her without creeping her out or making her think he was trying to get into her pants with his hypnotic, smoky eyes or whatever. He'd love to get into her pants, but he wouldn't put on an act to do it. He'd never been fake with her and wouldn't start now.

She was never shy about calling him on his shit, and he was glad that it hadn't changed. He was even happier to discover her body reflexively responding to his hadn't changed either.

Hello, hope, you sneaky son of a bitch. Where the fuck have you been hiding?

He'd found more points to add to the hope column. A spike of jealousy flashed in her eyes when she mentioned seeing him in photos with other women. She wouldn't be jealous if she didn't give a shit. Her keeping tabs on him was a good sign, too.

It was all evidence that Ted was right—she still had feelings for Zack. Ted also said she was ready to settle down with someone who loved and appreciated her. Was he right about that, too? It was no secret one of Zack's hobbies was fucking any willing and pretty girl he could, but the woman beside him made him want to change that. He wanted to be the one she came home to after a long day. The one she trusted with her secrets and knew all of his.

After the three weeks were up, would she want that, too?

He looked forward to catching up properly and hearing about what she'd been up to the last nineteen months. Did she live in the same apartment? Why wasn't she managing yet? Had her goals changed? Had she finally shed the toxic brainwashing that kept her hand out of the cookie jar most of her life? Was she better at saying yes to what she wanted?

When she said yes to joining him and his band on tour for two shows, he couldn't fucking believe it. There was no mistaking the excited glimmer in her eye when he invited her—like the devil on his shoulder had woken hers up from its slumber, they'd conspired together, and there was no stopping fate.

He hoped that part of her was still there, eagerly waiting for the chance to come out and play.

Mandy's long eyelashes fluttered in her sleep, her luscious pink lips parting with every soft exhale. The soft waves of her hair grazed the center of her back, and whenever she shifted in her sleep, he caught the faint scent of her jasmine shampoo.

She still looked strong and fit, but those hips he loved grabbing when taking her deep looked fuller and even more grabbable. He couldn't resist a glance at her tits, and they looked a little bigger too. Maybe there was a God, after all.

Thinking about what was hiding beneath her clothes made his cock spring to life beneath his. Yeah, he was a shameless pervert, but she didn't seem to mind when he was fucking her from behind in the back bedroom of a private jet. But here, now, in front of hundreds of passengers and a flight attendant passing out warm, wet towels, he had to keep his hands and dirty thoughts about other warm, wet things to himself.

A memory of Mandy naked on her knees stubbornly broke through anyway. *Holy. Fuck.*

It was dangerous to let his mind drift in that direction, so he told his cock to settle down. If he were going to win her back, two other organs needed to take the reins—his brain and heart.

He had to think of how to show her he'd changed and was ready to try again. And he wanted her to understand how much space she still owned in his heart.

As he watched her sleep, surrounded by her sweet scent, it was clearer than ever how much of it she'd claimed.

Zack slipped off his leather jacket and laid it over her chest and shoulders. She didn't look cold, but he still wanted her to feel his warmth on her body. And now, layered with her sweet scent, she'd also smell like him. It was something primal—a small, subtle way of marking her, claiming her—something he'd never craved with anyone else, but *oh*, he fucking craved it with her.

She shifted, her head knocking against the window. Her brows pinched together, but her eyes stayed closed as she tried to resettle. He pulled up the divider between them and slipped his arm behind her. Gently, he guided her head to his shoulder. To his surprise and relief, she let him.

The second her warm breath caressed his cheek, he was catapulted back to the first night she slept in his arms. Would he have that chance again? Or would he have to get by the rest of his life on nothing but memories?

Regardless of what came next, right now was perfect.

A loose strand of hair fell across her forehead. She released a contented sigh as he gently brushed it back, tucking herself further into his side. His heart thudded like a kick drum in his chest.

Even asleep, her body was drawn to his.

The flight attendant stopped beside his seat. "Can I get you anything, sir?"

"No, thank you." The flow of air stalled in his lungs as Mandy nuzzled his neck and relaxed in his arms. "I have everything I need."

18

Mandy

Mandy stood beside Zack at the baggage carousel, waiting for their luggage to appear on the belt amidst the chatter and chaos of hundreds of fellow travelers.

She'd woken up halfway through the flight with her head on his shoulder and his arm around her. After checking for drool, she sat up, but his strong arm stayed put. She didn't ask him to move it. Instead, she savored being held, making her feel calm and safe as they crossed the ominous black ripples of the vast Atlantic Ocean. No thoughts of plummeting thirty thousand feet before drowning in the dark sea.

No worries about anything, really.

It was a nice and welcome change.

The plane's wheels touching the ground broke the spell. She pulled away from Zack, gathered her things, and they merged with the passengers marching to baggage claim. The hustle and noise filled the silence between them as she fought to shake off the undeniably non-platonic feelings clinging as tightly as his scent on her clothes.

"Is that you?" He pointed to her emerald-green rolling suitcase with a paisley scarf tied to the handle.

"How'd you know?"

A corner of his mouth tipped up. "I saw you in the airport with it. I was too chicken shit to approach you, so I took about a hundred deep breaths in the bathroom before I could get on that plane."

Knowing she made someone so self-assured nervous caught her off guard. She knew he still cared, but not that she could still affect him like that.

Without overthinking and worrying about the consequences, she took two broad steps and wrapped him in a crushing embrace. His body stiffened before relaxing against hers. She smiled when he hugged her back, drawing her into the warmth of his chest like he was afraid she'd float away if he let go.

Zack's sigh ruffled her hair, the airport noise fading so far into the background that all she heard was his steady heartbeat beneath her cheek. The sound had settled her every night that she'd slept in his bed, achieving the impossible mission of shutting down the endless worries and "to-do" lists that loved to steal her sleep.

As they stood there in each other's arms, more memories tumbled in—their first kiss, laughing together at everything and nothing in his dressing room after sharing a joint, singing along to "Bohemian Rhapsody" with his bandmates on the limo ride to their Phoenix show.

She wondered if the same moments from their brief but intense time together were running wild in his head, too.

His lips grazed the shell of her ear. "I've missed you so fucking much."

His words and the heat of his shaky exhale ignited goosebumps on her skin. She was stupid for ever thinking what he felt was an infatuation that would fade. The warm flutters in her chest confirmed that nothing had faded for her either. And after months of nearly breaking under the stress of all she carried alone, she felt safe and grounded in his arms.

It wasn't supposed to happen this way.

She was supposed to run into him backstage with a groupie on his arm, making it easier to shift to something platonic. He wasn't supposed to rearrange his trip to ease her flight anxiety or hold her like he regretted ever letting her go.

Like he still loved her.

No.

I can't do this.

Their interactions on this trip needed to be about work and establishing a friendship. Anything more was impossible, and it would be unfair to make him think otherwise. Not only unfair but cruel, considering the circumstances. He had no clue about her deal-breaking secret, but she'd tell him everything when the time was right.

And Zack would never look at her, hold her, or think of her the same way again.

Mandy pulled out of the hug, slipped out of his jacket, and handed it back. "I missed you too."

She looked up at him, tears threatening to spill as her vision went murky. His features had taken on new meaning since their last time together. Every day, she saw the same moss-green eyes and strong chin on the face of her son. *Their* son.

Suddenly, the full gravity of her decision to keep Phoenix a secret hit like a bullet to the chest, stealing her breath. The tears of guilt and regret she struggled to hold back trailed down her cheeks.

His brows knitted as he took her face into his hands, wiping her tears with his thumbs. "Hey, don't cry. Come here."

He pulled her into another hug she didn't deserve but selfishly accepted. She didn't deserve more of his comfort after what she'd taken from him. Regardless of her concerns about his lifestyle and how it might affect Phoenix, he deserved the chance to decide whether he wanted to know his son. From afar, it'd been easier to rationalize her choices and decide for him.

Zack buried his face in the curve of her neck and breathed in. "Remember when we ordered French toast on the plane to Dallas, and you inhaled a cloud of powdered sugar?"

Fresh tears welled in her eyes, but she couldn't help laughing. "I was choking and drooling on myself. Not a good look."

He pulled back, cupping her cheek. "Even choking and drooling, you were the most beautiful woman I'd ever seen." The rough pad of his thumb stroked along her jawline, and her eyes fluttered shut. "Still are."

She stepped back. If she was going to make it through the next three weeks without losing her head or job, she needed to set clear boundaries—for both of them.

"Thanks for helping me during the flight, but we can't just pick up where we left off. I'm here to work. I need to focus on that and not get tangled up in old feelings."

He shook his head, an uncharacteristic seriousness in his expression. "They're not old for me." His eyes glistened in the light above their heads as they stood with their gazes locked. He'd cried the day she said goodbye, and like then, his pain gutted her. "I still—"

"Mandy!" Shane Marx strode toward them from the baggage claim entrance, clutching a briefcase. He set it down to shake her hand. "I recognize you from that *Alternative Press* article on your club. I thought I'd greet you properly as we embark on this adventure together. I hope you're as excited as I am."

She forced a smile, struggling to shake off the intense conversation he'd interrupted. "Absolutely."

"Super," Shane said, radiating enthusiasm. He thrust his palm out to Zack, and they shook hands. "Nice to see you, Mr. Maine. I guess you know my new assistant."

"We just met," she blurted. She didn't want him worrying about personal drama interfering with her duties. "I was just telling him how much I enjoyed their last album. Our planes must've landed at the same time."

Shane's brows pinched slightly before he nodded. She hoped he didn't sense any lingering weird energy between them. "Walk with me, Mandy, and I'll fill you in on today's agenda."

She held her hand out to Zack. "It was nice meeting you, Mr. Maine."

He took her hand, shaking it firmly, their palms sliding together as he let go. "Please call me Zack. And it was nice to meet you, too, Mandy. I'll see you around."

As she grabbed her luggage, two twenty-something guys walked up to Zack, begging for an autograph and photo. He said something that made them laugh before fulfilling their requests with a smile. That effortless charm was one of his best and worst qualities.

On their final day together, it'd worked too well on the half-dressed groupie—a memory she'd love to scrub from her brain. Although, holding on to it might help her shut down the feelings that didn't feel old for her either.

She followed her new boss to the glass exit doors of the terminal.

"I trust you've read the general schedule my secretary sent with the contract," he said.

"Of course." She studied it at home and on the plane and had it memorized. It helped her decide that the best day to tell Zack about Phoenix was after his show on their second day in Rome. He'd have two days off to process the news, so, hopefully, it wouldn't impact his work. And it gave them eight days to become reacquainted before she told him.

"Good. There are a few items to add."

She was distracted as Shane rattled off her additional tasks for the week. She couldn't verify that Zack was looking, but she swore his eyes were burning into her back as she walked away. The awareness made her skin tingle, and all she wanted to do was turn around, run into his arms, and kiss him until she forgot her name.

But that was a fantasy, and she was boringly, disappointingly rooted in reality.

It was eleven a.m., and the sun was high and bright above their heads as they approached a shiny black sedan parked at the curb.

Shane gestured to the tall, middle-aged driver with a black uniform and salt-and-pepper hair, who took her luggage and put it into the trunk. "This is Jesse. He'll take you to the hotel to check in, then drop you at the studio where the band's rehearsing. If they have last-minute requests, please handle them. Afterward, join me in the hotel conference room. We're meeting with the headliners' managers and local press. Take notes and run any errands that come up. Then, we'll join the bands and crew for the kick-off party. It can get rowdy once the drinking starts, so you can leave whenever you'd like."

"Got it." She waved at the driver. "Nice to meet you, Jesse."

Mandy climbed into the backseat as Shane answered a call on his mobile phone. She pulled her notebook from her bag and jotted down everything he'd said. Knowing Zack would likely be at the kick-off party, she appreciated the option to slip out early. She needed space to recharge her defenses after the feelings he stirred on the plane and at the airport.

As they drove through London, she stared wide-eyed out the windows as they passed famous landmarks she'd only seen in magazines and history books—Big Ben, London Bridge, the House of Parliament. On her time off, she planned to explore it all.

Shane ended his call and stuffed his phone into his suit pocket. "Jesse will wait for you in the hotel lot. Feel free to freshen up after the long flight before you head to the studio."

When he turned his head, she sniffed her shirt in case he said that because she was funky. She smelled nothing but Phoenix layered with leather, smoke, and a sexy hint of cologne from sleeping under Zack's jacket. The combination made her head swim and her chest ache.

She already missed them both.

Shane pulled something from his briefcase and passed it to her. She opened her palm to find a small mobile phone.

"Keep this on you always. You'll have plenty of time off, but as your contract states, I'll need you to be on call twenty-four-seven in case a musician has a midnight clothing crisis or something."

"Understood." She tucked the phone into her purse.

"You can use it for personal calls as well. The label's footing the bill, so go wild."

She laughed. "Thank you. I'm not someone who 'goes wild' with anything, but I appreciate that."

"Good to hear. I've had assistants who've indulged in the backstage temptations when they were on the clock, hence the need for the fraternizing clause in the contract."

The... what?

She'd read the major points of the contract before signing, but it was over thirty pages long and loaded with legalese. Afraid he'd rescind the offer if she took too long, she had it signed and overnighted to Shane's office the day it arrived.

There was a copy in her luggage, so she'd read it more thoroughly when she was in her room for the night. Though, she knew what the word "fraternizing" meant and had a pretty good idea of what the clause said—keep your hands off the talent. Despite the temporary hormonal hijacking on the plane, she intended to do just that.

"My mother's planning to visit me in Paris," she said, "but I promise it won't affect my work hours."

He shrugged. "Whatever you do on your time off is your business, as long as it doesn't breach the contract. I hope she has a wonderful trip."

The driver dropped them at the hotel entrance, and Shane left to make more calls. Mandy checked in at the front desk and followed the bellhop to her room. She hadn't stayed anywhere fancy enough for someone else to handle her luggage since her first Zack adventure. Judging by the soothing sounds of a live piano from the bar and the massive crystal chandelier in the lobby, this place was on another level of ritz.

When the door opened to her suite, she bit back a gasp. Her entire house would fit in the expansive room.

The bellhop deposited her luggage at the foot of the bed, and she slipped him a tip before he left. She stood inside the doorway, taking in every detail of the space.

A row of wide windows overlooked a river and the bustling city surrounding it. A silky black bedspread and impossibly fluffy, inviting pillows adorned the massive bed. There was a dining table, a plush red velvet sofa, and a gorgeous cherry wood desk beside the door.

"I can't believe I'm here," she whispered, disbelief and excitement bubbling through her.

A pang of homesickness struck as she marveled at the sights of an exciting new city. She missed her son. It was the middle of the night in Denver, so she couldn't call. She already missed the sounds of his laughter and the babbling that resembled actual words a little more every day. Hopefully, he'd save the real thing for her.

She wiped away a single tear and pushed aside the mom guilt. There was no time to fall apart. The driver was waiting, and she had to hit the ground running with the duties Shane had given her. She showered quickly before throwing on fresh clothes and returning to the lobby.

When the elevator opened, dozens of people were screaming outside the hotel. If she had to guess, they were happy screams, and most sounded female. Through the lobby's glass walls, she saw barricades set up to keep the screamers corralled.

She left through the double doors, heading toward the waiting car when that tingling awareness returned. Curiosity won over, and she turned to find Zack exiting a sleek black SUV. A huge bodybuilder-type stood beside him, and Zack laughed at something the guy said. He'd put on sunglasses since the airport, so she couldn't see his eyes, but she sensed his gaze on her. Her hand twitched to wave at him, but that would be stupid. Let him have his moment with his fans.

A high-pitched shriek from the crowd stole her attention. A skinny brunette with massive, impossibly perky tits bounced at the front of the fan cluster before letting out another ear-piercing squeal. Her cutoff shorts and halter top left nothing to the imagination. She suggestively licked her pouty, cherry-stained lips, and in case that wasn't enough of an invitation, she also blew Zack a kiss. His head never turned in the girl's direction, so he probably hadn't even noticed her advances. That was new.

As Mandy watched the girl try harder and scream louder to turn his head, something occurred to her—*Have I ever looked that hot?* If she had, that ship had sailed one decade, one pregnancy, and ten pounds ago. One of her biggest regrets was taking her pre-baby body for granted. If she'd known what was ahead, she would've worn more bikinis and miniskirts when she could pull it off.

Aside from the fan's firm, model-perfect body, she envied how comfortable the girl seemed in her skin and with her sexuality. Mandy avoided mirrors even when changing her clothes. Zack had helped her tap into a bold, naughty side she hadn't realized she possessed, but it was limited to him and behind closed doors. Now, that side was long gone—obliterated and buried beneath an avalanche of responsibilities and body issues.

She'd give anything to feel beautiful again. It would be so freeing to chase her desires without shame like the brazen, screaming fan clamoring for attention.

But she had to admit, she wished the girl's desires were aimed at someone else.

Of course, he was free to do whatever and whomever he pleased. Since they'd both be backstage, witnessing dirty deeds between him and one or several of these fans was a real possibility.

While she hated the idea of once again seeing him with someone else, on the bright side, it might make it easier to get over him. In the meantime, she'd have to keep a lid on her emotions to avoid alerting her boss or anyone else in their camp she and Zack used to... "Date" didn't feel like the right word. Whatever they were, it had to remain secret and not happen again. Their time on the plane reminded her how easy it was to get carried away with him, and she had to get better at shutting it down.

When Mandy arrived at the studio, hugging her trusty notebook and pen, at least a dozen people filled the hallways, chatting and laughing. She followed the slow-tempo drumbeats and sludgy guitar to the rehearsal space and found the band running through their biggest radio hit, "Sometimes Never."

Fury Fuel consisted of two fit, flannel-clad guys from Boston and Cassie Rose, the lead singer-guitarist who looked like Stevie Nicks in punk attire. Her waist-length platinum mane swayed behind her as she belted out lyrics about losing something you never really had. The words hit a little too close to home for Mandy's taste as she sat on a cushioned bench in the far corner of the room and waited for the band to finish. Judging by their sweaty faces, they'd been at it a while, so it wouldn't be long.

After two more songs, they abandoned their instruments, and Cassie grabbed a water bottle.

Mandy slapped on her warmest, friendliest smile and approached. "Hi, I'm Mandy Reid, Mr. Marx's touring assistant. You all sounded fantastic." She held out her hand, and Cassie was the first to shake it.

"Mr. Marx." Cassie giggled like she had a private joke. "I'm Cassie, but you can call me Cass. This is Felix and Roger."

The men took turns shaking Mandy's hand before someone in the hallway called them over.

"Can I get you anything?" Mandy grabbed a folded white towel from a table and held it out.

Cassie took it, dabbing her cheeks and forehead. "Thanks, but I'm good. Shane sent over enough food to feed a navy fleet. I just want to get back to the hotel and sleep off some of this fucking jetlag before the party. And he *hates* being called 'Mr. Marx.' He thinks he's way too cool for proper shit like that." She rolled her eyes.

Mandy grinned, liking her already. "Understood. Thanks for the tip."

"One thing you can do is to make sure Felix and Roger get to the arena on time. They can be such fucking slackers and need the occasional boot in the ass to get in line. Too much is riding on this tour for them to make us look unprofessional."

"You got it." Mandy jotted the task in her notebook. "Anything else?"

Cassie's eyes flicked to the empty hallway and back again. "I know we just met, but I need you to have my back. If someone talks shit about me or you overhear anything you think I should know, please tell me. Okay?"

Mandy wasn't sure how to interpret the vague request, but she nodded anyway. "Of course. It was great meeting you, Cass. I look forward to working together." She offered her hand again.

Cassie laughed and gave her a one-armed hug. "We're in shark territory now, honey. Us ladies need to stick together."

Again, Mandy was confused, but she smiled before searching for Felix and Roger to see if they needed anything. A short, beefy man who looked stoned out of his gourd informed her they'd left for the hotel.

With the first task complete, she returned to the car to meet Shane at the hotel's conference room.

"Hi, Jesse." She slid into the back seat and buckled in. "Thanks for waiting."

"No worries, miss. As long as I've got a Thermos of tea and a good book, I can wait in this car until the rest of my hair goes gray." He winked in the rearview mirror, and she smiled back.

As they pulled away from the curb, she took out the phone Shane had given her and called her mom. It was early in Colorado, but she'd be awake.

"Hello?" Her mom's familiar voice was like a warm hug.

"Hi, Mom. How's home?"

"Everything's great, honey. Enjoying my morning coffee. How's London?"

"London is..." Mandy watched the city sights flicker past her window as they drove along the Thames. "Amazing. I'm working, so I don't have much time, but I wanted to check in and tell you I landed safely. Is Phoenix up? I'd love to say hi."

"Of course. He was having a ball chattering with his toys, so he's still in his crib. One second."

Door hinges creaked, followed by her son's happy babbling. She smiled as bittersweet tears sprung to her eyes. The babbling grew louder, and she pictured his tiny hands clutching the receiver.

"Hey, Little Bug. Did you have nice dreams?"

He sneezed before the babbling continued.

"Bless you, sweetie," she said with a laugh. "I miss you so much. I hope you're having fun with Grandma."

She talked about her day, describing the gray clouds over the city and the blue river running through it. She told him about the pigeons pecking the grass as they passed a park. And she told him how much she loved him and couldn't wait to see him in two weeks. She kept an upbeat tone, even as her heart cracked from the distance between them.

"Mandy?" Her mom was back on the line. "I've got a diaper situation to handle, so I'll let you go. Don't worry about us, and enjoy this experience, okay?"

"Okay." Mandy wiped a tear from her cheek, and Jesse offered a warm, sympathetic smile in the rearview mirror. "I love you both. We'll talk again soon. Bye, Mom." She slipped the phone back into her purse.

"How old's your little one?" Jesse asked, his British accent thick and charming. He could make serious money narrating books. It'd be perfect for *The House at Pooh Corner*.

"Nine months."

"Ah, fun age. Must be tough to be so far, but babies are strong. I bet you are, too."

She nodded. "Please don't tell anyone about him."

"Not a problem, miss." He met her eyes in the mirror again. "You become a master of keeping secrets in my line of work, trust me."

The rest of the day went by in a blur of meetings, note-taking, phone calls, and shaking hands. Watching the three managers review performance schedules and discuss logistics for the upcoming shows and promotional events was thrilling.

In particular, Tomorrow Mourning's manager, Sophia Cruz, brought a no-nonsense, competent energy that commanded attention and respect. It was mesmerizing to watch her work, leaving no mystery as to the band's success. They were massively talented, sure, but that only got you so far. It takes knowledgeable, dedicated representation to have the chance to play in packed stadiums around the world.

Eliza Marsh was fifteen minutes late because of a phone call, but equally impressive. She demanded extra security for Killing Daisies and made it clear that if photos of Charlotte's baby were taken on this tour and sold, heads would roll. When Shane complained about the size of Cassie's dressing room compared to Sandra's, Eliza asked how many platinum albums Cassie had sold. That shut him up.

Mandy glowed inside as she watched her dream career play out, soaking up every detail.

After the final meeting, everyone headed to the ballroom for the kick-off party. She slipped her notebook into her handbag and trailed behind, mentally preparing herself for another Zack encounter.

Steady drumbeats echoed through the hallway leading to the ballroom like a giant's heartbeat. Inside the vast space, guests filled their plates at buffet tables set up along the far wall while a few dozen people danced to The Ramones in front of a DJ booth in the corner. Tables shrouded in black linen were filled with people in leather, flannel, or both, laughing, chatting, and drinking. Colorful mohawks and pierced faces dotted the room, adding to the punk rock wedding reception vibe.

Tyler Hall appeared in front of her, startling her. "Hey, Mandy." The volume of his voice was low as he offered his hand. "Zack told me you want to play it like we've never met, but for the record, I'm very glad to see you again."

She smiled, shaking his hand. "Glad to see you too. And congratulations on the wedding and baby."

"Thanks." He cracked a broad grin. Under his eyes were the telltale dark circles of life with a newborn. "A lot's changed since we saw you last. Congrats on your new gig. Shane seems cool."

"Thanks, he's been amazing. I've already learned a lot."

Adam Hyatt slung his arm around Tyler's shoulders, tipping his chin at her. "Hey. It's cool to meet you for the very first time ever." He sipped the beer clutched in his free hand.

She wrinkled her nose with a laugh. "Hi, Adam. Sorry to make it weird. I don't want people to think I'm here because someone called in a favor instead of what it is—a very strange small-world coincidence."

"Makes sense." He nodded, raising his bottle. "Can I get you a drink?"

She shook her head, expecting the other third of their band to pop up any second. "No, thanks. Still getting my bearings. How have you been?"

"Ty and I have been great," Adam said, the implication clear—Zack hadn't. "You?"

"Fine, thanks." Now, she wanted that drink.

Charlotte Hall came over in a green babydoll dress, looking ridiculously gorgeous with her long dark hair and chocolate-brown eyes. "Don't hog her all to yourselves, boys." She flashed a sweet smile as Tyler slid an arm around her waist. "I'm Charlotte. The red-headed freak skipping in our direction is Sandra."

Sandra Becker—one of the most talented and charismatic lead singers who'd ever lived—came bounding over from halfway across the room. "Don't leave me out of the huddle, fuckers. Hey, Mandy. I'm—"

"You don't need an introduction," Mandy gushed—something she rarely did, but Sandra was a rare breed of rockstar. "I'm a big fan. Of all of you, really. Your voice is phenomenal, Sandra, and I can't tell you how many times your lyrics have helped me through tough days."

Sandra beamed, her chin rising an inch at the compliment. "Phenomenal." She turned to her friends. "You hear that? My new best friend appreciates my pipes."

Charlotte's eyes rolled to the mile-high ceiling. "I heard her. Good thing you're super humble." She turned to Mandy. "She'll be insufferable all night, but I agree with you. The woman's got the goods."

The song ended, and a tall, handsome young guy with glasses came over. He looked vaguely familiar, but she couldn't place it.

"Have you ladies seen Amber?" he asked.

Charlotte and Sandra shook their heads in perfect unison. She'd observed over the years that band members were often like a single, synced-up machine even offstage.

"Mandy, this is my brother, Matthew," Tyler said. "Matty, this is Mandy."

Matthew's dark eyebrows jumped. "Oh, wow. Nice to meet you." He held out his hand.

She shook it, feeling awkward that she'd been a topic of conversation. "Nice meeting you, too."

"Let's find Amber so we can eat," Adam said, patting his flat stomach before his gaze slid to Mandy. "You should join us. Unless you have to sit with Cassie and the Dipshit Twins."

Tyler laughed and smacked his arm. "Shut up, dick. She has to work with them for three weeks." He looked at Mandy with a head shake. "They're not that bad. But yeah, you're welcome to sit at the cool kids' table with us."

Adam scoffed. "Who're you kidding, Ty? Once a nerdy band dweeb, always a nerdy band dweeb."

"Thanks, guys." Mandy shifted her stance, her eyes searching the room for Shane and their crew. Instead, she spotted Zack laughing with a ridiculously stunning blonde in a black leather jacket. No surprise there. "I'm going to mingle a bit. Have fun."

"It's nice to finally meet you, Mandy," Charlotte said, tucking a dark lock of hair behind her ear. "We'll see you around."

Sandra wrapped her arms around Mandy and squeezed. "Thanks for the ego boost, sweetie. We're super stoked to have you on the tour." She let her go, and the women headed in the direction Tyler and Adam had gone, disappearing into the growing crowd.

Mandy wandered to a table covered in freshly filled champagne glasses, the bubbles sparkling like glitter under the chandelier's lights above her head.

"Hey, stranger." Zack sidled up to her, their elbows bumping. "How was your first day?" His alluring scent instantly overtook the champagne's sweetness in the air.

"Exhilarating and exhausting. Yours?"

"Same, I guess." His body radiated a soothing warmth, and she reflexively leaned closer. "Want to dance?"

She barked a laugh at the mental image of him dancing to the gentle Cat Stevens ballad. "That would be fun but inappropriate. I have to pass."

His eyebrow quirked. "Inappropriate, huh?"

"Very. I know it's your middle name, but I have to be on my best behavior."

"Don't stress. I won't get you in trouble." He waved at someone across the room, and she followed his line of sight.

Tyler's brother, Matthew, was beside the pretty blonde Zack had been talking to. He beckoned Zack over before kissing the woman's cheek. She must be the

Amber he'd been looking for. Mandy shouldn't be relieved, but around Zack, she felt a lot of things she shouldn't.

When the woman turned, she realized it was Amber Jamison—the drummer for Killing Daisies. She was mega-talented, and Mandy couldn't wait to meet her.

This job had serious perks.

"Go ahead," she said. "Have fun with your friends. I'm going back to my room soon."

She also wanted to talk to Phoenix again as another wave of homesickness rolled in. Zack's resemblance to him was partly to blame. It was disorienting to have part of her son so close when he was so far.

And the worry that they'd been talking too long made her nervous. She scanned the room for Shane and found him sipping a martini and chatting with Cassie Rose across the room.

"Really?" Zack's head tipped to the side, a faint frown curving his lips. "I was hoping to catch up. You spent half the flight unconscious, so I think I deserve a five-hour raincheck."

She laughed, wincing at the nervous tremble in her voice. There was a lot they needed to talk about, and since her week one goal was establishing a friendship, she was on board.

"A catching up raincheck sounds great. Another time. Have fun tonight." *But not too much.* She told herself that her inner buzzkill had finished the thought, not the jealous ex who wished things were different.

She set her empty glass on the table as he joined his friends. A hand touched her elbow, and she spun around to find Sophia Cruz.

"Hi, Mandy." Sophia picked up a flute of champagne. "I was in work mode at the meeting, so I'm sorry we didn't get a chance to chat."

Mandy pressed her lips together to avoid gaping like an idiot. Sophia Cruz wanted to chat with *her*?! "Oh. It's fine. Honestly, you're a huge inspiration to me. I've read every interview you've ever done, and it was exciting to watch you in action." She was gushing like a silly fangirl for the second time that night, but she couldn't help it.

"I'm flattered. Thank you. Usually, my clients get all the glory, so I appreciate the ego stroke." Sophia grinned as she brought her glass to her crimson lips and sipped her champagne. "I overheard a certain bass-playing birdie saying you plan to get into management." She pulled a business card from her skirt pocket and offered it to Mandy. "This is my personal line. Call me if you'd like to pick my brain when the tour madness is over."

Mandy almost pinched herself to ensure the moment was real. "Wow, I'd love that." She hoped Zack hadn't set this up after she'd declined his offer, but regardless, it was too important to let pride rob her of the opportunity. "Thank you so much, Ms. Cruz."

"Sophia's fine." Her head tipped back as she drained her glass. "Now, if you'll excuse me, I have a few more hands to shake before I can kick off these heels, scrape off this makeup, and rest up for tomorrow." She winked. "See you around, Mandy."

How much did Sophia know about her relationship with Zack? Mandy didn't want preferential treatment but recognized that success often relies on who you know. She could handle being in the gray area as long as she didn't get a boost she hadn't earned.

She yawned, the long day catching up to her. Counting her brief party appearance as a success, she slipped out. Once back in her room, she locked the door and released a deep breath. After washing her face and changing into pajamas, she turned on the TV to help unwind her brain. Halfway through an episode of *Absolutely Fabulous*, the room phone rang.

She muted the TV and answered. "Hello?"

"Look out your window." Zack's familiar, silky baritone made her grin. It was quiet on his end, so she guessed he was back in his room, too. It was very unlike him to leave a party early.

She did as he said, pressing her hand to the glass. "What am I looking for exactly?"

"Follow the end of the bridge to the left. Do you see the three-story building with white lights around the windows?"

Her gaze followed his direction, and there it was. "Yes."

"Two hours of our raincheck will happen on the top floor tomorrow morning. A car will be downstairs to pick you up at nine."

There's that confidence again.

"Oh, really?" Her fingernail tapped a quick rhythm on the glass.

"You don't work until one, right?"

"How do you know my schedule?"

"What kind of stalker would I be if I gave away my secrets?" He laughed, and the edges of her mouth curled up, imagining him in his room staring out at the same beautiful sight. "You were reading it on the plane."

She'd sworn she caught his curious eyes drifting over to her notebook, and here was confirmation. Fortunately, she only used it for work, so nothing Phoenix-related was inside.

"What is it with you and breakfast?" Her voice was flirtier than she intended, and she bit her bottom lip, her nose scrunching.

He was quiet too long before his sigh crackled in the receiver. "Sweet dreams, beautiful."

19

Zack

As thin ribbons of steam rose from his coffee, Zack watched Mandy approach the front door of the café. He grinned at the flash of nervousness on her face. While he wanted her to relax around him and feel comfortable, knowing he could still get her flustered was an excellent sign.

He beckoned the waiter over to fill her mug so she'd arrive to a fresh, hot cup.

He'd been sitting there for half an hour to avoid raising suspicion if they left the hotel around the same time, his brain swirling with all the questions he wanted to ask and things he wanted to share.

She wanted to conceal their history, which was understandable. While he wished they didn't have to hide their connection, she didn't need anyone making crude assumptions about why she was there. Hopefully, Shane kept his mouth shut so she wouldn't find out that Zack had helped get her the job before he could tell her. *If* he ever told her.

When she reached the top of the stairs, she searched the room. The way her lips curled up when she spotted him instantly made his pulse race. He stood and pulled out her chair, acting like the gentleman they both knew he wasn't. For her, he would be.

"Hey, you." Taking a chance, he hugged her, pressing a soft kiss to her cheek before pulling back. "You look gorgeous."

She was in curve-hugging black slacks and an emerald-green blouse that dipped low enough in front to offer the tiniest peek of collarbone. He still didn't understand how she made that innocent spot so damn sexy and tempting.

"Thanks for the invite." She sat and browsed the menu. "I'm starving."

When the waiter returned, they both ordered English breakfasts.

"Are you excited for tomorrow's show?" She picked up her coffee, blowing on the steam before taking a quick, cautious sip.

"Always. It's a lot of work, but this job's still fun as hell. We've come a long way since the days of playing dive bars and backyard keggers."

"The arena's capacity is twenty thousand, so yeah. Not too many backyards can fit a crowd like that." She wiped a smudge of pink gloss from the rim of her mug.

"So," he said, stirring a spoonful of sugar into his cup, "what have you been up to the past year and a half? Give me the highlights."

Her full lips pursed, and she blew out a slow breath. "I bought a house. It's a little bigger than my old apartment, with a backyard that's sadly not seen any kegger action."

He laughed, setting down the spoon. "Let me guess. You have twice as many houseplants, a stuffed but organized bookshelf, and a CD collection that would make a hoarder blush."

A smile tugged at her lips. "Nailed it. Anyway, I was tired of paying someone else's mortgage by renting. It's a great investment."

"Is that why you haven't started managing yet?" It was none of his business, but he wanted to know why she'd set her dream aside. "Your savings went to buying the house?"

Her smile dropped, and she seemed grateful when the waiter interrupted to set down their plates and refill their coffees. When he left, she set a napkin in her lap and cleared her throat.

"Sophia approached me last night. She slipped me her business card and said I could call to pick her brain. I almost screamed."

"Good." Zack grinned despite being annoyed that she'd dodged the question. "I can't think of a better mentor."

They spent the next two hours chatting and laughing over way too much coffee. They stuck to safe topics like bands and movies they'd enjoyed since they'd last spoken. He talked about the progress of their new album and how much fun it'd been rehearsing with the members of Killing Daisies.

Other than the upheaval at the club, it sounded like Mandy's life had been pretty uneventful. No traveling or wild adventures to recount. It was a shame she hadn't stuck to her thirtieth-birthday vow to add more fun to her life.

He knew their time was over when she glanced at her watch, and her nose scrunched.

"I'll walk you back," he said. "We can separate a block away so no one sees us together."

One side of her mouth pulled up in a sweet, crooked smile, sending a rush of warmth sweeping through his chest.

She's so fucking beautiful.

"Thank you, Zack. This was nice."

They walked downstairs together, and outside the café, three young men were smoking cigarettes on the sidewalk. When one turned to face them, Zack froze.

"Are you motherfucking *kidding me*?!" Adrenaline spiked his blood, his fists curling at his sides, aching to crack bones. "Mandy, stay here."

"What's going on?"

"Just trust me." He stalked over to the group of dickheads, and the one who was seconds away from a fist to the face met his eye.

"Holy shit." The fuckwad's eyebrows shot up in surprise. "You're—"

"Take off the fucking shirt." Zack's molars ground together as he waited.

"What's wrong?" Mandy touched his shoulder, probably hoping to calm him before he did something stupid. Now, that was impossible.

"Nothing as long as this fucker listens before I bash his head in."

When she gasped, he knew she'd read the asshole's T-shirt. The words *Free Amy Carey* were printed across the chest above a mugshot of Tyler's ex-wife—the ex-wife who'd almost killed Tyler, his brother, and Charlotte. It was disgusting, and if the fuckwad didn't take it off, Zack would get his own mugshot.

"Zack, don't," she pleaded, her arms wrapping around his waist, "it isn't worth it."

"Take. It. Off," he growled through clenched teeth, stepping within swinging distance.

"Fine, dude." The guy removed the shirt, and his friend handed him the red flannel tied around his waist. "It was a joke."

"Hard to laugh with a broken jaw, so you made the right choice." Zack snatched the shirt and marched to the blue and white porta-potty beside the sidewalk, tossing it into the toilet. "Fucking asshole."

The men took off, disappearing inside a bar a few doors down.

As tempting as it was to chase the asshole down, Zack refused to let his temper get him into trouble. He'd been down that road before and didn't want to be that guy anymore. Instead, he stared at the ground as his limbs shook with pent-up rage that had nowhere to go, his breaths rapid and shallow. Finally, he took Mandy's hand, tugging her toward the hotel. He needed to get her back so he could take a run or find a punching bag to burn off the energy before he blew.

"Are you okay?" She stumbled, struggling to keep up. "Please, stop."

He pulled her into an alley away from prying eyes.

"No, I'm not fucking okay!" He slipped a pack of cigarettes from his pocket and lit one with trembling hands. He hadn't smoked in days and still planned to quit, but he needed something to help calm him before he put a fist through a window. "Three of my friends almost fucking died because of that *cunt*!"

"Oh, my god." She touched his face, the contact helping to ground him. "That's why I recognized Matthew at the party. I saw the news reports when it happened. I'm so sorry you all went through that."

He sucked the filter hard, an inch of paper crumbling into ash. "I hate that they have those fucked-up memories. I wish I was there to put that bitch in the ground."

Even a year later, his desire for revenge burned as fiercely as it did the day he received the call that three of his closest friends had nearly been killed. Charlotte took Rafael off the planet, but Amy was living in a fucking prison cell instead of rotting in a coffin like she deserved.

"Your friends are okay now." Her hands raked through his hair, her fingernails massaging his scalp in slow, comforting circles. The soothing touch made it easier to breathe, but he was still angry and shaking. "Those memories will fade, and they've built amazing lives for themselves." The ghost of a smile touched her lips. "It's sweet how protective you are of the people you love."

He scoffed, flicking his cigarette into the gutter. "Yeah, the ones who stick around."

She frowned, the light in her eyes dimming.

"Sorry. Fuck." He crushed his cigarette beneath his boot, grinding it into the concrete. "I'm an asshole. That T-shirt bullshit shook me, but I shouldn't take it out on you."

"I wanted to call when I saw it on the news, but—"

"Why didn't you?" He didn't want to make her feel bad, but a wound had been poked. It hurt that she didn't reach out during one of the hardest times of his life. "Hearing from you, thinking you still cared, would've meant a lot."

"Of course, I still cared. I knew your friends had your back. And I was afraid hearing from me would've added another layer of hurt to a terrible situation."

He shrugged, hoping to seem unaffected, but they both knew better. "It's fine. Let's get back. Long day ahead."

He took her hand, and they walked in silence, their fingers entwined, until they were a block from the hotel. He lifted her hand to his face and softly kissed her knuckles.

"See you at the show tomorrow," he said, releasing her. The high from spending time together had been obliterated. He wasn't ready to say goodbye but didn't want to drag her down with his grumpy bullshit.

"Thanks for another amazing breakfast." Mandy offered a faint smile before turning around. "No."

His brows furrowed.

She spun to face him. "You helped calm me on the plane, and I'm returning the favor by cheering you up. What's your favorite thing to do in London that takes less than..." She glanced at her watch. "Two hours?"

Zack scratched the stubble on his chin, grateful she wanted more time together but feeling like piss-poor company. Then, the perfect idea struck.

He stepped to the curb and hailed a cab. When it stopped, he stuck his head in the window and whispered their destination so Mandy wouldn't hear.

He turned to her, opening the back door. "Are you coming?"

A corner of her mouth hitched up, and she climbed in. She didn't ask where they were going and held his hand during the ride, his anger evaporating with every passing second. When the cab stopped, her eyes rounded as she realized where they were.

"The National Gallery?"

"Yup." He paid the driver and tugged her toward the entrance. "We don't have much time, but there's something I think you'll appreciate. We'll see that first."

As they walked through the echoing halls, it seemed more like a castle than an art museum—marble stairs, floor-to-ceiling columns, and gold-etched artwork on the walls. The high ceilings in some galleries had skylights, casting a soft, natural glow.

Her head was on a swivel as they walked, her eyes as big as a kid's in a toy store. He scanned the map he'd grabbed at the entrance and led her to the reason he'd brought her.

At the doorway to the room, he stopped. "Close your eyes."

Her brow arched, but she complied. He led her to the painting, positioning her to face it.

"Open them."

The second her eyes popped open, she gasped. Her fingertips slowly rose to her lips as her gaze swept over the canvas. "Zack. It's *Sunflowers*."

"When you said it was your favorite, I looked up where it was."

Tears glossed her eyes, but a broad, beautiful smile lit up her face as she studied the painting. "We were supposed to go somewhere to cheer *you* up."

"Seeing you happy makes me happy."

Her gaze slid from the painting to him, tears collecting on her lashes when she blinked.

She flung her arms around him, squeezing so tightly it was hard to breathe. "Just when I think I have you figured out, you surprise me."

He rested his chin on top of her head and hugged her back, savoring the feeling of being so close.

As Mandy pulled away, she pressed a kiss to his cheek. "Thank you. I'm so glad we did this."

He smiled, her eyes fixed on his even though her favorite painting in the world was two feet away. The touch of her soft lips lingered on his skin, tattooing itself as he fought the urge to taste them.

He touched the spot she'd kissed. "Me too."

20

Mandy

As Mandy worked through her tasks for the day, she never ran into Zack, but he endlessly ran through her mind. His thoughtfulness blew her away when he took her to the painting. Every time her mind replayed what he said, her heart fluttered like mad.

Seeing you happy makes me happy.

Those words turned her insides into warm caramel goo. When she said yes to breakfast, she'd expected to share a meal followed by a platonic "see you later," but like so much with him, things didn't go as expected.

One minute, his temper got the best of him—for good reason—and the next, he was hailing a cab to check a lifelong dream off of her list. His unpredictability was dizzying but thrilling. She relished the warm tingles in her belly whenever she wondered what he'd do or say next.

And no, they were *not* friendly tingles, even though they should be.

She returned the message one of Shane's clients had left about an upcoming Chicago gig, faxed a contract to his potential client in New York City, and delivered Cassie's dry cleaning to her suite.

After making the final checkmark on her list, Mandy had the rest of the night off. Her body was wiped, but her brain was wired. While sightseeing sounded fun, she'd forgotten her maps and guidebooks at home. They got missed in the rush to get Phoenix's things packed. Not wanting to spend her second night in a foreign country lost, she opted to stay in.

A good night's sleep was smart anyway since the first show was tomorrow. Plus, her breasts were sore from lack of pumping and feeding, and cold washcloths sounded like heaven.

There'd be other opportunities to explore London.

But when she hit the elevator button, returning to her room at eight p.m. suddenly felt pathetic. She wanted to talk to Phoenix, but he'd be down for his afternoon nap, so that was out. If she went upstairs, she'd end up hugging the shirt that smelled like him while crying her eyes out. Why waste a night in London sobbing in bed? Granted, the bed was nicer than any she'd ever slept on, but still. That was what the old, boring Mandy would do, and this was an opportunity to forge a new, more adventurous version.

Instead of taking the elevator, she turned toward the sounds of a piano filtering from the hotel bar. She'd embrace the fact that she could have a real drink again. The champagne on the plane and at the kick-off party hardly counted. She'd been breastfeeding for nine months, and although she'd miss that connection with her son, it was nice having her body back. She could do without the soreness, but a drink might help with that, too.

A handful of people sat at tables near the piano, but no one she recognized. She sat at the solid oak bar and grabbed the menu. She hadn't browsed a list of adult beverage options in ages, and the cocktails looked too fancy and complicated for her current mood. She focused on the wine list because that was what she'd missed most. Something dry, rich, and red sounded like heaven.

When the bartender came, Mandy ordered a French Cabernet—fitting for the start of this European adventure.

A young man with dark hair and a faded Bowie T-shirt slid into the seat beside her. "Put it on my room."

She looked him over—he was handsome and definitely her type, but she wasn't interested. And while flattered, she didn't want to give the wrong idea.

She met the bartender's eye. "No, I've got it." The bartender nodded, and Mandy turned to the stranger. "Thanks, but I prefer to pay for my drinks."

The stranger grinned, perfect white teeth flashing. "I won't argue. I saw a beautiful woman at the bar and couldn't resist." He held out his hand. "I'm Luke."

She looked closer, and it hit her. "Of course! Luke Rush. You play bass for Killing Daisies. I must be jetlagged." She shook his hand as the bartender set her wine glass in front of her. "Mandy."

His eyebrows raised. "*The* Mandy?"

She huffed a laugh. "I'm not famous. Is there a pop star with my name or something?"

He shook his head, his smile growing. "I heard you were touring with us; I just didn't know you were you."

Someone took the seat on her other side, and when leather and smoke hit her nose, she turned. Zack had mussed hair, and a faint shadow of a beard darkened his cheeks. He'd pushed his sunglasses on top of his head, and of course, he wore his leather jacket.

"Hey," she said, no other words forming in her brain.

"Hey." His gaze flicked to the approaching bartender. He ordered the same thing she had and said to charge their drinks to his room. His eyes on her mouth were too distracting to argue. Why did he have to be so damn hypnotizing? "What's up, Luke? I think Sandra was looking for you."

Luke laughed. "Yeah, right. You're just afraid of the competition." She turned to him, and he gave a conspiratorial wink. "I was about to invite her to my room."

Zack's homicidal glare seared into his face. "I'll invite her to your funeral if you don't get the fuck out of here."

"Easy, killer." She touched his arm, the heat of his skin radiating through the leather and warming her palm. "He's messing with you. He offered to buy me a drink, I declined, and you came over. End of story."

"Felt like a beginning to me." Luke placed a hand over his heart.

"Finish your drink and fuck off," Zack snapped. He was overreacting and being immature, but her libido didn't care. It was hot to witness how protective and territorial he was, despite the fact that she wasn't even his.

Luke laughed as he grabbed his drink and left his seat. "Later, guys. Nice meeting you, The Mandy."

She chuckled. "Bye, The Luke."

"What was that about?" Zack asked, his brows furrowed.

Not wanting to explain, she waved a dismissive hand. "How was your day?"

It was weird how domestic the question sounded—like she'd made pot roast, and he'd just come home from the office. That couldn't be further from their dynamic, and she was great with it. She'd never want what her parents had.

A sudden, sharp pang of guilt tightened her belly. Here she was, a world away from Phoenix, having drinks with his father. And reconnecting with Zack and her pre-mom self while he was clueless about their son back in Denver.

One thing she envied about her parents' relationship was its simplicity. This was far from simple.

"Long, but good." He sipped his wine and set his glass on the bar. The dark shadows beneath his eyes and the angry red pads of his fingers said he'd put in a hard day's work and needed to unwind. "We rehearsed downtown and did the usual crew huddle. You?"

"Also good." She told him about her day, and he listened despite his exhaustion.

The wine relaxed her as they went back and forth, talking excitedly about what the next days held and what sights they hoped to see in their downtime. Like on the plane and at breakfast, she was relieved he was still easy to talk to and down-to-earth. She'd worried he'd changed, or the issues that led to their breakup would've made it impossible to connect like this again.

Maybe enough time had passed for the hurts to settle far into the background, making a genuine, lasting friendship possible.

When their second glasses arrived, her eyelids were heavy, her muscles loose and warm. After eighteen months without alcohol, she was a lightweight.

"Are you hungry?" he asked.

"Not really, but the wine's going straight to my head, so I should eat something."

"Mine too. Aside from the champagne on the plane, I haven't had a drink in almost six weeks." He touched the tip of her nose with a grin. "You're a bad influence."

She hadn't expected that. Was it possible his hard-partying ways were behind him? She'd worried about what trouble it might lead to, hoping it was something he'd change—for his sake and Phoenix's.

"Why haven't you?"

He shrugged. "The guys thought I was overdoing it, and they were right. I'll have a drink or two sometimes, but I'm done being a reckless idiot."

She touched his wrist, earning a soft smile that brightened his tired eyes. "That's great to hear. I worried about you."

While she knew he'd never become as lost and broken as her brother, Zack's excessive drinking was one reason she'd called it quits. It would be an immense relief if the change stuck, but it still didn't mean they'd work as a couple.

"And I'm worried about you falling off your stool if you don't eat soon." He beckoned the bartender. "Two plates of French toast, please. Extra powdered sugar on hers."

A burst of giddy laughter escaped her lips. "You're ridiculous."

"Sorry, sir," the bartender said. "They don't serve breakfast until morning."

Zack slipped a hand into his pocket and pulled out his wallet. He slid two hundred-dollar bills across the bar. "Is it morning now?"

The bartender pocketed the cash with a nod. "I'll make it happen."

She shook her head, laughing at the exchange. "I repeat, you are *ridiculous.*"

"That's why you love me."

Her face fell, her laughter died, and the buoyant mood instantly fizzled.

Why did he have to say that? She returned to her wine, taking a deep drink.

"Sorry." The hurt in his eyes made her wish she could take back her reaction. "It just came out. I know you don't—"

"Want to watch a movie in my room?" She knew being alone in a room with him wasn't smart. A room with a bed, no less. Especially as the lulling effects of the wine set in, and he smelled more edible and tempting than anything on the fancy menu. But she needed to change the subject, and it was the first thing that popped into her head.

Friends watch movies together, right?

His head tilted as he scrutinized her expression, clearly digging for clues on what was happening in her brain. Good luck, since she didn't even know herself.

"I'd like that," he said. "You meant porn, right?"

Mandy spit out a mouthful of wine across the bar.

"Kidding!" He laughed as he grabbed a stack of napkins and wiped up her mess. "I'd love to watch a movie with you. Even one without silicone tits and horny pizza delivery guys."

"You're such a poet." She patted her lips on a napkin as she laughed, leaving behind a pale pink lipstick print. She rarely wore makeup because she didn't have time to fuss with it or anyone to impress, but being in a new country with a new job made it feel like a makeup day.

Soon, two plates of steaming French toast were placed in front of them, with a snowy mountain of powdered sugar piled on hers. She scooped off half and sprinkled it over Zack's plate.

"Now you can choke, too, smartass." She bumped his shoulder with hers and dug into her food. It smelled like cinnamon, vanilla, and rich maple syrup.

The first bite melted on her tongue and made her moan, her eyes sliding closed. She wasn't sure if it was worth two hundred bucks, but it might be the best thing she'd ever put in her mouth. Well, the second-best thing. She turned to Zack, and his Adam's apple bobbed on a hard swallow.

"Keep making noises like that and see what happens," he muttered, an unmistakable spark of desire flaring in his eyes.

After months of feeling frumpy and invisible, it was exhilarating to be the target of that intense, hungry gaze. She was used to playing the roles of daughter, mother, supervisor, and organizer, but Zack made her feel like a *woman*.

The wine made her feel bold, her head a little swimmy. "I bet that filthy mind of yours is conjuring up all kinds of creative uses for that powdered sugar."

His fist clenched around the base of his fork. "Careful." His tone was low and edged with heat. A warning.

With impeccable timing, as always, her mother's voice intruded, reminding her that good girls stay away from men with leather jackets and filthy mouths. Good girls stay out of trouble and certainly never ask for it.

Something about this man made her want to give a middle finger to that voice.

Craving another of his hungry looks, she dipped her defiant middle finger into the syrup on his plate, swirling it before bringing it to her mouth. His breathing sped up as she touched the fingertip to her tongue and sucked it clean.

"Are you done?" he rasped.

His shoulders tensed, a muscle in his jaw ticking. She felt the barely restrained energy rolling off him as he waited for a response. Knowing she had the power to inspire such a reaction was a hell of an ego boost.

She ate a few more bites before downing the rest of her wine and wiping her mouth. She took a moment to savor the sexual tension thickening the air. And to watch him sweat.

"Now I'm done."

"Good." He picked up the napkin with her lipstick kiss and slipped it into his pocket.

He stood, his fingers gripping her elbow and tugging her toward the door. She followed, struggling to keep up with his pace as her heart raced.

What the hell am I doing?

She should stop this. Giving in to their urges would only hurt them both. She was used to saying no to what she wanted, but with the man she'd missed and craved for so long, so close, nearly vibrating with desire for her, she couldn't form the word—or any other, for that matter.

He slammed the elevator button, and his hand locked tighter around her arm, his toe tapping out a quick staccato on the marble floor. Her eyes darted around, seeing no one from her crew.

The elevator dinged, and the doors slid open. He pulled her inside, and when another couple entered, Zack put a hand up. Whatever they saw in his expression made them step back out and wait for the next one.

His chest pressed to hers when the doors closed, walking her backward until she hit the wall.

"You've been teasing me since the goddamn plane." He seized her wrists in both hands and roughly pinned them to the wall above her head. Her breath caught in her throat at the delicious sensation of being trapped by his body and singed by the fire blazing in his eyes. His energy pulsed between them like he was angry, frustrated, and turned on all at once.

"I haven't," she squeaked out.

His dark chuckle echoed in the cramped space. "Don't play innocent now, baby."

Her head tipped back against the wall, and her eyes shut. She needed to resist, but that sweet endearment on his lips always made her crazy. Probably because he was often anything but sweet, like now when he had her at his mercy with eyes full of fire. The contradiction made her head spin.

"I saw how you looked at me on the plane." Zack's lips moved to her exposed neck, planting gentle kisses that left her trembling. "How you stared at my mouth with *need* in your eyes."

She whimpered. Overwhelmed by his scent, his heat, *him*, she fought to break loose from his grip on her wrists, but he only held tighter.

"What if I kiss you now?" he whispered, the damp warmth of his breath ghosting over her lips. "Would you stop me? Run away?"

Mandy forced herself to take a second to answer, allowing her brain to catch up. She couldn't risk getting caught by her boss, but she'd already memorized his schedule, and he was away from the hotel. Despite the thousand other reasons this was a terrible idea, her mouth ached for this man's kiss. The hold on her wrists wasn't enough—she wanted his hands on her tits, her ass, between her legs.

The doors slid open, and he pounded the button to close them and stop the car.

"Answer me," he snapped, the harsh command shooting straight to her clit. While she appreciated soft kisses and being called "baby," he obviously remembered that sometimes, she craved a rougher experience.

"I want it." Her whisper was as quiet as a breeze, but she knew damn well he heard it.

He turned his head, his ear an inch from her mouth. "I'm sorry, what? I didn't catch that." Always a fucking smartass, even as he made her wet and desperate for him.

"Kiss me, Zack." She was louder that time, nearly shouting her plea. "Fucking kiss me!"

A low growl cracked in his chest, and his lips crashed against hers. Her knees turned to jelly, but he held her wrists tighter, holding her up as his solid body pinned her to the wall.

His mouth slanted over hers, his tongue forcing her lips apart and plunging inside. She moaned at the forceful invasion as their tongues danced, the electric thrill of anticipation flooding her veins as his taste flooded her mouth. The heady combination of cinnamon, wine, and smoke made her mouth water as she sucked his plump bottom lip. As his body melted into hers, she hooked a leg around his hip, grinding against the thickening bulge in his jeans.

His head tipped back with a groan like she'd caused him pain. "Fuck, baby. I want you so bad I could scream." He released her hands and gripped her hips, pressing his erection against the seam of her pussy as his panted breaths grew louder in the space between them. "But it'll be a lot more fun making you scream."

An alarm sounded, masking her responding groan, startling them, and breaking the spell. He hit the button to open the doors, and the alarm quieted. In their place, alarm bells blared in her mind.

This is wrong.

You can't trust him.

When you tell him about Phoenix, he'll hate you.

His arm slipped around her waist.

"Stop." She stepped from his grasp, covering her face as she caught her breath. "What the hell am I doing?"

"Hey." A gentle hand touched her shoulder. "What's wrong?"

She smoothed her disheveled hair and took another broad step away, ignoring the question because she knew he wouldn't like the answer. "That was a mistake. I drank too much and got carried away. I'm sorry."

"Don't be sorry." He began reaching for her again but slipped his hands into his pockets instead. "We can slow down. A movie was a good idea."

"No. Being alone together right now is a *terrible* idea."

"I can control myself, Mandy."

"Clearly, I can't!" She exhaled a loud, shuddering breath. "I lose my head with you. If we get caught together, I'll lose my job."

The corners of his mouth turned down. "What are you talking about?"

"A clause in my contract says I can't be involved with anyone associated with the tour. I can get fired for what we just did."

"That's bullshit." He stepped closer. "I'll talk to Shane tomorrow and have him draw up a new contract without it."

"Don't you dare!" She stepped back, reestablishing some distance. "I don't want him or anyone on the crew knowing we have a... history."

He scoffed. "That kiss felt pretty present tense to me. It's all I've thought about since we broke up."

"The reasons we did haven't changed, so this was unfair of me. I'm sorry."

"For fuck's sake, stop apologizing!" He grasped his hair in his fists.

"I can't do that either. Because I have plenty to be sorry for." She couldn't tell him about Phoenix in a hotel elevator the night before the first show. But she needed to set clearer boundaries until she could. "I'm not the same person I was when we met. My life's more complicated now, and although I still have feelings for you, I have nothing to offer but friendship. Can we please try that?"

His lips pressed in a tight line as he shook his head. "That wasn't our last kiss. You know it as well as I do."

Mandy shut her eyes, trying like hell to muster the patience and self-control that usually came easily. "It has to be this way. Can you please just be my friend? Isn't it better than nothing?"

He shifted his stance, but his penetrating green eyes never left hers. Their connection was as strong as ever—maybe even stronger. Still, it had to be this way.

"Wait." His head cocked. "You said *reasons* we broke up. Wasn't it only about the distance?"

Shit.

"No." This was not the time or place for this discussion either, but he deserved her honesty. "It wasn't only the distance."

"If it was about the booze, I have it handled. And if you're worried about other women... Getting wasted isn't the only thing I haven't done for six weeks. I haven't touched or even *thought* about anyone else." He closed the distance between them in three slow, deliberate steps, taking her face into his hands. "I'm ready to be the man you deserve. I've watched my best friends find something real, and I want that, too. I can't be the lonely fuck-up anymore. I'm ready for more, and I've never wanted it with anyone but you."

Tears sprang to her eyes at his perfect words. It was everything she wanted to be true. But she'd trusted him once, and he broke her heart. And if he truly was ready for her but not Phoenix, their relationship would still be doomed.

If, by some miracle, he felt the same when all her cards were on the table and they rebuilt their broken trust, maybe there was hope. In the meantime, if they were friends, she could judge how changed he was.

"Monday night after your show," she said, "we can sit with a bottle of wine and talk about everything. I promise. For now, all I can offer is friendship. Can we start there?"

The elevator opened and closed again.

His eyes narrowed, studying her. "Fine. If that's how you want it." He thrust out his hand, his expression suspiciously blank. "Friends?"

She hesitated a second before pressing her palm to his and shaking it. He tightened his grip, and she gasped when he tugged her closer, her feet stumbling until their faces were inches apart.

"I have enough friends, Mandy. Maybe some things about you have changed, but one thing sure as fuck hasn't. You're still too stuck in your head to admit what you want and too afraid to fucking take it."

She yanked her hand away and staggered back. "And you're still too hung up on what *you* want to face reality. We didn't work then, and we can't work now. I shouldn't have teased you in the bar or kissed you. I was a jerk for leading you on."

He slammed a button on the wall, and the elevator doors opened on the top floor. "Do you remember the last thing I said when you told me our phone calls had to stop?"

She nodded, her eyes fixed on his. Of course, she remembered. Every detail of their time together was branded on her brain whether she wanted them to be or not.

"Don't regret me," she said.

"Do you?" His voice trembled a little, softened by vulnerability and probably fear of how she'd respond.

She shook her head without hesitation, unable to speak as tears pricked her eyes. Knowing she'd never have what she really wanted tore her apart, but she'd never regretted a second with him.

"Good." He pressed the button for her floor and stepped out of the elevator. "Don't start now."

21

Zack

Throughout the afternoon soundcheck, the elevator kiss replayed in Zack's mind like a favorite song. He didn't miss a single note and added a flair to the opening bassline of "Savage" that had a few roadies in the setup crew pausing their work to watch.

He hadn't played that well in a long time, and the pleased grins and nods Tyler and Adam aimed in his direction confirmed it. As they prepared to hit the stage to kick-off the European tour, he held on to that energy and the hope that the kiss had sparked a new beginning.

Mandy pulling away afterward disappointed him, but he wasn't deterred. And her apologizing for kissing him back while grinding against his cock was laughable.

She'd blamed the wine for getting carried away. He knew from ample experience that alcohol turns down the noise in your head that prevents you from accepting inconvenient truths—something she'd always struggled with. It was clear she wanted him as much as he wanted her, but that fucking noise inside her brain kept talking her out of it.

Why did she keep resisting what she obviously wanted?

Was it the fear of getting caught and fired? Maybe. But he'd never let that happen. Money and fame talk, and Zack had a fuckload more of both than Shane Marx.

She might want to see for herself that he'd stopped drinking himself stupid and would keep his hands off other women. That wouldn't be a problem.

The brainwashing bullshit from her childhood was likely part of her resistance too. He'd hoped she'd kicked it by now, but being manipulated to believe your only choices in life were to conform or burn in hell is a serious mind fuck.

He'd shed that toxic, Puritanical bullshit ages ago, but when she opened up to him on their first night together, he recognized her struggle, and it stirred something inside him. Their time was short, but he wanted to help her shed it, too, like some twisted, heretical avenger.

Of course, her issue might not be as major as it seemed, and she'd taken something small and overthought it to death. If that were the case, he'd be frustrated by their wasted time, but at least it'd easily be dealt with.

Regardless of the reason for her resistance, the breakup was over more than distance. She promised they'd talk it out next week, and he'd sure as fuck hold her to it. Patience was still a struggle, so hopefully, he could get her to open up sooner.

First, she had to feel comfortable. Going along with the friendship she asked for might help. As tough as it would be to keep his hands and mouth to himself after that mind-blowing kiss, he'd slow his approach to avoid scaring her off for good.

Friends. It was bullshit, but he could do that. Even though the things he wanted to do to her were anything but friendly.

"Ten minutes, gentlemen," the stage manager barked over the backstage chatter and crowd noise. Killing Daisies' set got the arena nice and riled up, and now, it was their turn at bat.

Tyler slid an arm around Adam and Zack's shoulders. "Ready to blow away twenty thousand Brits?"

"Fuck yeah, brother." Adam bounced on the balls of his feet. "Let's kick this tour off right."

Zack scanned the backstage crowd, hoping to spot Mandy. He'd only seen her a few times throughout the day and never from close enough to offer anything beyond a quick wave when no one was looking. She had work shit to handle after the opener's set, but he hoped she'd watch him tonight.

A bony finger jabbed into his ribcage, and he turned to find Sandra.

"Good luck topping our masterpiece performance." Her lips curled in a teasing smirk. "If you guys put people to sleep, I'll wake their asses up when I join you."

Zack flipped her off. "Keep dreaming, princess. You warmed them up; we're about to set them on fucking fire." He leaned close to her ear. "Have you seen Mandy around?"

She aimed a thumb behind her. "She was taking sandwiches to Tweedledum and Tweedledumber's dressing room. Want me to get her?"

No one liked the guys in Fury Fuel. They seemed fine at first but were pretty fucking full of themselves for an opening band with only two albums that weren't even halfway to gold. The lead singer, Cassie Rose, was cool, and it was clear she carried the two dickheads with her talent. Hopefully, Mandy would mostly work with her.

"Five minutes," the stage manager announced.

"Guess not." Sandra put out her fist, and the guys bumped it. "I love giving you shit, but you're the band I've cranked the loudest since album one. Have a killer show, guys. See you out there."

The house lights went off, and the crowd's din grew into a unified roar, shaking the walls. Adam went out first, the crowd going wilder as he waved and took his place at the drum kit. Zack took a deep breath and walked onto the stage, waving at the sold-out arena before grabbing his bass.

Seeing and hearing that many people lose their shit over what they'd created never got old.

Tyler joined them, grabbing his guitar and taking the center-stage mic. "Looking good tonight, London." He grinned at the surge of high-pitched whistles and shrieks from the ladies in the crowd. "This first one's for my incredible wife and her band." The responding roar vibrated the stage beneath their feet. "They're the toughest act to follow, but we'll do our best. Kick it off, Zacky."

Halfway through his bass intro, Adam's drums joined in. Zack's chin lifted, and he spotted Mandy on the side of the stage. She smiled when their eyes met and gave him a sweet little wave as her head bobbed to the beat. Her hips swayed, and, to his surprise, her mouth began moving as she sang along to Tyler's lyrics.

She knows this song.

"Long Time Alone" was off the album they'd released after their breakup. He was staring at proof she'd listened to it. Not once or twice, but enough to know the fucking words.

She'd kept part of him in her life all this time.

He wasn't sure exactly what it meant, but it meant something.

Six songs in, Sandra joined them for their cover of INXS's "Need You Tonight." He turned toward where Mandy was standing, and his gaze latched to hers, excited for her reaction. When Tyler played the first chords, her eyes snapped wide. Zack smiled, giving a quick nod of recognition.

The song was for her. He wanted to reach her through music and have her recognize that he'd remembered everything she loved. That he'd never let her go.

She knew every word but wasn't singing along. She wasn't moving at all, and her smile was gone. Did he fuck this up too?

Cassie tapped her shoulder, saying something in her ear before Mandy followed her backstage and disappeared.

The rest of the song was a blur, and his gaze kept drifting back to her empty spot. When he botched a note, he shook it off and returned his focus to his instrument. He had a job to do. He'd find her later to ask what happened.

After the show, he searched for her backstage with no luck. The afterparty was in full swing, but the lure of beer, babes, and bong hits didn't tempt him. He needed to find out why Mandy reacted that way to the song.

Zack's wallet and hotel key were in his dressing room, so he headed there to grab them and bail. He opened the door to find a sight that would normally inspire an internal high-five and kick off an incredible night. Instead, it sent him spinning into panic mode.

A petite but well-endowed chick lay sideways on his couch buck-ass naked. Her dark hair partially covered her tits, her hard pink nipples peering through the strands.

It was common for roadies to hand out backstage passes to pretty women who begged for them, but that stopped now.

"Great show, Zack." She let her knee fall to the side, exposing herself to his view. Her British accent was thick and vaguely familiar, so it was possible they'd hooked up the last time he was in London. "You deserve a reward for all your hard work."

His head snapped to the left. She was hot and all, but he wasn't interested. The fear Mandy would see her and get the wrong idea had his heart pounding in his throat.

"Wow." He picked up the pile of clothes beside her and shoved them into her hands, careful not to make contact. "I appreciate the offer, honey, but you need to put these on and go. Now."

Before she could argue, he walked out, shutting the door behind him.

Then, it hit him—was she the reason Mandy left?

What if she'd been waiting to talk about whatever upset her during the song, and she stumbled on Tits-out Tara or whatever the fuck her name was?

Now, instead of being nervous, he was pissed.

"Who the fuck is in charge of security back here?" His bellowing voice silenced the hallway chatter.

Within seconds, a massive wall of muscle appeared in a black "Security" T-shirt. "Is there a problem, Mr. Maine?"

The chatter picked back up, and Zack shoved a finger in the guy's face. "Yes, there's a fucking problem. A naked woman's in my room without an invitation to be there. If it happens again, you'll be tearing tickets for Vanilla Fucking Ice. Got me?"

"Yes, sir." The guy's head reared back, obviously confused, but Zack didn't need him to understand—he needed him to listen. "Sorry for the breach. It won't happen again." He escorted the now-dressed and equally baffled woman out of the dressing room and toward the exit.

"Killer show, Zack." Amber, the drummer for Killing Daisies and Tyler's future sister-in-law, tapped his shoulder with her drumsticks. "Matty and I are about to sneak off to share a joint. Want to join us?"

It was tempting as his heart rioted in his chest. He didn't want Mandy thinking he'd asked the naked woman to be on his goddamn couch flashing her cooch. If that were the case, he needed to set her straight.

"Thanks, but I'm about to bail."

Her eyebrows jumped. "*You* are turning down a joint and ditching out on a party? Where are you going that'll top all of this?"

She gestured to the dozens of people drinking and laughing around them while L7 blasted from a stereo. He'd partied plenty. What he wanted more of was time with Mandy. He only had nineteen days left to win her back and didn't want to waste a second.

"Back to the hotel. Have a few shots for me, yeah?"

She shrugged. "Suit yourself. Later."

On the ride back to the hotel, he had the driver stop at a pastry shop. Fifteen minutes later, he headed up to his suite with a bag loaded with London's best desserts. After a quick shower, he grabbed the bag and took a deep, steadying breath while waiting for the elevator to Mandy's floor.

He needed answers about her leaving and couldn't wait a week to find out why he was getting friend-zoned. Hopefully, she'd be willing to talk after she was nice and sugared-up.

Once the obstacle was behind them, they could give a relationship a real shot. If she still wouldn't talk after a bellyful of Sticky Toffee Pudding and Spotted Dick, he needed to add another item to his list of shit to change:

5. Figure out how the fuck to be patient.

22

Mandy

The tour's first show was a wild, high-energy ride that went off with only three bumps.

The first came with Felix and Roger. After banging on the door of their shared suite, some busty, half-dressed woman answered. Mandy kicked her out along with her equally busty friend. Then, she dialed up her stern mom voice while dragging the hungover men from their beds. They reeked of cigarettes, sweat, and sex—a combination she once found hot but now turned her stomach.

After the douchey duo was showered and dressed, she got them to the show with fifteen minutes to spare. Cassie was right—they were lazy idiots taking for granted their massive opportunity by succumbing to temptation and shirking duties. It was a story Mandy had seen play out a hundred times. A harsh wake up call was likely in the cards someday, but it would likely come too late, reducing these talented men with potential to broke has-been clichés.

Once, Ted warned her that Zack might end up suffering that fate. She never worried about that. While he indulged plenty in backstage temptations, the band was his priority—he'd *never* let them down. And his bandmates loved him too much to let him go too far over the edge.

From what he said last night, they'd stopped him from doing that six weeks ago, and he'd changed his ways. And his claim about abstaining from sex for that long was surprisingly believable. She hadn't seen him even glance at any women fighting for his attention outside the hotel or in the front row at tonight's show. And while his kisses were always intense, the way he attacked her mouth in the elevator was like he was starving for it. Maybe Tyler and Adam had also helped him shed that nasty old habit of bedding women who didn't deserve him.

If they'd helped him grow in those ways, how would they react to the news that Zack was a father? Would they push him to clean up his act further or back him up if he decided he wanted nothing to do with Phoenix? Since Tyler was now a father, she'd bet on the former, but she didn't know him well enough to be certain.

The changes were encouraging, and hopefully, they'd stick, but Zack was still far from being a trustworthy role model. But, as Ted suggested, if a meeting between Zack and Phoenix went well and they built a connection, Phoenix might offer extra motivation to become one.

The second bump of the day came when Tomorrow Mourning played "Need You Tonight." It'd been her favorite song since college, and Zack's nod and pointed glance said it wasn't a coincidence. Twenty thousand people filled that arena, but the song was for her.

Just as his sweet and rough sides were perfect contradictions, so was this very public yet still secretive declaration of love. And it was an acknowledgment that he'd held on to the parts of her she'd shared so freely when they met because of how safe he made her feel.

It shouldn't have woken up the flutters in her chest that made her want to ignore every reason to stay away. Their scorching elevator kiss had looped through her mind all day, and right then, she wanted to run onto the stage and put it to shame.

But it also hurt knowing they'd lose this intense, beautiful connection if her secret drove him away. This might be the last time she felt so seen and wanted. The edges of her mouth tipped down as her throat tightened.

She was startled when Cassie touched her shoulder, asking for help with a stuck zipper. After savoring one more moment of watching him play her song, Mandy reluctantly tore her gaze from Zack.

As Mandy tugged at the fabric jammed between the metal teeth, Cassie glanced over her shoulder. "Be careful."

At first, Mandy assumed she was referring to the task at hand. "I won't snag your skin, don't worry." The fabric came loose, and she dragged the zipper to the base of Cassie's spine.

"I meant what just happened out there." Cassie let her short plaid dress drop to her feet before kicking it away. "If you want the crew to take you seriously, you have to be more subtle. No more googly eyes or everyone will think you got this job with your tits instead of your wits."

Damn. Had she been that obvious? If Cassie noticed, did anyone else?

Mandy handed her the folded T-shirt and patchwork skirt that sat on the vanity. "I don't know what you're talking about."

Cassie's eyebrow cocked. "Don't bullshit a bullshitter, hon. He's cute and all, but not worth getting canned over." She fluffed her hair in the mirror. "Shane said to tell you that you're free the rest of the night. Thanks for your help today. See you later, Lover Girl." With a wink, Cassie turned on her heel and strutted out the door, disappearing into the sea of hallway revelers.

The third and final bump came when Mandy went into Zack's dressing room to leave him a note to call her later. The brunette that'd been screeching outside the hotel was naked on his couch, waiting for him.

Mandy bolted from the room as tears flooded her eyes.

After all the sweet things he'd said and assurances he'd changed, he does *this*?! Had he actually abstained from sex for six weeks, or had he lied to her face? And why did he play her song and look at her like that while his post-show plans were naked and waiting?

Maybe he'd accepted that friendship was all they'd have, and the song was the start of that shift. It's what she said she wanted, after all.

Regardless, seeing proof he'd moved on so quickly after their kiss was a crushing disappointment. After their breakup, he'd done the same, so it shouldn't surprise her. Yes, he was single. She'd rejected him both times, so he didn't owe her anything.

But those facts didn't make it hurt less.

On the ride back to the hotel, the words she'd read in the contract the night before had replayed in her mind: *Any intimate relationship with members of the bands, management company, or crew will result in immediate termination.*

Cassie was right. Mandy needed to be more mindful of her behavior, or she'd waste this once-in-a-lifetime opportunity. If that happened, she'd never forgive herself. She couldn't have him anyway, so getting hung up on one kiss was ridiculous. She had to keep things platonic, as planned.

Now that she was back in her room, she kicked off her shoes, slipped off her shirt, and removed her bra. Releasing her sore, swollen breasts from their too-tight, black lace prison was nearly orgasmic. She tossed the nursing pads irritating her skin all day into the trash. Hopefully, she wouldn't need them much longer. She changed into the black silk pajamas she got last Christmas and slipped a fresh pair of pads into her comfy sports bra to avoid staining her PJs.

The urge to wash the day off her face was strong, so she dumped the contents of her cosmetics bag onto the bed and plucked a bottle of face wash and a jar of moisturizer from the pile. She scrubbed her skin before rinsing off the plum-scented face wash over the bathroom sink and patting her face dry.

Aside from the bumps, her first three days of work were exhilarating. Running errands around London allowed her to explore the city and meet locals in the industry. She enjoyed getting to know Cassie and helping her prep for the show.

Working alongside Shane revealed the complexities of her dream job. Since he coordinated client and company calls according to time zones, he worked in bursts throughout the day and night. He argued with arena staff about budgetary issues, crew members asked him questions, and he had to be available for any band support he couldn't pass off to Mandy. He balanced work with his home life, calling his wife after dinner to ask about her day. When his upset preteen daughter called that afternoon, he had to leave a meeting to calm her down.

There was much more to the role than Mandy thought, but nothing she couldn't handle. In fact, she was even more excited to get started on her own.

Zack had taken up more headspace on this trip than she'd anticipated, but that would change now that he'd moved on. She'd shove aside the feelings he'd stirred, rededicate herself to a friendship, and avoid him like the plague whenever his naked women were around.

She applied a thick layer of moisturizer to her face and glanced at the clock. It was past midnight in London, so her parents were getting ready for dinner. She dialed their number while staring at the glorious sight of London at night. Tiny lights twinkled on the river below as cars drove across bridges bigger and grander than any she'd ever seen. Crowds of people looked like colorful ants as they moved through the streets and along sidewalks crammed with lit-up shops and cafés.

"Hello?" Her mom's cheerful voice brought her back to Earth.

"Hey, Mom. How's home?" The sound of Phoenix's babbling instantly brought tears to her eyes. This was already a very emotional trip, and it'd just begun. Her arms ached to feel the weight of his wiggly little body.

"Everything's great. How's London?"

Mandy shared the highlights from her first days working for Shane, her words rushing out and her free hand gesturing wildly as she described the experience. Despite the lows, most of it'd been the exhilarating, educational experience she'd hoped for.

"Sounds nice," her mom said. "Your father says hi."

Mandy hadn't heard any other voices besides her son's, so she doubted it. "Can I talk to Phoenix? I miss him so much."

"One second."

He let out a joyful shriek into the receiver, making her grin.

"Hey, Little Bug." She sat on the edge of her bed. "I miss you. Are you having fun with Grandma?"

She smiled, blinking back tears as she listened to his string of almost-words. He made letter combinations that vaguely sounded like "Mama," but it was wishful thinking. It wouldn't be long before he was carrying on conversations and cracking jokes like his dad.

"When you get to Paris, I'll bring you something special from my trip, okay?" For a second, Zack flashed in her mind. No, she wouldn't be bringing Phoenix a father, but maybe, somehow, they'd forge a bond. Even if Zack sent birthday cards and called occasionally, it would add something special to Phoenix's life.

"Mandy, we have to go. I have a Women's Club dinner to prepare for, and the ladies will *flip* when they see Phoenix. We'll talk again tomorrow. Say goodbye to him."

"Okay." The first tears fell at having to say another goodbye. She wiped them away as loud breathing in the receiver made her laugh. "You're trying to eat that phone, aren't you, buddy? Have fun with Grandma and her friends. I love you so much." She made a kissing sound before the line went dead.

She set the phone back in its cradle, and as a fierce wave of emotion hit, she crumpled to the floor. All the joy from her trip so far evaporated, and she just wanted to jump on a plane back to Denver.

A soft knock on the door startled her. She wanted to ignore it, but in case it was Shane or someone else from the crew who needed something, she had to answer.

She splashed cold water on her face, blew her nose, and opened the door.

Her stomach plummeted.

Zack stood in the hallway with a blue shopping bag, his smile slipping when he saw her. In her rush, she didn't think to check the peephole.

"Shit, Mandy." He touched her cheek, his brows knitted. "Are you okay?"

"Yeah, I'm just watching a sad movie. *Beaches.* Gets me every time." She hated lying, but it was unavoidable.

His hand returned to his side as he glanced inside her room. "The TV's off." *Damn.*

She stared at the blank screen, rubbing the back of her neck. Her emotions from the call were so fresh that she couldn't think straight. "Yeah, it just ended."

"Mmhm." He wasn't buying it, and they both knew it. "A wise and ridiculously gorgeous woman once told me honesty's always better, even when it stings."

She rolled her eyes, impressed he'd remembered her words and irritated he'd tossed them back at her. "Fine. There was no movie. I'm a little homesick, I guess. Why aren't you at the afterparty?"

"Wasn't in the mood." He frowned, his feet shifting. "I came to see if you wanted to grab some food, and I brought dessert for after." He raised the bag. "It might cheer you up to get out."

"That's not a good idea." She was surprised he wasn't still banging away with his very hot, very naked new friend.

"If you saw the girl in my room..." He exhaled a loud breath. "I didn't invite her or want her there. And I gave security hell for letting her in. It'll take them a while to catch up to the fact that I don't want that anymore."

"Oh." A warm wave of relief washed over her as she uttered the only word that came to mind. And she felt like a jerk for jumping to conclusions.

"I was telling the truth about wanting something real. I'm done with empty sex."

In her emotionally fragile state, she didn't know what to do with that.

"It still seems reckless to be alone together." She wrapped an arm around herself, her gaze darting to the empty hallway. While sharing a late-night meal wouldn't technically break the fraternizing clause, it didn't seem wise to be spotted with Zack, especially on day three. *Night* three.

"Right. You're worried about Shane finding out," he said as if reading her mind. "How about we order room service in my suite?"

She bit back a laugh. "Someone seeing me go into your room would be even worse." She also didn't trust herself to be alone with him after the elevator debacle. But if they were going to build a genuine friendship, avoidance wasn't the way.

He glanced down both sides of the hallway. "Your room, then. Everyone's at the arena, so no one's around to narc on us." A corner of his mouth rose in that way that always made her want to do the opposite of whatever her inner Fun Police said.

With a resigned sigh, she stepped back, his smile growing at his victory as he walked inside.

"Nice digs," he said, taking in the space. His gaze landed on the mess she'd made of her room—clothes tossed onto the bed, toiletries scattered beside them, and the pile of candy wrappers on the nightstand. "And it's nice to see you're human now."

Mandy scoffed, shoving the toiletries into the bag, zipping it up, and tossing it and the clothes into her opened suitcase. "I'm not as neat as I used to be."

I'm not a lot of things I used to be.

"Don't sweat it. My luggage threw up all over my room, too." He sat at the dining table and grabbed the room service menu. "What sounds good?"

She appreciated how casually this was starting. It would be much easier to veer toward friendship if the sexual tension faded into the background and maybe, eventually, disappeared. With him smelling like sexy aftershave and his hair ruffled and damp from a post-show shower, it wouldn't be easy.

She scooped up the candy wrappers—which had contained at least seven hundred calories of chocolate caramel balls—and dropped them into the trashcan.

"A salad, I guess." For once, her mother's voice in her head approved of one of her choices.

Zack's nose scrunched. "You're not as neat, *and* you've turned into a rabbit?"

She swiped the menu from his hand as he laughed. The second she saw the fish and chips, her mouth watered. As a bonus, it was probably the most unsexy food on the menu, hopefully making it easier to keep the vibe platonic.

"Fine," she said. "Fish and chips. When in Rome. Well, London."

"Wise choice. I'll make it two." He grabbed the phone and relayed their order.

"And a beer," she added. It would complement the meal and sounded good after the long day. But she'd stick to one after yesterday's wine had made it too easy to get carried away.

"And two lagers, please," he said into the phone. "Thanks."

When he hung up, she took the seat across from his. He studied her for a moment. Being scrutinized after falling apart over missing their son made her squirm in the cool leather-padded chair like a suspect under interrogation.

"Is that really why you were crying?" he asked. "You're homesick?"

She shrugged. "I've never been this far from my regular life before. It's exciting but overwhelming." It was as close to the truth as she'd get. "I'll adjust. It's only a few weeks anyway."

He rubbed his chin, his calloused fingertips moving back and forth over the five o'clock shadow that looked ridiculously sexy no matter what time it was. She remembered he did that when deep in thought.

Hoping to avoid a heavy discussion about whatever was brewing in his head, she changed the subject. "The guys didn't give you crap for leaving early?"

"Nah. Ty was about to head back here to crash with Charlotte and their kid, and Adam's having international phone sex with Kyla."

Hearing her name made Mandy even more uncomfortable. She didn't want to think about James Sutter or the awful things he'd said. And despite Zack's denial on the plane, she still couldn't shake the suspicion that the phone call had somehow played a part in why she was sitting in a London suite with him.

"Tyler and Adam... Are they happy?" she asked.

A broad smile stretched his face. "Yeah, they're really fucking happy. The bastards." He laughed before the joy in his expression vanished. "It's impossible not to envy what they have."

"Really?" She sat straighter, wondering if he meant he envied the romantic connections of the couples or the family life Tyler and Charlotte had built. She wanted it so badly to be the latter. If he'd warmed up to children from being around Tyler's daughter, her confession would be so much easier.

"Sure. Not the kid shit, of course. Ty's baby's part of the family now, so I'm trying to like it. But the constant crying and annoying interruptions when we're trying to work are already getting old. And it sucks watching my used-to-be-fun friend walk around like a fucking zombie. I don't know why anyone would throw a garbage bomb like that into their life."

Her heart sunk like a leaden weight in her chest.

"Oh." Mandy fought to keep her expression neutral as his words looped in her head.

Garbage bomb?!

He called the baby "it."

"What I meant was—"

A knock at the door cut him off. It was a welcome interruption, giving her a chance to regain her composure.

How was she supposed to tell someone who despised "kid shit" that he was a father?

Maybe this whole "establish a friendship first" idea was all wrong. Maybe it was kinder never to tell him at all.

She opened the door for room service, and the attendant wheeled in a silver cart that smelled like the ocean and salty French fries. Zack slipped the guy a tip and lifted the silver domes off their plates as the door closed.

The fear of his reaction to finding out about Phoenix wasn't the only reason she felt seconds away from falling apart. Even though she'd known since before the trip that being with Zack was impossible, the part of her that refused to let him go held on to hope that, someday, somehow, they'd find a way.

Newspaper lined their plates, napkins and utensils tucked between bottles of ketchup and malt vinegar. Everything looked delicious, but her stomach tied in knots as the tiny bubble of hope she'd held onto burst.

There would never be a second chance for them.

It was over.

Zack dug into his food, chasing a few bites with a swig of lager. "Aren't you hungry?"

She poured a blob of ketchup on her plate. "Yeah, this looks great."

Their lives were fundamentally incompatible now, and there was no changing it. Tears stung the corners of her eyes as she poked at her food, but she quickly blinked them back.

He set down his fork. "Why do I feel like you're lying again?"

Needing a moment to collect her thoughts, she cut a piece of fish, doused it in malt vinegar, and chewed. The probably delicious food was like ashes on her tongue.

He still hates kids.

Would he think of Phoenix as a garbage bomb that she'd dropped into his life?

Despite that possibility, she came on this trip with a goal. It would be easier to keep Phoenix a secret, but that was the coward's way out.

She'd been a coward long enough.

In five days, she'd introduce him to a whole new reality. And she'd be saying goodbye to all the incredible things he made her feel.

She took a long, cool sip of beer to steady herself before again opting for a subject change.

"Do you promise you didn't set this job up for me?" She was deflecting, but it was a legitimate question. One that would conveniently mask the actual reasons she was too upset to eat.

He brought the mouth of his bottle to his lips and took a long pull before meeting her gaze. "Why don't you think you're worthy of this opportunity?"

"Promise me, Zack. Promise me, and I'll drop it for the rest of the tour."

He set his bottle on the table, giving her his full attention. "I promise you got this job because you're incredible at what you do. It's a shame you had to leave the club, but this can be the bridge between that and your dream job. I'm happy for you."

At least she could put that worry to rest. She nodded, dragging a French fry through the puddle of ketchup on her plate. "Thanks. I'm happy for me, too. The club isn't what it was after Ted sold it, so it was time for a change anyway."

His warm palm covered the back of her hand. "Your new boss there..." Her chin lifted, and she looked into his eyes. Something dark and dangerous brewed in their depths, making her shiver. "He didn't hurt you, did he?"

Mandy shook her head, and his tense shoulders loosened. "It was mostly words, but I'm fine."

"Mostly?" His shoulders stiffened again, his white-knuckled fist clenched on the table.

"I appreciate your concern, but I can fight my own battles. He touched my face once and grabbed my arm. I didn't get groped or whatever else you're worried about."

"He grabbed your fucking *arm*?!" he gritted out, a muscle popping in his clamped jaw.

He was acting like a Neanderthal, but damn if it didn't turn her on. Imagining him breaking that asshole's face made her skin flush with heat.

It bothered her that, besides the long scratch on his car from her key, James Jerkwad Sutter got away with treating her like he did. There was no doubt in her mind he'd behave that way with the female staff at all the places he owned, but what could she do?

"I'm fine." She touched his cheek, hoping to reassure him. "I promise. If it makes you feel better, I keyed his car."

His jaw relaxed beneath her fingertips as he smiled. "That's my girl."

She let the comment slide and smiled back, grateful he'd let it go.

Then, the pain of having to let *him* go returned, her chest tight and the backs of her eyelids stinging. She wouldn't be his girl for long. His feelings about Tyler's kid made a meeting unlikely, but she'd still let him know about Phoenix. She'd tell him, he'd be furious, and that would be that.

She dreaded the loss of his sweet protectiveness, hungry looks, and passionate kisses. And how he looked at her like no one else existed. Even with no makeup and lotion all over her face, it seemed like he only saw the very best version of her.

But he was here now, and she'd revel in these last days of connection before everything changed.

When they finished their food, he set their empty dishes on the tray and rolled it into the hallway. He grabbed his shopping bag before returning to his seat.

Zack waggled his eyebrows. "You hungry for some Spotted Dick?"

"Excuse me?" she sputtered, her eyes snapping wide.

His lips curled in a cheeky grin as he pulled out a takeout container and set it in front of her. "I've been dying to say that since I bought it."

"Of course you have. I was worried you'd contracted a very unfortunate STD." One thing she hoped never changed about him was his sense of humor. Even when his jokes were immature and crass, he somehow made them charming. "That's really what it's called?" She opened the container to find a cake-like mound with dark spots and a pale yellow drizzle.

He held his hand over his heart. "I swear on the queen."

She dug a fork into the dessert. "It smells like lemon and vanilla."

"So do you, sweetheart." He pinched off a piece and popped it into his mouth. "You are what you eat."

She chuckled. "I was almost flattered until you implied that I'm a spotted dick." She took a bite. It had an unusual flavor and texture, but it was delicious. "This is great. Thank you."

"You should do your first time in Europe right, trying what every country's famous for. I got you chocolates too. They're shaped like Big Ben."

Again, his thoughtfulness touched her. So did his knee under the table as it rested against hers. When he didn't move it, she looked at him, not moving away either.

He grabbed a fork, poking at the cake before setting his fork down with a clatter. "I don't know how to do this."

"How to do what?"

"Pretend I don't want to kiss you and pick up where we left off in the elevator. I don't just mean sex. I mean holding you and feeling connected to you again. Feeling like this thing between us isn't all in my head. Tell me I'm not alone."

Mandy frowned, wanting the same impossible things but knowing damn well it didn't matter. She had to do what was best for Phoenix while trying not to hurt Zack. She struggled to keep her true feelings locked up tight while, as usual, he let his roam free without concern for consequences.

"Like I said before, we can't." She pushed the food aside. "This was nice, but we should call it a night."

He chewed his bottom lip as he watched her. "Sure. Big day tomorrow and all that."

"Exactly."

He crossed his arms over his broad chest, not budging from his seat. "Why did you leave the show when we played that song? It was for you."

"I know." She pulled in a slow inhale and let it out. "Cassie needed help. And then I needed to catch my breath, I guess. I appreciate the sweet gesture, but I can't be who you want me to be."

"I want you to be yourself."

She nodded slowly. "I know. But what if the people we are now aren't compatible?"

His responding grimace made it clear he wouldn't accept that. When she shared her secret, he wouldn't have a choice. "Are you in love with someone else?"

"No."

"And you still have feelings for me."

He framed it like a statement, not a question, and she nodded in response.

"Then nothing else matters." He reached across the table to take her hand. "Can we set aside whatever's holding you back until the tour's over and pretend it doesn't exist? I've missed you all this time and know you missed me, too. We're finally in the same place, and I'm supposed to just accept we can't be together because there's some mysterious wall between us?"

"Zack..."

"I want to see you every second I can and fall asleep holding you. When we return to our lives, I don't want us to regret our wasted time. Whatever's in the way, I can handle it. Even if I end up hurt, at least I won't have regrets."

If only that were true.

His words brought fresh tears to her eyes as the knots tightened in her stomach. Inside, she battled the intense urge to leap into his lap and pretend their obstacles didn't exist. To live in a fantasy world where she woke up feeling safe and loved in his arms without fretting over consequences.

Instead, she had to accept that friendship was all they could have. And that she'd likely lose that after telling him about Phoenix.

"I'm sorry. I can't." She released his hand, walking around him to get to the door. She made sure the hallway was empty before holding the door open. "Thanks for dinner. And the Spotted Dick."

"Sure."

He left his chair, approaching her with slow steps. When he didn't make another joke, she knew he was even more hurt than he was letting on. She held her breath as he leaned in and softly kissed her cheek. It took every ounce of her restraint not to grab him with both hands and never let go.

"Sweet dreams, beautiful."

When the door clicked shut behind him, the room fell into a cold, empty silence.

She missed him already.

Mandy was sick to death of saying no to what she wanted. She'd been doing it her whole life for one reason or another. Her determination to change that on her thirtieth birthday was cast aside after finding out she was pregnant, but maybe she used that as a convenient excuse to stay in the safe zone.

Saying yes came with the risk of pain and disappointment, but even fleeting moments of bliss that became beautiful memories would be worth that risk.

She caught a whisper of his scent in the air and glanced at the dessert and chocolates he'd brought. Since sitting beside her on the plane, Zack's sweet gestures had made her feel special and treasured. And they reminded her that her needs mattered, too.

This might be their last chance to experience their rare, beautiful connection. And her last chance to love him and feel his love in return. Being together was impossible, but could she set their obstacles aside so they'd have a proper goodbye?

He was right—if they missed out on the time they could spend together, they'd regret it. Even if a temporary fling was all they'd have, at least they'd have new memories to hold on to when they returned to their lives after the tour. It might give them both the closure they need to move on.

If it was goodbye, at least it would be a goodbye without regrets.

As he'd said before walking out, she didn't know how to do this either—to pretend she didn't want to kiss him until the world and her endless, stifling worries disappeared. She didn't know how to pretend she didn't want him or crave their connection.

A faint smile touched her lips as the last threads of her resolve snapped.

Mandy opened her suitcase, grabbing the blouse and skirt on top. She changed quickly and slipped on her shoes.

Maybe it was time to stop pretending.

23

Zack

Zack shuffled into his suite and flopped onto his bed, fully clothed. As all the air left his lungs in a long sigh, someone knocked at his door.

"Fucking hell."

He pictured Adam standing there with a six-pack, probably bored, lonely, and pumped with post-show adrenaline. The sting of another rejection left Zack exhausted, depressed, and ready to crash, so he ignored it.

When another, louder knock came, he slid off the bed and shuffled toward the door. "Fine, asshole. I'm coming."

When he opened it, Mandy stood in the hallway with a shaky smile.

"Hey." His brows knitted as he held the door, wondering what she wanted. "Sorry about the asshole thing. I thought it was Adam."

Without a word, she closed the distance between them, her fists curling into the front of his T-shirt. His breath hitched as she tugged him closer and crushed her lips to his. A groan rumbled in his throat as her soft lips parted and her tongue pushed inside his mouth.

It was too good to be true. If he'd had more than one beer, he'd swear he was hallucinating.

"Tell me you want this as much as I do," he whispered against her lips.

She kicked the door shut behind her, the automatic lock clicking into place. "I do. I want this. I just think—"

He touched a fingertip to her lips. "Judging by the way you just kissed me, you didn't come to my room to think." He grabbed her ass in both hands, lifting her, and she wrapped her legs around his waist. "So stop fucking thinking."

Before she could talk herself out of this again, he cupped the back of her neck and pulled her mouth to his. She surrendered to the kiss with a low, desperate moan that shot straight to his stiffening cock.

With Mandy's thighs squeezing his hips, there was no more wondering—she wanted him. There was no space in his head to worry about consequences. Even if lust were all she felt and she woke up in the morning regretting him, he'd make damn sure the night was one she'd never forget.

He wanted to haunt her dreams, to be the face popping up in her fantasies whenever those slender fingers slipped beneath her panties to rub one out. It was only fair because her face was the only one he saw when his eyes were closed.

She might break his heart tomorrow, but having her in his arms now, her body calling to his with the primal need for connection, made any pain that came after completely fucking worth it.

He flipped on the lights as they entered the kitchen, and she abruptly broke the kiss.

"Turn them off."

"I want to see you." It'd been so long, and he wanted to drink her in, every inch of bare skin.

She shook her head, a flash of panic in her expression. "No. Please."

Zack searched her face, trying like hell to figure out the struggle behind her eyes. Before he could get answers, she broke his concentration with another kiss, her soft tongue sweeping inside his mouth.

With their lips fused, he felt around for the switch and flipped the lights back off. He walked them to the kitchen counter, setting her ass on the cool gray marble. He reached underneath her skirt, hooked his fingers on the sides of her panties, and slid them down her legs. Her hands splayed behind her, her eyes hazy and lust-drunk as she watched him.

Desire looked beautiful on her.

He parted her knees and moved between them, pressing the aching hardness in his jeans against the heat of her core to watch her squirm. "I want to taste you so badly, my fucking mouth is watering." He licked her tongue and pushed her skirt up her thighs, the fabric gathering above the tiny patch of dark hair between her legs.

When he pressed the pad of his index finger to her clit, she hissed through her teeth. With a slow, teasing slide, he traced the slippery inner lips of her pussy. His cock throbbed, begging to be inside her. Hopefully, they'd get there, but he wasn't about to get carried away and scare her off again like in the elevator. Instead, he'd take his time, savoring every second.

When he brought the finger to his mouth and sucked it clean, she groaned.

Her hand fisted in the front of his shirt. "Why do you have to be so damn irresistible?"

A slow grin curved his lips, pleased to hear that. "So I can take that safe little shell you built around yourself..." He leaned in, kissing and sucking the skin above her pulse point. "And smash it to fucking pieces."

He dipped his head between her legs, licking a trail up her center before taking her clit between his lips and gently sucking it into his mouth. As he devoured her, his guttural groans of agony and bliss were buried in her wet flesh.

She was drenched for him. Her fingernails dug into his scalp as he lapped at the slick, sweet arousal between her legs. With two fingers, he circled her entrance, but she grabbed his wrist.

"No," she said quickly. "Not inside, okay? Just your mouth."

His eyebrows pulled together as, again, he struggled to figure her out. "Did I hurt you?"

"No, just... please."

The only light was the glow from the city outside the windows. He thought he saw tears glistening in her eyes, but it was too dim to be sure.

"Everything okay?" Then, a possibility entered his mind that made lava flood his veins. "Did someone else hurt you?"

Did her old boss do something after all? Or an ex? If *anyone* touched her without permission, he'd fucking kill them. Tear their limbs from their body with his bare hands and burn the pieces.

"No." Her voice was strained with what sounded like impatience. "No one hurt me. I've missed your tongue so fucking much."

He calmed, satisfied, and relieved it was the truth. The raw need in her gaze made it impossible to argue, so he buried his face between her legs and feasted. He sucked her slick lips into his mouth, grazing the sensitive flesh with his teeth as her panted breaths and sexy little whimpers spurred him on. He sealed his entire mouth over her pussy and thrust his tongue as deep as it would go, pinning her thighs to the marble as she squirmed.

Mandy bucked her hips, begging for more. She needed to come, and he *needed* to make her.

"God, I love it when you fuck my mouth." He pressed a gentle kiss to her inner thigh. "Your body's so good at telling me what you want."

She shouted a curse as her trembling hands fisted in his hair.

He returned his attention to her clit, their eyes locking as her control slipped, and she gave in to the pleasure. He wanted to fuck her with his fingers and work her G-spot, remembering how much she loved it, but he wouldn't cross the line she'd drawn. She didn't owe him an explanation, but he hoped to get one anyway to understand.

"Oh, fuck, Zack," she groaned, his name on her lips making him ravenous.

He gripped the flesh of her hips and French-kissed her aching pussy until she was screaming and clawing at his scalp.

"That's it, baby," he cooed against her sensitive flesh. "Let go. I've got you."

After a few more swipes of his tongue on her clit, she broke in his arms. Her hips bucked against his insatiable mouth, and her thighs squeezed the sides of his face. Her muscles flexed and twitched against him as he drank his fill.

No, fuck that. He'd *never* be full of her. He already wanted more.

She cried out, her palms slapping the cold marble beneath her. Gradually, her muscles relaxed. Her body melted in his hold as her peak receded. With a heavy, satisfied sigh, she lay back on the counter, her legs dangling over his shoulders.

"Holy shit." Her hand slapped over her eyes. "I can't even see straight."

He chuckled with satisfaction as he kissed a trail along her inner thighs, the damp heat of her pussy searing his skin. "Then keep those pretty eyes closed and just feel."

24

Mandy

Mandy's eyes followed Zack's mouth as his lips returned to the apex of her thighs. His tongue darted out for one last glide over her clit, the tiny bead over-sensitive from her climax. She shivered at the sensation.

"Wow." Her chest rose and fell with panted breaths. "That was... I can't think either."

He raised his chin, his fingertips stroking her inner thigh. "Good. That brain's been doing cartwheels for fucking days. It can use the break."

A held-back smile made her lips twitch. He wasn't wrong.

"Mandy..." He stood to his full, impressive height, a pensive line notched between his brows. "Why don't you want my fingers inside you?"

Anxiety churned in the pit of her stomach, her mouth going dry. "Can we not talk about this?" She sat up, drawing her knees together. "You're killing my afterglow."

She'd never have to explain with no chance for a future together. She could continue hiding the changes to her body and never have to see the disappointment on his face. She reached for him, but he stepped back.

The crease between his brows sunk further as he scrutinized her expression. "Okay. Why can't I look at you with the lights on? You never hid from me before."

Heat flared in her cheeks. The dim light was a blessing, masking the evidence of her shame. "I've... gained some weight since then. My body's changed since you saw it last."

"Is that all?" Zack huffed a loud breath, his tight features relaxing. She wished that was the only reason she wanted to hide. "Baby, I thought you got hurt and had a scar or something. Do you think I give a shit about a few more curves? You're beautiful."

She hugged herself as tears pricked the backs of her eyelids. She knew he meant it, but his opinion would change if he saw the parts of herself that she was desperate to keep locked away.

How did she ever think she could do this?

The bliss of shutting off her mind and focusing on how he made her feel had fizzled out, drowned by the insecurities she couldn't shake.

This was a mistake. She was too different now to be the bold, fearless woman he hoped to draw out again. Even for one night, it was impossible. Instead, he was stuck with a fragile, disappointing mess.

Now, she wanted to run.

She touched his chest, pushing him back a few steps as she slid off the counter. "I'm sorry, but I have to go." She blinked back the tears threatening to spill, not wanting him to see her cry.

"Mandy."

She picked her underwear off the floor and slid it back on. As her eyelids stung, the shame morphed into anger. The urge to lash out made ugly, hurtful words burn in her throat.

"Mandy." His tone was sharp as the light switch clicked, illuminating the room and the grim set of his jaw. "Stop shutting me out and talk to me."

"How can you possibly think I'm beautiful?" she snapped. "I've seen photos of the women decorating your arm at awards shows. I see the skinny young girls outside screaming for your attention. And offering themselves up in your dressing room." Then, she thought of what was sure to get him to drop his questions. "And I saw the bitch draped all over your lap our last day together."

Zack's eyes darted around, searching his brain for a memory or an excuse. He was pretty drunk that night, so either made sense. "What the hell are you talking about?"

"I saw you! The blonde with huge fake tits who'd been pawing you every chance she got, trying to drag you away. I came back from the bar, and she was in your damn lap. Her lips were on your neck, whispering in your ear. I ran to the bathroom and threw up, I was so upset. You told me you wouldn't even *look* at anyone else, and I was so disappointed in you. And mad at myself for getting wrapped up in the fantasy that I could ever be enough for someone like you."

"No." The corners of his mouth drooped. "That's not what happened."

She scoffed, even more pissed at his denial. His *lie*. "Even now, you can't tell me the truth?"

"I am. Yeah, she got in my lap and tried to get me to leave with her, but I told her to fuck off. Ask Tyler. He was sitting across from me."

She rolled her eyes, unconvinced. "Like he wouldn't back up your lie."

"Not Ty. He's like my brother, but he's not a liar. He'd say it wasn't his business or some shit to brush it off."

Zack's frown deepened as he shook his head, looking wounded by her accusation. Was it possible she'd been mistaken?

"I swear on my life," he said. "It happened, but it wasn't like I could get rough with her and shove her off. Once she got the hint, she left, and I went looking for you."

Could that be true? Did she assume the worst and punish him over a stupid misunderstanding?

Tears spilled down her cheeks, the memory painfully fresh of him knocking on the bathroom door while she cried, crushed that it was over. And knowing that she'd never be able to trust someone surrounded by temptation because she wasn't enough to hold his attention for longer than a few days. She was sure he'd already grown bored with her and found someone prettier and easier in every way. She'd done the same thing a few hours ago with the woman in his dressing room.

"Once I met you, I didn't want anyone else." He sank to his knees at her feet, wrapping his arms around her middle. "I know I'm a fuck-up. I know I'm hard to care about and even harder to trust. But please believe me, I'd never hurt you."

He was telling the truth. She saw it in his eyes. Why did she so easily believe he was that heartless? She just ran like a coward without giving him the chance to defend himself.

After peeling herself off the bathroom floor that night, she washed her face and slapped on a brave mask. She told him she wasn't feeling well and needed an earlier flight home. She thought the final glimpse she'd have of Zack was through the back window of that cab as her heart broke into pieces. But here he was, baring his soul and desperate to hold on to her.

Would anyone ever love her as fiercely as the man literally on his knees for her?

His fingertips slipped underneath her shirt, and she jumped back, breaking loose from his hold. She couldn't bear to see the disappointment and disgust on his face if he touched her saggy belly or saw the silvery stretch marks on her hips and stomach.

Instead, hurt overtook his features at her rejection, his pain slicing through her heart. She kneeled in front of him, taking his sad, brutally handsome face in her hands.

"I believe you." She pressed her lips to his, and he groaned, leaning into her touch until she broke the kiss. "And I'm sorry I ran without letting you explain. You're not a fuck-up, and I hate that you think you're hard to care about. It's never been hard for me."

It would be easier to stay away if it was.

"If you thought I cheated," he said, "why did you start taking my calls?"

After eight days of trying to let him go, she realized it was futile and picked up.

"Despite my hurt, I cherished our connection. Your voice in those messages made me realize how much I missed you and how attached I'd become. If all we could have was a long-distance friendship, it was better than nothing. In the end, it just wasn't enough."

It would be a relief when she could stop telling half-truths. She couldn't tell him about Phoenix the night before a show when he was already hurting. But giving in to the pull between them before retreating had to stop. It was cruel and unfair to both of them.

The truth couldn't wait five more days.

She would tell him tomorrow.

"All this time," he whispered.

"All this time, what?"

He sat on the floor with his knees raised, forming his own wall between them. "We could've been talking every night. I could've flown to see you every chance I got, flown you to see me. It could've worked, Mandy. I thought miles were the only reason you didn't want me."

She shook her head. She never stopped wanting him. That wasn't the problem. And the distance, his drinking, and the handsy groupie weren't the only reasons she cut him out of her life.

With their bodies apart, her head cleared. When Zack found out her life now came with a child, he wouldn't want her. It was cruel to give him false hope when he didn't have the full picture, so it was better to end this now.

"We have to stop," she said. "We got carried away, and I don't want to hurt you worse than I already have."

She pushed off the floor, another wave of tears threatening to spill as he sat there, broken. She'd broken him. Again. And there'd be more pain to contend with once she told him about their son.

She bent at the waist and pressed a soft kiss to his forehead. "I'm so sorry."

His hands raked through his hair. "Stop fucking saying that." His chin lifted, and he hugged her knees, knocking her off balance so she fell into his lap, straddling him. Their faces were nearly touching, forcing her to witness every bit of the pain in his red-rimmed eyes. "How do I fix this? Tell me how to fix it, and I'll do it. *Anything.*"

"Too much has changed." Her body, her responsibilities, her life. As much as she wanted to cling to this intense, beautiful thing between them, they no longer fit into each other's lives. Maybe they never did, and it'd all been a silly, impossible fantasy. "Like I said during our last call, you need to find someone who can give you everything I can't."

He pulled her face to his and kissed her until all the reasons this was reckless and stupid vanished like a cloud of smoke. With tears dotting his lashes, he broke the kiss.

"I love you, Mandy. I never stopped loving you." His chest jumped beneath her with a choked sob. "I can't. Please don't fucking ask me to let you go again."

His lips captured hers. He tasted like salt, their tears mingling.

I love you too. The words burned in her throat, fighting to meet the air, but it would only mean more torture for both of them.

His fingers slipped beneath her shirt and up her ribcage, and again, she grabbed his wrist to stop him.

"Why won't you let me touch you, baby?" His lips found her throat, the gentleness of his kisses making her want to relent. She craved his touch but couldn't shake the image of what his face would look like when he saw the parts of her that made her feel ugly.

She pushed his shoulders to the ground. Her fingers drifted down his chest, pausing at the waistband of his jeans before unbuttoning them.

"What are you doing?" The gravel in his voice said her distraction was working.

They were done talking.

"Close your eyes," she whispered.

His brows pinched together before he obeyed.

She unzipped his jeans and slid them down his legs with his black cotton boxers. His impressive cock sprung free, hard as steel and begging for her mouth. She swirled her tongue around the head in a slow circle, and his body went rigid.

"Looks like you're wet for me too." She licked the bead of moisture on the slit, the salt of him exploding on her tongue. "If you could touch between my legs, you'd feel how wet I am, and it's all your fucking fault."

He groaned deep in his chest, his fists slamming against the hardwood beneath him. "Show me. I want inside you so badly, I could fucking die."

Usually, her mother's words killed these moments, but this time, it was the voice of James fucking Sutter. *You're on the wrong side of thirty, probably have stretch marks all over the body that I bet was hot and tight before you shit out that kid.*

If Zack's fingers or cock slipped inside her, he would discover she wasn't tight or hot in the ways that mattered. And he'd regret everything that'd happened since getting on that plane.

But tonight, they both needed this. So, she'd be with him in every way she could.

Mandy slipped her fingers between her legs, gathering her wetness and touching her fingertips to his lips. She pushed inside his mouth, his tongue circling her fingers, collecting every last drop. He sucked them clean, and then, she couldn't wait another second to suck him.

She shifted back between his legs, her head dipping to lick his shaft from base to tip with the flat of her tongue. "It's your turn to stop thinking and just feel." Her fingers curled around his heated flesh as she kissed and suckled the head of his cock.

Her lips slipped down his length, and she hollowed her cheeks as she withdrew, sucking him hard. His breaths grew heavy as their gazes fused. He watched her teasing the head again with her tongue before taking him deep into her throat.

"Fucking hell, I love watching you swallow my cock." His fingers stroked her cheek, and she bobbed on the tip as it swelled in her mouth. "Turn around so you can fuck my face while you suck me."

The image made her bite back a moan, but she shook her head. "I want to focus on you, and your talented tongue would make that impossible."

A wicked grin curled his lips. "Talented, huh?"

"And you fucking know it, you cocky prick."

His chest jumped as they laughed. She knew he liked it when she cursed and when she teased him back. He *really* liked it when she did both.

She wrapped her fist around his length and stroked, making him gasp. His eyes went dark, and she bent forward, kissing the crown before pushing it past her lips. With her hand and mouth working together, she tugged him closer and closer to the edge. Soon, the muscles in his hips twitched, and his back arched off the floor. She took him as deep as he'd go and cupped his balls in her free hand, kneading the silky flesh.

"Fuck, fuck, *fuck*!" His fists pounded the floor again. "If you don't want to swallow, pull off now."

That he was already close to exploding further proved he'd abstained for a while. The man could go for hours. She shook her head, sucking him while her hand jerked in quickening pulses below the head. Her body remembered what he liked without having to think.

Before Zack, she never understood the hype about giving blowjobs. But the power coursing through her as he lost control from the pleasure she gave was heady and intoxicating.

With a roaring groan, hot, spurting ropes of his release hit her throat. His flavor coated her tongue before she swallowed hard. His fingers tangled in her hair, his hips jerking as the final salty drops pooled on her tongue. She swallowed again, savoring his taste.

Was it cruel to give him pleasure, knowing afterward, she could only offer pain? Of course, it was. But their bodies communicated on a level she didn't fully understand—like they demanded to connect, to merge, and she was no longer behind the controls. If anyone had said that to her, she'd think it was a flimsy excuse to rationalize terrible choices, but it was true.

"Take a shower with me." He took her hand, lacing their fingers together.

The thought of being naked beside his perfect, chiseled body deflated all the bliss she'd felt seconds before.

"I have to get back to my room. I told my parents I'd call before I went to bed."

Thinking about her parents made the unsettling tingle of anxiety creep back in. Her mom and Phoenix were flying to Paris in ten days.

"Why won't you let me in?" Sadness tainted Zack's usually upbeat tone, and she couldn't handle another emotionally draining discussion. "Why do you react like I burn you every time I touch you?"

She untangled their fingers and stood. "Find me tomorrow."

Enough delaying the inevitable and skirting around the truth. He deserved to know why she kept hiding her body and wouldn't let him in so he'd stop blaming himself. Once he knew about Phoenix, she'd fill in the remaining gaps and answer all the questions she kept dodging.

He sat up. "Tell me now. Whatever it is, it doesn't matter."

She huffed a humorless laugh. "After your show, after my work is done, find me. I'll tell you everything, I promise."

He stared, his eyes searching her face like they'd done countless times since he sat beside her on the plane. Sometimes, he saw right through her. Now, his frustration was evident as his lips pressed into a grim line, his expression tight, because her secrets were buried too deeply for him to see.

"Stay with me," he said. "If whatever you have to say might change things between us, give us one more night where things are like this."

"Zack..." This was a dangerous game. She'd already let things go too far.

"Let me hold you while you fall asleep and wake up to you in my bed. If you want me to beg, I will."

It would only make their inevitable goodbye even harder, but if this were what he wanted, she'd give it to him. She wanted it, too, more than she should. Loving him this much was foolish and dangerous, but her stupid heart didn't seem to care.

Without another word, Mandy walked into his bedroom. She was done with words, done with tears. But she wasn't done with him.

She took off her skirt and folded it, setting it on his dresser. "Do you have a T-shirt I can wear?"

"If I say no, will you sleep without one?" His sad eyes muted his cheeky, half-hearted grin. Like he already knew her answer but had to ask in case she was willing to be skin-to-skin.

She shook her head, and he gave a resigned nod. He rifled through his luggage and grabbed a folded black T-shirt from the top.

"Do you have one you've already worn?" She wanted one more night enveloped in his scent and warmth in every way.

Even in the scant light, she saw his eyes darken. He grabbed a shirt off the back of a chair and gave it to her. She went into the bathroom and locked the door. Once she undid the buttons on her blouse, she slid it off.

She stared at her feet for a few breaths before looking into the mirror.

All she saw were flaws. It was like waging a war with her mind whenever she looked at herself naked. She was in love with the life she'd brought into the world but repulsed by the damage done to her body.

How could she ever feel the gaze or touch of someone again without wanting to cover up and hide?

She grabbed Zack's T-shirt, bringing it to her nose and taking a deep, torturous hit into her lungs of smoke, leather, and the man she loved. After slipping it over her head, his essence surrounded her, clinging to her skin. She brushed her teeth with his spare toothbrush, washed her face, and returned to his bedroom.

He pulled back the sheets, and she climbed into his bed, settling under the covers. He used the bathroom and returned, smelling of mint and soap. He joined her in the bed and hooked an arm around her waist, dragging her against his warm chest with her back to his front. It was how they'd slept their first night together—another sweet, dizzying hit of déjà vu.

His lips caressed the shell of her ear. "Remember how I said I saw you in the airport before our flight?"

She nodded.

"You had tears in your eyes, baby. You looked so fucking sad, I wanted to shove my way through the crowds and hold you." He gently brushed the hair off her cheek. "Does the thing you have to tell me have anything to do with why you were crying?"

She sniffed, her eyes stinging and her throat going tight. Unable to speak, she nodded again.

He pressed a kiss to the side of her neck that lingered, accelerating her pulse and making her heart swell almost to bursting. "There's nothing you can say that would make me stop loving you." He kissed the spot again, his arms locking around her like a cage she never wanted to leave.

In his arms, she felt beautiful, treasured, and safe in a way she never had before they met. She was certain he was her only chance at feeling deeply, truly loved, and it was such a loud and cruel *fuck you* from the universe that it was temporary.

Tomorrow, she'd give it all up so that he'd know that a part of him was living, breathing, and tossing tiny socks on the other side of the world.

"*Nothing*," he said again, leaving no room to argue.

The finality in his tone didn't offer comfort since he didn't know what secret she held.

When he did, this would all be over.

Mandy listened as his breathing slowed, and he drifted off to sleep. Her mind replayed every second they'd shared since they collided as she carried an armload of CDs in Rollin' Rockies. Looking back, it was a fitting introduction. She tried to do too much at once, being the perfect worker bee while everyone around her danced and laughed. Zack Maine strolled along with his head high and not a care in the world, literally crashing his way into her life.

Bit by bit, he'd burrowed beneath her skin and taken up permanent residence in her heart. She'd never evict him, but tomorrow, she had to prepare for him to rip himself free and never look back. As she fell asleep, five words echoed in her mind.

You're going to regret me.

25

Zack

The mystery of what Mandy had to tell him had haunted Zack all day. During the interviews with local press, his thoughts wandered, and he mostly gave one-word answers to questions tossed his way. The photographer for the band's shoot outside the arena kept reminding him not to scowl or stare into space.

The afternoon soundcheck went by in a blur, and now, as he dressed for the show that began in twenty minutes, he'd put on two different shoes. He toed off the black-and-red sneaker on his right and kicked it across the room before putting on the black boot to match the left.

He couldn't take that stage without knowing what was wrong.

He yanked the door open, grabbed the nearest roadie, and slipped him fifty bucks to hunt Mandy down and bring her to his dressing room. Obviously, he still hadn't cracked the code for learning patience.

Soon, there was a soft knock at the door, and every muscle in his body clenched with nerves. He didn't want stressful shit in his head while he played, but this was worse. Not knowing was eating him up inside.

"Come in," he called out. It was time to end the maddening mystery, and he wasn't taking no for an answer.

Mandy inched inside with cautious, shuffling steps, her face pale and fingers trembling.

What the fuck is going on?

"I have to get back to work," she said, her voice as unsteady as her hands.

Fury Fuel and their crew were back at the hotel for an interview, so he knew it was bullshit.

"Close the door and lock it."

"Zack, please." She must've seen it on his face—he needed this to end now. "Don't."

"Close the fucking door, Mandy." There was no heat behind his words, only an exhausted plea.

She sighed and closed the door behind her, clicking the lock. "You have to be on stage in a few minutes. We'll talk as soon as the show's over, I promise."

She looked gorgeous, as always, in a black silk button-up shirt and gray slacks. A tiny silver heart charm hung from a thin chain around her neck, dipping beneath the collar of her shirt. He wanted to memorize every detail in case whatever she revealed was as bad as she made it seem.

If he was about to lose her, he wanted one more moment of soaking her in.

She dabbed a corner of her eye. "I can't do this now."

"No. *I* can't do this. The waiting's making me fucking crazy. There's no way I'll be able to focus out there with this question hanging over my head. Put me out of my goddamn misery and tell me so we can put whatever it is behind us."

She dragged a hand over her face, all the air evacuating her lungs in a loud rush.

Then, something a few inches lower snagged his attention, and his gaze dropped to her chest. Two dark circles of moisture appeared, slowly expanding over her breasts.

"Oh, shit." He pointed to her blouse, confusion replacing the anxiety over her secret. "Mandy..."

She looked down and sucked in a gasp, covering herself with one arm. "Oh, my god."

"Are you okay?" he asked, struggling to make sense of this.

"I'm fine. I'm just..." Her eyes darted around the room, searching for something.

On reflex, he grabbed a clean Tomorrow Mourning T-shirt from the back of the couch and handed it to her. "What the fuck is going on with you?"

His brain caught on a memory. The same thing happened to Charlotte when her baby cried. But that didn't apply here. Was there another reason this happened to women he was clueless about? He should've paid attention in health class.

All the remaining color drained from her face as she unbuttoned the top of her shirt, averting her eyes. "Please turn around."

He did, although he was dying to see more of her skin. "I've seen you naked before."

She scoffed as if what he said was ridiculous, but he didn't ask why. He was too busy trying to figure out what had happened. He heard her pull several tissues from the box on the coffee table, probably to wipe away whatever the hell had made a mess of her shirt.

"Okay," she said, "you can turn around."

She wore his T-shirt, her folded blouse in the crook of her arm. Her face said she knew damn well he wasn't leaving without an explanation, so he stayed quiet and waited.

"Zack… I have to tell you something."

"Yeah." He barked a humorless laugh. "No shit." He didn't even try to hide his frustration.

Someone knocked at the door, and she jumped.

"Go time, Zack," Tyler said on the other side of the door.

"In a second."

"Now." Tyler's voice was more urgent, and when Zack glanced at the clock, he knew why. They took the stage in ten minutes.

"Fuck off!"

She flinched, making him regret his outburst. "We'll do this later. Get out there."

"Aren't you watching the show?" He frowned, frustrated with her stalling but also disappointed she wouldn't be on the side of the stage while he played.

After a second, she nodded. "If you still want me to after I tell you, I will."

Then, the realization hit him like a truck.

No.

It couldn't be that.

Please don't let it be that.

"Mandy..." Zack's heart pounded in his ears like an amplified kick drum dialed up to eleven. It can't be true. She would've said something by now. But nothing else made sense.

"Do you have a..." He swallowed past the sudden tightness in his throat like an invisible hand was strangling the shit out of him. Once the last word was out, everything would change.

He could feel it now, the full gravity of her confession.

The last word of his question almost choked him before he let it out. "Baby?"

Her eyes slid shut, shimmering with tears when they opened again. All doubt left his mind. He knew. Her nod was unnecessary; the truth was written all over her face.

Someone pounded on the door. "Zack, *now!*" This time, it was Adam.

Zack stomped over, his blood on fire. He nearly tore the door off its hinges as he yanked it open. "Give us a goddamn minute, or I'll rip off your fucking nuts and feed them to you!"

He slammed the door in Adam's stunned face, and she jumped.

"How old?" His strained voice was almost a whisper.

"You need to get out there."

He kept his tone as gentle as he could muster while she stared at the floor. "How old is your kid, Mandy?"

Finally, her chin lifted. "Nine months."

He did the quick math in his head before his stomach plummeted like an elevator with severed cables.

Tears trailed her cheeks, and her teeth clamped so hard on her bottom lip he worried she'd bleed. "I wasn't with anyone else." It was another thing that didn't need to be said. Every detail of her reaction left no doubt the baby was his. He'd been struggling to read her since the plane, and now, the hiding was over.

He sucked in a shuddering breath as the world he knew cracked around him. "How the fuck could you keep this from me?!"

Prickly heat simmered beneath his skin. He was furious. She'd kept this massive fucking secret for almost two years while he was oblivious! Would she have ever told him if she wasn't here, being pushed to confess?

Her deepening frown and damp eyes reflected pain he wasn't ready to soothe.

"What the fuck am I supposed to do with this?" he mumbled to himself.

"I'm so sorry." She roughly wiped the tears from her face.

He huffed a demented laugh. "*Sorry*?! Holy fuck. How could you do this to me?"

Metal rattled in the doorknob, and the door swung wide. Before Zack could react, Tyler seized his collar and yanked him into the hallway, dragging him to where Adam waited by the steps leading up to the stage.

"What the fuck is your problem?!" Tyler screamed the words in Zack's face before releasing him. It didn't faze him. Nothing did. He was numb, in shock. Tyler's voice lowered as people stared. "You going to delay a show over a god-damn lover's spat?"

"She has a baby." Zack needed a fucking drink. And about ten more to chase it with.

Tyler's eyes blew wide. "What the ever-loving fuck?"

"Holy shit." Adam leaned in. "Is it yours?"

Zack nodded, his brain pinging in a thousand different directions but settling on nothing.

"That's a mind fuck and a half," Tyler said. "I'm sorry, brother. She had no right to put this on you five goddamn minutes before we go on."

"She had no choice." Zack had demanded the truth. And her wet shirt made any more stalling impossible so that part wasn't her fault. There were plenty of other things to be angry about, but not that.

"Sorry to be selfish," Adam said, "but you can't let this fuck-up the show. All those people paid to see us, and the contract's riding on it. Get your head in the game. We'll talk later."

"It'll be okay." Tyler clapped Zack's shoulder, but the touch barely registered. He was numb all over, disconnected from everything and everyone around him. "We've got you."

The crowd's roar was distant as they approached the stage, garbled like he was underwater. It made sense because this sure as fuck felt like drowning.

The lights went out, and the stage manager gave them the cue to walk, but everything went by in a muddled haze. Fortunately, muscle memory took over as Zack waved to the crowd, kicking off the first song with a bass solo that vibrated the rafters above their heads and had the audience screaming.

He wouldn't disappoint his friends or the fans who'd made the band what they were because of his mistakes.

But that wasn't right.

Nothing with Mandy had ever felt like a mistake. Even hurt and pissed, he still craved her the same. He wanted to feel her eyes on him as he played and run into her arms after he set down his instrument. He wanted to take her back to his room to have another night, another morning with her soft lips on his skin and their bodies tangled together.

Tyler was right—this was a brutal mind fuck.

After the third song, Zack checked the sides of the stage for her but only found the usual faces of the crew and the contest winners who'd won a VIP meet-and-greet with the bands.

A kid.

A *baby*.

He didn't even know if it was a boy or a girl. What was the kid's name?

He thought back to the broken condom on their last morning together. They were in a hotel room in Phoenix, and when he pulled out after finishing, the outside of the condom was slippery and coated in thick white streaks. He knew immediately what'd happened. Surprisingly, it was the first condom that'd broken in all his years of fucking like a maniac. He was just tested, so they were safe in that regard. And Mandy said her period started in a few days, so getting pregnant was basically impossible. Something about her eggs being on their way out or some shit.

Obviously, science had other plans. And a seriously fucked-up sense of humor.

Layered with the shock was anger. Did she ever plan on telling him he was a fucking father? She'd been in Denver all this time, a single mom, struggling to pay bills when he could've been helping her out. He didn't have what it took to be an actual parent, but he had money—lots of it. He could've bought her a house and ensured she and her kid had everything they needed.

No. Not her kid.

Their kid.

It would take a long time before that reality sunk in.

His fingers fumbled on a chord change, and Tyler shot him a worried look. During Adam's drum solo on the next song, Tyler jogged over to Zack, getting so close their foreheads nearly touched.

"You good? Stupid question, I know."

Zack shook his head. No, he wasn't good. He was so far from fucking good that *good* might as well be on goddamn Jupiter.

"We have your back, brother." Tyler turned away from the crowd, set a hand on Zack's shoulder, and squeezed. "Always. You can fall apart later. Now, you need to focus on getting through the show."

Tyler returned to his microphone, and the sounds of his guitar filled the arena. His lyrics echoed in the vast space while Adam and Zack kept the rhythm steady behind him.

Zack was lucky to have these men in his corner, ready to stand alongside him and take on whatever challenges he faced as if they were their own. He'd need it since he was seconds away from bashing his bass against the stage until it was nothing but splinters.

When he checked the side of the stage again, Mandy was there. She still had sad eyes but seeing her in his T-shirt made his heart skip.

Sad eyes.

The airport.

As puzzle pieces connected, he knew why she'd been crying before boarding the plane. She had to leave her baby behind. And she had to do that because Zack rearranged her life to get her back into his.

Would he take it back, knowing what he knew now? That was impossible to answer with the shock so fresh.

As he played on autopilot, he grasped for more answers, digging into his mind to pull out the other things that didn't make sense.

She didn't want him to touch her stomach. She didn't let him take off her clothes or see her with the lights on. And every time he tried to get inside her, she said no. He struggled to remember exactly what she'd said. Something about her weight, her body being changed.

Another puzzle piece clicked into place, and a wave of hurt overtook him. Not for himself this time, but for her. Was she embarrassed by her body now? Had a boyfriend told her she was anything less than perfect? She said no one had hurt her, but now, he was certain that it wasn't true—there were different kinds of hurt.

With so much he still needed to know, he hoped like fuck she'd finally give him all the answers.

When the song ended, he glanced back to where she'd been standing. Her spot was empty, and she was nowhere to be seen. A hollow, suffocating feeling in his chest made it hard to breathe, worsened by the fear that he'd never be able to fill it back up again.

— ◆ —

"Hi, Zack." The teenage girl with cropped black hair shook his held-out palm. "I can't believe I'm shaking your hand!" She smiled, baring her braces-covered teeth.

She was a winner of the meet-the-bands contest, which raised money for Safe Start, a women's shelter in Portland and Charlotte's favorite charity. The organization helped addicts recover and get back on their feet. If it hadn't been for supporting the worthy cause and agreeing weeks ago to meet the winners, he would've already bailed.

"Cool to meet you too." He signed autographs and took photos, plastering on a fake smile while fighting the urge to hunt down the nearest bottle of strong liquor and smother the emotions he had no fucking clue how to deal with.

Tyler leaned close, his voice low so only they'd hear. "Go. We'll finish up here, and if you need to talk, I'll be in the hotel bar."

Zack scoffed. "I'll beat you there."

If there was ever an excuse to have a stiff drink, he'd found it.

Twenty minutes later, with a half-full glass of expensive whiskey, he stared blankly at the wall beside him. He'd taken a booth in the furthest, darkest corner of the bar to avoid being recognized and hassled, stewing in his thoughts that were flying in all directions.

Tyler slid into the seat across from him, clutching a pint of beer. "Talk."

Zack raked a trembling hand through his hair. "What the fuck am I supposed to do with this, Ty? I can't be a..." The word lodged in his throat, and he took a long, burning swallow of whiskey to dislodge it. "I can't be someone's father. Fucking look at me! I'm a goddamn mess. I can't change diapers and teach someone to tie their shoes, brush their teeth, or drive a car. I can't comfort someone when they scrape their knee or teach them right from fucking wrong when I've spent over a decade of my life drinking, smoking, and fucking anything with fluttering eyelashes and a pulse."

He took another deep pull from his glass, lighting a fiery trail down his throat and into his belly. After hours of feeling numb with shock, he welcomed the familiar burn. "We were getting so close again. Every fucking thing about her I've been aching for, *craving* so badly it hurt, was still there. She's even more incredible than I remembered. I don't want to lose her again, but how can I be in her life if I can't be a father?"

He knew the answer. After he was quiet for a few moments, Tyler spoke.

"You never give yourself credit, Zack. You always cling to your roughest edges, but there's more to you than that. If you want to be a father, you're capable. You have to be willing to put someone else's needs above yours. I've seen you do it with Mandy, so I know you can. You helped get her that job to better her life, even though you might end up hurt again. You flew here with her because she'd be afraid, and you wanted to comfort her. And you've never failed your friends when we've needed you."

Zack drained his glass and coughed at the stinging heat. "I never wanted this, Ty."

"I know. It's probably why she didn't tell you, not that it makes it okay. But you never wanted a relationship until you met her, and I know damn well you don't regret taking that leap, even after this. The woman you love has spent all this time pouring everything she's got into a life you created together. That kid is part of you. The least you could do is arrange to meet them and see how you feel. If you give it a chance, you might surprise yourself again."

Zack pushed his empty glass aside. "There's more. I think she's ashamed of her body. She's still beautiful to me, but every time I've tried to touch her stomach or take off her clothes, she freaks out and stops me. It breaks my fucking heart to imagine what thoughts are running through her head."

Tyler nodded and sipped his beer. "Charlotte struggles with that, too. She got a few stretch marks, and her skin isn't as tight as she wishes it was. But she's never been more beautiful to me because of what made those changes. She dealt with morning sickness, back pain, foot cramps, and labor that looked so painful, I know for fucking sure I wouldn't have been able to handle it. She's a goddamn warrior. For nine months, she grew this person who smiles and grabs my finger in her little fist like she knows she owns me." He laughed, his eyes glistening in the dim light. "I remind her of those things every time I see her frown at her belly in the mirror or try to hide her body from me."

As the liquor took hold, the tension between Zack's shoulders loosened, and he sank back in his seat. "I appreciate everything you're saying, Ty. But I still don't know what the fuck I'm going to do."

"You'll figure it out. All of it. New things are thrown at Charlotte and me every day with our kid, and somehow, we make it work. All you need is love." A corner of his mouth lifted.

"Don't start quoting the fucking Beatles, you sappy shit." Zack balled up a bar napkin and tossed it at his friend's head.

Tyler laughed, dodging it. "Couldn't resist."

They both froze when Mandy appeared beside the table.

"Adam told me you were here," she said, her voice small and timid. "Can we talk?"

Tyler's pointed glare in her direction instantly put Zack on edge. "Next time you want to drop a bomb on his head, could you not do it seconds before he has a fucking show to do?"

"Ty, don't." Zack shot him a look that told him to shut up and mind his business. Although he appreciated his friend's protectiveness, advice, and the shoulder to bitch on, he didn't want Tyler's frustration aimed at her. Zack softened his tone. "Just go. I'll see you in the morning."

Her gaze slid to Tyler, her eyes so fucking sad and full of regret it was impossible to miss. "I'm sorry."

He gave a curt nod, picked up his beer, and left. She slid into the empty side of the booth.

"Boy or girl?" Zack would ask every question buzzing in his brain, and now, she would answer them.

The waitress came by, and Mandy ordered a glass of Cabernet. He ordered another whiskey—a double this time—before the waitress walked away.

"A boy."

He nodded slowly, letting that sink in.

He had a son.

The waitress set their drinks on the table and disappeared.

"What's his name?"

Mandy met his gaze before taking a long sip of wine. "Phoenix."

"Oh, fuck." He slapped a hand over his eyes. Did she seriously name him after the city where the condom broke? He wasn't sure how to feel about that yet, and there were more questions to get through.

"Does he have a middle name?" he asked, swirling the dark liquid in his glass.

"Zachary."

He swallowed thickly, setting down the glass.

She named him after me.

His eyes squeezed shut as he pinched the bridge of his nose. He suddenly wasn't in the mood for more questions. He couldn't take it. After draining his glass in three deep swallows, he signaled to the waitress for another.

Two sips into the next drink, another question begged for release. He pulled in a deep, steeling breath and let it out. "Why?"

A crease dipped between her eyes like she wasn't sure what he was asking.

"Why didn't you tell me?" he clarified. "What happened to honesty's always better, even when it stings?"

She stared at the burgundy liquid in her glass. "I knew you didn't want kids. That toddler eating pancakes grossed you out, and you said you never wanted to be a father. And I'm sorry to say this, but you deserve to know everything."

"Just say it."

"When I decided to have him, I called to tell you. You were wasted. I didn't try again because I was afraid of what it would do to our son if someday you wanted to be in his life and didn't change. You know what I went through with my brother. My parents and I begged him to get sober and make a better life for himself, only to be crushed again and again. I couldn't put Phoenix or myself through that if you overdoing it became something worse."

It wasn't easy to hear, but he couldn't fault her for that.

"Your lifestyle isn't kid-friendly," she continued, "and that's okay. All that matters to me is that you're happy. You didn't ask for this. I chose to keep him. I've been doing this on my own all this time, and you only need to be as involved as you want to be, if at all. No pressure. Nothing really has to change for you, Zack."

He ran a hand over his head, processing that. How was it possible for nothing to change? Even if he decided he couldn't be in the kid's life, he wouldn't let her shoulder the financial burden alone anymore. That was a good place to start.

"I'll call my business manager in the morning and have him set up monthly payments. And back pay for all the time before now."

She squared her shoulders, scowling like he'd offended her. "I don't want your money."

"What if that's all I can give?" His voice broke, and he cleared his throat before continuing. This felt too much like a goodbye, and the liquor made it easy for his emotions to bleed in. "I'm just not sure what else I can handle yet."

"Like I said, it's up to you." She sipped her wine, her eyes fixed on his above the rim. "You don't have to decide anything right now."

"What..." Zack shifted in his seat, his knee bouncing beneath the table. "Um, what's he like?"

She smiled, her eyes sparkling in the light from the lamp above the table. "He's funny like you. Always laughing, and oh, my god, his laugh is so great." She chuckled, looking off into the distance. "He loves peaches and bananas but hates carrots with a passion. And socks. He hates wearing them but likes throwing them for some reason. His favorite book is *The House at Pooh Corner.* He hands it to me at bedtime and slaps it with his little hand."

"Pooh?"

She laughed again, wiping a tiny tear from the corner of her eye. "As in Winnie. Not shit."

He couldn't help laughing, surprising them both. "I know about Winnie the Pooh, Mandy. I didn't grow up on Mars. Does he like music?"

The question made her smile grow. "I play your albums in the car. He claps, and his little legs jump to the beat. It's so damn cute."

"That's why you knew the words to 'Long Time Alone.'"

She nodded, her smile dissolving. "It was a way to have you in our lives without interfering with yours."

A lump lodged in his throat. She'd never let him go. And she wanted their son to know him in the only way possible without getting hurt by Zack's lifestyle and possible rejection. He filed it away with the rest of the things he was still too stunned to process.

"Fortunately," she continued, "your band is amazing. It would've been awful if his father played country music."

He gave a dramatic shudder, and she laughed.

Her smile dimmed, but the light in her eyes didn't. "He looks like you."

His knee stopped bouncing. "Do you have a picture?"

She nodded, digging into her purse and sliding a glossy photograph across the table. "I have one in my locket, too, but this one's more recent."

His chest jumped with a sharp inhale, shocked at what he saw. She wasn't kidding—he looked like Zack. His eyes were the same shade of green, same broad nose, same chin. If he'd had the tiniest glimmer of doubt that her baby was his, it would've been snuffed out for good.

"He does. He looks just like me."

Mandy reached across the table, her soft hand covering the one holding the photo. "I know you didn't want this, but we made an amazing kid. That sweet smell you noticed on the plane was him. I held him so tightly before I said goodbye." She stopped to catch her breath, dabbing her eyes with her napkin.

"I'm sorry you had to leave him to come here." He skimmed his thumb along her wrist, guilt burning in his gut.

With her confession, he was tempted to come clean about helping her get the job, but the possibility of her bolting and hating him was too high to risk. Besides, one heavy conversation was all he could handle.

"I'm a good mom, Zack. I give him everything I can, plus some. He's my entire world. But I came here, and this thing between us woke up and grew, and I feel like the worst person alive for holding on to this secret while we both fell under the delusion we could ever be part of each other's world for longer than these beautiful but temporary moments."

"Don't say that." He couldn't let her give up on them before he'd let this new reality sink in. Maybe Tyler was right, and he'd somehow come around to the idea of being in his kid's life.

She sniffed, dabbing her eyes again with her free hand. "I've been unfair to you, and you've been nothing but honest and kind to me. I understand if you want me to leave right now and keep my distance for the rest of the tour. Then, you never have to see me again if that's what you want." She let him go, her fingers wrapping around the stem of her glass.

He didn't want that. There was so much confusion, and the shock was too fresh to know what he did want, but he couldn't go the rest of the tour or the rest of his life without seeing her again.

As he stared at the photo in his hands, he imagined Mandy's life back in Denver with their son. He wasn't sure how to picture himself wedged into it. He'd only held a baby once—for, like, ten seconds after Anna Jude was born. Could he even fit in with the life she'd built for her and Phoenix? He understood they were a matched set, and he couldn't have her if he didn't want to be a father.

His eyes shut as a realization bashed him over the head, a few more puzzle pieces clicking into place. He didn't know shit about kids, but he knew they were expensive.

"That's why you aren't managing, isn't it?"

She nodded, chewing at her bottom lip.

"You know I would've given you *anything*." He leaned forward. "You didn't have to give up your dream for him. Why didn't you come to me?"

"I didn't want your fucking charity."

"Not charity. Child support, if nothing else."

"Why would I ask you to pay for something, some*one* you never wanted? I thought it was better for all of us to cut ties and move on. But I came to realize it was wrong to decide for you. I was being a coward. I planned to tell you but didn't know when or how. Then, it felt like the universe put this opportunity in front of me so I could tell you in person."

It wasn't the universe. It was him.

He'd triggered all of this by not being as honest as she thought.

A few more puzzle pieces were trying to connect in his brain, but the whiskey made the edges fuzzy. "Is he the biggest reason you stopped talking to me?"

Her eyes narrowed. "I don't like how you phrased that, but yes. You didn't want kids, and I decided I did. So, you and I became impossible." She raised her glass to her lips. "You moved on pretty quickly anyway."

"What are you talking about?"

"Two days after I told you we were over, I saw a tabloid photo of you with a bikini-clad blonde on some beach." She chugged the rest of her wine and waved the waitress down for another.

"Mandy, don't get drunk because you're pissed at me."

She scoffed. "Look who's fucking talking."

The waitress brought the wine, shooting them weird looks before scurrying off. Don't people fight over secret kids and relationship drama every day in this place?

"The blonde was my cousin in Miami. Adam was there, but they cut him out of the shot. I'm no saint, but those fucking vultures get off on making me look like more of a scumbag than I've ever been." He shook his head. "One thing I love most about you is you don't believe the bullshit people say about me. When did that change?"

They were quiet for a while, sipping their drinks and avoiding eye contact.

Finally, she broke the silence.

"I'm sorry that I assumed the worst again when I should've talked to you. And that I didn't tell you about Phoenix."

Trust didn't come easily for her. Even though that photo was innocent, plenty followed that weren't. It wasn't because he was over Mandy—not even close—and he didn't want to go back down that road by losing her again.

"Come back to my room." Zack pushed his glass aside and took her hand, her eyes wide with surprise. "I can't guarantee I'll wake up ready to be a dad. Fuck, that's weird to say." He took a breath and another drink before continuing. "I can't guarantee that, but I promise to try. I don't want to lose this." He gestured between them. "I'll try my best to be who you need me to be while we figure out the rest."

After a beat, she nodded. "Let me grab my bag from my room first, okay?"

"I'll walk you up."

He signed the check, and they stepped inside the elevator. When the doors slid shut, he laced their fingers together. They rode up to her floor in silence. Maybe they'd both had their fill of words for a while.

In her room, she stuffed her toothbrush and clean clothes into her backpack. He hitched it over his shoulder before taking her hand again. It was risky, but he needed the comfort, and the hallways were empty anyway.

They made their way back to his room. He set her backpack on the couch and sank into the cushion beside it.

"Want a beer?" she asked. "Because I could really fucking use a beer."

"You've been around me so much, you're starting to sound like me."

Mandy laughed as she went into the kitchen. His elbow hit her backpack, knocking it to the floor. Something solid hit the ground, and he picked it up. It looked like the voice recorder Tyler used to record ideas for lyrics when a pen wasn't handy. Knowing her, she used it for tour notes to help her stay organized. Curious, he pushed play.

26

Mandy

The voice coming from the other room sent an icy shudder up Mandy's spine.

I only tried to fuck you because I pity you.

She bolted toward the sound to find Zack listening to the tape she'd made of James fucking Sutter laying out how ugly and worthless she was.

You're on the wrong side of thirty, probably have stretch marks all over the body that I bet was hot and tight before you shit out that kid.

"Stop the tape." Tears flooded her eyes as she hugged herself, desperate for it to stop. She lunged for the recorder, but he held it out of her grasp, his face unreadable through the blur of tears.

If you couldn't even keep the man dumb enough to dump his load inside you, you won't be able to keep anyone. Those tiny wrinkles around your eyes and mouth will only get deeper, making you unfuckable and unlovable, until you die alone.

Zack's face flamed red, and he stopped the tape with a resounding click. He'd already heard it all—every cruel, hateful word. She ripped the machine from his grasp and stuffed it into her backpack.

"You had no right to listen to that!" She wiped at the tears sliding to her chin. "How could you go through my goddamn stuff behind my back?"

His chest rose and fell with ragged, shallow breaths. "It fell out of your bag. Was that your fucking boss?" There was danger in his tone, but not for her.

"My *former* boss. Not that it's any of your business." She'd brought the recorder in case her current boss was a fast talker, and she needed help keeping track of his requests. If he had been, she would've recorded over that garbage, so she'd never have to hear it again.

"Mandy…"

"Don't!" Her hand shot up between them. "Don't you dare look at me with pity in your eyes over that!"

He reached out and took her hand into his, pressing his lips to her knuckles. She considered pulling away, but the fraught conversation downstairs and the words on the tape had scrubbed her raw, and she craved the comfort.

"You know he only said those things to hurt you, right? None of that's true."

She scoffed. "How would you know? You haven't seen my stretch marks, loose belly, saggy tits, or the cellulite on my hips that magically appeared during pregnancy and never went away. Or the way my—"

"Stop." He stood up and stepped closer, touching a finger to her lips. "Kick whatever you were about to say out of your fucking head because it isn't true. Even if it is, I don't care. You could've sprouted a tail, and I'd still want you. There's nothing about you that isn't beautiful to me."

Her chest heaved, a brutal sob crashing through her. He pulled her into his arms, and she let it all out—the torment of hating her body, anger at herself for letting those feelings grow and fester after that asshole planted those seeds in her head. Guilt for being so far from Phoenix. And grief for all the times she could've been held like this if only she'd believed in Zack instead of talking herself out of what her heart wanted.

She buried her face in his neck as a gentle hand stroked between her shoulder blades.

"Do you know what I see when I look at you?" He breathed the words against her cheek. She stayed quiet, listening while the tears fell. "I see someone who's had to be strong for so long that she doesn't know how to let go and trust. Someone who's worked so hard caring for other people, there's nothing left for herself." His hand stilled. "Mandy, please look at me."

She slowly raised her chin and met his gaze.

"I see the woman I love." He wiped away her tears with his thumbs, cupping her cheeks. "A woman so beautiful, intelligent, and strong, I can't believe I'm lucky enough to breathe the same fucking air. No matter what happens after our time here is up, I need you to know that wherever you go and whatever you do, you'll always have my heart in your fucking pocket."

She looped her arms around his neck and brought his face to hers, their lips pressing together without urgency or heat, just soothing and slow. He moaned into her mouth as his warm body pressed to hers, holding her against his chest like he'd never let her go. She didn't want him to. She wanted to freeze the moment and lock it away, giving her a piece of him to cling to no matter what the future held and what he decided.

He angled his face, their tongues tangling. She felt his desperation, his need, and she needed him too.

Her head swam as she forgot to breathe, feeling his hunger for her in every frenzied sweep of his tongue. His hands slid down her back, gripping her ass and pulling her against the thick hardness in his jeans. It was her turn to moan, the vibration buzzing across their lips.

"Can you feel what you do to me?" His kisses moved from her mouth, tracing her jawline. "I missed you every fucking day, every second." As he kissed and sucked the sensitive flesh of her neck, she hooked a leg around his hip and rubbed herself against him, desperate for sweet friction against her core. "If you give me a chance, I'll never hurt you again."

He couldn't promise that. If he ever hurt or rejected Phoenix, it would hurt her.

There was no guarantee he wouldn't do that.

Of course, her choices weren't perfect. No parent got everything right, and there was no guarantee her decisions wouldn't break her son's heart someday.

"We'll take it one step at a time," she whispered as he sucked her earlobe into his mouth and released it with a slow drag of his teeth.

With her body and mind running on separate tracks, she surrendered to the pull she felt whenever Zack was close. They were like two crazy, imperfect magnets drawn together in a way that grew stronger every second.

With her final secrets out, it was time to stop running from what she wanted and follow her heart, regardless of the consequences.

He took her face into his hands again, and their eyes locked. "I love you, Mandy. I fucking love you so much it feels like my chest is splitting apart."

His words did the opposite to her, mending something inside her that was broken long before they met. She saw the honesty in his eyes and couldn't hold the words back another second.

"I love you too."

He sucked in a sharp, shuddering breath. "Say it again."

"I love you, Zack. I've loved you since that last night in Arizona when I fell asleep in your arms. That's why I named him Phoenix. He was created there by two people who loved each other despite their obstacles."

Unshed tears glistened in his eyes. "Fuck, baby..."

"No matter what you decide, my heart's in your fucking pocket too."

Their lips collided again, and this kiss was more urgent and needy. She tugged his shirt over his head and fumbled with the button on his jeans. He grabbed the hem of her shirt, but she stopped him, her face hot as panic threatened to destroy the perfect moment.

"Turn the light off first."

He shook his head, his expression stern as a muscle ticked in his jaw. "Not this time. Get that bastard's words out of your head."

He went for her hem again, and her hands covered his. After a second's hesitation, she let go. Her body was the last thing she'd been hiding from him, and it was time to let go and trust. He slipped the T-shirt over her head and released a heavy breath as his gaze raked over every inch of her bare skin.

The urge to cover herself was strong, but she fought it. If he wanted her, he'd have to accept the changes in her body. She hoped that someday, she'd learn to accept them herself.

She could only imagine what was going through his mind. He'd slept with models and actresses. She looked for disappointment or disgust on his face but didn't see it. Maybe he was hiding it to spare her feelings.

He sank to his knees.

"What are you doing?" She didn't want her sagging belly at his eye level, imagining how repulsed he must be. Her palm slid over her stomach.

"Stop." He eased her hand back to her side.

He leaned forward and planted a line of kisses above the waistband of her skirt. It was hard to crowd out the embarrassment, but the awareness of how close he was to her pussy made her pulse race.

"Don't ever hide from me," he said. "Not anymore. You're the sexiest fucking woman I've ever seen. If you think that's just a line to make you feel better, look in my eyes. You can see the truth in my eyes, can't you?"

She scrutinized every detail in his expression—the raw sincerity in his eyes, the subtle pinch of his brows, and the firm, straight line of his mouth. There was no sign of deception or the repulsion she'd been worried about. Only reverence and lust.

Yes, she saw the truth.

Mandy nodded her head. She recognized the truth in everything he'd said, and now, he wanted her. He thought she was beautiful.

And he loved her—another unmistakable truth.

"Then let me take care of you." He grabbed the waistband of her skirt and tugged it down, letting the fabric pool at her feet. She stood in nothing but her simple black bra and matching panties. The way he looked at her with love and lust had those panties drenched.

Feeling bold, she unhooked her bra and let it fall to the ground between them.

"Holy shit," he whispered, rising to his feet. He teased her nipple with the tip of his tongue before taking it into his mouth and sucking hard. His eyebrows drew together, and he swallowed, pulling back with something like surprise on his face.

Then, she realized what had happened.

She slapped her hands over her eyes, embarrassment setting her face on fire.

"Oh, my god." Her hands muffled her words. "I should've warned you. I just stopped breastfeeding, so there's still... Yeah." She reached for her bra, figuring fun time was over after that mortifying moment she'd love to bleach from her brain.

"Don't you dare." He snatched the bra and tossed it across the room. "I got on my knees because I wanted to taste you, and I guess I did."

They laughed together as she landed a playful smack on his arm.

"It's fine," he said with no sign of a lie or impending freak out in his expression. "That's a first for me, and I wasn't expecting it. It was actually… kind of hot."

"Really?" Her eyes snapped wide. When she let herself get past the initial embarrassment, she had to agree—it was kind of hot. Sharing an experience that he'd never had made it even hotter. She didn't think he had any "firsts" left.

"Yeah. Is that weird to say?"

She huffed a laugh. "Nothing you say surprises me anymore. And you're the kinkiest guy I've ever been with, so you finding that hot doesn't surprise me either."

He returned to his knees. "We might revisit that, but now, I need to taste you *here*." His hand cupped her between her legs, her clit throbbing against his palm and begging to be stroked.

"Do it." She dragged her fingers through the soft, dark locks of his hair. "I want your mouth on me *now*."

He slid her panties down her legs with a slow, teasing drag. "Are you wet for me?"

His fingertips ghosted over the skin on the backs of her legs, igniting goosebumps. Her brain turned to mush, and all her thoughts silenced as she focused on his touch. When she didn't answer, he slapped her ass, and she yelped.

So, he remembered something else she liked.

"Answer me," he demanded, his tone sharp.

"Yes," she breathed, a wave of pleasure rolling through her at the lingering sting. "Yes, I'm fucking wet. For you. Only for you."

"You know what happens if you lie to me."

Fantasy and reality bled together. Heat simmered in her chest, sinking until it settled low in her belly.

Mandy plunged two fingers inside her pussy and smeared her arousal across his lips. "Believe me now?" She lifted a brow.

She watched the pink tip of his tongue emerge, gliding along the glistening trail. His eyes closed, a low, feral hum rumbling in his throat.

"Fuck, I missed that taste," he rasped. "I'm going to fucking *devour* you, baby. Worship you. Make you come in my mouth and scream my name until you finally accept that you're mine and I'm yours."

Again, this was part of the fantasy because they both knew it was already true.

She grew wetter at the words that were like the man who'd said them—filthy but sweet. "Fucking do it." Her pulse thumped in her neck. "*Please.*"

Zack grabbed her ass with both hands and pulled her to his face, dragging the flat of his tongue along the seam of her pussy and plunging inside. She groaned, using her grip on his hair to grind against his mouth. He hummed against her clit in approval. Another sharp smack landed on her ass, and she gasped at the delicious combination of pleasure and pain.

He was relentless, feasting between her legs until she was crying out with an orgasm that made glittering stars burst behind her eyelids. When she relaxed, he leaned back, and she whimpered in protest at the loss of his warm, wet mouth.

She looked down to find his face shimmering with her arousal—his cheeks, lips, and chin displaying the evidence of what he did to her. How amazing he made her feel.

"Get on the bed and spread your legs for me." He rose to his feet, his breathing heavy. She obeyed, lying on her back and parting her knees wide, the anticipation and the aftershocks of her orgasm making her dizzy.

He stalked to the bed, his pants unbuttoned but clinging to his hips. Her eyes tracked his movements as he fixed that. With his zipper pinched between two fingers, he brought it down in a slow, torturous drag. Her mouth watered, craving the feel of him slipping past her lips and fucking her throat like the night before.

"You look so beautiful lying there," he said, "naked, wet, and waiting for me."

He slid his jeans and boxers down his legs and kicked them aside. At last, they were both bare. The worries over what he'd think about her body faded into the background. Like so many fears, it was scarier in her mind. Facing it head-on was the first step to conquering it.

She should've known she was safe to give all of herself to him without judgment and would accept all of him in return.

Her eyes drank in every inch of his naked flesh. "It's easy to be wet when you look like that."

She groaned at the sight of all that ink and muscle. The man was even hotter than she remembered, which seemed impossible. She'd masturbated to the memory of him naked and hard countless times.

Now, she got the real thing and planned to savor every second.

Zack planted his elbows on the edge of the bed and leaned forward, his hooded gaze fixed between her legs. Again, it was tempting to cover herself and hide, but nothing in his eyes or expression looked anything less than mesmerized. He trailed a finger from her clit to her needy pussy as it pulsed, begging to be filled. He circled her entrance, slipping inside to the first knuckle.

She shut down the voice inside her head that said he could tell she was looser and that it wouldn't feel as good for him.

"I can't wait to feel this pretty pussy stretch and squeeze my cock." He added the tip of a second finger. "You're so fucking tight. I don't think you're ready for me yet."

They'd promised never to be fake with each other, and it didn't sound like a lie. The last threads of tension in her belly unfurled.

He leaned in further, dipping his head between her legs and latching onto her clit. He gently sucked, his tongue lapping at the sensitive nub as her fingernails bit into her thighs. After her first orgasm, the sensation was too much and not enough.

"I'm ready," she panted. "*Please.*"

She was done with teasing and foreplay—she needed to be fucked.

"Patience, baby." His strong fingers slid deeper, twisting inside as her pussy gripped his knuckles. She moaned at the delicious stretch. "Almost there."

Mandy grinned, knowing exactly how to snap his resolve.

"Wanna know why I'm so tight?" she asked, a teasing lilt to her tone.

He nodded with her clit between his lips before releasing her flesh with a soft pop. "Tell me."

"Because no one's fucked me since you."

He stilled, and their gazes locked, his eyes flaring with hunger. "Why not?"

She raked a hand through his hair, tugging at the roots. "You're the best I've ever had, so what was the point? No one else could *ever* fuck me like you can."

A growl rumbled in his chest like a savage animal was trapped inside. It was, and she'd taunted it before setting it loose.

She knew he'd appreciate that. Especially because it was true.

"I'm on the Pill," she said, "so if you're clean, I want you to fuck me bare and raw."

Again, fire blazed in his eyes as he crawled up her body. He lined up their hips and sank his weight on her, pressing her into the mattress. The warm, velvety steel of his cock nestled against her belly, the weight of his balls resting on her clit.

"You know just what to say to get what you want, don't you, smart girl?" He traced her lips with the tip of his tongue and pulled back before she could capture his mouth in a kiss. "Well, guess what? It fucking worked."

He slid down her body far enough for his cock to fall between her legs. With an upward snap of his hips, the thick crown nudged at her opening. Her tender skin burned at the intrusion, and he rocked back and forth with shallow thrusts, slickening his movements. She muttered curses between panted breaths, desperate for him to sink deeper.

"You're doing so good," he cooed. "Can you take a little more?"

Sweat beaded at her temples. "Fuck, *yes*. I want all of it."

Zack pressed a soft kiss between her eyes. "I've never done this bare before. You're the first." He pushed inside another agonizing inch. His words and the burning need incinerating her core made tears sting her eyes. "And I want you to be the last."

He slid to the hilt, and they groaned in unison as his balls slapped her skin. Feeling thoroughly filled overwhelmed her senses. And the way he combined dirty words with sweet ones that set off flutters in her chest was disorienting. She felt too much all at once, her mind clambering to catch up.

"You feel so goddamn good. I'm not going to last." His mouth found her neck, licking, sucking, and biting her skin. "But before I get there, you're going to come all over my cock." A rush of her arousal slickened his movements.

"Make me," she rasped.

His rhythm quickened, their hips pounding together without restraint. He hooked an elbow under her knee and angled his hips to sink deeper. The desperate cry that escaped her lips sounded foreign to her ears—like a wounded animal begging for mercy. That's exactly what she was.

"*Fuck*." Her fingernails bit into his shoulders, and he hummed his approval. "You're so deep. You feel so fucking good."

"Listen to that filthy mouth." He released her knee and grabbed her hips, dragging her against him to straddle his lap. "I think I might've corrupted you a little."

A low, gravelly laugh rose from her throat. The shameless vixen locked inside her had officially come out to play. "That's what I get for falling in love with a sexy bad boy in a leather jacket."

A corner of his mouth hitched up. "And look what I get for falling in love with a sexy good girl who loves angry rock music and French toast." He grabbed her ass, grinding her clit against the base of his cock. "I think I made out better in the deal."

She smiled as pleasure sent sparks of heat where their bodies connected. She slipped her hands behind his neck, pulling him in for a deep, consuming kiss that set fire to her blood. As she drew back, she sucked his plump bottom lip, dragging her teeth along his flesh. "I love tasting myself on your lips."

"Mmm. I guess we'll see." Zack grabbed her breast and squeezed, two creamy white drops falling to the skin below her nipple. She watched as he dipped his head, lapping them up before his Adam's apple jumped on a hard swallow. "Every inch of your body feels and tastes like fucking heaven."

She claimed his mouth in a kiss so deep and hungry she clung to his back to stay upright. Again, she tasted herself on his tongue, mingling with the salt from their sweat and a sweetness that made her cheeks flush with heat. He was worshipping her, as promised. Devouring until she was hollowed out before filling the empty spaces with all the best parts of him. All the parts she loved, even the ones that drove her crazy.

With his hands on her hips, he lifted her and pulled her back onto his lap, his cock sinking inside without resistance. She rocked her hips, the ridge of his flared crown rubbing her G-spot as she rode him.

His chin tipped down. "Look at us, baby." His voice was a deep rumble, husky and spiked with lust.

Her gaze dropped to where their bodies were joined as his thick cock disappeared between the glistening pink lips of her pussy. She whimpered at the erotic display and the feeling of him dragging out and sliding back inside her.

"It's so fucking beautiful," she said.

Their chins lifted in unison, their eyes connecting.

"So are you." His hand fisted in her hair, his gaze unwavering. "So fucking beautiful."

His words tossed fuel on the fire burning in her chest, and she surrendered to the flames, letting them consume her. "I love you," she breathed as he drove deep inside her.

He pressed their foreheads together as a slow grin crept across his lips. "I'll never get tired of hearing you say that. I love you too."

The electric sparks of pleasure gathered between her legs, gradually building until her inner muscles clamped around him, and again, shimmering stars burst behind her eyes. She moaned from deep in her chest, and he didn't slow his pace or change his rhythm. Just as she hit her peak, another wave rolled in.

He stuck two fingers in his mouth, wetting them. "That's it, gorgeous." He pressed his slick fingertips to her clit, making tight circles that had her whimpering and agonizingly close to the edge again. She rode his cock faster, chasing her release.

His free hand fisted in her hair, his teeth grazing the skin beneath her ear. "Come for me," he ordered, his low, rumbling growl vibrating through her core.

"Oh, fuck!" Mandy threw her head back and screamed as her orgasm crashed over her. He groaned and bucked his hips to meet her thrusts, fucking her hard as she let go. Warm bursts of pleasure exploded through her with such intensity that her vision went hazy at the edges.

She'd never experienced something so powerful, every cell glowing as a tear trailed her cheek.

Holy fuck.

Discovering that she could reach such euphoric heights gave her a new appreciation for her body. And Zack's skills.

As her climax gradually receded, he released her clit. It pulsed as her hips rocked faster, their bodies slick with sweat. She spread her legs wider, sinking him deeper, and he whimpered in her ear.

A blissed-out grin tugged at her lips. He was close to the edge and desperate. Perfect.

She fisted his hair, bringing his face to hers. "Come for me."

He groaned, and when she pressed their sweat-drenched foreheads together, all that existed were those gorgeous green eyes that bore right through her. The intensity of his gaze branded itself in her memory—loving and lustful in equal measure.

Seconds later, the hot, jetting bursts of his release filled her, their hips slamming together until his muscles relaxed, and he collapsed onto his back.

Zack pulled her against his damp chest, breathing like he'd run a mile. Their bodies stayed connected as they came back to Earth.

"You. Are. Amazing." He kissed the top of her head as she traced a few tattoos he didn't have the last time they were together. "It's so fucking sexy to watch you come apart in my arms."

"Ditto. That was incredible. *You* are incredible."

"I have my moments." He chuckled, his chest jumping beneath her ear.

"If I ask you a question..." A nagging worry intruded on her afterglow, and she wanted it settled. "Do you promise to tell the truth, even if you think it would hurt me?"

He was quiet, his heartbeats quickening beneath her ear. "Of course."

She traced a black line of ink over his collarbone. "Do I feel different down there? Looser?"

He cupped her chin, forcing her to look him in the eyes. "No. Your pussy is perfect. I promise you feel even better than I remember, which is saying a lot. I fucked my fist to the memory of sliding between your legs more times than I could ever count. And if we didn't need sleep, I'd be kicking off round two."

She smiled, satisfied by his thorough, unsurprisingly graphic answer, and returned her cheek to his chest. The new tattoo on his left pec was a delicate, thin-line musical note with the pale shadow of a broken heart beside it.

"What does this mean?" Her head sank as he sighed.

"I got it after we broke up. Music connected us. And the broken heart..."

He didn't need to finish.

"I know I've said it a lot, but..." She pressed a kiss to the ink on his chest. "I'm sorry. For everything."

There were some very heavy conversations and decisions in their future, but at least tonight, they'd revel in the comfort and pleasure no one else could bring.

He kissed her forehead. "I know, baby. So am I."

27

Zack

After calling his business manager to send money to Mandy for Phoenix, Zack felt lighter, not just in his wallet. The more he repeated the name, the cooler it sounded.

Phoenix.

A mythical creature that was reborn from the ashes of its past. Zack could relate. He was working to burn down the worst parts of himself—his selfishness, immaturity, and self-destructive bullshit—to become someone capable of being part of their lives.

Giving her a shitload of money was a start. Mandy would argue when it showed in her account, but he wasn't taking it back. She and Phoenix needed it, and he had it—simple. She'd earned it by doing everything for their kid while Zack was oblivious, getting wasted and chasing supermodels.

There was a knock on the door of his suite, and of course, he hoped it was Mandy. She'd left early for work, and it was almost noon, so she might want to have lunch together. It was something normal couples did, right? He didn't think he'd ever be half of anything considered normal, but he'd try his best for her.

He opened it to find Tyler holding Anna Jude, a black leather bag slung over his shoulder.

"She was begging to see you," Tyler said. "I think you really connected with that fist bump."

Zack snickered, moving aside as they walked in. "Hey, chicks love me. Even ones without teeth, apparently."

Tyler sat on the carpet with his knees bent. He set the baby on his lap, facing him. "Want to know one of the most important things to do with babies?"

"Keep them home so no one else has to deal with their crying?" Zack sat on the couch, regretting the words as soon as they tumbled out. Shit-talking kids was another old habit he'd have to break.

Tyler shot daggers at him. "You'll be crying if you say anything remotely mean about my daughter." He was always protective of his people, but that energy doubled when he fell for Charlotte and tripled when Anna Jude was born.

Zack had felt protective of Mandy since the day they met when some raging asshole pushed her. And when he heard the hideous shit her boss said to her on that tape, he wanted to beat that fucker to death until nothing remained but a puddle of red goo. Would he feel that protectiveness for his son? Or had he lost his chance to develop the instinct because he'd missed Phoenix's first months? Her reasons for keeping him a secret all made sense, but it was time they'd never get back.

"Sorry, Ty. Are you going to tell me or what?" he asked, bringing it back to Tyler's question.

"Eye contact." Tyler stared at Anna Jude as if to demonstrate. "Looking into their eyes makes them feel safe and bonded with you." He lifted an index finger and stroked the baby's chubby little cheek. "She gets to feel my warmth and learn my smell, and it teaches her which humans to go to when she's hungry or cold. Although, she prefers Charlotte by a mile. Who can blame her?" He smiled, tiny fists rising in the air between them.

"Is she trying to punch you in the face?"

Tyler's shoulders shook with laughter. "I'm trying so hard not to call you an idiot for saying that, but since you don't know shit about babies, I'll hold it back."

Zack scoffed because he'd basically said it anyway. "So, why's she throwing fists and sticking out her tongue?"

"She's only two months old, so it's all instinct and reflexes when they're this young. She's learning what her body can do. The tongue thing is because she's hungry. Which I planned for." Tyler dug into the bag at his side, pulled out a bottle full of milk, and held it out to Zack. "You're treating my daughter to lunch."

His eyebrows hiked up his forehead. "Are you goddamn kidding me?"

Tyler stood with the baby, walking to the couch.

"I can't, Ty. I'll fucking break her or drop her or something."

Tyler tapped Zack's ankle with his boot. "Don't be an ass. You're too afraid of me to hurt her. Keep her head tucked against your elbow for support like this." He held the baby to his chest with the crook of his elbow as a pillow. "Your turn. You need to feel what this is like. It might help you decide what you can handle."

Zack's pulse kicked up at the reminder of the decision he had to make—meet his kid someday and try to be in his life or let Mandy go and never know his son.

What Tyler said made sense. Zack had missed out on this tiny, helpless, fist-throwing phase and had no idea what to expect with his kid. Regardless, this was a baby step he had to take if he was going to take a step toward his baby.

"If she shits on me, I'll sue your ass."

"Fair enough." Tyler laughed, setting Anna Jude in Zack's arms. "Perfect."

Zack's hands shook as he adjusted to the feeling. She weighed almost nothing, and her wide blue eyes were fixed on his face. Her tongue pushed out again, and she shoved her fist in her mouth.

Tyler handed him the bottle. "Put it to her lips gently, and she'll do the rest."

He was right. As soon as Zack offered it, she wrapped her lips around the rubber tip and drank. It was weird—like she was some alien creature who couldn't walk or talk but somehow knew how to survive.

As the nerves settled, he found it sort of calming. The baby smelled nice—like baby powder and lavender. He was worried she'd smell like puke or nasty diapers. And he felt her tiny little breaths on his hand as she drank, making her seem more real than just the screaming thing that made Tyler and Charlotte tired.

"Am I doing it right?" he asked, not as nervous anymore but still unsure.

Tyler sat beside him and clapped a hand on his shoulder. "You're doing great, bud."

Anna Jude's eyelids drooped when she was halfway through the bottle.

"Is she crashing out?" Zack asked with a grin.

"Yeah, when she hits the bottle hard, that happens." Tyler nudged his elbow. "Hey, you have that in common."

Zack laughed, tempted to flip off his friend, but his hands were busy.

There was a knock at the door.

"Shit."

"I'll get it." Tyler got up and answered it.

When the door opened, Zack heard Mandy's voice before she walked inside with Tyler.

The second she saw Zack with the baby, her feet froze. Tears glossed her eyes, but she blinked hard, clearing them. He set down the bottle since Anna Jude would rather sleep than eat.

"This is not what I expected to see." Her hand covered her mouth, disbelief layered with the warmth in her expression. "I wanted to take you to lunch, but I guess you're already spoken for."

He tipped his chin toward the phone. "We can do room service if that's cool."

"Sure." She nodded, grabbing the menu and browsing it.

"Can you order since my hands are busy?" Zack surprised himself that his first thought wasn't to hand the baby off. She was still passed out with a tiny puddle of bubbling white in the corner of her mouth. It was gross but could've been worse. "Please get me a turkey club if they have it."

"Tyler?" She chewed her bottom lip as her eyes flicked to him and back to the menu.

"I just ate," he said without looking at her, "but I'll take one of those massive shortbread cookies. Thanks."

The tension between them from the pre-show drama needed to be squashed. They were two of Zack's favorite people and had to get along.

She called in the order with hers before sitting beside him on the couch.

Tyler aimed his thumb at the door. "Are you guys good for like fifteen minutes? I promised Charlotte I'd grab her some chocolate in the gift shop."

Mandy grinned. "My kind of girl." When she turned to Tyler, her smile slipped, a crease dipping between her brows. "I'm sorry about upsetting Zack before the show."

Tyler waved it off, meeting her gaze. "Old news. We're good. Especially if you make sure he doesn't try to put my kid in the dishwasher or something."

She laughed, the notch of tension between her eyebrows smoothing. "Deal."

Zack relaxed against the back of the couch, relieved to have that behind them.

When Tyler left, she rested her cheek on Zack's shoulder, gazing down at Anna Jude. "Those two make beautiful babies."

"Yeah, she's alright." He kissed the top of Mandy's head as she snuggled closer.

"So did we."

After a moment, he nodded. He'd seen Phoenix's picture, and while he'd never considered a baby beautiful, the kid had enough of her features to qualify.

Anna Jude's eyes popped open, and she stared up at him.

"Uh, hi."

Her tiny chin crinkled, her eyes screwed shut, and her face turned bright red. He fucking knew he'd break Tyler's kid.

"What do I do?" He turned his head to find Mandy's lips turned up in a sweet grin.

"What did you do when I cried last night?"

He grimaced at the memory of her pain after listening to that fucking asshole's insults about her body. What did he do to help her?

Searching his brain, he remembered holding her to his chest, so that's what he did. He carefully positioned the wailing baby with her chin on his shoulder like he'd seen Tyler and Charlotte do. Mandy held her hands up in case he fumbled, but he didn't.

With Anna Jude's chest pressed to his, he swayed in his seat. It was another thing he'd seen Tyler do. His friend had only been a dad for two months, but he was great at it. Zack knew he'd never compare, but he wouldn't be so clueless with practice and copying what other people did.

Mandy rubbed Anna Jude's back. "Did she burp after you fed her?"

"I didn't hear anything. Is it supposed to be loud?"

She snickered against the crook of his neck. "Sometimes." She dug through Tyler's bag, grabbing a white cloth and putting it on his shoulder beneath the still-screaming baby's chin. "Pat her back like this."

He copied her movement, and a loud burp that seemed impossible to come from something so small roared in his ear. "Dude! That was really fucking gross." They laughed. "And kind of impressive." Anna Jude stopped crying, so he stopped swaying, but he rubbed her back again like Mandy had done.

"I've heard you do worse." Her head rested against his shoulder again. "Zack?"

"Yeah."

"Phoenix is coming to visit me in Paris."

His hand stilled, the air stalling in his lungs. That was the last thing he'd expected to hear, and his overloaded brain struggled to grasp the full gravity of what she'd said.

"Who's bringing him?"

"My mom." She squeezed his knee before drawing tiny circles on the spot with her fingernails. "I didn't intend it as an ambush, I promise. We talked about it before I was hired and before I knew you'd be on the tour. If you aren't ready to meet one or both of them, it's okay. I don't want to push you."

Was he ready to meet their son? The idea twisted his stomach into knots. Without a doubt, her judgy, uptight, super-Catholic mom would hate him. Hell, she probably already did, and they hadn't even met. Fortunately, Mandy was strong-minded enough not to let anyone's opinion sway her, but if he made a lousy impression on Phoenix, it might be a deal-breaker.

Maybe this surprise babysitting job was some sort of test or practice run.

"Did you and Tyler set this up?" With his free hand, he gestured to the baby on his chest. He wouldn't put it past either of them to push him to get over his baby allergy with a baptism by fire. And monster burps.

"No, I swear." Her head shook against his shoulder. "I think he's trying to help. It's sweet how much your friends love and trust you."

Her words sank in as the three of them sat in their warm, quiet huddle. Tyler left him with the most important thing in his life. Sure, Mandy was there, but he'd let Zack hold, feed, and comfort her. Tyler didn't give away that kind of trust easily, and Zack was honored by his friend's faith in him.

"I understand why you didn't tell me," he said. "I was such a mess, I made it impossible. I wouldn't have been good for either of you, and you did the right thing. If you feel guilty about it, don't." He turned his head, pressing a soft kiss to her temple. "I want to meet him." His tone was certain, and his decision was final.

He wanted to meet his son. And he wanted to see the side of Mandy he hadn't yet—as a mother to their child. He wasn't psyched to meet her mom, but he'd do his best not to fuck it up.

Her fingers slid into his hair as she smiled, caressing the back of his neck. "Good. I can't wait to introduce you."

Someone knocked at the door, and she answered. The room service attendant wheeled in a silver cart, and Mandy slipped him some cash before he left. She handed Zack half of his turkey club, and he took a huge bite. Shreds of lettuce and tomato seeds fell from the bottom onto his lap and all over Anna Jude's back.

"Your sandwich needs a diaper, too." Mandy laughed and took it back, wrapping the bottom in a napkin.

"Cute," he said, tossing a piece of lettuce in her direction.

There was another knock, and she answered, returning with Tyler. He took one look at Zack and tipped forward, laughing his ass off.

"Did you make a salad on my kid's back?" Tyler picked lettuce off Anna Jude and tossed it on the cart.

"Sorry. Sandwich failure. She's otherwise untainted by my dumbassery, I swear."

Mandy bit into her Cornish pasty. "He did great. Even stopped her from crying and got her to burp."

"That was fucking wild," Zack said with a chuckle. "She burps like a full-grown man."

Tyler grinned with pride and picked up his cookie, taking a bite. "When she's old enough, I'll teach her to punch like one, too." He scarfed down the rest of his cookie before taking the baby. "We're out. Good seeing you, Mandy." He raised his chin at Zack as he slung his bag over his shoulder. "Be ready to leave in an hour, man. Thanks for watching her."

"Yeah, it was..." Zack nodded as it dawned on him. "Surprisingly okay."

Sure, it was only a few minutes, and he had experienced help as a backup, but he did it—he kept a baby alive and happy without freaking out. Maybe he could do this.

When Tyler left, they sat at the table and returned to their lunches.

"I'll miss you tomorrow," Zack said. "We have a long fucking bus ride, and I want to see your face light up when we arrive in Rome. I hate that we have to keep sneaking around."

"I wish we could travel together, too, but..." One side of her mouth curled up. "At first, the sneaking around made me nervous, but now I think it's kind of hot."

They'd had a few close calls in the hallways between their rooms, but when she attacked him immediately afterward, it became clear she found the whiff of danger exhilarating.

His brow lifted. "Maybe we've unlocked a new kink of yours."

"Maybe." She grinned, biting into her pasty and licking a blob of sauce from her lip. "Sneaking or not, I love experiencing exciting new places with you."

"If we can make this work, I'll take you anywhere you want." He finished his sandwich in six bites and set their empty dishes on the tray.

"This was nice." She stood, fisting the front of his T-shirt and tugging him close for a kiss. "I have to wrangle Felix and Roger for the event. See you soon."

The bands had a four-hour record signing scheduled at a local music store before they were leaving for Rome. He loved meeting fans but would rather spend more time alone with Mandy before Phoenix arrived in Paris in eight days.

After she left, he stuffed his clothes into his suitcase and set it by the door. He wasn't looking forward to spending twenty hours on a bus without her, but it would be a good chance to catch up on sleep and hang with his bandmates.

The thought shocked him, but he also wanted to spend more time around Anna Jude. He could ask Tyler and Charlotte baby questions and watch how they take care of her more closely. Since she was born, he'd tried to ignore the annoying inconvenience, but now it was clear what an asshole move it was. She was family as much as Tyler was, and by avoiding her, he'd missed opportunities to learn how to care for a helpless little human.

Before this trip, he told himself he'd do *anything* to win Mandy back so they'd have a future together. He couldn't have predicted it would take figuring out how to be a father, but here they were. And he wouldn't only be doing it for her but for Phoenix, too. He deserved another parent in his life who did everything possible to keep him safe and happy. Zack couldn't imagine not having his father to lean on when he was growing up, and he'd do his best to be that solid, accepting presence for his son.

It wouldn't be easy.

But they were worth it.

28

Zack

"Eighty thousand dollars?!" Mandy pushed inside Zack's suite while he stood in his boxers, holding the door open. After making up for all the time apart traveling between London and Rome, she left his room at six that morning. Since it was a little past four, she must've just finished her work for the day, prepping for tomorrow's show.

"Hello to you, too."

"Take it back," she said.

"My hello?"

Her eyes narrowed. "Don't be cute. The money. It's too much."

"It's yours. And on the first of every month, you'll get more. You've bought every diaper, bottle, and toy for nine months. You did all the work, had zero free time, and lost sleep on all the nights you were the only one there when he cried. It's your money. And his."

She crossed her arms, her pretty pink mouth set in a hard, stubborn line. "Is it because you feel guilty or feel sorry for me?"

"Neither. Well, maybe a little guilty, but that's not what this is. I want our kid to have a nice house, go to good schools, and have everything he needs without you being stressed and working yourself to death."

She glared like he'd offended her. "We don't live in a mansion, but I'm proud of my house. I bought it on my own. And it's in a safe neighborhood with great schools. I don't need you swooping in to be the hero because you think what I've done for him isn't good enough."

How the hell did she get that from what he'd said? When she was this worked up, he had to think harder before opening his mouth. And she had to stop misreading good intentions and assuming the worst.

"Mandy, that is *not* what I said. I know you're a great mom and that you've done your best. I'm lucky enough to make ridiculous money doing something I love, and I want to help. The burden isn't just yours anymore."

"The *burden*?!" Her cheeks flamed red, and she looked poised to slap him. "My son is not a fucking burden!"

"You know damn well that's not what I meant. I feel like you're picking a fight, trying to make me the asshole, and I don't understand why. I told you I'd try to figure out how to fit into your lives, and this is me trying. Let me do the right thing."

She went quiet, her chin dropping to her chest as she stared at the carpet. "You're right. I've done my best, but sometimes I worry it's not enough. The money's incredibly generous, but it hit a nerve. I'm sorry I got defensive."

Sensing the fight leave her, he took a cautious step closer. "Other than your parents babysitting so you can work, who else has helped you with him?"

She shook her head, confirming his suspicion that the answer was *no one.* As amazing as she was, she didn't easily let people in. Aside from his core friend group, neither did he, which was why they had loneliness in common when they met. They had people who loved them but shared a soul-deep ache for someone to lean on and cherish, fully accepting each other, flaws and all. Now, it was within reach if they overcame their remaining hurdles.

"I promise, your best is more than enough." He squeezed her shoulder, the muscles rigid beneath his fingertips. "I love that you're strong on your own. You don't need a damn thing from me, and I've never wondered if you're using me for my money or status. *Never.*"

Her chin lifted. "I hate that you've had to worry about that before."

"I get enough perks to sweeten the awful shit, but yeah. That part sucks." He stepped closer, clasping his hands at the small of her back. "But you don't get dazzled by the things about my life that, for other women I've met, are the only draw. You see who I am and somehow love me anyway."

"Somehow?" She set a hand over his heart. "It's not a hard thing to do. And if you spend time with Phoenix, he'll love you, too. He doesn't care that you can buy him a mansion. He cares that you'll try your best to be part of his life if you're ready."

"You're keeping the money." His firm tone left no room to argue. "Even if it's an emergency savings or a college fund, I want him to have it."

"Okay. Thank you."

The edges of Zack's mouth rose at the victory. "Was that so hard?"

She landed a playful swat on his chest. With the heavy talk behind them, they could switch gears and prepare for the fun night ahead.

"Did you bring a nice dress on the trip?"

Her head cocked. "Yeah, why?"

"Put it on." Zack pressed his lips to the center of her forehead. "I'm taking you out. You left early for work, and I had band shit all day, so we didn't get a chance to sightsee. I want to show you Rome, and we're running out of time." His last five words made his stomach sink.

The downward curve of her mouth said she didn't like them either.

They'd run out of time in Phoenix on their first, perfect week together, and he hated feeling like it was happening again. And like that first time, he wanted to do all he could to make her smile and fall so hard for him that she didn't want to let go.

While Mandy got ready in her room, he put on his suit. It was jet-black and tailored to fit him perfectly. He wore a dark gray button-up shirt underneath and pulled a black silk tie from his suitcase. After lifting his collar, he used the Windsor knot his dad taught him to finish the look.

He could almost hear his dad's voice as he tightened the knot: *Every man should be able to tie a tie and throw a punch.* He was a minister and didn't condone violence, but he grew up on the south side of Chicago and ran with a rough crowd before "finding Jesus." He always used that phrase, like the dude was playing hide-and-go-seek or some shit. Gary Maine understood the darker side of the world and believed being able to protect yourself and the people you love was essential. Zack had no use for his dad's preachings but was thankful to know how to tie a tie and break a nose.

He considered calling his dad to tell him about Phoenix, but that was an in-person chat that would wait until Zack was back in Portland.

The knock made him grin. His woman was right outside, and without a doubt, she was looking hot as hell.

He gasped when he opened the door before letting out a low, appreciative whistle. Mandy looked even more stunning than he'd imagined. Her hair was up, accentuating her kissable neck, and a few loose tendrils grazed her collarbone. The silky, sleeveless black dress dipped low in front to showcase her ample cleavage, the hemline a few inches above her knees. Her long, gorgeous legs were bare to the shiny red heels on her feet.

He seized her wrist and tugged her to his chest, shutting the door behind her.

"Fuck, baby," he breathed against her mouth. "You look beautiful. Hot. All the words that mean fucking gorgeous."

She chuckled as her hand slipped around his tie, trapping it in her fist. "Ditto. For such a dirty boy, you clean up nicely."

A growling hum vibrated his chest, his cock stirring. "You haven't seen dirty yet, sweetheart. When I get you back here, you'll ache in all the best places for *days*."

His hand trailed down her back and slipped under her dress, cupping her ass. Two fingers slipped beneath her panties, and her breath hitched when he grazed the soft, puckered hole he hadn't explored yet. Later, he would. He wanted to claim every sweet entrance of her body for himself, drowning her in pleasure as he did.

A pretty shade of pink bloomed on her cheeks. "If we don't leave now, I'm going to bend over that fucking table so you can show me."

His eyes shut in bliss. Why was it so goddamn sexy when this woman said naughty things? Probably because it meant he'd slithered under her skin.

Corrupted her.

Tonight, there would be a lot more where that came from.

They left the hotel separately, rejoining outside an ivy-covered wine bar two blocks south. Rome was perfect for wanderers who chose adventure over plans and surprises over structure. Hand-in-hand, Zack led Mandy along the sidewalks filled with locals speaking their beautiful language and travelers carrying shopping bags. People sipped espresso at counters or sat at outdoor tables spooning gelato into their mouths.

He never would've considered himself romantic, but this city breathed it. Rome was all about art, love, and passion, from the majestic arches of ancient buildings to the couples stealing kisses on park benches.

There wasn't anyone else in the world he'd rather share it with than the woman beside him.

When they reached the restaurant, he held the door open for her. During the band's last tour in Italy, the guys had dinner there three nights in a row because it was the best food they'd ever had.

Inside, candlelight flickered at a few dozen tables covered in black tablecloths. The scents of garlic, basil, and freshly baked bread filled the air, making his stomach growl. Layered with the din of conversation, the lulling sounds of a violin gave the place an even fancier feel, but that didn't matter. They were there for the amazing food, and he wanted to show her he could do this—be the guy who opens doors, pulls out chairs, and plans dates that don't involve beer and peanuts.

A young man with tanned skin and dark, slicked-back hair greeted them. "Buona sera, signor y signore."

"Buona sera," they said in unison before sharing a smile. When in Rome...

He led them to a table underneath a painting of the Trevi Fountain. They were far enough from the violinist to hear each other talk, and despite Mandy looking so fucking edible, that's what Zack wanted to do more than anything. He still had a million questions.

The waiter came over, and Zack ordered a bottle of Barolo. She liked dry reds, so she'd have the best one in the country. When the waiter left, Zack shifted his leg under the table so their knees would touch. A corner of her mouth curled up.

"This is nice." She sipped from her water glass. "This trip has been overwhelming in so many ways, most of them good. It'll be strange to return to my normal life."

He shook his head, his stomach sinking at the huge fucking question mark about the future. "Please don't. I get stressed thinking about what's next and want tonight to be stress-free. Can we focus on now? Now is perfect."

When the wine was poured, Mandy swirled her glass and took a sip. Her eyes shut, and a soft moan purred in her throat.

"Speaking of perfect." She licked a stray drop of wine from her lip and took his hand. "Now *is* perfect. Thank you for bringing me here. I appreciate you showing me how it'll be if we make this work, and I promise, no more stress tonight. Just incredible wine and food, more catching up, and later... a whole lot of naked."

He grinned, lifting her hand to his lips and kissing her knuckles. "How did a dickhead like me get so fucking lucky?"

She squeezed his hand. "I was thinking the same thing, but I didn't call myself a dickhead."

They laughed, sipping their wine as the candle flickered beside the bottle, casting long shadows on the wall beneath the painting.

The waiter returned, but they'd barely glanced at their menus.

Mandy scanned hers before her gaze slid to Zack. "So many amazing choices, I can't decide. Order me your favorite thing."

He ordered two plates of cacio e pepe, a basket of fresh rosemary focaccia, and a Caprese salad to share. She wasn't leaving Rome without trying their homemade mozzarella.

They talked and laughed, finishing the bottle of wine and starting another while savoring every bite of their food. She kept making sexy little moaning sounds in her throat whenever she took the first bite of something, and he was grateful for the cloth napkin and long tablecloth concealing his hard-on.

For the last course of the incredible meal, they sipped cappuccinos and shared a plate of the best tiramisu in the city. He looked forward to tasting espresso and chocolate on her lips.

After dinner, they held hands as they walked along the Tiber River, swapping stories and stealing kisses. They'd had a few days of heavy conversations, so they stuck to the light, easy stuff—funny work anecdotes, new bands they'd discovered, and concerts they'd attended.

Her smile grew whenever he asked questions about Phoenix, a subject becoming less stressful with every detail she shared. He was thankful for anything or anyone who made her light up like that. She talked about her plan to take Phoenix to the zoo and out for ice cream for his first birthday and how she wanted to take him to Disneyland when he was a little older. She described her thirty-six-hour labor and how happy she was when the doctor put him in her arms.

For the first time that night, an unexpected pang of sadness pierced the center of Zack's chest. He stopped walking. "Who was with you when he was born?"

She turned to face him, the corners of her mouth tipped down. "My mom. Ted and his wife Ella came later."

He imagined her lying in a hospital bed, afraid and in pain. If he hadn't been such a selfish, anti-kid fuck-up, he could've been there for her. Even if he hadn't been ready to be a father, he could've helped her through it like he helped her on the plane. When Charlotte had Anna Jude, her room was filled with people who loved her, and Mandy deserved the same.

His hands slipped around her waist, pulling her closer. "I'm sorry I wasn't there to hold your hand." He kissed her before she could apologize again. They'd both made mistakes, but he hoped she felt in his kiss that he wanted to put them in the past. He touched his forehead to hers. "If you ever need me now, I'll be there. Okay?"

"You can't promise that before you've met Phoenix and decided what you can handle. But I appreciate where your heart is." She smiled, kissing him again while the city life carried on around them.

As they walked back toward the hotel, the city lights danced on the water. The scents of tomato sauce and oregano wafted onto the sidewalk from pizzerias, and people walked their dogs, enjoying the warm summer night. Zack led

Mandy to a sweets shop where he bought her a dozen chocolates from the best chocolatier in Italy and his mom's amaretto cookies, as promised.

When they exited the shop, the sounds of a street performer's accordion offered the perfect soundtrack to their stroll.

The city was magical at night, but what came next was best done indoors.

Mandy shared a fantasy on their first night together that was only possible with established trust and boundaries. Back then, it was impossible—seven days weren't enough.

But now, if she were ready... he would make her fantasy come true.

29

Mandy

They separated a block from the hotel, and Mandy went in first, waving at a few crew members before taking the elevator to the top floor. The hallway was empty, so she let herself into Zack's room, checking her hair and makeup in the mirror beside the door as she waited.

A broad smile lit up her face. The pale gray eyeshadow on her lids brought out the green flecks in her eyes, a whisper of blush accentuated her cheekbones, and the Petal Pink gloss made her lips look plump and freshly kissed. His gaze had dropped to her cleavage plenty at dinner, the appreciative flare of his pupils making her ache for his touch.

She felt beautiful, desirable, and alive in every way.

It wasn't just his influence that helped her embrace her changed body. Stepping outside her predictable routines, ignoring the toxic lies she'd been taught, and prioritizing her needs helped, too. She deserved to feel pleasure and explore her desires. A few extra pounds and some stretch marks didn't make her less worthy of touch and connection. She was through allowing her brain to concoct "reasons" to hold her back from fully living.

As she smoothed a few flyaways on the crown of her head, the click of the lock startled her. Her heart raced as she stared at the door, ready to pounce. Zack stepped inside, and once the door was shut and locked, his chest collided with hers, backing her into the wall. He looked even more handsome and dangerous in his dark suit than in his usual faded denim and leather. But with or without clothes, every inch of the man oozed sex, swagger, and power.

He dipped his head to kiss her shoulder, and his fingertips slipped beneath the strap of her dress. "Are you in the mood for something a little…" He let the strap glide down her arm. "Intense?"

She licked her lips, nodding slowly at the word. She knew what that meant. They'd never had the chance to explore the fantasy she'd shared their first night together, but she trusted him.

"Do anything you want to me." She grabbed his tie in her fist, shivers of anticipation and a dash of fear skating up her spine. "I'm all yours."

The low, growling hum in his throat said he approved of her word choice. With one swift motion, his mouth was on hers, his greedy tongue parting her lips. The other strap of her dress slipped off, and he stepped back to let the fabric pool at her feet.

She stood with her back to the wall in red lace panties and a black strapless bra working overtime to support her swollen tits.

"You're so fucking beautiful, baby." He stepped closer and kissed the tops of her breasts, making his way up her chest and settling on her neck with sensual licks and gentle nips of his teeth. "You bet your ass you're all mine." His hand slipped behind her, roughly grabbing a cheek covered in red lace.

"I want you to hurt me," she rasped. "And use me."

He seized her elbow and spun her around, her forehead pressed against the cool wall. Her heart leaped to her throat, her breath quickening. She stilled, her senses on high alert after making the request she knew damn well he'd fulfill.

A sharp smack on the ass cheek he'd grabbed made her breath catch. He followed it with one on the other side, hard enough to sting.

"Do you trust me?" His hot breath ghosted over her bare shoulder.

"Completely," she replied without a second's hesitation.

"That's my girl." He pressed a soft kiss beneath her ear, and his warm exhale made her shudder. As he moved, the stiff fabric of his suit coat was rough against her skin. "You let go, and I'll catch you."

No one else she'd been with had figured out what she liked, and it killed the vibe to spell it out. But Zack knew. He studied her reactions, looking for signs something felt good. She was certain he'd do the same with pain, trusting him to take her right to the edge without going too far.

He moved to his knees behind her, and flames licked her face. Two loud smacks landed on her ass, and she moaned at the delicious sting. A warm, blissful rush swept through her, her pulse surging in anticipation of the next strike.

"You make the sexiest fucking sounds for me." His smooth lips grazed her burning flesh, soothing the pain with gentle kisses. His mouth and breath on her ass felt so intimate and naughty her knees wobbled. "Ready to give me more?"

When the pain faded, his teeth sank into her flesh. She gasped, a stream of curses tumbling from her lips as the pain intensified. He pulled away with a biting suck that would definitely bruise. Pain throbbed in the spot. He said she'd be sore in all the best places for days, and she could already tell sitting would be unpleasant for a while.

"Will you let me in here tonight?" Zack ran his tongue up the lace-covered crack before circling her hole through the fabric.

Her fingernails scraped a trail on the wall as she focused on the sensation. They'd tried anal sex once before, in Dallas, but after his finger was inside, she was too afraid to continue. He was gentle, and it didn't hurt, but the intrusive thoughts that often kept her from trying something new bled into the moment. They made the act feel dirty and wrong. But those thoughts weren't hers; now, she was better at shutting them down to embrace new experiences.

She nodded against the wall. "Yes. I said I want you to hurt me, but please be careful there and go slow."

He stood up, the heat of his solid body against her bare back making her sigh with pleasure. "I would *never* hurt you. Not in a bad way." A hand slapped her hip, and she yelped. "I know what you can take. If I ever go too far, what do you say?"

She swallowed thickly, the ache between her legs building, spreading.

"Tell me, Mandy. Say it."

"No." Her thighs squeezed together, desperate to ease the pressure. "I say no, and you stop."

"Good girl." He stroked a knuckle along her cheek and softly kissed her temple. "You ready to play?"

Her blood simmered beneath her skin at the gentle praise and wicked taunt in his words.

"Yes," she whispered.

He grabbed the lace at her hips and tore it from her body, tossing it aside. He unhooked her bra, and his hands covered her heavy breasts, kneading the sore, swollen flesh. His teeth sank into the crook of her neck, and the rush of pleasure-pain made her grind her ass against the bulge behind his zipper.

"Look how fucking hungry you are for my cock." He thrust forward, pinning her hips to the wall and sliding his erection along her crack, teasing her with a taste of the friction she craved. "Rubbing against me like a shameless whore."

She groaned. Somehow, he knew the sinful words she dreaded in her younger years sounded like heaven on his lips. He wielded them in a way that redefined their meaning, giving them the power to stoke her desire.

"Take off my shirt." The command rolled off his tongue like erotic poetry.

She turned around, and her trembling fingers fumbled with his tie and then the buttons of his shirt, eager to expose his warm, inked skin. Her lips parted with a soft sigh when she reached the last button. She dragged the fabric over his shoulders and off, tossing it to the floor.

Her hand rose to touch his muscled chest, but he seized her wrist and spun her back around to face the wall. Fabric rustled behind her, piquing her curiosity. She glanced over her shoulder to see he'd picked up his tie from the pile on the floor.

He slapped her right hip, startling her. "Did I say you could look at me?" he growled in her ear, the sharpness in his tone making her hands shake. He pulled her wrists together at her lower back. Warm silk circled them before squeezing tight, almost too tight. "Maybe I should've blindfolded those pretty hazel eyes instead."

"No, I want to see you."

"The feeling's mutual, gorgeous." His rough fingertips stroked between her shoulder blades, tracing her spine and slipping along the crack of her ass. "Now that you're done hiding from me, I can't get enough."

Mandy grinned, warmth rising to her cheeks. She was done hiding and had never felt so free and unashamed.

He spun her around, claiming her lips before bending forward and tossing her over his shoulder as if she weighed nothing.

"You're going to throw your back out," she protested.

Two smacks landed on each ass cheek, harder than before, and she could only imagine the shade of red he'd painted there. She bit her bottom lip, breathing through the pain.

"Don't insult me, sweetheart. And if you insult yourself again, I'll make you regret it."

The ominous threat made her core clench with need.

And made her want to push him.

As he carried her into the living room, she was so wet that her arousal was probably dripping down his chest. Knowing Zack, he'd rub it into his skin and lap it off his fingers.

He set her on her feet in front of the black leather couch and left the room without a word. After a few minutes, he returned with a single glass of red wine. He sat on the cushion facing her, glass in hand.

"On your knees."

Adrenaline spiked her blood as her heart thudded against her ribcage. "Or what?"

As she'd hoped, her bratty defiance added fresh tinder to the fire raging behind his eyes.

He grabbed her jaw hard enough to bruise, tugging her face within an inch of his. "Or I'll make that ass red and purple beneath my palm, take you right to the edge with my tongue, and I won't let you come no matter how much you beg."

She wanted none of that. Except maybe the first one.

She sank to the floor and sat back on her heels. It was tricky with her hands tied behind her, but he looked pleased when she settled between his thighs, a barely-there smile pulling at the edges of his mouth.

He set down his wine, took the hair tie out of her updo, and tied it back in a low ponytail. With a knuckle to her chin, he slid his thumb across her bottom lip. "You're going to take my cock into this pretty mouth until you choke, understand?"

Unable to resist giving him another push, Mandy shook her head. "Only filthy sluts do things like that." She lifted a challenging eyebrow. "Are you going to make me?"

A low, rabid growl rumbled in his chest, his cool green eyes darkening into deep emerald pools. His fist clamped around her throat, and he yanked her up on her knees. "You are a filthy slut, and you'll take my cock anywhere I want to fucking put it. Do you understand me?"

She swallowed beneath his hold as she nodded her head, her inner thighs growing slick. Her hands shook in their binds as he released her throat. She knew he'd never hurt her, but the whiff of danger turned her insides molten. Instead of wondering what was wrong with her for feeling that way, she clicked off her brain to enjoy the ride.

"You're shaking, baby." Zack reached into his lap, unbuckled, unbuttoned, and unzipped until she was staring at black cotton boxers. "Are you scared?"

"Yes," she answered quickly.

"Smart girl." He reached beneath his waistband and pulled out his impressive erection, the head pink, swollen, and begging for her mouth. "You should be."

He wrapped her hair around his fist, pulling her face into his lap. Heat from the smooth skin of his shaft warmed her cheeks, and the spicy, masculine scent of his cologne surrounded her. She was desperate to bathe the sensitive flesh with her tongue but couldn't resist giving him one last shove.

His thick fingers curled around his cock, giving it two long strokes. "Open your mouth."

She kept her lips tightly pursed and shook her head.

He slapped her cheek with the rigid crown, making her gasp. "Do you really want to test my patience?"

Yes. Yes, she did.

When she still didn't open, he slapped the other cheek with the head of his cock, harder than the first. When she didn't budge, he hauled her onto his lap and spanked her so hard a shuddered cry escaped her lips. It hurt like a bastard, and her eyes watered, but she didn't tell him to stop. He paused as if waiting for it, but she kept her lips sealed.

Once the pain receded, pleasure rolled in. Her tense muscles relaxed, and she'd never been so at peace and agonizingly turned on all at once.

"I wish you could see how pretty your skin looks. You made me paint it red because you can't play nice." His fierce slaps moved to the backs of her thighs, each strike making her flinch. A scream clawed at her throat as the agony climbed higher and higher. "Are you ready to behave?"

The swollen crown of his cock prodded the side of her left breast, leaving a slippery trail of precum on her skin. There was no question of how badly he wanted her, and it was a heady sensation like nothing else.

"Yes," she whispered. A rough finger dragged along the wetness between her legs, and she moaned, writhing against his touch, begging for more. "I promise. I'll do anything."

His dark, rumbling chuckle shook their bodies. "You think I'll give you what you want when you don't do what you're told?"

The finger circled her entrance, and the tip slipped inside, stilling, teasing as her inner walls clenched around it with need. Two fingers pushed inside, and she whimpered—a pathetic sound that made him chuckle again like he was enjoying every second of driving her fucking crazy.

His fingers withdrew and moved to her backside, circling the tight ring of muscle. "You don't get to come until my cock is buried here." His finger was lubed with her arousal, and he slid inside to the first knuckle and withdrew. "I get to be the first and last one to do it because I'm going to wreck you, Mandy." His tongue circled the shell of her ear before grazing it with his teeth. "The thought of fucking someone else will make you sick because no one will ever know your body—fucking *worship it*—like I do."

As if to prove his point, his other hand slipped between their bodies and found her clit. He pinched it between his fingers, and she groaned like a wounded animal.

He hummed low in his throat, pleased with her reaction. "No one else can draw those sexy sounds from your lips like I can."

Zack was right. She was so consumed by desire that she let her body sing for him and only him.

He released the sensitive nub, two fingers slipping inside her without warning. "No one else will ever touch this pussy again because it's mine." He slowly fucked her with his fingers before settling on her G-spot and stroking with quick pulses, tugging her to the edge.

She groaned again when his fingers were gone, the sound low and desperate.

He set her back on her knees. "Now it's time for you to take what's yours."

Her bound hands tingled with pins and needles, but the almost painful sensation only added to the intensity. He picked up the glass and took a long sip, watching her from above the rim. He leaned forward and pressed his lips to hers before angling his head and letting a mouthful of wine flood her tongue.

He seized her throat, his grip tightening. "Swallow." It was a struggle to swallow past his hold, but when she did, his lips curled up at the edges like he was pleased. "Now that you have the practice, wrap your lips around my cock and get ready to swallow again."

The thought of tasting him made her clit throb. She flicked the tip of her tongue along the extra sensitive spot on the underside of the head. He hissed through his teeth at the contact, his eyelids heavy with lust.

Her trapped hands twitched with the need to grip and stroke him, but she focused on the sensation of his silky flesh slipping between her lips. She took the crown into her mouth and gave it a gentle suck before releasing it with a wet pop. His taste mingled with the wine on her tongue, ramping up her desire.

His chest rose and fell with heavy breaths while he watched her explore the most intimate parts of his body with her mouth. "That's it. You're doing such a good job," he cooed.

The contrast with the gruff, demanding tyrant he was moments before made her head swim. And made her thighs squeeze together with the need to get fucked and used.

He took another sip of wine, sitting back on the couch like an arrogant king on a throne. "If it's too much, tap my ankle. Understand?" He set the glass on the coffee table.

She tensed, knowing what that meant—she'd be unable to speak because her mouth would be full.

"Yes." She sat back on her heels and waited, her heart galloping in her chest.

Zack wrapped her hair in his fist again, gripping his cock in the other. He pulled her face to his lap and pushed the flared crown past her lips. He released his shaft and lifted his hips off the couch, sliding his erection into her mouth until he hit the back of her throat.

"Fucking hell," he breathed. "You like swallowing my cock?"

She nodded enthusiastically, and whatever he saw in her eyes made him grin. With another snap of his hips, she choked and nearly gagged, but she relaxed her throat as he fucked it without mercy.

Tears sprung to her eyes, and she breathed through her nose while he took what he wanted—what she'd demanded he take. Being controlled by force was intense and a little frightening, even with the trust they'd established.

But once she surrendered instead of fighting it, something inside her shifted.

Her mind blanked, and all that existed were their connected bodies and the gravelly, animalistic sounds he made as his climax neared. Again, she refused to question why she loved every second.

As the salt of his precum coated her tongue, it took all her restraint not to jump into his lap and ride him hard.

Zack released his grip on her hair, and she pulled air deeply into her lungs. "You're doing so well, baby." He wiped the tears of bliss sliding down her cheeks with his thumbs. "You're so pretty when you let me use you like a whore."

Hearing that shouldn't make her want him more. He did use women—a fact she didn't like but tried not to judge. The women used him right back, as she'd planned to do the night they met. But he wasn't using Mandy, not really. He knew damn well she loved this game as much as he did. If she said no right now, it would end. If he thought she wasn't enjoying herself, it would end. He knew what she wanted and needed, and she trusted him to give it to her.

Saliva dripped to her chin, and she wiped it off on his knee. "Is that the best you can do?"

His gaze narrowed in a glare as his lips twitched. "Challenge accepted."

He grabbed her face in both hands, getting to his feet and feeding her his cock. His pants and boxers brushed against her knees as they fell to the floor. She breathed through her nose and swiped the underside of his shaft with the flat of her tongue as he slid to the back of her throat.

His hips snapped forward as he fucked her mouth with quick, deep, unrelenting thrusts. "How's that? Hard enough for you?"

She moaned around his length, saliva sliding off her chin and onto her chest.

"I'm going to fill that pretty throat, and if you spill a single drop, you'll do it all over again until you get it right."

His fingers dug into her scalp, and she savored the bite of pain.

"Fuck!" With a grunt, his seed burst on her tongue and slipped down her throat. Her jaw ached around his girth, but it was exhilarating not to be treated like an innocent, fragile thing.

The experience was a thousand times better than in her fantasies.

When he was finished, his hand wrapped around her throat, tighter than before. "Swallow for me, baby."

Mandy sat back on her heels and tipped her chin up so he could watch her throat jump beneath his palm. With a satisfied sigh, he released her, collapsing backward on the couch, his breathing ragged and face glistening with sweat.

"Jesus Fucking Christ, woman." He wiped his forehead with the back of his wrist. "You're a goddamn treasure."

She added 'blasphemy' to her internal, running list of things that had no right to be as hot as they were. Things she never knew turned her on until this cocky rockstar walked into her life.

He leaned forward, touching a knuckle to her chin. "Do you have any fucking idea what you're doing to me?"

"I'm more interested in what you're about to do to me."

Together, they smiled, their lust-drunk gazes locked.

"Turn around," he said, his tone gentle.

When she did, he untied her numb hands. She clenched her fists and released them a few times to get the blood moving again.

"You okay?" he asked, stroking her hip.

She turned to face him, bending at the waist to kiss his cheek. "Never better." It was the truth. And they were just getting started.

"Good. Bend over the arm of the couch and wait for me."

He walked to the bedroom while she got into position, waiting while her mind buzzed with the possibilities. Since her ass was in the air, she wouldn't be an anal virgin much longer. The thought was thrilling, but fear of the pain and backing out again if it still felt like the wrong kind of dirty remained.

"Eyes down," he ordered. She obeyed, staring at the cushion below her face. "Good girl. Looks like you're not in the mood to argue anymore, hmm?"

"No more arguing," she promised, "but I'm not opposed to begging if that's what it takes to get you to fuck me."

"And you say I'm the one who needs to learn patience."

A sharp swat on her backside made her yelp with surprise. The white-hot pain was more intense than what his hand had done. When her head turned, he forced it back down with his palm.

"It's a riding crop, sweetheart," he explained. Something smooth and cool glided over her spine, making her shiver. "I paid a visit to the adult shop up the street and got a few toys I think you'll like." Six quick snaps cracked in the air, and fire licked the backs of her thighs.

"Fuck, Zack," she panted.

"Mmm... I don't know what I love more—hearing you say my name or hearing you say 'fuck'." His fingertips raked over the small of her back in gentle strokes. "Still doing okay?"

"Yes." She nodded, her elbows braced against the couch cushion. "More."

Six more slaps stung the already tender flesh of her ass, and she moaned, slipping a hand between her legs and cupping her aching pussy.

"Dirty fucking girl." The cool leather ran along the crack of her ass and slapped her fingers. "I thought I made it clear this pussy is mine. Don't you fucking touch it again without permission."

She whimpered and shamelessly ground herself against the toy, desperate for relief. It lifted from her skin before slapping against the wet flesh.

Mandy bit back a scream as he did it again, harder, flames igniting between her legs and spreading like wildfire. "Fucking hell!"

She sensed his movements behind her and stilled, waiting. He pressed a kiss to the wetness between her legs as her flesh screamed from the delicious burn. Sweat beaded at her temples, her head tipping back as glorious waves of pleasure rolled through her.

"There's that word again, naughty girl." His breath on her wet slit was almost too much to take. "And after making me come so hard I was afraid I'd pass out, you deserve a reward." That's all the warning she had before his warm, wet tongue slipped inside her.

She bit down on her forearm, muffling the savage roar climbing up her throat. He continued licking and sucking the sensitive flesh between her legs until she was about to burst. He pulled away, and she groaned in protest. Something nudged inside her, but it was colder and more rigid than his cock.

She froze, the muscles in her thighs taut. "What is that?"

"Another treat from the adult shop."

Something buzzed behind her, and whatever he held to her pussy slid inside in one smooth push. She moaned at the feeling that was both a relief and a torturous tease. He adjusted the toy, and the vibration hit her clit. Her muscles tensed before the pleasure took hold.

Zack leaned forward, brushing her hair off her neck and whispering, "Does that feel good?"

"Fuck yes. Don't you dare stop."

He kissed the center of her back. "Who's the bossy one now?"

A wet finger circled the tight ring of her backside. When he slipped half his finger inside, she focused on the vibrations working her clit instead of the stinging burn of his invasion.

She glanced over her shoulder. "I like that."

"Good." His finger sank a little deeper. "Relax and let me in. I won't hurt you."

Mandy took a few deep breaths, letting her body relax. Soon, two lubed fingers were inside her, twisting and sliding as they opened her up. It was further than they got before, and she breathed through it, letting the sensations crowd out all thoughts. It didn't feel wrong this time, but it felt dirty in all the best ways.

"Lie on your back," he said, his tone as gentle as a caress. The toy and his fingers withdrew.

She lay across the couch cushions, the top of her head brushing the armrest. Zack got to his knees between her spread legs and slipped a large pillow underneath her ass. He pressed the toy to the slick entrance of her pussy and pushed it inside before the buzzing returned. She was so wet it moved in slow, torturous slides with no resistance.

"I think you can handle a little more." He clicked a button at the top. The vibrations on her clit intensified, and within seconds, tingly warmth spread through her core. She clung to his sturdy shoulders, her fingernails digging into his skin. Right when she was about to come, he pulled out the toy.

"No!" she gritted out. "More. *Please.* I was so close."

"What did I tell you?" He landed another sharp slap on the side of her hip, startling her and making her more desperate all at once.

"Remind me." Irritation spiked her tone.

He chuckled darkly as he drizzled lube on his palm and stroked his shaft with slow, smooth slides. "You don't get to come until I'm buried inside this virgin ass. And guess what...?"

She held her breath, waiting, her need to climax almost unbearable.

The head of his cock nudged at the hole he'd prepared at the same time the toy slid back inside her pussy.

"You're ready for me." He pushed inside past the tip, and she sucked in a stuttered breath.

Her tight ring of muscle gradually stretched to accommodate his girth. As the burning sensation almost became too much, the vibration attacked her clit, stimulating the sensitive bead until she was seconds from unraveling. Another inch slipped inside her ass, and she tensed.

"Shh..." He stroked her hip. "Just relax." He leaned back and pulled the toy out a few inches before slowly fucking her with it. "Focus on the toy and let me in."

She shut out the burn and zeroed in on the toy rubbing her G-spot. "That feels so good."

His hips surged forward, and once seated to the hilt, his balls slapped her skin. His feral, satisfied groan in her ear and the sensation of being thoroughly, blissfully filled for the first time tipped her over the edge.

She cried out as she came, a fiery rush of pleasure exploding through her as her inner muscles clenched and fluttered around the toy. The only thing that would've made it better was if he'd had two cocks.

"Fucking hell, baby." His voice was deep and gritty. "I'm not going to last after that."

He sank back inside, driving into her in smooth strokes that still burned a little, but the lingering bliss of her climax overrode the discomfort. "I've never fucked anyone bare here either. I was saving it for you, and I didn't even know it."

How something and someone so filthy could be so sweet would never stop surprising her.

"I waited for you, too," she said, her breath stilted by his movements. His hips and quads bumped against her sore spots, but it only heightened the pleasure coursing through her. "You've made me feel more than anyone ever has or ever could."

That sentiment applied to both bad feelings and good. No one ever had the power to break her heart like he did. No one else had ever made her come so hard that the world blurred. And she'd never experienced love like this. Their son owned half of her heart, and in a few intense and beautiful days, Zack had reclaimed the rest.

His strokes quickened, and he roared as he filled her ass with his release. Rough fingertips bit into her hips, still tender from his slaps. After one final thrust, his weight pressed her into the cushions as all the tension left his body. Breathing wasn't easy, but she wasn't ready for the moment to end.

"Fuck, you're perfect." He kissed the crown of her head before he pulled out and got to his feet. He offered a hand, helping her up. A wave of dizziness struck, and she gripped the back of the couch.

"You okay?" A crease of concern dipped between his brows.

She nodded, miles beyond *okay*. "My legs are rubber, and my head's swimming, but yeah. That was amazing."

He laughed. "That's one word for it." With an arm behind her knees, he scooped her off her feet. Wetness slid out of her backside, but she didn't care. She was floating in a sex-drunk haze, and nothing fazed her.

Zack carried her into the shower and washed every inch of her body, tenderly rubbing soap into her skin and rinsing it off under the rushing water. He washed her hair and raked conditioner through the strands while peppering kisses everywhere he could reach. She'd never felt so loved and treasured.

She cupped his damp face in her hands. "I love you, Zachary Maine." Steam surrounded them like clouds, which fit since the sensation overwhelming her felt like floating.

"I love you too, baby." His fingertips drifted across the skin of her bare shoulder. "Thank you for trusting me."

She kissed him, warm flutters stirring in her chest. "Thank you for being someone I can trust. And for knowing what I want and need even when I don't."

After they'd dried off with the hotel's fluffy white towels, he picked her up again like a newlywed headed for a doorway. He was probably trying to prove a point after her "don't throw out your back" comment, but regardless, it was hot and pretty damn romantic.

He set her on the bed, lay beside her, and held her close. With a deeply contented sigh, her entire body relaxed in his arms.

They kissed for what seemed like hours. It was gentle, slow, and soothing after their intense experience.

In between kisses, he told her again that he loved her. She was the first and only woman who'd heard those words from his lips, and if Mandy had her way, she'd be the last. He wasn't the marrying type, and she could live with that, but if things went well when he met their son, they could build a life together that would work for everyone. It may not end up looking traditional, but neither were they.

Still, a stubborn voice in her head insisted he was never meant to be a father. But she'd seen his changes firsthand and had faith that he could rise to the role if he wanted to.

If he changed his mind about trying, this would all end. And it would hurt even worse than their first breakup because her heart would break for Phoenix, too.

As with so many things in their relationship, only time would tell. Everything would change when he met Phoenix, for better or worse. In the meantime, she'd focus on the present, savoring every beautiful moment with Zack as if it were the last.

30

Zack

Their final days in Rome went by in an incredible, dizzying blur of music, sex, and adventure. Zack got to share the sights of the most beautiful city in the world with the most beautiful woman in the world, and he'd never been happier. They worked hard on show and event days, and he loved seeing Mandy's wild, curious side come out when her task list was done and it was time to play hard.

Now, the wild, carefree time was over.

Phoenix had been in Paris for two days, but Mandy's mom had scheduled a bunch of touristy shit for the three of them during Mandy's time off. He'd hardly seen her and hadn't had a chance to meet Phoenix.

Until now.

As he paced the floor outside Mandy's Paris suite, Zack got plenty of odd looks from other guests and hotel staff. He didn't give a shit. The only two people whose opinions mattered to him were waiting inside. It would take a lot of courage to knock on that door because there was no going back once he did.

He was going to meet his son. And unfortunately, Mandy's mother—the woman who helped instill shame and insecurities in the woman he loved. He'd prefer to avoid her altogether, but she was important to Mandy, so he'd act like a gentleman for her sake.

He wiped his sweaty palms on his jeans. Neither introduction would be easy, but he had to suck it up, knock, and get on with it. Hopefully, it would only get easier once the initial terror had passed.

He took a few deep breaths and knocked softly in case Phoenix was asleep. A few seconds later, Mandy opened the door with a sweet smile like the one she had when she woke up in his arms that morning.

"Hey, you," she whispered, "come in."

Zack walked inside her suite and spotted the playpen beside the bed. His heart thundered in his chest as he looked around. "Where's your mom?"

She shut the door with a light click. "Grabbing coffee and croissants. I thought it would be easier for you to meet him without that added stress."

He released his held breath, appreciating how well she knew him. "Thank you." He turned toward the mesh walls of the playpen and inched closer. A pale blue sock covered a tiny foot in the corner.

"He's asleep, but he'll be up any second." She took Zack's hand and laced their fingers together. "Come here."

She guided him toward the playpen until they were standing beside it.

A lump lodged in his throat at the sight of the baby sleeping inside. Like in the photo, he had Zack's broad nose and square chin. He had Mandy's silky brown hair, long eyelashes, and the same smooth, pale skin that made her look like an angel. The sleeping face blurred as tears stung Zack's eyes.

A heaviness settled into his chest, the weight of everything this meant striking at once.

I'm a father.

He thought of all the ways his dad had supported him—offering advice and encouragement, cheering the loudest at his first gig, and giving him swift kicks in the ass when needed. Could Zack be that person for Phoenix?

This monumental responsibility might be the start of a new beginning or end in disaster.

What if his own son hated him? What if Phoenix was so used to the way his life is that he doesn't want someone new butting in? What if Zack wasn't good enough at being a parent, and Mandy pulled away before cutting him out of their lives again?

She kissed his cheek, snapping him out of it. "He's going to love you like I do," she said, as if reading his mind. "I know you can do this. Take your time."

Phoenix's eyes slid open and landed on her.

"Hey, Little Bug. I want you to meet someone."

Zack's chest tightened, and his hands shook. This was it. If he fucked this up, he'd lose them both. She squeezed his hand before letting go.

Mandy bent at the waist, scooping the baby into her arms. "Phoenix, this is your... This is Zack." She stroked the baby's hand as he clung to her. "Can you say hi?" She waved, and his tiny hand lifted, copying her motion. "Since he learned that, he waves at every human, bird, and dog that passes our window at home."

Zack offered a shaky grin. "Hi, Phoenix." He reached into his pocket and pulled out the small stuffed frog he'd bought in the hotel gift shop. "Do you like frogs?"

She smiled as he held out the toy, and Phoenix took it. "Thank you, Zack. That was sweet."

He shrugged. "It was only twenty bucks."

"The money doesn't matter, but the thought does." She touched his cheek while Phoenix stuck the toy frog in his mouth and chewed on its face. "Do you want to hold him?"

Zack's hands still trembled, but he remembered how scary it was to hold Anna Jude at first. After a while, it got easier. He'd even held her a few times when he hung out with Tyler and Charlotte after shows, knowing he'd need the practice.

He nodded and held out his hands.

"He's not as fragile as Anna Jude, but he can land a sneak head butt or slap if you aren't quick." She laughed as she passed Phoenix to Zack. "Babies are a trip."

As he held Phoenix to his chest, two curious green eyes stared up at him like they were trying to figure out who the hell he was. If he hadn't been around a lot of men aside from Mandy's dad and Ted, his confusion made sense.

"Nice to meet you, little dude." Zack smiled as the mutual staring contest continued. Phoenix was more alert than Anna Jude, like he was actually listening and trying to understand what they said. "Your mom told me a lot of nice things about you. I'm with you; carrots are bullsh—" He caught himself, and she laughed. "Gross. Carrots are gross."

Mandy wiped a single tear from her cheek, her smile bright and beautiful. "I've imagined this moment so much, I can't believe it's real. It's strange seeing you together."

"Good strange?"

"The best kind." She kissed his cheek as the door swung open. Her eyes widened before she spun around. "Mom, I said to give us an hour."

A woman with dark blonde hair streaked with gray and a pissy scowl stopped a few feet inside the door. She held a Styrofoam coffee cup and a small brown paper bag, sizing him up with a look that said she didn't approve of what she found.

"So, you're the mysterious Zack." She said his name like it was bitter on her tongue. "I'm Jill. And that little boy and his mother mean more to me than anything."

Phoenix's little hand waved in the air, his other hand clutching the frog.

"Mom, be nice." Mandy took the coffee and paper bag, setting them on the small table by the window. "Yes, this is Zack, but there's no mystery. He's smart, successful, and good to me."

That made him smile. It was nice to know she was on his side. It was already obvious her mother might never get there.

This rude witch is important to them. Play nice.

He moved Phoenix to his hip and held out his hand. "It's nice to meet you, Jill."

She stared at his hand like it was diseased before crossing her arms over her chest. "Have you ever held a baby before today? Or changed a diaper?"

Mandy's eyes rolled as she sat at the table. "I told you not to come up yet because they deserved some time to get to know each other before your third degree."

Phoenix made fussy noises, probably because of the sudden tension in the room. His nose scrunched, and his bottom lip curled like Anna Jude's before she cried. If that happened, it would only give her mom more fuel to think he was a clueless loser.

Mandy said he loved to laugh. Zack sucked his cheeks in like a fish, crossing his eyes to make it extra ridiculous. Phoenix let out a loud, unrestrained burst of laughter that shook his little body. She was right—the kid had an amazing laugh. They both smiled at their private joke while the women argued.

Phoenix's smile reminded him of his dad—their round cheeks even puffed out the same way. Reality sunk in a little deeper. This tiny person was a link between his world and hers that could never be undone. To his surprise, that was more comforting than scary.

As Mandy listened to her mom rattle on about the importance of appropriate role models in a kid's life, she rubbed her temples, her shoulders hunched forward. He wanted to gag and throw up a middle finger, but that wouldn't fly here.

"One of my best friends just had a baby," he said, answering Jill's question while interrupting the argument that accomplished nothing but exhausting Mandy. "And I've held her a few times and fed her. No diapers yet, but I have a strong stomach, and I'm willing to learn."

Mandy pulled a croissant from the bag and took a bite, chasing it with a sip of coffee. She ripped the pastry in half and offered him a piece.

"Thanks, baby." He bit into it, a few crumbs falling to his shirt. Phoenix grabbed a large crumb and stuck it in his mouth. "Shit. Err, crap. Can he eat that?"

Mandy's lips quirked. "It's fine. You want a piece, sweetie?" She offered the baby a chunk of her pastry, but he snatched Zack's instead and jammed it in his mouth. She laughed, pulling it out and tearing off a smaller piece to replace it with.

"I'll take the one he drooled on." She swapped her dry one for his.

"So, you still curse, I see." The wrinkles framing Jill's mouth deepened. "And you call my daughter 'baby' after knowing her for... what? A couple weeks total?"

"Mom!" Mandy's stern tone made Phoenix whimper. She turned to him, rubbing his back as Zack held him tighter. "It's okay, sweetheart. Mommy's not mad. Granny's just being a hard ass."

Jill scoffed. "So now you have my daughter using foul language? What other delightful things have you influenced her with?"

Mandy's head whipped toward her mother. "Stop it." Forced calm chilled her words, but her face flushed red. "Do you honestly think I'm so weak I'd let a man dictate who I am? If so, pot, meet kettle."

"Mandy Marie! Don't you dare disrespect me in front of this degenerate!"

"*Degenerate*?!" Zack's face heated as he fought the urge to lash out. "You don't even know me, lady. Mandy's willing to give me a shot at getting to know Phoenix. You don't have to like me for that to happen, but we should try to get along for their sake."

He'd never met a girl's parents before, and now he knew he wasn't missing out. Things were going great before she butted into their time together. He'd never have another chance to make a first impression on Phoenix, and she was ruining it.

Phoenix fussed again, squirming in his arms. Zack swayed and bounced while rubbing his back. It worked on Anna Jude, and fortunately, it worked on Phoenix, too. Soon, he settled, resting his warm cheek on Zack's chest, directly over his heart.

The lump returned to his throat, and when his gaze slid to Mandy, her damp eyes glistened as she smiled. They deserved this moment, and he'd ignore the invader to hold on to it a little longer. He set down the rest of his croissant and took the chair by the window.

He kept rubbing Phoenix's back while he chomped on the toy frog again. His jaw slowed as his tiny eyelids fluttered and shut, the weight of his small body pressing into Zack's chest.

As Phoenix fell asleep in his arms, Zack felt something inside him rearrange. The puddle of drool collecting on his shirt didn't bother him. Jill's homicidal glare lasering his face didn't faze him either.

If Mandy and Phoenix were happy and safe, nothing else mattered.

She bent over and kissed Zack's forehead. "You're doing great."

Jill sighed. "Fine. He isn't completely useless." She turned to him. "Am I correct in assuming you'll start helping them financially so my daughter can stop stressing about bills?"

Mandy responded before he could. "He gave me eighty thousand dollars."

Jill released a shuddered breath, her eyes bulging.

That's right, lady. Want some salt and pepper for the foot you just stuck in your mouth?

"And more will come every month until Phoenix turns eighteen," Mandy continued. It wasn't her mom's business, but he suspected she said it to shut her up. And make her eat her words a little.

Jill sat at the edge of the bed. "That's something. You live in Portland, correct?"

He nodded as Phoenix stirred and grabbed a fistful of Zack's shirt in his chubby, wet hand. "Yeah, we'll figure out what this will look like after the tour."

"What it will look like?" Jill sputtered, her eyes darting to Mandy and back to him. "You either move to Denver, or you lose them. Isn't that the long and short of it?"

"Mom, stop." Mandy's jaw clenched, her calm tone faltering. "Now that I'm not at the club, I can figure out my next steps."

Jill's eyes snapped wide. "I hope you aren't suggesting you might move with my grandson to Oregon! Mandy, be serious. You hardly know this man."

Zack took a deep breath to calm the fire racing through his blood. "She's smart enough to figure out what she wants to do. You should trust her to make the best decision for her and *our* son."

It was petty, but he wanted to remind her Phoenix wasn't only Mandy's. Jill needed to get that through her thick, judgmental skull and keep the fuck out of it.

"And she's my daughter. She's smart, but I see how sucked in she was by you the first time. I'd hoped she'd let it go, but clearly, you've orchestrated this 'job' of hers to yank her back into your life."

Fuck.

So, Jill was rude and critical but not stupid. He didn't want to keep lying to Mandy, but now he was even more determined to keep the truth hidden. If Jill found out, she'd have another weapon in her fight to break them apart.

"I love him," Mandy said, fortunately evading her mother's accusation. "I'm thirty-two years old and capable of making my own decisions. I appreciate you flying here with Phoenix and look forward to spending time with you. But right now, if you're going to be rude to Zack, you need to leave. Take a walk or go to your room until you cool off."

That last line sounded like a mom scolding a misbehaving kid, and he snickered. Fitting since Jill was acting like one.

"I'm not going anywhere." Jill shook her head, her gaze flicking to Zack. "Your father's a minister, correct?"

He nodded, his chin brushing against the soft hair on Phoenix's head.

"What does he think of how you live? Does he know you got my daughter pregnant? Does he know she was so disgusted by your lifestyle that she kept her son away from you all this time?"

Her words were like a fist to the chest. He hated that she was right, but so was Mandy for keeping Phoenix a secret for as long as she did. Instead of beating himself up or letting Jill take another turn, he was determined to focus on the future.

"Mom, that's enough!" Mandy got to her feet and opened the door. "You need to go. I'll find you later, but they deserve time together without you ruining it."

Phoenix's head rose, and his bottom lip curled out. Tears filled his eyes, and he started to cry. Zack stood, swaying as he wiped tears from Phoenix's cheeks. Anger simmered in his gut to see this helpless, innocent person upset by his grandmother's raging nonsense.

"It's okay, buddy," he said. "The angry lady's leaving."

Jill strode toward the door before turning to her daughter. "He won't stick around. When he gets bored, he'll find some younger, prettier woman with fewer complications and leave you and Phoenix in the dust."

He couldn't hold his tongue after that. "Stop right there. Say whatever the hell you want about me, but don't you dare talk to her like that. There's no one prettier than her, and you're an asshole for saying otherwise."

Jill's face and neck flushed red, her homicidal glare returning. Before she spouted any more bullshit, he continued.

"I love your daughter. I won't stand here and listen to you insult her or judge me when you haven't even tried to get to know me. Hell, you wouldn't even shake my hand like a decent human being. You need to leave. Now."

Jill's eyes slid to Mandy, her head shaking. "You hear how he talks to your mother? See his temper? What's he going to say to Phoenix if he breaks or spills something? You cannot be with this man or trust him with your son."

"Mom—"

"He's my son too, whether you like it or not." He cut Mandy off before she could respond to such an insulting fucking dig. Phoenix stopped crying, his eyes rimmed with pink as he stared up at Zack. "I would *never* hurt either of them. Yeah, my dad's a minister, and he taught me people earn respect. They aren't entitled to it. You made up your mind about me before you even walked in here. I've made a hell of a lot of mistakes, but I'm loyal to people I love and don't let *anyone* talk to them or about them like you did to Mandy. So don't shovel it if you can't take it."

Jill's mouth hung open like a dead bullfrog's.

"Mom, I know how much you love me and Phoenix," Mandy said with an exhausted sigh, "and I appreciate all the help you've given me. Without you, I don't know how I would've made it through the past year." She swung the door wider. "But he's right. You need to leave now."

The beaming smile Mandy wore when he first arrived had vanished. They'd probably had these fights before, and he'd be damned if she ever had to deal with her mom's bullshit alone again.

When Jill stomped out, Mandy shut the door behind her and stared at it, her shoulders taut with tension.

"Sorry I called your mom an asshole."

She huffed a laugh, turning around and wiping a tear from her cheek. "She was being an asshole. Thank you for defending me, but I wish you didn't have to."

He held out his free arm. "Come here."

She hugged his waist and planted a kiss on Phoenix's cheek. "It wasn't supposed to be like this. I wanted today to be perfect. For all of us."

"Hey." He bumped his hip against hers as Phoenix babbled, waving his frog in the air. "It's another thing we'll get right the second time. Let's say our second chance at a perfect day starts... Now."

She chuckled softly, the sadness in her expression starting to lift. "I'm in. I can't believe I have my two favorite guys in the same place. I won't let anyone spoil that."

An idea occurred to him that might make her feel better.

"Why don't we get the tour photographer to snap some shots of us like last time?" He laughed as Phoenix opened his mouth in a wide yawn. It made Zack yawn, too, and he had to yank his head back when Phoenix tried to jam the toy frog into his mouth. She was right—babies are a trip. "He's a friend, so I'll make sure he keeps it from Shane and your crew."

Her lips curled up. "I would love that."

"Good. I'll go change into a shirt with less drool on it."

She took Phoenix and sat on the bed with him in her lap. As Zack headed for the door, Phoenix tossed the toy frog across the room.

Zack furrowed his brow. "Doesn't he like it?"

"He throws everything." She shrugged. "It's his latest quirk."

Zack picked up the toy and handed it back to Phoenix. His little laugh filled the room as he tossed it again. It landed on the dresser, a front leg dangling over the edge. It was at least eight feet away—the kid had a hell of a throwing arm.

"Usually, I correct him, but I'll make an exception." Her bright smile was back in full force. He'd seen her happy before, but there was an extra glow with Phoenix around, making her even more beautiful. "He's playing with you."

"Like fetch?" Zack got the toy and stuck it back into Phoenix's tiny, outstretched palm. A second later, it struck the back of the door with a loud smack before sliding to the floor. "I guess that makes me the dog."

Phoenix folded forward as he laughed, his round cheeks turning pink. He was probably laughing at the sound of the frog hitting the door, but his timing made it seem like he got the joke. They laughed with him, making Phoenix laugh even harder while his little arms waved in the air.

This was how it was supposed to be.

Zack was grateful for another chance at a do-over. He wasn't stupid enough to think everything about being a parent would be this fun and easy, but as long as moments like this broke up the tough parts, he could do it.

31

Mandy

While Shane sat at the desk in his suite, rattling off her tasks for the day, Mandy grinned like a lovesick fool as she jotted them down. Her heart still glowed from yesterday's (mostly) successful first meeting between Zack and Phoenix. Seeing them together, connecting and becoming more comfortable with each other, was better than she'd ever imagined in her wishful daydreams.

Even remembering the awful things her mom said didn't burst her bubble. Only five days remained before they headed home to Denver, and she intended to help everyone get on a better track before then. Even if forced cordiality were all her mom could manage, it would be an improvement.

"My seventeenth wedding anniversary is tomorrow," Shane said.

Mandy's pen moved across the page before her chin tipped up. "Congratulations."

"Thank you. I don't know how she's put up with me all these years, but I'm a grateful and lucky man. Please have flowers delivered to her office around noon."

"What are her favorites?"

He shrugged as an incoming call buzzed on the phone in his palm. He checked the number before slipping the phone into his pocket. "I should know that, but sadly, I'm clueless. Send whatever flowers you like. I'm sure she'll love them. And have them write something sweet on the card. I'm not terribly romantic, so whatever you come up with is fine."

Mandy would be hurt if a guy who'd been with her that long couldn't name her favorite flowers or think of a sweet sentiment for an anniversary, but every woman and relationship was different. It was unfair to judge.

"Got it. Anything else?"

He rifled through his briefcase and handed her a stack of paperwork to fax and a list of phone calls and messages to return. "That's everything until the usual pre-show prep, which you're incredible at. Cassie and the guys have nothing but praise."

She smiled, her cheeks warming at the compliment. "That's nice to hear. I've enjoyed working with all of you as well. And I promise your wife will *love* her bouquet."

"I'm sure she will." He clicked his briefcase shut and stood. "Enjoy the rest of the afternoon."

She intended to.

After two rounds of morning sex, Zack had invited her to join him and his friends for lunch at a café a few blocks from the hotel. They all wanted to meet Phoenix, and she looked forward to getting to know them better.

Once she'd completed her tasks for Shane, she returned to the hotel and knocked twice before opening her mom's door.

"Are you alone?" her mom asked as Mandy stepped inside.

"Interesting greeting." Mandy waved at her son sitting on a blanket, stacking plastic blocks. "Hello to you, little one."

"I just wondered if—"

"No, Mom. Zack's not here, but I'm joining him and his friends for lunch so they can meet Phoenix. You're welcome to come too if you can be nice."

A burst of air escaped her lips. "I'll pass."

"I figured. You've wanted to hit that art museum up the street anyway, which would be more fun without a baby." She packed enough diapers, formula, wipes, and toys for a few hours into the diaper bag. "Want me to bring you something back?"

"No, thank you."

Her mom wiped invisible crumbs off the table and dropped them into the trash. Her set jaw and stiff movements meant she still wasn't ready to drop her lousy attitude. Mandy didn't have the time or patience to deal with it, so she strapped Phoenix into his stroller, stuffed the diaper bag into the basket beneath it, and headed for the door.

"We'll see you later, then. I need to leave for work at four-thirty."

"I'll be here." Her mom snatched a blue onesie from the bed and folded it neatly, her gaze never meeting Mandy's.

The snub stung, but hopefully, the time apart would do everyone good. With a quick goodbye, she walked Phoenix to the elevator and out of the hotel.

The weather was perfect for a stroll—the sun was high and bright, the sky cloudless and blue. She gazed up at the Eiffel Tower, still in disbelief that she was in Paris, a city she'd only seen in her guidebooks and daydreams. Phoenix waved at every bird and dog they passed along with every person who offered a friendly smile before waving back. When they reached the red brick café, the hostess led them to a back room with high cathedral ceilings. Stained glass windows throughout the perimeter cast brilliant splashes of transparent color on every wall. It reminded her of the church she went to growing up, minus the depressing organ music and bleeding Jesus statues.

Zack's bandmates sat around a large wooden table with Charlotte, Amber, and Sandra, their laughter and spirited conversation echoing in the space. Their voices quieted, and every head turned toward the doorway.

"Hey, you two!" Zack pushed away from the table and greeted her with a kiss. "I missed you."

She chuckled against his lips. "I left your room four hours ago." She kissed him back. "But I missed you too."

He unbuckled Phoenix from his stroller and picked him up. His little head was on a swivel as he took in all the new faces in the room.

Adam walked over. "Holy fucking shit," he muttered as he smacked Zack's arm. "He's like your tiny twin."

Mandy laughed, grateful her mom wasn't there to hear the colorful language. There were worse things than cursing. All Mandy cared about was his friends being kind and accepting of her and her son.

"Seriously!" Charlotte rushed over, touching Phoenix's cheek. "You're much cuter, though. I can't wait to introduce you to my Anna Jude."

"Where is she?" Mandy asked.

"Taking a nap in our room," Tyler replied. "Charlotte's dad's been doing most of the babysitting, but my brother Matthew's watching her today. It'll be nice to have both hands free to eat with."

"We got Phoenix welcome to the family gifts." Amber walked over, clutching a white paper bag covered in cartoon elephants. "I hope he likes them."

"That's very sweet. Thank you." Mandy pulled a blanket from the stroller basket and laid it on the carpet before taking the bag. She set Phoenix on the blanket and sat beside him. "Do you want to open it, sweetie?"

He snatched a piece of blue tissue paper from the top and jammed it into his mouth. Everyone laughed as she took the wet paper away and set it on the table. She held the bag open, and he reached inside, tugging out a tiny black T-shirt. She unfolded it to read the words *And you thought my dad was a loud pain in the ass*.

Again, the room filled with laughter, the sound warming her chest.

"That one's from me," Sandra said. "No offense whatsoever to that perfect little sweetheart, but I embrace all opportunities to take a dig at Zack." She laughed at his raised middle finger and gave one right back.

"Understood," Mandy said. Working around them for the past couple of weeks taught her that this group's dynamic was more like loving, playful siblings than just friends. It was sweet and made her long for the fun, simpler times with her brother before he lost his way. "No offense taken, and thank you."

Phoenix reached into the bag again and pulled out an empty photo album with a map of Europe on the cover.

"From me and Ty," Charlotte said. "You can put your photos and little keepsakes from the trip inside."

"Thank you both." Mandy took the book before he started shredding the pages. "That's really thoughtful." He was too young to remember the trip, so it would be a perfect thing to give him when he was old enough to appreciate it.

Next, he pulled a small toy drum from the bag.

"Of course, that's from me." Amber smiled. "The kid's got music in his DNA, and no one's cooler than drummers."

Everyone except Adam groaned, which made Phoenix's eyes flit around the room as if trying to read their faces.

"Whatever, bitch," Sandra playfully shoved Amber's shoulder. "Anyone can hit shit with sticks. At least I don't look like Animal from The Muppets on speed when I play."

"Hey, without the bass, every other instrument would sound soulless and dull." Zack sat beside Phoenix. "My shit gets hearts racing and heads bobbing."

"You're all amazing and essential," Mandy said, entertained by their good-natured smack-talk and eager to show her gratitude. "Thanks so much for the gifts." She pulled a burp cloth from the diaper bag and wiped drool from Phoenix's chin. "We have plenty of time to figure out what instruments he wants to learn. I played piano and violin, so if he chooses those, I've got him covered."

Adam swiped two spoons from the table and kneeled beside Zack. He played a fast, rhythmic beat on the toy drum that had Phoenix mesmerized, his muscles frozen as he watched. When Adam was done, he passed Phoenix the spoons. His tiny hands clutched the silver handles, banging away on the drum with strikes that lacked rhythm but not volume. When he was done, his fingers opened, and fortunately, he dropped the spoons instead of throwing them.

"That was awesome!" Zack held his hand up in front of Phoenix. "High-five?"

Mandy laughed. "He doesn't know that yet."

"Phoenix, watch." Zack held his hand up to Adam, and he slapped it. "See? High-five." Zack lifted his palm, grabbed Phoenix's wrist, and helped him slap it. "Want to try?" Zack held up his palm again, waiting.

Phoenix grinned, his little body teetering forward as he slapped Zack's hand. Everyone in the room cheered, and Phoenix did it again, eating up the attention.

Zack's smile—beaming with pride at teaching their son something new—was one of the most beautiful things she'd ever witnessed.

"He's a genius." Zack glanced at Tyler with a teasing smirk. "Let's see your kid do that."

"She can't," Charlotte said, "but her mom can open a can of whoop ass on you if you keep talking crap."

The conversations were easy and stress-free as they passed around heaping plates of delicious French food. Everyone took turns holding Phoenix, treating him like family. If only he had this all the time—surrounded by these fun, talented, big-hearted people who instantly adored him because they loved his father. And they'd all welcomed her into the fold despite her mistakes and all the pain she'd caused their friend.

If she and Phoenix moved to Portland, they'd have this.

She watched how comfortable he was in Zack's lap, poking a tiny finger into the food on his plate while Zack laughed it off and handed him a spoon. For a long time, she'd doubted this day would ever come, and here it was. She never would've thought he'd take to the role so well and so quickly because, again, she'd underestimated him.

If only they had more time.

A pang of sadness struck, her chest going tight. There was so much they'd all be losing when they returned to Denver. The three of them deserved more than a week to be a family.

She rested her head on Zack's shoulder while he chatted and laughed with his friends. She'd miss having this strong man to lean on who'd seen her best and worst sides, accepting her completely. The man who'd forgiven her mistakes and learned from his own, changing into someone she could imagine a future with.

What if the distance made it impossible to maintain their connection, and they drifted apart? Phone calls wouldn't be enough. A visit every few months wouldn't be enough. She wanted his arms around her every night and his gentle forehead kisses every morning. She wanted to watch his bond with Phoenix grow, and for their son to have someone else to love and protect him.

As she took her last bite of bourbon bread pudding, the work phone in her pocket vibrated, pulling her from her thoughts. Zack gave a quick nod of understanding, and she stepped away from the table, answering the call in the quiet hallway.

"Hello?"

"Are you close to the hotel?" Cassie's words came out in a rush.

"A few blocks away, why? Are you okay?"

"Nope. Totally panicking. I woke up with a sore throat, and I need you to get me honey, licorice root tea, decaf green tea, zinc, and menthol lozenges."

Mandy made a mental note of her list. "Got it. I'm sorry you're panicking, but you just need to get through two more shows before your vocal cords and the rest of you get a nice break. Need anything else?"

"No. Please hurry." The line went dead.

She slipped her phone into her pocket and returned to the dining room. "Sorry, everyone, but I have to get some stuff for Cassie." She picked Phoenix's things off the floor and stuffed them into the diaper bag. "I'm glad you all got to meet Phoenix. This was great."

Zack frowned. "You have to go already?"

"Sorry, duty calls." She held out her hands to take Phoenix. "I hope my mom's in her room."

"Can he stay?" Zack asked. "We were all going to hang in Ty's room for a bit. He and Charlotte can be my backup, so I don't do another stupid thing."

He'd handed Phoenix a piece of crab meat during lunch, but she snatched it before he stuck it in his mouth. Understandably, Zack didn't know not to feed babies shellfish until they were over a year old. Plus, if Phoenix was allergic like her mother, having to treat his reaction in a foreign country wasn't ideal.

Zack had a lot to learn, but aside from that minor bump, he was off to a great start.

"I can drop him off with your mom before we leave for soundcheck," he said, his tone and expression free of hesitation.

Another confrontation between him and her mother made her uneasy, but her guys should spend as much time together as possible. And it would be an opportunity for him to learn how to take care of Phoenix's needs without her hovering.

She gave Charlotte a questioning look with raised brows and got a reassuring nod in return. "Okay. Call me if you need anything." She bent at the waist and kissed him. "Thank you." She pressed a kiss to Phoenix's soft cheek. "No projectile vomiting or diaper blowouts, okay? Go easy on him."

Zack quirked an eyebrow, and she kissed him again before saying goodbye to everyone else.

She hit the pharmacy and natural food store to get everything on her list before carrying the shopping bags to Cassie's suite. She knocked, surprised when Shane opened the door.

"Thanks, Mandy," he said, taking the bags. "We can't have a singer with a scratchy voice. Hopefully, this stuff works."

Soft music played in the room, layered with running water.

She peeked inside but didn't see Cassie. "Do you want me to come in and make the tea?"

He shook his head. "Got it handled. She's taking a hot shower now, hoping the steam helps relax her vocal cords. We'll see you at soundcheck."

Before she could say anything else, he shut the door.

Okaaay.

It seemed odd that he was there during her shower, but he'd been a very involved manager, and a lot was riding on Cassie nailing the show. In his place, Mandy would do the same.

Trusting he had it handled, she took the elevator to her mom's floor. If work didn't need her, at least she could play referee if her mom laid into Zack again. After two knocks, she let herself in with her key.

"Back already?" her mom called from the open bathroom. She came out in a white bathrobe with a towel piled on her head, her mouth drooping at the corners. "Where's Phoenix?"

"With Zack and his friends. He'll drop him off before soundcheck."

Her mom's eyes blew wide. "You trusted him *alone* with my grandson?!"

"Yes, Mom." Mandy set a hand on her hip with an exasperated sigh. "I'm trusting Phoenix's father to take care of him. Don't say it like I'm out of my mind."

"You'd have to be!" She tugged the towel off her head and tossed it to the floor. "What if he—"

Fortunately, a knock at the door cut her off.

Her mom dashed to the bathroom, slamming the door shut before the lock clicked.

Mandy opened the suite door to find Zack and Phoenix. They were smiling, and aside from the chocolate smeared on Phoenix's cheeks and the fact that Zack was wearing a different shirt, they looked like she'd left them.

Take that, Mom.

She stood aside, and he pushed the stroller into the room. "Did you guys have fun?"

"Yup. He pissed on me when I changed his diaper and poked his finger in Anna Jude's nose, but otherwise, no problems."

She laughed. "I should've warned you about the pee thing. He's gotten me plenty of times, too, so consider it a rite of passage."

"Like a gross baptism." He kissed her forehead. "I'm honored. Where's your mom?"

"Getting dressed." She didn't want to shove him out, but avoiding a clash would be wise, considering her mom's attitude. "I'll get him cleaned up and ready for his nap. See you after the show?"

He nodded and gave her a proper kiss on the mouth that made her eyes flutter closed and her heart skip. "See you tonight."

She would *never* get tired of hearing those words tumble from his lips.

The bathroom door swung open, and her mom took Phoenix out of the stroller. "He looks like he's in one piece. Miracles happen."

Those unnecessary digs, on the other hand, Mandy was definitely tired of.

"Mom, stop. He did fine."

Her mom pulled a baby wipe from the diaper bag and cleaned Phoenix's face and hands. "Sure. Feeding him sugar before naptime is a brilliant idea."

She scanned Zack from his mussed dark hair to his combat boots, her nose scrunching. "Do you have to dress like a thrift store Satanist when you're around my grandson?"

Mandy turned to him with a dramatic eye roll. "You better go. Have a good soundcheck."

"Thrift Store Satanist would be a killer name for a metal band." His lips curled in a smirk, and Mandy stifled a laugh. "Great seeing you again, Jill."

"Don't patronize me," her mom snapped back.

"Later, little man." He held up his hand to Phoenix, earning a high-five and a sweet little laugh before he walked out.

Mandy locked the door behind him. She changed Phoenix into his pajamas while singing her favorite Tom Petty song, "Wildflowers," to help them both settle.

Her mom sat with a magazine at the table, nearly ripping the pages as she flipped them. "You're making a huge mistake."

"I don't have the energy or time to fight with you." Mandy rocked Phoenix in her arms, singing softly as he fell asleep. Even though her voice was calm, frustration lit a bonfire in her gut.

Why couldn't her mom set aside her preconceived notions and give Zack a chance? If they built a future together, would she ever stop putting him down and picking fights in front of Phoenix? She'd always been critical but never so verbally aggressive. It was an ugly side Mandy hadn't seen before—one she wished would return to hibernation and never wake up.

When Phoenix was asleep, she set him into the playpen. "Thanks for watching him." Mandy sighed, grabbing her purse and leaving without another word. She couldn't think of a single one that would do any good.

32

Mandy

After Mandy once again dragged Felix and Roger out of their beds for their second to last show of the tour, the pre-show soundcheck went off without a hitch. Zack and his band had a charity event with Killing Daisies across town, making it easier to focus on work. She ironed Cassie's dress, ran Shane's errands, and prepared the dressing rooms for pre- and post-show festivities.

After completing her tasks, she had free time until her seven o'clock meeting with Shane to review last-minute details before the show.

It was the perfect opportunity to see Phoenix before he went down for the night and to clear the air with her mom. Mandy couldn't believe how cruel she'd been to Zack, in front of Phoenix no less. If they didn't get along, the rest of their time in Paris would be tainted.

In her mom's room, Mandy found her and Phoenix watching cartoons on the bed. He was clutching the stuffed frog Zack had given him. She picked up her son and held him to her chest, letting his familiar scent and warmth soothe her before another heated conversation.

"Everything okay, sweetheart?" her mom asked.

Mandy sat beside her mother with her back against the headboard. "You need to apologize to Zack."

Her mom scoffed, gawking at Mandy like she'd sprouted a second head. "You can't be serious. After the way he spoke to me?"

"He's trying, unlike you. Think of the first impression you made. You walked in, glaring daggers at him, ready to strike. You wouldn't even shake his hand. You weren't any better when he dropped Phoenix off this afternoon."

She huffed, crossing her arms like a petulant toddler. "I don't know what you see in him. I raised you better than this."

"You raised me to fall in line, so it's killing you that instead, I'm thinking for myself." The words tumbled out before her brain caught up, but she meant every word. After years of locking up her feelings, it felt good to stand up for herself. "I'll never live up to your expectations because I'm not the perfect daughter you've created in your head. I have to live my own life."

"It's not only your life I'm worried about. He'll hurt Phoenix, too. I'm certain of it. When he does, get ready for the Texas-sized 'I told you so.'"

Phoenix hummed as he blew spit bubbles. Fortunately, he was young enough to be oblivious to his grandmother's relentless drive to tear down his father.

"He makes life exciting. I like that he's unpredictable, and I never know where the day will take us. He's sweet, protective, and surprisingly romantic. And I help ground him. We balance each other out." She brushed loose hair off Phoenix's forehead. "And he surrounds himself with amazing people. His friends have been so welcoming, treating both of us like family."

"I've seen the half-dressed girls screaming for him outside. I'm sure they're pretty welcoming, too. How long will it take for that temptation to be too strong to resist?"

She understood why her mother would worry about that, but Mandy was through doubting him and assuming the worst. Zack loved her. He wanted to be with her. She didn't doubt those facts, and he'd earned back her trust. It could work this time if they didn't let outside influences like her mother ruin it.

"I was wrong about what I saw before we broke up. He wasn't with anyone else. I underestimated him like you are and never gave him a chance to explain the truth."

"Sure, he wasn't." Her mom's eyes rolled. "You might believe his lies, but I don't."

Phoenix turned to face Mandy, and she smiled, pulling him in for a hug. She'd never judge someone he loved if they were good to him. And when her son was grown, she'd trust him to make his own choices.

"I love him, Mom." She planted a soft kiss on Phoenix's forehead. "He's changed a lot, and I trust him now. He's good for me. And I think he'll be good for Phoenix, too. Otherwise, I wouldn't be pursuing this. If you weren't so blinded by your unfair judgments, you would've seen how great Zack was with him. He soothed him when he cried and made him laugh. He took care of him today without my help. He even bought Phoenix the toy frog he won't let go of. My son deserves to have his dad in his life, and I deserve to be with someone who makes me happy. This can work. But you have to give him a chance."

Her mom craned her neck, finally meeting Mandy's gaze. "I promise I'll do what's best for you and Phoenix. And I'm sorry I lost my temper. Can we try to enjoy our last few days here?"

"Of course." She rested her cheek on her mother's shoulder, grateful to have the matter settled. "Thank you."

"How about we hit the Eiffel Tower tomorrow night? Phoenix would love to see it lit up and sparkling."

Mandy nodded and turned to the TV, laughing at Wile E. Coyote's attempt to drop an anvil on the roadrunner. "Sounds great."

Phoenix crawled down Mandy's legs and pulled off her left sock. She laughed, and when Phoenix chucked the sock onto the TV, her mom laughed, too.

Mandy shook her head as he yanked off and tossed her other sock. "What is it with you and socks, huh?" She tickled his ribs, and his laughter obliterated the lingering gloom in the air, his cheeks turning pink.

"Where is Mr. Wonderful anyway?" her mom asked, a sarcastic edge to her tone Mandy ignored.

She glanced at the wall clock. "With his band, getting ready for the show. Speaking of which..." She grabbed a still-giggling Phoenix and covered his face in kisses before returning him to her mom. "I have to meet Shane soon and be available during the show if anyone needs anything. I'll see you two in the morning."

Mandy went to her room, changed her clothes, and met her driver down-stairs. She made it to the arena thirty minutes early. Shane wasn't in his usual spot backstage, so she decided to check on Cassie and try again at seven.

When she reached Cassie's dressing room, music played behind the door. She knocked, but there was no answer, so she cracked the door and peeked inside, gasping at what she saw.

Cassie sat on the vanity table in a black lace slip with her legs spread wide. Shane Marx's hips pressed between her thighs, their mouths fused.

Cassie's eyes snapped wide when she spotted Mandy. She broke the kiss and pushed him away. "Shit!" She straightened her clothes before sliding off the table.

Shane's head whipped toward the door, his face red and tense as he stepped back. "You should've knocked."

"I did. You didn't hear me." Mandy walked to the stereo and shut off the music, her hands shaking. "I wanted to see if she needed anything before our meeting at seven."

"Nope." Cassie wiped the smeared lipstick off her mouth. Something in her eyes was off. Was she ashamed? If she wasn't, she should be. So should he, only double. "All good."

"Right." Shane cleared his throat, wiping a smudge of red lipstick from his mouth. "Well, this is awkward."

That wasn't the word she'd choose. He'd been married for almost two decades. He had Mandy send the poor woman anniversary flowers, for fuck's sake. And they had three kids at home. What kind of monster cheats on his wife and risks breaking up his family?

Cassie slipped on her show dress and bolted for the door. "I need a drink."

When she left, a heavy silence descended. Shane tucked his shirt into his pants and smoothed his disheveled hair in the mirror.

"Has this been going on the entire tour?" She felt bold and protective of his wife, who was probably oblivious.

His gaze narrowed. "It isn't your business, but yes. Cassie and I have had an... interest in one another for a while, and we wanted to see how things would be away from home before we did anything drastic."

She bit back a scoff. Sticking his tongue into a mouth that wasn't his wife's was pretty fucking drastic. Why did so many men in their industry have to be disgusting and disappointing?

"You're right. It isn't my business. Can we go over the schedule and tomorrow's list? I'm pretty tired all of a sudden." And sick. Sick and fucking tired of scumbags like him having power over her. He hid it better than James Sutter, but they were cut from the same rotten cloth.

She was more grateful than ever to have found a guy like Zack.

He was *nothing* like them.

A nagging thought scratched at the back of her mind as she remembered the look on Cassie's face before she hurried out. Shane's power and influence could make or break her band's career. Did he use that power to get Cassie into his bed, or did she have genuine feelings for him?

Mandy's stomach roiled at the realization that what she'd walked in on and how low he'd sunk might be even worse than she first thought.

"Make sure Felix and Roger are ready to go on." He moved to the door, his hand stilling on the knob. "It probably goes without saying, but if you tell anyone about this, your hopes for a managing career will be over."

The flow of air into her lungs halted.

How was she here again—with her future in the hands of another selfish, despicable prick?

"After that..." She shook her head. "I wouldn't expect any less from you."

He walked out, and she covered her face with her hands, forcing herself to take a few deep breaths. The band went on in twenty minutes, and she had a job to do. She made sure Felix and Roger were ready and in position at the bottom of the backstage steps.

On her way back to Cassie's dressing room to check if she was ready, a hand clamped around her wrist, tugging her into a dark closet full of coats and gear. She gasped, her pulse spiking as someone kicked the door shut.

"I couldn't resist," a deep, familiar voice whispered in her ear before letting her go.

"Dammit, Zack!" She shoved him into a shelf loaded with folded towels. "What the fuck?!"

"Sorry to scare you, baby." He cupped her cheeks, pulling her in for a kiss. "I missed you today."

"I missed you too, but I'm working. I have to find Cassie." She wasn't looking forward to facing her again, but she had no choice. Part of Mandy's job was ensuring Cassie had everything she needed before the show, from bottled water to polished boots.

His thumb stroked her cheek. "Everything okay?"

"Let's talk later." She kissed him to stop further prodding, and she needed the comfort.

As her lips parted, he broke the kiss. "There's something I have to talk to you about, too. Kyla's in town, and there are some things you should know before you run into her."

Mandy's brows knitted at the frustratingly vague statement. "Sure. I have to go. Have a great show. I'll watch if I can."

She cracked the door and slipped out when the hallway was empty. Cassie was already by the stage steps with Roger and Felix, her eyes sliding to Mandy. She offered a sad smile and a shrug before running her fingers through her wavy golden mane and turning back to her bandmates.

"Mandy."

She glanced behind her to find Shane ending a call and tucking his phone into his pocket. "Take the rest of the night off. Cassie's idea. She worried you were upset and might want to spend time with your boyfriend."

She felt the color drain from her face. "What are you talking about?"

He chuckled, his obnoxious smirk reminding her too much of the boss she'd ditched to be here. "Do you think I'm blind, stupid, or both? Instead of firing you for breaching the fraternization clause, let's call it extra motivation to keep your mouth shut."

Her hands twitched with the urge to punch his stupid, cheating face. Apparently, the fraternization clause didn't apply to him.

There was only one more show after tonight. Then, she'd never have to see him again. James Jerkwad Sutter had given her plenty of practice at smiling through misery to get her job done, so she'd get through this.

"Enjoy the show," he said with a wave and another arrogant smirk.

Fuck that guy and the fucking horse he rode in on. And fuck Cassie for fucking someone who had a fucking wife at home.

Zack would be proud of her internal curse-filled rant.

With her schedule wiped for the next few hours, she'd take that asshole Shane's advice and enjoy the show. Phoenix and her mom were asleep, and it'd be nice to cap off the shitty night with incredible music.

The house lights died, and the crowd went nuts as Fury Fuel took the stage. That performance, she'd skip. She couldn't stomach the idea of watching Cassie sing about love and loyalty like a damn hypocrite.

Instead, she drifted through the crowded hallway, looking for Zack.

"Mandy!" Charlotte stood outside the Killing Daisies dressing room, waving her over.

"Hey, Charlotte." She plastered on a fake smile, but the slight squint in Charlotte's eyes said she wasn't fooled. "Excited for the show?"

"Hell, yes. We're blowing off steam before our set. Come join us."

"Not too much steam, I hope." Eliza Marsh grinned as her high heels clicked down the hallway. Over the past few weeks, Mandy had observed how attentive she was to the band's needs and how protective of their privacy and safety—the kind of manager Mandy would be. "Do my Daisies need anything before showtime?"

Charlotte shook her head. "We're all set, thanks. Enjoy the show!"

As Eliza walked off, Charlotte beckoned Mandy into the room.

Amber and Sandra played the board game *Guess Who* on a small card table, laughing their asses off. When Mandy looked closer, she saw that they'd replaced the game's faces with taped-up photos of musicians and cartoon characters.

"Hey, girl!" Amber waved before flipping down her Freddie Mercury card. "Done with work for the night?"

Mandy sat on the chair by the vanity table. "Yeah, just finished."

Sandra did the same squinty-eyed thing Charlotte had done. "Did Zack do something stupid? You look hella bummed."

Her terrible poker face strikes again. "Not Zack. Although he dragged me into a supply closet, which could've gotten me in trouble."

"Hot." Amber fanned herself. "I still can't believe you guys have a kid. Phoenix is so damn cute. And after you left, Zack kept giving him high-fives and making him laugh. I'm not a huge baby person, but it was adorable."

Mandy nodded, a smile curling the edges of her mouth. "Yeah. Zack's been great with him. He has a lot to learn, but he'll get there."

"Tyler was fucking clueless about babies too," Charlotte said, "but he read a ton of books while I was pregnant and even signed us up for newborn classes. It was sweet. Zack will figure it out, and he has all of us to back him up."

An unexpected surge of emotion struck Mandy like a tidal wave, and tears flooded her eyes. She slapped her hand over her mouth as a sob escaped. "I'm so sorry. I don't know why I'm crying." It'd been an emotionally fraught day, filled with highs and lows, but she was usually better at keeping a lid on her emotions, especially at work.

All three women surrounded her, squeezing her in the center of the first group hug she'd ever received. It was as warm and comforting as a steaming mocha latte in winter. Of course, it made her cry even harder before erupting in a fit of laughter like an unstable wacko.

She wiped her tears, and Amber left the huddle to grab a box of tissues. Sandra slid to the floor at Mandy's feet, and Charlotte pulled up a chair beside her.

"Spill it, sweetie." Amber set the tissues in Mandy's lap and sat on her other side. "Between the three of us, we've been through plenty of shit that led to hysterical crying, so let it out."

Mandy sniffed. "Nothing I say leaves this room?"

Sandra scoffed, giving her knee a reassuring squeeze. "You won't find more loyal, secret-keeping bitches than the ones right here. You can trust us."

Mandy described what she walked in on between Cassie and Shane. She told them about his threats and that he knew about her and Zack, putting her job, reputation, and future at risk.

As she spoke, all three women looked poised to fight—their expressions tight and shoulders tense. While it was risky to trust people she didn't know well, Zack trusted them. That was enough for her. Getting the stressful situation off her chest was an immense relief—much better than going with her default mode of holding it in and letting it fester.

"So," Amber said, "I pin him down, Sandra grabs the scissors, and Charlotte snips off his balls?"

Sandra's bottom lip curled out. "Why does Charlotte get the fun part?"

Mandy laughed, wiping away the last of her tears. "Shouldn't I get to do the snipping?" She tossed her wad of used tissues into the trashcan. "I can't shake the look on Cassie's face. I'm not sure she wanted it as much as he did."

Amber shot to her feet and her face reddened, fists clenched at her sides. "Do you mean he fucking *forced* her?!"

"No, no, no." Mandy flapped her hands as if they'd erase the misunderstanding. "She looked like a willing participant, but I wonder if she's doing it because she has feelings for him or because of what he can do for her. I feel sick even saying that." She touched her churning stomach.

"Either's possible." Charlotte slid an arm around Mandy's shoulders. "Sadly, some women find it easier to use favors to get ahead while the rest of us hustle and sweat. I'm sorry you're dealing with this bullshit. Especially after the non-sense with your last boss. There are *way* too many gross assholes in the music biz."

"And not enough fed-up chicks wielding scissors," Amber added, miming a cutting motion. "Talk about an effective deterrent."

Mandy laughed, appreciating the graphic yet strangely cathartic mental image.

"Are you going to tell Zack?" Sandra asked.

"I was going to, but probably not. I don't want him to say anything to Sophia or anyone else. Or to worry that Shane might try something with me."

Amber grabbed two beers from the fridge and popped the caps. "Here, girl. It is sooo beer thirty." She handed Mandy a bottle and took a drink from the other.

It was ice cold and hoppy with a hint of bitterness.

"Damn." Mandy glanced at the label. She'd never heard of High Notes, but they'd give any Colorado brewer a run for their money. "This is incredible."

Amber grinned. "My fiancé owns the brewery. This is his summer ale."

"I miss beer." Charlotte sighed before nudging Mandy's elbow. "Don't make any plans later because we're taking you dancing. Our guitar tech Molly's coming, too. You'll love her."

"The nightclub up the street has the most fabulous drag queens in the world," Sandra added. "And Cosmopolitans so strong, they could remove paint. Amber and I went with Luke a couple of nights ago, and shit got wild."

"Ugh." Amber touched her head. "Don't remind me. I'm pretty sure I peed in the street while eating a cheeseburger. Not my finest moment."

"Glad I missed that one," Charlotte said with a laugh. "Anyway, you can use a fun night out, and my cousin Kyla's in town."

Mandy perked up. She was excited to meet her. Kyla cared enough about Zack to reach out to a stranger to help him, and when James was a creep, she stayed on the line to make sure Mandy was okay. Those details alone said a lot about her character.

"And Tyler's staying in to watch Anna Jude," Charlotte added. "Have Zack bring Phoenix and his sleep stuff to our suite, and the guys can have a baby party."

Laughter filled the room, delivering the final, fatal blow to Mandy's sour mood. This is what she'd been missing out on all these years. Letting people into her life came with risk, but it was worth it if the reward was laughter and support before she asked for it and right when she needed it most.

"My mom's got him tonight, so he's set, but I'd love to go dancing."

"Speaking of your mom," Charlotte said, "how are she and Zack getting along?"

Mandy blew out a long, slow breath to ease the rising frustration. "She's been so unfair to him. She hates his clothes, his job, the way he talks... He's tried so hard to be polite, but if they can't get along, I don't know what to do."

Amber raised her bottle. "My dad's a slut-shaming homophobe with two gay kids. I know all about jerk parents and their shitty judgments. Sorry you're dealing with that."

"Thanks." Mandy clinked their bottles together. "My mom's got the slut-shaming thing too. When a girl at my high school was assaulted at a party, my mom said, 'See? That's why I don't let you go to parties. Who's going to want her now?'"

"Fuck, man." The edges of Amber's mouth tipped down in an angry grimace. "Sorry to be blunt, but your mom's an asshole."

The other women nodded in agreement, and Mandy joined them. Sometimes, her mom was an asshole. But she was also an amazing, attentive grandmother and, usually, a kind and helpful mother. Mandy owed her a lot for everything she'd done for her and Phoenix. The contrasts made the situation even more aggravating.

"So, it's settled." Sandra poked Mandy's knee. "Girls' night out in the City of Lights. Friends, Parisians, countrymen, hold on to your asses."

"You're such a nerd." Amber finished her beer and tossed the bottle in the trash.

"Thanks, you guys." Mandy glanced at her watch and stood. "Almost stage time." After years at the club, shutting off her internal showtime clock was impossible.

Sandra punched the air. "Fuck yeah, it is! Are you watching us or hiding in another supply closet with Bass Boy?"

Mandy laughed at the cute nickname. "Wouldn't miss it. Bass Boy can wait."

"Our crowd can't, so we're out of here." Charlotte got up and pulled Mandy in for another hug. "I know we're new to you, but you can come to any of us with anything." She stepped back, gripping Mandy's shoulders, her expression serious. "*Anything*. Even Zack stuff. Just because he's been our friend longer doesn't mean you can't trust us with your secrets."

"Well, it's official," Sandra said. "You got the Charlotte trust speech, so you're one of us now. Welcome to the club. Instead of punch and pie, we have booze, chocolate, and dirty jokes."

Amber checked her makeup in the mirror. "And if you ever need a tampon or help hiding a body, we've got you covered."

Someone knocked on the door before a male head peeked through, "Ten minutes, ladies!" It was Luke, their bassist, who'd hit on her at the hotel bar in London. His eyes slid to her, and he smiled. "Hey, it's The Mandy! If you hook me up with Cassie Rose, I'll be your best friend."

She laughed. "I'll put in a good word for you, The Luke."

"Awesome." He held the door open. "The rest of you, get moving. Our crowd awaits."

"Keep your pantaloons on." Sandra hugged Mandy on her way out the door, Charlotte trailing behind. "See you after the show!"

Amber hugged her last. "Thanks for trusting us. Sandra said welcome to the club, but really, we're a family. No matter what, you and Phoenix are part of it, too."

Again, Mandy was on the verge of tears, but they were happy ones this time. "Thanks, Amber."

Before talking to them, she didn't think she could feel any worse, and now, she couldn't imagine feeling lighter and more excited for what was ahead.

Killing Daisies put on a flawless, dynamic performance, as always. When it was over, they invited her back to their dressing room for drinks before the guys went on. She couldn't remember the last time she'd laughed so much or felt so young and free.

They joined her at the side of the stage before Tomorrow Mourning's set kicked off. She stood between Charlotte and Luke, anticipation bubbling through her as the arena darkened.

The vast space exploded with noise. Crowds had roared every time the band went on over the past three weeks, but this was on another level—like the love from their fans formed an intense wall of sound that electrified the air. When Zack took the stage, he shot a grin in Mandy's direction, and she blew him a kiss. What was the point in hiding now with the dirt she had on Shane? If he fired her, she wouldn't hesitate to call his wife.

Zack's eyebrows jumped at her boldness. She felt a thrilling charge whenever she surprised him. One of the many things he'd taught her was that predictability was overrated.

His eyes slid to Luke beside her, shooting the fellow bassist a pointed *she's mine* glare. Witnessing his possessiveness gave her a charge, too. He had nothing to fear, of course, but it was thrilling to feel claimed by someone millions of women would kill to touch.

Adam and Tyler took their places, but her gaze never wavered.

Damn, he's fine.

Mandy's attraction to musicians began in high school at her first rock show, but how her body responded to watching Zack play was miles beyond attraction. If she were wearing panties, they'd be soaked once his fingers started working those strings. With his hair drenched in sweat, black T-shirt clinging to his muscled chest, and powerful hands clutching his black and silver bass guitar, her insides were melty goo.

Maybe she'd drag *him* into a closet to soothe the needy ache building between her legs.

The women and Luke danced and sang along, cheering Charlotte on when she joined the band for a punked-up cover of David Bowie's "Changes."

When the encore's final notes died out, the guys left their instruments to the roadies and descended the stage steps. Tyler swept Charlotte into his arms, kissing her hard before they disappeared down the hallway. Adam searched the faces in the backstage crowd before zipping off. Zack met Mandy's eyes and tipped his chin to the right.

She grinned at another chance to sneak around, following a few steps behind. He turned the corner and opened a door, checking inside before beckoning her to join him. He locked the door behind them and flipped on the light.

The empty dressing room was under construction. Large chunks of plaster were missing from the walls, buckets of paint were scattered around the room, and the only furniture was a raggedy brown couch covered in dust.

"We are *not* having sex in here." Her fingers curled in his sweat-dampened T-shirt. "No matter how badly I want you."

"Hold that thought, baby." His hands covered hers, stopping her from going any further. "Remember when I said we needed to talk?"

Damn. She had forgotten. Since he'd halted her advances twice, it must be serious.

So much for her great mood.

"What's wrong?"

He ran a shaky hand through his hair. "There's something you should know, but I really fucking don't want to tell you because it'll bother you and might ruin your night. Maybe even the rest of your trip."

"You're scaring me now." She wanted to get comfortable for this and glanced at the dusty couch before deciding that standing was better. Plus, it would make it easier to exit if she needed to. "I'm a big girl, Zack. Spit it out."

"I had sex with Kyla."

Mandy's stomach backflipped, her blood going cold. "*What*?! When?"

Kyla had only been in Paris for a few hours, and he'd been with his band.

Or had he? If he lied and cheated, she'd *never* forgive him.

She inhaled deeply through her nose. Instead of letting her thoughts spiral into thinking the worst, she gave him a chance to explain.

"The day of Ty's wedding. After the reception."

She exhaled her held breath. That was almost a year ago. She was relieved but still didn't like it. "But she's with Adam. Wasn't he pissed?"

A nervous laugh burst from his lips as he rubbed the back of his neck. "They weren't together yet. He was there, too. And we even kind of..."

Her eyebrow arched. "Kind of what?"

"Well..."

"Zack," she snapped, tired of the stalling.

"Sucked each other off."

Her eyes bulged, and her mouth fell open. It would've shocked her less if he'd said they'd done naked handstands on the White House roof.

"You *what*?"

He averted his gaze and paced the room. "It was just a little bit, not like we finished or anything. Not with each other, at least. And there was some jerking involved. Kyla asked for it."

"Stop moving." She walked to him, grabbing his shoulders. What the ever-loving hell was she supposed to do with this information? "Are you bisexual now? Or maybe you've always been, and I didn't know. It's fine, of course, I just—"

"No." His lips twitched with a held-back smile. "I'm not bi, just willing to try anything once, and she had a fantasy. We haven't touched each other since, and honestly, she bugs me."

"Why?"

"She's always at our place, cooking shit and walking around in Adam's shirts and boxers like she fucking lives there. Technically, she does now, but still."

Mandy shrugged, failing to see his problem. "She's his girlfriend, Zack. Do you think Adam would have a problem if I made breakfast and walked around your place in your clothes?"

His lips twisted. "I guess not."

"Is there another reason she bugs you? Are you still attracted to her?"

"The answer to your second question is no. She's pretty and all, but she's no Mandy."

She smiled, still unsure how to feel but appreciating the compliment. "And my first question?"

"I feel like a third wheel when she's around. I miss hanging with Adam without her popping in and snatching up all his attention. Even on this tour, he's always on the phone with her. And they're moving to a new place together when we get back, so I'll probably only see him for band shit."

She set a hand on his chest. "You sound like a jealous boyfriend."

"I am *not* bi."

Mandy laughed. "I'm teasing, sorry. I know how close you and Adam have always been, so it makes sense you'd miss the days when you didn't have to share him." Her eyebrow lifted. "Or when you shared women with him."

She knew of Zack's reputation when they met. While she didn't like imagining him fucking dozens of women, she wasn't about to judge him for all the crazy things he did before they were official.

Were they official now? They hadn't really defined their relationship, but it felt official.

While labels and rules weren't fun or sexy, they needed to discuss boundaries soon and at least loosely define what they were.

"I don't miss that crazy shit." He shook his head, his gaze sincere. "You're enough for me. And I'm sorry to shove this at you right before you meet her. I've wanted to tell you all day, but we haven't had much time alone."

"I'm going out with her later. And the other girls. It'll be weird, but I'm glad you told me."

"No more secrets, baby." He grabbed her hips, pulling her closer. "It was a stupid threesome. A few hours of fun led to them liking each other, and now they're solid. I don't have feelings for her and never did."

"You just fucked her."

"Yes. It meant nothing. Also, I might be getting hard after hearing you say 'fuck.'"

She landed a playful slap on his chest before steering the conversation back into less playful territory. "Do you honestly think you can handle being monogamous long-term? What if you decide one day you need more variety?"

He took her hands, threading their fingers together. "I only want you. I know there's nothing I'm missing, nothing I wish I'd tried. I'm game if you want to try anything, but I don't think I can share you."

"There's plenty I want to try, but only with you." She stroked his wrist with her thumb, building up the courage to voice a nagging worry she wanted to put behind her. "Since we're being honest, I'm afraid you'll get bored with me. I don't have nearly as much experience."

"Experienced or not, the best sex I've ever had has been with you. No contest."

She smiled, the tension in her shoulders unfurling as the worry dissolved. "Ditto."

"I know. I have a gift."

She laughed, her eyes rolling to the half-painted ceiling. "But not the gift of modesty. And I'll try to keep things interesting." Feeling brazen, she slid their joined hands between her legs.

His breath hitched, the black of his pupils edging out the gorgeous green.

"You're bare under your skirt?" he whispered, a throaty growl spiking his words with lust. "Nothing boring about that." Their hands separated, and his strong, talented fingers slipped inside her. "Mmm... Baby, you're *so fucking wet.* What's been going on in that pretty head of yours?"

Her hand grazed his crotch before cupping his erection, flattered he was already hard. "If my knees wouldn't get covered in paint and dust, I'd show you."

Zack's head tipped back with a groan. "I chose the wrong fucking room." He brought his fingers to his lips, her arousal glistening on the tips. She watched as he sucked them clean.

Why is it so damn hot when he does that?

"Let's put a pin in this," she said. "I'm not ditching the ladies to ride you on a dusty couch."

A disappointed grunt rumbled his throat. "Right. You have plans. As much as I want you all to myself tonight, I'm glad you like my friends. You deserve a night out, and I know they'll have your back if some handsy French dude tries anything."

She thought Charlotte, Amber, and Sandra were great, but hopefully, knowing Kyla had been with Zack wouldn't screw with her mind. Wrapping her head around him fooling around with Adam would take some time, too. She had to admit, imagining that was hot. So, there were two things she and Kyla had in common.

"I can take care of myself."

"I know. But isn't it nice sometimes not to have to?"

A corner of Mandy's mouth curled up. "Yes. It is."

She cherished her independence and had more than proven she was strong and capable of anything she set her mind to. But there was peace with letting go and accepting the help and comfort she'd lacked until now.

"Go have fun with the girls, but later tonight…" He dragged his tongue across her bottom lip and kissed her. Tasting herself on his lips made her want whatever would finish that sentence to happen right fucking now. "You're all mine."

She opened the door before either of them got carried away, and he followed her into the hallway, staying a few steps behind.

"Hey, Mandy!" A young, dark-haired woman who resembled Charlotte ran over and hugged her. "It's so good to meet you!"

Mandy's arms stayed at her sides before giving the strange woman a half-assed squeeze. "Hi." Who the hell was this chick, and how did she know her name? "Do I know you?"

The woman laughed. "I should've led with that instead of tackling you. I'm Kyla."

"Oh. Right. Hi."

Kyla's eyebrows dipped, and Adam rushed up behind her, hooking an arm around her waist.

"What's up, Mandy? Glad you guys can finally hang out."

"Me too!" Kyla beamed. She was ridiculously pretty and just as enthusiastic. And her body was perfect—of course. Mandy's stomach roiled at the thought of this gorgeous little nymph in bed with Zack. She tugged at the hem of her blouse which was suddenly too clingy and tight. "I've heard the new job's going great."

Mandy shrugged, struggling to keep her thoughts off her face. "Yeah, I'm learning a ton. The band I'm working with is nice."

Except for the lead singer, who's fucking my boss behind his wife's back.

Her skin felt hot. Tiny beads of sweat tickled the back of her neck.

Kyla frowned. "Are you okay?"

"Sure." Mandy fanned herself. "Just warm in here."

Zack touched his palm to her forehead. "The AC's blasting. Do you feel sick?"

"Stop fussing over me." She swatted his hand away. "I'm fine."

Kyla's head cocked. "Do you feel weird because I overheard the phone call with your shithead boss or..." Her throat jumped on a hard swallow. "Did you hear something that bothered you?"

Zack tucked Mandy against his side, and she appreciated the comforting contact even though images of him naked with Kyla still taunted her. "She knows. I told her about our post-reception, uh, events. I don't want secrets between us."

Kyla's eyes popped wide. "Wow. Good for you, Zack." She turned to Mandy. "It meant nothing, I promise. There's never been weirdness between us since, and I have zero interest in anyone but Adam."

Zack raised a hand as if taking an oath in court. "And I have zero interest in her or ever touching a dude again."

Adam snorted. "So, you told her that, too."

Kyla blushed as her eyes slid back to Mandy. "I give them props for letting me check that fantasy off my list, and I hope it isn't weird for you."

Damn. She was gorgeous, smart enough to have earned the word "doctor" before her name, sexually adventurous, and incredibly considerate—no flaws to be seen.

But Zack didn't want this pretty veterinarian. He wanted Mandy.

She shook her head to clear it of the old, distorted perceptions that caused nothing but pain. "If I let his crazy past bother me, I'd get nothing done." She had to accept he'd been with perfect tens in all ways, but what mattered was he'd chosen her *now*. She was intelligent, sexually adventurous, and beautiful, too—facts that sank in deeper every day.

They all laughed, lightening the tension in the air.

"And now," Zack kissed her cheek, "she'll be part of my crazy future."

"That's so sweet." Kyla put a hand over her heart. "I'm happy for you guys. And I need to hear all about little Phoenix! I hope you have pictures."

Mandy nodded, her shoulders relaxing. "In my purse. I'll show you later. Should we find the other ladies and see if they're ready to go?"

"Definitely." Kyla grabbed Adam's hand, and they headed toward the action and noise of the backstage afterparty.

"Have fun," Zack said, "but be safe."

The hallway was still empty, so she grabbed his collar and pulled him in for a kiss.

"I love you, you freaky weirdo," she whispered against his lips. "I'll see you tonight."

33

Mandy

The morning light filtered through the curtains in Zack's suite, and Mandy groaned. Pain throbbed behind her eyes, and her ears rang from hours of dancing beside speakers blaring thumping dance beats. She threw the blankets over her head.

"Morning, sunshine."

She peeked out from beneath her cocoon to find Zack dressed and putting on his watch.

"Five Cosmopolitans was probably one too many." She forced herself to sit, and the room wobbled. "But I had so much fun. I love your friends. I needed that and didn't even know it."

"They're your friends now, too, and I'm glad you had a good time. So did I when you woke me up at three and jumped my bones."

She grinned, heat rising to her cheeks at the memory of him gripping her hips and fucking her from behind. "That was fun. I'm glad I got my kicks before the headache set in. Where are you going?"

"I'm meeting Adam and Kyla for breakfast." He dug through his backpack and pulled out a small bottle, dumping two white pills in his hand. "They invited you too, but I know you have plans." He filled a glass with water in the bathroom and gave it to her with the pills. "Sorry your head hurts, baby. That's what happens when you party with rockstars." He pressed a gentle kiss to her temple. "Your mother would not approve."

"Shit! My mom!" Her head swung to the right a bit too fast, and it felt like someone had kicked her in the brain. She was meeting her mom and Phoenix at the café next door at eight-thirty. "What time is it?"

"Seven twenty. You're good. You got in late, so I let you sleep as long as possible. I was about to wake you up."

She smiled at his thoughtfulness despite the pounding headache. "Thank you. I'll shower and chug some coffee so I can feel human. And maybe..."

His head tipped to the side as he buckled his belt. "Maybe what?"

"You'll take a raincheck with Adam and Kyla to join us?" She tossed back the pills and drained the glass in four deep swallows. While she worried it was a terrible idea, she wanted to give her mom one last chance to be civil.

His chest fell with a heavy exhale as he sat beside her. "You know I want to spend every second I can with you before your flight. And Phoenix. But he shouldn't see two people who care about him fighting and hurling insults."

"I'm sorry about my mom."

"Not your fault. Anyway, I'd love to take you and Phoenix to lunch. Or maybe the zoo? The one here's supposed to be amazing. He'd love the sloths and meerkats. And he can see some real frogs since he likes the one I got him."

"Correction: He *loves* the one you got him. I don't think he's let it go since. You can get away that long?"

"The radio interview was canceled, so after our breakfast shit, the rest of my day's yours. Meet me back here when you're ready."

She smiled and leaned over for a kiss. "Then let the breakfast shit commence."

"First, I got you something." He grabbed an envelope from the dresser and handed it to her.

She sat straighter and tore the seal. Her fingers slid inside and pulled out two plane tickets from Denver to Portland—one for her and one for Phoenix.

"I'm not trying to pressure you to move," he explained. "I want you both to meet my family. And I want to show you my city to see if maybe—"

"Thank you." Her smile grew as she held the tickets to her chest. "I'd love to see where you grew up, and I'll keep an open mind. I promise." The most they'd talked about the possibility of her moving was during the argument with her mom, but they were on the same page.

Mandy got dressed, swept her hair into a ponytail, and brushed her teeth. Everything Zack had said and done since she woke up swirled in her mind. He didn't want Phoenix to see two people he cared about fighting. He wanted to show him the animals at the zoo. Zack got her medicine and water for her headache without being asked and kept an eye on the clock so she wouldn't be late for her obligations.

When she left the bathroom, he was sitting on the bed, tying his boots.

"Hey," she said.

His chin lifted, a question in his eyes.

"Thank you for being so good to us."

His brow crinkled. "What do you mean?"

She straddled his waist, threading her fingers through his hair. "You didn't want Phoenix to be scared by arguing. You calmed him down, made him laugh, and taught him how to high-five." Her eyes remained fused to his, needing her words to soak into his bones so he would understand his worth and stop underestimating himself. "And you want to take him to the zoo to make him happy. You have everything it takes to be a great dad, and I appreciate you trying so hard. I'm proud of you."

Tears shined in his eyes as he smiled. "Thank you."

"And you've been so patient and sweet, getting me out of my head when I spin out. Helping me go for what I want and need without pressuring me. You've been honest, present, and faithful. Everything it takes to be a good..." She bit her lip, searching for the right word. It was too soon for "partner" and "lover" lacked depth. "Boyfriend?"

Really, he was a few notches above that, but the perfect term to describe his role in her life didn't exist.

He laughed, blinking until his eyes cleared. "If you want to slap a label on me, I'm good with that one."

He cradled her face in his palms, kissing her until she forgot about the pain in her head or the mistakes of their past. This could work if they focused on what mattered and what came next. After the tour, they could fly back and forth for a while, getting by on nightly and naughty phone calls until they decided their next steps. If she fell in love with Portland, they could build a life there, surrounded by his family and incredible friends. Phoenix would meet his other grandparents. And visit Mandy's parents and Ted as often as possible.

Everything standing between them three weeks ago had fallen away.

Now, they could be a family.

They said their goodbyes, and she pressed the elevator button for the bottom floor. When the doors opened, Cassie Rose stood alone inside in blue silk pajamas, her eyes widening on Mandy before dropping to the floor.

Okay. Obviously, this was going to be awkward.

Mandy took a deep breath and stepped inside.

Her questions about what she saw between Cassie and Shane sat locked and loaded on her tongue. They might not get another chance to speak privately, so she felt compelled to seek answers. And to be there for Cassie if she needed support.

"Cassie, are you okay?" The question might be strange, but it seemed like a good place to start.

She hugged an arm around herself. "Why wouldn't I be?"

"When I walked in on you with Shane, how you looked at me made me wonder." Mandy's eyes roamed her face, scrutinizing her tight expression. "Did you want that, or was he taking advantage of you?"

Cassie barked a humorless laugh. "Didn't I look like I wanted it? I don't let just anyone feel me up."

"That wasn't what I was implying. I mean, did he pressure you?"

Cassie rolled her eyes as the elevator rattled. "Look, Mandy. You're not some naïve kid, so I'll be straight with you. We work in an industry run by men. They make the rules of the game, and we follow them if we know what's good for us. Our dreams are locked behind heavy doors, and they hold all the keys. I'm out of stupid analogies, but you get what I'm saying."

Mandy touched her stomach as it churned with nausea that had nothing to do with her hangover. "It sounds like you felt pressured to trade sex for opportunities."

Cassie shrugged. "Call it what you will. I want a successful music career more than anything in the world, and I'll do whatever it takes to get it. He offered me a key, and I took it."

In some ways, she was right. Rich, powerful men were the gatekeepers in the music business, and women had to work ten times as hard to gain a foothold and earn respect. It isn't easy to pass up a shortcut when you're tired of struggling.

Still, Mandy didn't know whether to hug her out of pity or slap her for failing to see her worth. "You can report him."

Cassie laughed, with humor this time. "Right. Who would listen? I'm supposed to kiss my career goodbye, let people tear me down and call me a slutty liar looking for a payday? Shane's one of the world's biggest reps, and who the fuck am I? No one yet. He has the power to change that, and I'm not stupid enough to pass up my chance when I'm still young, hot, and talented enough to have a real shot at being a star."

Sadly, Cassie was right about that, too. If she spoke out about his abuse of power, she'd be risking her career while his would likely come out unscathed. For that reason alone, Mandy wouldn't tell anyone else about what she'd seen because he wasn't the only one who'd suffer. If Cassie ever wanted to out him for being a predatory creep, it was up to her.

"You're worth more than this," Mandy said.

"Am I? I'd rather be dead than go back to the trailer trash town I came from. At least Shane's nice to me. It's not so bad."

"He has a wife. And kids. That doesn't bother you?"

The elevator door opened at the café, but Mandy sent it back to the top floor to continue the conversation.

"Of course, it bothers me!" Crimson flared in Cassie's cheeks, her eyes wet with unshed tears. "I've met his kids, and his wife's a fucking saint. But I didn't make promises to them. He did. And I'm not the first or last girl he's fooled around with. The others are off making millions and traveling the world. It's my fucking turn."

That might be the saddest thing Mandy had ever heard. When she made it, she'd do everything possible to ensure the artists she represented felt safe and respected. Success should come from talent and hard work, not whatever the hell this was. The more balance strong women bring to the business, the better off everyone will be. She was even more impressed by Sophia and Eliza's accomplishments and more grateful than ever for the male managers she knew who'd never take advantage of their position.

"When you make it huge," Mandy said, "and I know you will because you're incredible... Wouldn't you rather know you earned it?"

Cassie scoffed, wiping her eyes on her sleeve. "You can judge me and claim you'd never get on your knees to get ahead, but we both know it isn't true."

Mandy's head jerked back. "What the hell are you talking about? You think I'd use Zack to boost my career? I'd *never* do that. I've said no every time he's offered to pull strings."

Cassie lowered her chin, raising her eyebrows like she wasn't sure if Mandy was lying or just plain stupid. "Zack got you this job. You know that, right?"

Mandy's stomach dropped to the floor, the throbbing behind her eyes going full jackhammer as she processed the words. "No. My old boss gave me Shane's number for the interview. He and Zack don't even know each other."

The doors opened, and she slammed the button for the bottom floor again. They'd ride it all damn day if that's what it took to get everything out in the open.

"It's easy to get a phone number, Mandy. All I know is that Zack got Shane's number from Sophia Cruz and had her tell Shane to hire you. Shane knows it pays to be on her good side, so he gave you the job. He didn't interview anyone else."

Mandy's hands trembled as ice water flooded her veins, her breath stalling.

Was it possible? Had Zack been lying to her this entire time?

"That can't be true. I asked him twice if he had anything to do with getting me this job, and he said no." More than that, he *promised* he didn't.

"I take back what I said about you not being naïve." Cassie stepped forward as the elevator dinged and the doors opened. "He's a lying user like the rest of them. Do the job, take the money, and build a good life for yourself. You're worth more than this."

As the doors slid shut, Mandy felt like someone had slammed her in the face with a shovel. Tears streamed down her cheeks as she rode the elevator back to her floor. She needed to pull herself together before meeting her mom and Phoenix.

He lied to me.

She asked Zack point blank on the plane if he'd gotten her the job, and he denied it. And again in her room. He had three whole weeks to come clean and hadn't said a word, promising they'd have no more secrets between them. Would he have ever told her?

What else had he lied about?

How could she ever trust someone who lied to her face so easily?

And he even got sweet, loyal *Ted* to lie for him?!

Zack manipulated her and the people she cared about to squirm his way back into her life, and like a desperate, lonely fool, she fell for it.

Was *any* of it real?

Along with the pain of his betrayal, the job she was so proud to have earned was tainted. She had no desire to deal with him, Shane, or Cassie again. Only one show remained, but it would take everything she had to get through tomorrow without breaking.

She wiped her face with trembling hands, leaning back against the elevator wall for support.

He was supposed to be different from the James Sutters and Shane Marxes of the world. But like them, Zack selfishly used his privilege to get what he wanted, no matter the cost.

This time, the cost was the family she foolishly believed they'd have together.

And like she'd done with James and Shane, she'd do whatever it took to avoid getting hurt again.

34

Zack

As much as Zack dreaded knocking on that door, he did it. Mandy left his suite at eight-fifteen and never made it back. It was almost noon. Hopefully, she didn't get called into work, killing their date with the sloths and frogs. Since she wasn't in her room, this was the next logical but super shitty place to check.

Jill answered the door with the same disgusted scowl as every other time she'd seen him. If she wasn't careful, it might become permanent.

"Mandy isn't here." She held a steaming cup of tea, and he wouldn't put it past her to throw it in his face. "Neither is Phoenix."

When she said nothing else, he asked, "Where did they go?"

"Come in here, Zack." She beckoned him inside.

Was this a trap? Was she about to offer him muffins laced with rat poison or some shit?

He hesitated in the doorway before walking in.

Hopefully, they could have a truce so she'd stop being such a pain in his ass and cut Mandy some slack. He could only imagine what Jill said about him when he wasn't around.

"Have a seat." She gestured to the chair by the window and sat across from it, setting her cup on the table. "Do you know what my daughter said when she returned home from her first little adventure with you?"

So, no truce. No beating around the bush, either.

"Enlighten me."

"At least I tried. Mandy gave you a chance to prove yourself worthy, and you failed. And despite your attempts to convince her you've changed, I don't doubt you'll fail again. Since she looked upset this morning, I'm guessing you already have."

Upset? She was fine when she left his room. Better than fine—she was beaming with fucking joy. Did something happen during breakfast with her mom and Phoenix? When he found her, he'd find out. First, he had to ditch scowly, judgy Jill.

He stood. "Look, lady—"

"Save it." She held a hand up and gestured to his chair again.

He sighed before sitting back down. If it were anyone else, he'd tell them where to shove it. He hated forcing himself to be respectful when someone refused to do the same.

"But not only Mandy will be hurt this time," she continued. "Think about your son. Would you rather he had a father who was always gone and behaved like a drunken caveman, or would he be better off with Steven, who makes an excellent living as a stockbroker, is a better role model, and can provide stability and security you cannot?"

He squinted, confused and suspicious as fuck. "Steven? Who the hell's that?"

"I'm not surprised she didn't mention him." Jill pinched the string dangling from her cup and dunked the tea bag a few times, darkening the liquid. "He's a good man from a good family. Phoenix has played with his daughter, and if things worked out, he'd have a big sister and a father who's always around."

Zack bit his tongue, holding back the stream of curse words he'd love to darken the holier-than-thou air in the room with. "You don't know what I can give her. I can buy her a house, pay for Phoenix to go to fucking Harvard if he wants to. There's *nothing* I wouldn't do for her. For them. I'm trying to be a better man, but you're so stuck in your ignorant, bullshit opinions you won't bother to see it."

She shook her head, frowning and looking unconvinced, as expected. "If you love her, let her go. Let them both go. A leopard can't change his spots. You've covered them up to fool her, but I see who you are. Your sinful life of excess will lead to nothing but pain and disappointment for my daughter and grandson. I won't let you drag them down with you."

He stood again, over with this conversation before it began. "Good thing her decisions aren't up to you."

"Steven wants more children. Has Mandy told you she does as well? I know Phoenix was a mistake you never wanted, so will you deny him siblings because of your selfishness? Steven can give them everything you named, plus a life free of disappointment and compromising their needs."

"Don't call my son a mistake." His heart pounded in his chest, his mouth dry. "Mandy and I will figure out our future together. *Our* future. Get used to that because she doesn't love that guy. She loves me."

"I'll offer some more food for thought." Jill plucked the tea bag from her cup and dropped it into the trashcan beneath the table with a wet thunk. "What if commitment makes you feel shackled, and you grow bored and change your mind? Do you honestly think you can handle midnight feedings, tantrums, and disciplining a child when you have none yourself? And I've witnessed your temper."

"I would *never* hurt them, so don't even go there."

She arched a brow. "Everyone has limits. And how do you think my daughter will feel when you're going to meet Phoenix's friends' parents and his preschool teacher looking like a hungover Hell's Angel? Speaking of which, do you really believe you'll stay sober so they can rely on you to run to the store for milk? Or drive to the hospital if Phoenix breaks his arm?"

"I've changed. None of that's an issue anymore."

Jill's head shook as she let out a bitter laugh. "Don't kid yourself. People like you don't change. I've seen it with my son. You're both weak. Everything's fine and dandy before life dishes out more than you can take. You'll turn to the bottle or pills or whatever offers an easy escape from dull, mundane reality. My advice is to carry on with your wild, carefree life. But first, let them go."

He scrubbed a hand over his face. As much as he tried to brush off everything she said as lies and nonsense, some of her words burrowed beneath his skin.

What if this Steven guy was better for Mandy and Phoenix? If she wanted more kids, could Zack get on board with that? If they were as awesome as Phoenix, he could, but what if two ended up being more than he could handle? And it would mean leaving her to do twice the work whenever he had to travel. How would she begin a new career if he was gone so much?

If Jill hoped to make him doubt everything he was certain about before walking in, she'd succeeded.

He left his seat. "I wish I could say it was nice to meet you, but you're about as pleasant as a boot to the balls. Have a safe flight home, Jill."

He got the hell out of there before she said another word. His toe tapped the hallway carpet as he waited for the elevator. When it dinged and opened, Mandy stood in front of him. Her wide eyes were red-rimmed, and her face was flushed. Phoenix was in a stroller, holding his frog and smiling up at Zack.

"Hey, buddy." He waved at Phoenix. Mandy's gaze dropped to the floor, and he touched her chin to lift it. "Baby, what's wrong?"

"Not here." Her bottom lip trembled as she pushed the stroller out of the elevator. "I'll put him down for his nap and meet you in your room."

So, lunch and the zoo were off.

What the fuck happened?

Phoenix thrust his arms out, his tiny fingers reaching for Zack. He smiled, unbuckling the stroller before picking him up. It was still strange to be part of a family he didn't even know he had a few weeks ago, but it felt more natural every time Phoenix smiled at him or asked for his attention.

It warmed something in his chest to be wanted by someone so innocent and pure, who didn't lie or fake anything. Whatever feelings Phoenix had, he made them known by crying, babbling, smiling, fussing, or laughing. Zack used to think babies were stupid and annoying, but the fact that they were always so honest was pretty damn cool.

Phoenix's mom, on the other hand, was harder to read. She was clearly upset but fighting to keep it under control, most likely for Phoenix's sake.

She tried to take him, but Zack shook his head.

"Let me help. Your mom doesn't scare me. Though, she gave it a hell of a shot."

Mandy frowned, her eyes finally meeting his. "Why did you come to her room?"

"I was looking for you." He took a chance and touched her cheek, but she jerked from his grasp and pulled away. "Mandy, what the—"

"I said not here." Tears glossed her eyes as she took Phoenix. "Say goodbye to Zack, sweetie." Her voice trembled, the sadness painting every syllable ripping at his heart.

Zack held up his hand. "High-five?"

Phoenix smacked his palm with a wide, almost toothless grin. Zack wrapped him in a one-armed hug and kissed the top of his head as Mandy stared at the door. His heart cracked at being so close to her while she clearly wanted nothing to do with him.

"Later, little dude." He waved, and Phoenix waved back as she opened the door to Jill's room. "I'll see you soon?"

Mandy gave a terse nod, disappeared behind the door, and left him in the hallway, feeling like someone had ejected him from his own life.

A few hours ago, she was happy.

When she left his room, she was excited about their future. She was excited to take Phoenix to Portland.

All of that was real.

What happened between leaving his room and finishing breakfast with Phoenix and her mom? Jill knew something was up with Mandy, but she was clueless about the details, too. Because if it were over something he'd done, she would've thrown it in his face like a rancid tomato.

He took the elevator back to his suite and collapsed onto the couch, feeling exhausted even though the day was only half over. A bag of chocolate roses sat on the coffee table—the last gift of sweets he bought to help Mandy savor her first European adventure. Three weeks had zipped by, and hopefully, he could fix whatever had upset her before the trip ended on a sour note.

It felt like hours had passed before there was a knock at his door. He opened it to find Mandy looking even more miserable than moments before—her skin was pale, her eyes puffy like she'd been crying. She sat on the couch, and he settled a few cushions away, giving her space.

"Do you want something to drink or—"

"You lied to me."

"Lied?" His brows furrowed. "About what?"

"You got me the job. Cassie told me. All this time, I thought I earned it on my own while everyone around me thinks I'm only here because I fucked you."

Her sharp, heated words were a kick to the gut.

There was no use denying it. He'd really fucked-up this time.

As she stared, waiting for a response, his pulse thrummed in his ears, and it was hard to breathe. He forced air into his lungs as his vision blurred at the edges. Remembering Charlotte and Matthew's descriptions of panic attacks, this felt the same. Elbows braced on knees, he took a few deep breaths. This conversation was too important to lose his shit and spin out.

"Mandy, no." He scooted a little closer, and she moved further away. "I mean, yes, I called Sophia and asked her to get you an interview with Shane, but—"

"The *only* interview he gave. Because of Sophia's status, he just handed it to me. And I looked like a fucking fool, pretending I didn't know you while *everyone* knew the truth, probably laughing behind my back. Even your friends must've known!"

"I..." He rubbed the back of his neck with an unsteady hand, searching for the right words. "I didn't know he didn't interview anyone else. I only asked that he hold off on hiring anyone until he interviewed you. I knew you'd blow him away."

"That makes it okay? And to make things worse, you asked *Ted* to lie for you!" Her hands fisted in her lap, her knuckles bleached. "You manipulated me! Toyed with my life. What made you think you had the right to do that?"

"Your new boss hurt you, Mandy!" A spike of pain shot through his clenched jaw, the anger over finding out she was in danger bubbling to the surface. "Kyla told me what he said. I heard the vile shit he spewed in that recording. You weren't safe. You needed to leave and go after your dream."

She threw up her hands, her cheeks flaming. "Again, you don't have the fucking right to decide how I live my life! I was trying to get out of there but had to stay until I found another job. Phoenix is counting on me, and I couldn't go without a paycheck."

"Now you have enough money to start managing, even if finding clients and earning a decent commission takes a while. I'm sorry I lied, but I'm not sorry you can finally have what you want."

"I wanted *you*!" Tears slipped down her cheeks, her voice breaking. "But you messed with my life so I'd be near you again, knowing how easy it is to charm your way into my bed. And I was so fucking lonely and missed you so much that I made it even easier this time."

No.

That was all wrong. He had to turn this around fast.

"Baby, please stop." It took every bit of his restraint not to lunge forward to hold her. "That's not true."

She roughly wiped at tears. "Of course, it is. I fell in love with you even harder this time, thinking we'd be a family. It makes this so much fucking worse because you hurt Phoenix too." She bent forward, her hands covering her face as her shoulders quaked with sobs.

"Mandy, no." Her words and the heartbreak lacing every word pummeled his chest. "It wasn't like that. I wanted a second chance, but more than that, I wanted you to be safe, happy, and not struggling to get by. Knowing about Phoenix, I'm even more glad I did it. What if that shithead hurt you? Or fired you because you wouldn't screw him?"

When she looked up, tears streaked her face, dark eyeliner smeared in the corners of her eyes. "Those would've been my problems to solve. You don't get to act like some puppet master hero because you want to fix everything broken in my life!"

"I'm sorry. I should've told you. I didn't want you to think you didn't deserve that job because you do."

"You know what I deserve? People who know how hard it is for me to trust and don't fucking lie to me. People who don't fool me into thinking my heart's safe with them when everything that led me there is based on a goddamn lie."

With every word, he felt her slipping away. Even worse, he didn't have enough relationship experience to have the foggiest fucking clue how to stop it. He was furious with himself for not coming clean. Instead, she had to hear someone else's version of the truth.

"I'll do anything it takes to fix this," he begged. "I want to go back to our perfect morning when we talked about making this work. When you said I had everything it took to be a great dad and appreciated how hard I've worked to figure it out. We *can* be a family. I want that, too. I want to put a ring on your finger and have all the beautiful, sock-throwing babies you want. I used to think those things were prisons, but I was so fucking wrong. I just never saw you coming. But you opened my stupid, blind eyes to what life can be, and I can't go back."

"Please, stop." She swiped a knuckle beneath her eyes. "I can't be with someone I can't trust. Now, I'm questioning everything you've done and said. What was true, and what wasn't? We gave this a second chance. I don't have it in me to give you another."

"Don't say that." Tears stung the corners of his eyes as her watery gaze fell to the carpet. "Everything else was the truth, I swear. I know I fucked-up, but this can't be the end for us."

"You can have as much or as little contact with Phoenix as you want." She sniffed, her tone flat and emotionless as her detached mask slipped on. "He loved having you around, so I hope you'll find a way to be in his life. Even if it's just calling him once in a while."

A sob cracked in Zack's chest, and he slid closer, taking her hand. "Please don't do this. I love you. All of this was real, I promise. Don't make me let you go again. I can't!"

She leaned forward and pressed her lips to his, but it didn't feel like forgiveness.

It felt like goodbye.

Her hand slipped from his as she stood and walked out the door.

As he replayed her words in his head, one thing was obvious. She swore she'd never do it, but it was exactly what he deserved.

Now, she regretted him.

35

Mandy

Five hours. That's all that remained of this job Mandy had been so excited for, and now every task on her list felt like torture. Felix and Roger must've sensed her foul mood because they were at the arena an hour early for soundcheck, sober, smiling, and ready for the stage.

She knocked on Cassie's dressing room door, waiting for her "Come in" before walking inside. Mandy wasn't about to walk in on another vulgar display of infidelity and exploitation.

Cassie sat at the vanity table, applying a rose-colored blush to her cheeks with a large makeup brush. "Lock it, please."

Their eyes met in the mirror, and Mandy nodded, locking the door.

Cassie spun around in her chair. "I owe you a fucking massive apology, Mandy. I didn't know you and Zack had a kid. And I saw your resume in Shane's room. You deserved this job. Hell, you deserve Shane's job. You sure as fuck have more integrity than him. I had no right to suggest you were just some bimbo Zack wanted to help. Especially since I've seen plenty of proof that isn't true."

Mandy shook her head, hugging her clipboard over the gnawing ache in her chest. "It's fine. He should've told me the truth. Doesn't matter now."

Of course, it mattered. Maybe someday, it wouldn't hurt so much, but right then, it took everything she had not to run back to her room, lock the door, and bawl her eyes out until it was time to fly home.

"Please tell me you didn't break up because of the shit I said." Cassie frowned, her shoulders slumped forward. "Throughout the tour, I saw how you looked at each other. I think I lashed out at you because I wish the men in my life looked at me like that. Somehow, you found love in this crazy fucking world of ours. Don't let it get away because some jealous fame whore took her issues out on you in an elevator."

"You're not a fame whore." She sat beside Cassie with a weary sigh. Being reminded of the love she'd just lost was another knife to the heart, but like every time she'd dealt with difficult things, she didn't have the luxury of falling apart. "You're like walking sunshine, and it's been fun working with you despite the not-so-fun moments. I hope someday you find someone who'll love and appreciate you."

Cassie's face brightened. "Walking sunshine. I like that. Maybe it'll be a song title on my solo album."

"Solo, huh?" Mandy's eyebrows rose at the unexpected news. "Good for you."

"Yeah, I'm sick of Felix and Roger's slacker bullshit, and Shane scored me a killer deal. As soon as I signed, I ended things with him. I realize using him was shitty and un-feminist as hell, but at least I got what I wanted. And I had a P.I. take photos of the two of us together for insurance. If he fucks with my career or yours, I'll mail them straight to the media and his wife. Hopefully, she figures him out on her own."

Mandy didn't know how to respond. It would be easy to continue judging Cassie for using her body to get ahead, but what was the point? Both women were doing their best in difficult circumstances. Mandy had her own tough choices and consequences to live with.

She glanced at her watch. "Do you need anything from me before show-time?"

Cassie stood, opening her arms wide. "Just a hug."

Mandy got up, and they wrapped their arms around each other. They both needed comfort after a long, eventful, and exhausting three weeks.

"Have a great show tonight," Mandy said, letting her go. "If you're ever in Denver, call me. I'd love to see you again." She walked to the door, and as she turned the handle, Cassie's voice stopped her.

"Hey, Mandy."

"Yeah?"

"The contract I signed is for one album." A smile tugged at the edges of her glossy red mouth. "If I blow up, I'm firing Shane. If you're managing when that happens..." Her smile grew. "*You* call *me*."

⁕

While Fury Fuel did their soundcheck, Mandy packed up Felix and Roger's dressing room before doing the same for Cassie. The band was flying back to Boston early in the morning, so Shane had asked her to get all their things together and on the bus before the show. She was startled by a voice in the doorway as she folded the last of Cassie's pleather miniskirts and tucked it into a suitcase.

"Hey, Mandy."

She turned to find Adam, and her heart sank. The last thing she needed was another heavy conversation. A frown pulled at the corners of his mouth as he walked in and closed the door, clutching a white paper bag.

"Hi." Feeling awkward, she crossed her arms over her chest. "Do you need something?"

He held out the bag. "Zack wanted you to have this. He figured you didn't want to see him and didn't want to make you uncomfortable at work."

She took the bag and peered inside. Foil-wrapped, flower-shaped candies filled it—the final chocolates from their final stop. She shoved down the surge of emotion rising in her throat. "Thanks, Adam. Please thank him for me."

He sighed, sinking into the velvet-lined chair by the vanity table. "He told me not to throw my two cents at you, but this is fucked. Zack's spent the last year and a half in so much fucking pain over losing you. When he knew he'd see you again, he worked hard to get his shit together because he thought you were out of his league. He changed to be ready to give you everything. And you have a kid together. That man hated kids three weeks ago, and now he won't shut up about how great Phoenix is. He forgave you for not telling him, so forgive him for doing something stupid with good intentions."

She set the chocolates on the vanity, tears blurring her vision. "I'm sorry I hurt him. I wish it were as simple as brushing it off and forgiving him, but he broke my trust."

And since he orchestrated this second chance by using sweet, loyal Ted as a pawn, he didn't deserve a third. When she returned to Denver, she'd sit down with her friend and hear the full truth.

"I get that. But since I've known him, I've never seen him happier than he was with you and Phoenix. You're good for each other."

She'd thought they were, too, but her broken heart said otherwise. "He's lucky to have you, Adam. Thanks for the talk. And the chocolate."

"He'd kick my ass if he knew I said any of that, but he's like my brother. I had to try. Take care of yourself, Mandy. I really hope to see you again."

He left with a wave, and she grabbed the bag, unwrapped a candy, and chomped off a dark chocolate caramel rosebud. The sugary perfection melted on her tongue. Like always, Zack knew exactly what she liked.

Knowing he was just a few rooms away triggered a tugging feeling in her chest.

But feelings couldn't erase his betrayal. Listening to her heart instead of her brain got her into this mess. Soon, she'd be home, and life would return to normal. Well, a new normal. With the money she'd made and the check from Ted, she could focus on starting her dream career. She'd reach out to the band that made the demo Ash gave her and invite them to be her first clients. It would be a welcome distraction from the heartbreak that would worsen before it got better.

Now, she needed to get through the last day of the most exhilarating, exhausting, and heart-wrenching three weeks of her life.

36

Zack

Zack bolted upright from where he'd passed out on the floor of his Paris suite, coughing, sputtering, and soaked with water. Sandra hovered above him, holding an empty, overturned ice bucket, tiny droplets dripping from the rim.

"What the fuck, Sandra?!" Zack shook out his drenched hair and got to his feet.

Her head tilted, a pile of long red curls falling over her shoulder. "I shocked you out of your drunken stupor. It always worked on my stepdad."

"I'm not drunk."

She blinked. "You're not?"

"No." He wrung out the hem of his shirt, creating a dark puddle on the beige carpet. At least his jeans were dry.

Sandra shrugged. "Oops."

Adam emerged from the bedroom and handed Zack a dry T-shirt and a towel. "Sorry, man. It's almost time to leave for the arena, and we just assumed—"

"That I went right back to being a weak, stupid piece of shit?" He peeled off his drenched shirt and tossed it at Adam.

The assumption was fair given his history, and he'd been tempted since Mandy left, but he didn't give in.

He'd slept like shit, so after soundcheck, Zack returned to his room. As he shuffled to the bed to rest before the show, he remembered lying there with her, and his knees buckled. He collapsed in a pathetic, tear-soaked heap on the floor before eventually crashing out. Only sleep offered a break from the feeling of his chest being ripped open and hollowed out.

He hadn't left the spot until the water bucket alarm clock shocked him awake.

"Sorry to disappoint you." He slipped the dry shirt over his head and toweled off his hair.

"Disappoint me?" Adam wrapped him in a hug. "I'm so fucking proud of you, man."

Sandra squeezed them both. "Me too. It couldn't have been easy to resist getting blitzed."

It wasn't. But after what he'd done, their pride was undeserved. Sure, he avoided his old vices, but his dishonest bullshit drove away the woman he loved. It wouldn't be long before that Steven fucker or some other guy realized how amazing she was and swooped in.

"You okay?" Adam squeezed his shoulder.

"Nope." Tears trailed to Zack's chin as he sank into the massive black leather couch beside the wall of windows, looking out over Paris. "I'm pretty fucking far from okay. But I'll pull it together for the show."

Sandra pulled a baggie from her purse, setting it in his lap as she sat beside him. "Eat this. Carbs won't mend a broken heart, but they try their best."

In the bag was a croissant loaded with sliced deli meat and cheese. Though he hadn't eaten in at least twelve hours, his stomach was too twisted with nerves and misery to touch it.

"I dropped off the chocolate roses after soundcheck." Adam sat on his other side. "She said to say thanks."

"How did she look?" Zack rubbed his forehead, remembering the devastation on her face before she left his room.

"She'll be okay." Adam's dodge of the question said it all. "A hot shower might make you feel better. Or a quick run. We don't have to be at the arena for another hour. We thought we'd have to drag your ass out of bed and pour coffee down your throat. Glad we don't."

Zack scoffed. He was struggling to stay upright, so running was out. He'd be lucky to get through the last three weeks of shows without having a nervous breakdown in front of thirty thousand witnesses. And he wasn't about to go inside the shower that looked too much like the one in Rome he'd shared with Mandy after fulfilling her fantasy of giving up control. The flash of memory was another kick in the gut.

She let him take control because she trusted him completely.

It wasn't easy for her to do, and in the end, he'd proven he wasn't worthy.

"Sandra's bucket shower was enough." Zack dragged a hand through his damp hair.

"Again, sorry about that." Her nose wrinkled. "To make up for it, we'll help you pack for tomorrow, so you don't have to worry about it."

"On it." Adam got up, gathered all the T-shirts and jeans scattered around the room, and stuffed them into a suitcase.

The next day, they'd be on a bus heading for Berlin, leaving Paris and all that happened there in the rearview. It already felt like a wishful fever dream, but the brutal, relentless ache in his chest confirmed it'd all been real. Including the fact that he'd blown his last chance with the love of his life.

She's gone.

It's over.

He'd fucked-up so completely that he deserved every bit of the pain gluing him to that couch.

"Then I'm on caffeine duty." Sandra headed for the minibar and set up the coffeemaker. "We could all use a jolt before showtime, and the backstage sludge is revolting."

Zack's jaw clamped shut, his molars grinding. "Why the fuck didn't I tell her the truth when I had the chance?"

Sandra and Adam stopped what they were doing and turned to him.

"Because love makes people do stupid things," she said, returning to the couch. "But you can't give up. A lot's happened for her in the last few weeks. It would overwhelm anyone. Once she's back in Denver and has had time for her head to clear, reach out."

Zack shook his head, wishing it were that simple. "You didn't hear her, Sandra. She's done with me. I had so many fucking chances to tell her the truth, and I didn't. She asked me outright if I helped her get the job, and I lied to her face. I don't deserve another shot because I'd just fuck it up again."

It killed him that Jill was right—he hurt them as predicted, and they deserved better. He betrayed Mandy by lying and robbed Phoenix of the chance to have his parents together.

"I'm with Curly Top." Adam set the luggage by the door. "Three weeks. Give her three weeks to cool off and yourself three weeks to figure out how to make it right. And I'm sorry to bring this up, but..."

Zack groaned, his head falling back against the cushion. "Fucking *what*?"

"I'm relieved you didn't backslide and get drunk because we need your focus on work."

He knew that, but the last thing he needed was a reminder of the pressure to perform flawless sets on top of everything else. Or the reminder that for twenty-one more days, he'd be on the other side of the world from the two people who owned his heart.

"I swear to Christ, Adam, if you mention that goddamn contract," he said through clenched teeth, "I'll fucking snap. I know I can't fuck-up. I'll be at every soundcheck, signing, and stupid goddamn interview and give everything I've got for the rest of the tour. Just please shut the fuck up about it."

"Understood." Adam's hands raised. "Sorry. Let's get some coffee and food in your grumpy ass and head for the arena."

Zack took a few bites of the sandwich and guzzled two mugs of coffee just to make them happy. As he tied his boots, an intense wave of grief crashed over him. He'd give his left arm just to hear Mandy's voice. Or Phoenix's infectious laugh. Instead, he'd have to settle for their echoes in his mind as he put one shuffling boot in front of the other, slapped on a smile, and got to work.

37

Mandy

In her suite, all of Mandy's luggage sat packed and stacked alongside Phoenix's and her mother's. Her job was done, and their flight home was only three hours away. Her mom was doing a little last-minute sightseeing, and Mandy appreciated the peace to collect herself.

Phoenix sat in his playpen, happily babbling to his stuffed frog like best friends planning an adventure. Fortunately, he wasn't old enough to understand how royally she'd screwed up his chances of having his father in his life every day. If she'd been stronger, she would've stuck to the original plan and built a friendship with Zack instead of giving in to her emotions. She'd still do her best to encourage a bond between them, but it would be a second-rate version of the one she'd hoped for.

Someone knocked at the door, and she set down the backpack she'd organized for the plane. The part of her that felt empty and lonelier than ever hoped it was Zack, but leaving would be a thousand times harder if it were. She despised goodbyes—more than ever after this trip.

The new friend she'd called an hour ago was there instead.

Charlotte offered a sympathetic smile before hugging her tight. "I know this is a dumb question, but are you okay?"

Tears welled in Mandy's raw, puffy eyes, but she refused to cry. If she started again, she might never stop. "I will be. Thanks for coming. I know this is an awful favor, and I'm sorry. I just can't—" A brutal sob seized her throat, cutting her off.

Charlotte hugged tighter. "It's okay. Like you, I'm tough as hell and here to help you through this. Then, I'll help him."

Zack deserved the chance to say goodbye to his son, but Mandy couldn't bear to witness it. She might cave in and take him back, leaving herself vulnerable to being hurt again. So, like a coward, she asked Charlotte to take Phoenix up to give them time together.

Charlotte walked over to the playpen and grinned. "Good morning, handsome. Are you excited to ride in the airplane?"

He waved at her, and she waved back. He held his frog in the air, and she took it, making it hop and ribbit along the edges of his playpen while he giggled.

"I hope our next one's a boy. And exactly like this one." Charlotte touched the tip of his nose with the frog and held it out. He took it back, hugging it to his chest. "I'll need about three years to prepare first. Thank goddess for IUDs." She sat on the bed, and Mandy joined her.

"I want more someday, too. Maybe things worked out for the best." Despite what Zack said about wanting to get married and have as many kids as she wanted, she was certain it was a desperate, last-ditch effort to hold on to her. He'd never said those things before.

As her mom kept reminding her, Steven would have another kid tomorrow if he could. Although he was nice, Mandy's heart was too bruised to give him a real chance. Besides, there was no spark. She knew exactly what it felt like to journey from sparks to deeply, madly in love and wouldn't settle for anything less.

"For what it's worth," Charlotte said, "his intentions were good. He should've told you the truth when you arrived, but I understand why he didn't. It doesn't excuse it, but all this is new to him. Doing the right thing is hard when you're making it up as you go."

"If he lied about that to my face, he might've lied about everything that made me fall in love with him. Without trust, it can't work."

Charlotte nodded slowly, the beginnings of a frown tugging at her lips. "Tyler and I broke up once over trust issues. He didn't tell me something he should've, and I flipped. I thought nothing could change my mind, but that weirdo sat on my porch in the rain, professing his love through my door and apologizing for everything he'd ever done to hurt me. And he slept on that cold concrete slab because he wanted to know I was safe." She touched her chest, letting out a slow breath. "Forgiving him was the best decision I ever made. He's the one I belong with. I'm not saying it's the same for you and Zack, but when you get home, think about all you'll be giving up if you don't give him a chance to make things right."

She was glad that Charlotte found happiness through forgiveness, but it didn't change Mandy's mind. "I appreciate what you're saying, but I can't. I'd be setting myself up for more disappointment and wasted time."

Charlotte's chin dipped, holding her gaze. "Can you honestly tell me it feels like you wasted time with him? You know what real love feels like. You have your son. Before the tour, I sat with Zack at my kitchen table, and he told me about all his fears of messing this up. Of not being good enough for you. He wanted it to work *so badly* that he jumped at what he thought was his best shot. He was a bonehead for not coming clean. But that bonehead loves you with his whole heart. He'd do anything for you. And for Phoenix. Most people go their whole lives without ever finding that."

Mandy blinked back a fresh wave of tears and sniffed. She knew exactly what she was losing, but there was no fixing what he'd broken. "We need to leave for the airport soon."

Charlotte glanced at her watch. "Shit." She stood, looking down into the playpen. "Okay, mister. Grab Froggie Mercury, and let's go visit your...?" She looked at Mandy, her eyebrows raised in question.

"Zack." Even saying his name was like a jagged spear through her heart. "He never asked Phoenix to call him 'Dad,' so I'm leaving it up to him to decide if and when he's ready."

Charlotte's gaze warmed with sympathy before they hugged again. "I'll miss you, girl! I wish we could go to each other's houses for coffee while the babies babble and toss socks and toys at each other."

Mandy laughed, wishing for the same. She almost had it but was left with another disappointment to swallow instead. "Next time you're in Denver, it's a date."

Charlotte let her go and picked up Phoenix. "You're a lot bigger than my Anna Jude. No wonder your mom has such sick biceps." She bumped Mandy's hip with her own on the walk to the door.

Mandy waved at Phoenix until the door shut between them. The second the elevator dinged, she crumpled to the floor and fell apart.

38

Zack

Zack had hoped to find Mandy outside his suite door, but the sight of Phoenix hugging his frog was just as welcome.

"Hey, little dude." Zack hoped he didn't look as ragged and beaten down as he felt. "What a nice surprise."

When Phoenix tipped forward and reached for him, Charlotte drew in a shaky inhale, her eyes glossy in the overhead light. Zack took him into his arms and held him close.

Over the baby's shoulder, Zack's eyes met Charlotte's. She shook her head, a silent confirmation that Mandy wasn't coming. She'd avoided him before and after last night's show, and it wouldn't have been right to hunt her down and cause a scene. So, the only goodbye they'd have was the depressing as fuck kiss on his couch before she walked out of his life.

"She wanted you to have the chance to say goodbye to him," Charlotte explained, tears dotting her dark lashes, "but knew it would be too hard, so I'm happy to help."

"Thank you." His chest warmed with gratitude for his friend, a welcome break from feeling cold, empty, and hopeless.

"Aunt Charlotte will take any chance she gets to poke this little one's belly." She did, and Phoenix giggled before chomping on his frog. "Do you want me to leave so you can have a minute?"

Zack shook his head, knowing he wouldn't be able to keep his shit together without her keeping him grounded. He already felt the prickle of tears gathering behind his eyelids.

"Let's sit down, yeah?" He sniffed as he set Phoenix on the carpet and sat beside him. "Your frog looks like he's ready for a nap."

Phoenix threw the frog over the back of the couch and laughed when it smacked the coffee table. Zack crawled on all fours to pick it up, sticking it in his mouth before crawling back and dropping it at Phoenix's feet, making him laugh even harder. They kept at it, almost breaking a lamp and knocking over a fake plant, but replaceable things didn't matter when this might be all the time they had together for a while.

The final leg of the tour would last the next three weeks. Once the band signed the new contract, it would be more traveling, endless hours in the studio, and more lonely nights in lonely hotel beds.

"You're great with him, Zack." Charlotte stroked a knuckle along Phoenix's cheek. "Even though you shouldn't teach him that it's okay to throw things."

Zack grinned despite the grief ripping him apart from the inside. "You've clearly never heard of sports."

She laughed and shoved his arm.

"Did you see that, Phoenix?" He pointed at Charlotte. "Aunt Charlotte thinks throwing things is bad, but pushing is okay. Hell of a role model."

"Well, damn. You found my one flaw."

Phoenix babbled as he removed his left sock and threw it in the air. It landed on Charlotte's head.

"Not cool, kid." She plucked the sock from her hair and put it back on his foot.

Zack shrugged. "He's a rebel like his dad."

Phoenix pulled the sock off again and threw it at Zack. "Dack."

Zack and Charlotte froze.

"What did he say?" she whispered for no good reason.

"Dack!" Off came the other sock.

Zack glanced at her. "Was that real or babbling?"

"Dack!"

Once might've been a fluke. Twice, a coincidence. That third time was unmistakable.

"Holy crap, it's like Dad and Zack squished together," Charlotte said, swallowing hard like there was a lump trapped in her throat too. "I hate to spoil the moment, but Mandy's going to be incredibly bummed that she missed his first word. And that it wasn't Mama. Personally, I'd riot."

"Then don't tell her." He pulled Phoenix into his lap as the joy of witnessing the milestone mingled with the misery of all he was losing. Of all the words and names Phoenix could've said, he chose his. "She doesn't need another reason to be disappointed."

Charlotte glared. "It's so hard not to push you again. That's what got you in trouble in the first place. She'd rather hear the truth than have you conceal shit to spare her feelings."

Her words triggered a memory. On its heels was a smack-upside-the-head moment of clarity.

I am such a fucking idiot.

"Honesty is always better," he said, "even when it stings."

"Exactly! Is that from some philosopher or something?"

"Yeah. Mandy Marie Reid. She said that right after we met. She told me what she needed on day one. All I had to do was listen, and I couldn't even do that."

A long string of drool slid from Phoenix's chin, and Zack wiped it off with his hand and onto his jeans. He hadn't even hesitated to do something he would've found disgusting a few weeks ago. If he'd ever doubted being around Phoenix had changed him, his proof was drying on his pocket.

Charlotte checked her watch and sighed. "I hate to say it, but we have to go. Airport time."

Zack smiled through the tears blurring his vision as he picked up Phoenix one last time. "It's been real, kid. Can I get one more Dack for the road?"

"Bahbahbah."

"Close enough." He hugged Phoenix to his chest, not ready to let go. "I'll visit you soon, okay? Take care of your mom for me."

Charlotte wiped the corners of her eyes. "Okay, bud. Say bye-bye to...?" Her gaze slid to Zack.

"Dad." He kissed Phoenix's forehead. "Bye-bye, Phoenix." Zack gave him one last hug as tears slipped to his chin. "I love you."

In his twenty-eight years, he'd only said those words to his parents, Mandy, and now, Phoenix. He loved his friends but never felt compelled to say it out loud. They knew. But he wanted Phoenix to hear it, to know he was created by two people who'd always be there for him. Two people who loved him without condition.

Even if he didn't understand the words, hopefully, he felt them.

Charlotte whimpered, fanning her eyes with her free hand. "I'll come right back, okay? And I'll bring Adam and Ty for reinforcements. Hang in there until then." She hugged him from the side. "You'll be okay. I promise."

When they left, Zack collapsed on the couch and cried like he hadn't since he was ten and broke his leg jumping off the roof of his dad's truck. He'd give anything to trade in his broken heart for a broken bone. This hurt so much worse and would be a lot harder to fix.

And he knew that, like a broken bone, even if it healed, it would never be whole again.

39

Zack

In his Paris suite, a glass of Zack's favorite brand of whiskey sat on the table in front of him, but he hadn't touched it. He'd failed enough lately and wasn't about to let old habits bleed back in. Maybe he ordered it without intending to drink it to prove Jill wrong or to assure himself the changes he'd made would stick. That they weren't just a ploy to get Mandy back—he genuinely wanted to be a better man. There was no bigger test than having old vices within reach as Mandy's plane was taking off, moving further away with every second that passed.

And Phoenix gave him a new reason to stay strong. Zack would never be a clean-cut stockbroker, but he wanted to be someone his son would be proud of and look up to. Lying to Mandy was a mistake and a terrible example of how to treat the people you love.

An apology wasn't enough.

He couldn't let this be how things ended—everyone returning to their lives as if nothing had changed. He needed to stop beating himself up over his failures and decide how to correct them.

First, he needed to shut off Jill's voice in his head, saying Mandy and Phoenix were better off and to let them go. He pushed the glass aside and called the only person who could do a better job than the whiskey.

"Hey, Mom. Is Dad there?"

"Hello to you, too, Zachary. He isn't. Can I help you with something?"

"I…" His throat went tight, his voice breaking as the gravity of his mistakes crashed over him like an avalanche. "Mom, I fucked-up."

"What happened? You can talk to me."

His fingertip tapped the whiskey glass. "Can you put your judgments about my life aside if I do?"

She was quiet for a moment. "Yes. I'm sorry if I've made you feel otherwise. Go on."

"I have a kid."

There was a gasp on the other line, followed by a shattering sound. "Did I hear you correctly? You have a *child*?"

"Yeah. A son. He'll be one in September. Did something break?"

"A plate. It's nothing. Please tell me this boy isn't the product of some backstage dalliance with a ridiculous groupie." She cleared her throat. "I'm sorry. That was definitely judgmental. Go on."

"Mandy's the mother."

Another gasp, followed by a whimper, then sniffling. His dad wouldn't have cried, but maybe Zack needed to hear an emotional reaction to his problems instead of his father's logical one. It was comforting while his own emotions were so raw. Without numbing them out, they stayed uncomfortably close to the surface every second he was awake.

"Oh, son. You've never spoken about a woman the way you spoke about her. And when you did, you lit up like I hadn't seen in years. Make it work this time, no matter what it requires."

"I lied to her. My intentions were good, but I don't think I can fix it."

"Of course, you can. Show her you're willing to sacrifice for her. And your son. My lord, I can't believe I'm saying that to you. Zachary, you have a *son*." She started crying again, but he knew they were happy tears. She never thought he'd settle down and give her grandkids and was jealous of her friends who had them. Knowing her, she'd run to Toys R Us after they hung up to start the spoiling.

"The one sacrifice I'd have to make…" He stared at the dark liquid in his glass. "I can't turn my back on my best friends and this thing we created together."

"Oh, sweetheart. Choose the child you created with the love of your life."

Over thirteen years, he'd built something with Adam and Tyler that became so much bigger than they'd ever thought possible. When the band started, they were three weirdo kids jamming in Zack's garage whenever his parents were busy with church duties. Tyler was the most naturally talented by a mile, challenging Adam and Zack to practice until their hands bled to reach his level.

They became a tight, coordinated unit commanding stages across the globe. They were about to sign a seven-figure contract, get to work on the next album, and plan the next tour. He loved his career and was proud of what they'd accomplished.

How could he give that up?

He pinched the bridge of his nose, tears dampening his fingertips. "I don't know if I can."

"If you don't, you'll regret it the rest of your life. One day, you'll find out she moved on. *Your son* will call someone else 'Dad.' Someone else will teach him how to be a man."

"Her mom's been trying to set her up with some perfect stockbroker douchebag. Maybe she's better off with him. Maybe they both are."

"Zachary Alexander Maine, stop talking like that! Even if it doesn't work out with Mandy, that boy will always be your son. It's up to you whether you're a strong, reliable presence in his life or a stranger who sends checks once a year in a birthday card."

There was no perfect solution. Either way, he'd hurt people he loved.

"No matter what I do, I'll disappoint people."

"You're an important part of that band, son. And I'm proud of your talent and success. I know it sounds harsh, but you can be replaced. There's no replacement for you in your son's life. Even if she marries Mr. Perfect, *you* are that boy's father." She blew her nose. "What's the baby's name?"

"Phoenix Zachary." Saying the name made the corners of his mouth turn up. Judging by the sounds on the other end of the line, it did the opposite for his mother—she pulled in a shaky breath and sniffed before blowing her nose again. "For a kid, he's pretty great."

"You met him?!"

He filled her in on their time together in Paris. He even told her about the arguments he'd had with Jill and the awful things she said.

"That woman better pray we're never in the same room together." Her angry mama bear tone made him smile. "I appreciate we share similar beliefs, but she has no right to judge you like that. Or to say Phoenix would be better off without you. That's rubbish."

"Are you all done judging me then?"

She was quiet for a few beats. "I'll try. I haven't always been as present and accepting as I should've been, but I love you, Zachary. And no matter what I think about your choices, I will always be on your side. Always."

"I love you too. Thanks, Mom."

"Thank me by bringing over my amaretto cookies and photos of my grandson. Call when you get home so I know you're safe. Goodbye, sweetheart."

After hanging up, his gaze shifted to the sky outside his window. He wondered if Phoenix was anxious on the plane like his mom and wanted to know when they landed safely. And he regretted not being there to hold Mandy's hand on the flight.

The entire situation was fucked, but one bright spot was knowing he was capable of so much more than he'd thought. His dad and friends were right all along.

After the call, he needed fresh air to clear his head, so he walked down to the lobby. At the exit, something on the ground caught his eye. He bent over and picked up a familiar stuffed green frog.

Phoenix must've dropped it when they left the hotel. The green fur blurred as tears flooded Zack's eyes. He'd cried more in the last twenty-four hours than in the last fifteen years. He thought about how Phoenix laughed when he tossed it around the room, and Zack fetched it over and over like a Labrador. He needed more moments like that—pure, unhurried time that brought each other joy and deepened their connection. He wanted to watch Phoenix grow up, not settle for occasional phone calls and flat, one-dimensional glimpses in photographs.

He pocketed the toy and spent the next two hours wandering the streets of Paris. While waiting for a light to change, the neon sign outside a tattoo shop snagged his attention. A design had been kicking around his head for days, and without a second's hesitation, he headed inside to get it done.

Two hours later, with the fresh ink stinging under a layer of ointment and thin plastic film, he walked some more, trying to figure out how to fix what he'd broken. He thought about his last conversation with Mandy, the goodbye with Phoenix, and the talk with his mom.

When he returned to his hotel, he knew what to do. He found Tyler and Adam finishing dinner in the hotel restaurant and took an empty seat at their table.

"Where the hell have you been?" Tyler wiped his mouth on a napkin.

"Bus leaves for Berlin in an hour," Adam mumbled around a hefty bite of his sandwich. "We were starting to worry."

Zack leaned his elbows on the table and took a deep, steadying breath. "This is my last tour."

Adam's sandwich fell through his fingers and onto his plate in a messy pile.

Tyler's dark eyebrows pinched together. "What the fuck are you talking about?"

Zack's gaze shifted between the two men—the best friends he'd ever had.

He loved the life they built together, but his wants and needs weren't the only ones that mattered anymore. His mom was right—if he didn't do everything possible to make it work with Mandy and Phoenix, he'd regret it for the rest of his life.

"I'm not signing the contract," Zack said, "and I'm moving to Denver. I'm sorry to do this to you, but I have to choose between you and them. I choose them."

Tyler looked conflicted, his lips pressed in a grim line, the crease between his brows deepening. "What if we can figure out a long-distance solution? You can fly to Portland when we need to write. It's, what, a two-and-a-half-hour flight? And when it's time to cut a new album, you can record your parts in Denver or fly in on weekends."

"We've never worked that way, Ty." Zack held his friend's gaze, watching the opposing flashes of protest and understanding play out behind his eyes. "You get an idea at midnight, we're at your place by twelve-thirty, and three new songs are done before the sun's up. I'll call around and help you find someone the label will approve so the contract isn't at risk. Don't let me hold you back."

"Bullshit." Adam shoved his plate aside. "We've changed things for Ty since his kid popped out, and we can change things for you if you need to move to fucking Colorado."

"We can and will." Tyler's eyes stayed on Zack, his jaw ticking. "I understand where you're coming from. I wouldn't want to be away from Charlotte and Anna Jude for a day, let alone weeks at a time. Our lives are evolving, and we can figure out how to make everyone happy without crashing this thing we built into a fucking brick wall."

"Exactly. This is goddamn ridiculous," Adam hissed. "You are *not* quitting the band."

Zack wouldn't drag them down by his choices. And he wouldn't spend half his life on airplanes zipping back and forth between the only life he'd known and the one he didn't think he wanted until he had a taste of it.

"I'm sorry, but..." Zack pushed back in his chair and stood. "I just did."

40

Mandy

Mandy's toe bounced as she dialed the phone number on the back of the Toxic Shade demo tape Ash had given her.

She was doing this.

The day after returning from Paris, she called Sophia, and they talked for over an hour. Mandy's hand had cramped from all the notes she'd taken about approaching new clients, drawing up contracts, and commanding respect from stubborn, gate-keeping men who want to perpetuate the industry's toxic culture—people like her recent ex-bosses. Sophia shared stories of guys she'd encountered during her career who made James and Shane seem like angels.

This wasn't a job for weak, shrinking violets, and Mandy was neither.

She'd spent the two days since that call preparing for this one. It was a welcome distraction from her heartbreak and the aggravating uncertainty about how to fix it.

"Hello?" The voice was deep and unmistakably that of the lead singer of the band she'd played on repeat all morning. Music played in the background at his house, but she heard him fine.

"Hi, this is Mandy Reid. Jerry, right? Ash gave me your tape a while back, and I—"

"Mandy! Yeah, I know who you are. I've been going to Rollin' Rockies since I got my first fake ID."

She smiled. "There's no way I was manning the door. I would've caught it."

He laughed, the background music quieting. "So, what's up? Did you like the tape?"

"I absolutely loved it. Sorry I took so long to reach out. I'm calling to see if you still need a manager."

A lighter clicked, followed by a deep inhale. "Shit, yeah, we do. It feels like we're stuck in rock and roll limbo hell until we get one."

"I'd love to represent your band, Jerry. I'm new to the role, but no one will work harder for you. I have connections to get you the airplay and stage time you need to grow your audience. Then, we'll work on scoring you a record deal." She chewed her bottom lip, his silence making her nervous. "Are you willing to take a chance on me?"

"Shit, we totally would. Problem is, we're moving to Seattle in a few weeks. We figured we'd chase the last ripples of the grunge wave before it's over for good."

Every ounce of her excitement deflated. "Seattle?"

"Yeah. Otherwise, it'd be an easy yes. Sorry to disappoint you. You should look us up if you're ever in the Northwest."

"I will. Thanks, Jerry. Good luck with the move."

She hung up and stared at her kitchen wall with slumped shoulders, reeling from yet another massive disappointment in her life.

If she didn't find a band in the next few months that would earn her a decent commission, she'd have to find another day job before the tour money ran out.

And she'd have no choice but to give up the dream for good.

She wasn't touching the money from Zack because it was for Phoenix. As promised, a deposit appeared in her account on the first of the month, but he hadn't called or reached out. To be fair, neither had she. Every time she considered picking up the phone, she chickened out.

Phoenix's cries echoed through the house.

"I'm coming, Little Bug." She walked to her son's bedroom, lifting him from his crib. "Did you have a nice nap?" She held him close and rubbed his back, but he wouldn't settle. His red-rimmed eyes searched the room as he continued bawling. "What are you looking for?"

Since he was three months old, he'd had a favorite blanket or toy that soothed him, and it changed every few weeks. Lately, his favorite toy was the stuffed frog Zack gave him, but she hadn't seen it since they left the hotel in Paris.

"Are you looking for the frog you got from your d—" She cleared her throat, hoping to dislodge the lump forming there. "The one you got from Zack. Where did that little bugger go?"

She walked into her room and sank to her knees with the screaming baby in her arms, digging through the luggage she hadn't had the energy to unpack. In truth, she wasn't ready to let go of the trip and put everything that happened behind her.

She wasn't willing to accept that she might never see Zack again. And that Phoenix might grow up with only her stories and photos to tell him who his father was. He wasn't just the leather-jacketed bad boy in magazines and music videos.

He was the love of her life. And when given the opportunity, he was an incredible dad. She felt certain he'd find a way to be in their son's life because their bond was undeniable.

Despite his mistake, his intentions were good. Despite his, Adam's, and Charlotte's insistence that was the case, it hadn't sunken in until she had a long talk with Ted. Everything Zack said aligned with Ted's account, and surprisingly, he encouraged her to give Zack another chance. The lengths he'd gone to for her safety and happiness impressed Ted and earned his respect.

And once he heard how well Zack and Phoenix got along, he pleaded with her to forgive him so they could be a family.

While her reaction to Zack's dishonesty was justified, she shouldn't have shut him out. His protectiveness was one of the qualities she loved most about him, and it set everything in motion. He'd forgiven her for her massive secret, but she'd failed to offer the same grace for his.

Again, Mandy had underestimated him, and again, she talked herself out of the life she wanted. He probably hadn't reached out because he was tired of having to defend himself. And why would he want to be with someone who kept pushing him away?

When she reached the bottom of her suitcase and came up empty, tears pricked her eyes. With Phoenix crying in her ear, she plopped down on the floor and joined him. He tucked his head into her neck, and she rocked them both forward and back, trying to soothe a hollow, gnawing ache that might never go away.

Phoenix's lip curled down in a pout. "Dack."

She gasped. Was that an actual *word*? His babbling was usually more of a string of vowels and consonants, but that was plain as day.

"Did you say... Dack?" A baby book she'd read said "z" is one of the hardest letter sounds to make. Was he trying to say what she thought he was trying to say?

He cried louder, punching his knee with his tiny, angry fist. "Dack!"

She grabbed a photo Zack's friend had taken of the three of them in Paris to confirm her suspicion. "Is this Dack?"

"Dack!" He slapped Zack's face in the photo, and again, she joined him on the floor to cry it out together.

His first word. He'd only known Zack for a week, and he was asking for him. Of course, he was. Zack was funny and kind, with a magnetic personality that made life more fun.

"I know, sweetheart." She held him against her chest, his tiny, racing heart-beat fluttering over hers. "I'm sorry he isn't here with us."

She almost didn't hear the knock at the door over his crying, but she pushed off the floor to answer it. For a fleeting second, she imagined a handsome, dark-haired rockstar on her porch, but she was more likely to find her neighbor's dogshit after treating Zack like exactly that.

Go ahead, Fido. Do your worst. I deserve it.

She opened the door to find her mom's frowning face.

"What's wrong with my grandson?" She reached for the baby, taking him into her arms and bouncing him on her hip. "I could hear his screaming from the driveway."

"He woke up from his nap crying and hasn't stopped. I think he wants his toy frog." Mentioning Zack would start an argument she didn't have the energy or patience for. "Have you seen it in any of your stuff?"

"No." Her mom's nose wrinkled. "Phoenix kept dropping it on the hotel room floor, and it was full of germs. Good riddance."

Mandy grimaced at her callousness, throwing up her hands. "He drops all his toys. You don't like the frog because of who gave it to him."

"Guilty."

Phoenix's face reddened, and his fists balled tightly as he wailed.

Mandy dug through his bag, pulling out a stuffed penguin with a bowtie. "What about Mr. Fancypants? He came all the way from Antarctica to be your friend." She made the penguin dance on his knee. He grabbed the toy and tossed it across the room, but not in his usual playful way. More like he wanted to chuck the penguin straight back to the icy wasteland hell from whence it came. As he cried even louder, she took him back. "I'm sorry you're upset, sweetheart. Are you cutting a new tooth?"

"Dack," he pleaded through his tears.

Her mom's head cocked before she shook it. "I'll... grab a ring from the freezer."

"No, I've got it."

On the way to the kitchen, Mandy blew a loud raspberry into his neck—usually, a foolproof way to end the crying and trigger his amazing laugh. It didn't work. She grabbed a teething ring from the freezer and gave it to him, but he chucked it to the floor. She held him flush against her chest, bouncing and rubbing his back.

"I miss him too," she whispered in his ear. Of course, she didn't mean the frog. Zack and Phoenix built a genuine connection, and it shattered her heart to know her son was hurting, too.

"Why were you crying?" her mom asked, brushing hair from Mandy's face.

Mandy plopped onto the couch. "I know you don't want to hear it, but I miss Zack." Fresh tears spilled down her cheeks, and she wiped them away.

Her mom sat beside her, taking Phoenix into her lap. "Phoenix deserves a good man in his life, even if that man isn't his father by blood. You deserve better, too. I'm glad he finally understands that."

Mandy's gaze narrowed. "What do you mean he finally understands?"

Her mom bounced Phoenix on her knee before waving a dismissive hand. "It doesn't matter. All that matters now is the future. I ran into Steven at church, and he'd love to see you both now that you're back."

Mandy's tears dried on her cheeks as she scrutinized her mother's suspiciously neutral expression. "What did you say to Zack when he came to your room looking for me?"

"Nothing he didn't already know."

"Such as?"

She sighed as if the question irritated her. "That being a father takes more than writing checks and playing house for a week. He's not going to shuttle Phoenix to soccer and go to PTA meetings. I told him it's best if he returns to his ridiculous, sinful lifestyle so you can be with someone like Steven who'd give Phoenix siblings and be a decent role model."

Mandy gaped at her mother, speechless, as anger set her skin on fire.

Was that why he hadn't called? When they broke up before, he left message after message, so his silence was a surprise and disappointment.

Was he at home thinking they were better off without him?

Mandy took the baby, marched to the front door, and swung it wide. "Get out."

Phoenix quieted, his gaze darting between them.

"Mandy Marie!"

"I'm grateful for everything you've done for us, but you had *no right* to make Zack feel like he wasn't good enough for us. I love him. He loves me. It's my fault he didn't get to know Phoenix before and learn how to be a father, but he was trying so hard. You didn't even attempt to see it or give him credit. You judged him like you judge me and everyone else who doesn't live exactly like you do."

"He's a loser, Mandy! All the money in the world won't change that."

Mandy kicked the door shut. "I don't give a flying *fuck* about his money. He's a good man who followed his dreams and became successful because he's talented and works his ass off. He's an incredible friend, willing to drop anything when they need him. And I've never been with someone who makes me feel so treasured and beautiful. You make me feel fat and inadequate."

Her mom's face flushed with red. "Stop this right now!"

"He showed me everything I missed out on by being brainwashed into feeling afraid and ashamed of anything that felt good." She opened the door again. "You betrayed me and Phoenix by making Zack think we're better off without him. If he stays away because of it, then you robbed my son of his father and me of a future with the only man I've ever loved. You need to leave."

Her mom stood, smoothing the front of her flowery pink blouse. "If trying to save my daughter from herself is a betrayal, fine. If you get back together, it'll be your worst mistake. When you figure that out, don't come crying on my doorstep, asking for forgiveness for the horrible things you just said."

"Don't worry, Mom. I won't be asking you for anything else."

Her mom's eyes darted between Mandy and Phoenix before lingering on him with a tight frown. "We'll see about that." She stomped out the door with her head held undeservedly high.

Mandy shut and locked the door, smiling at Phoenix so he wouldn't worry. "What do you think, Nixy? Can we fix this?"

He smiled back, his chubby pink cheeks lifting. She gave another neck raspberry a shot, and this time, his head tipped back as he giggled. The tension from arguing with her mom melted away, and in its place, ideas rushed in—possible ways of mending what her mother, Zack's insecurities, and Mandy's trust issues had broken.

"Phoenix..." A wide grin bloomed on her face at the possibilities ahead. "It's time we had a brand-new start."

41

Zack

Zack white-knuckled the steering wheel of his rental car as he sat outside Mandy's house. The place had her written all over it—the grass-green siding with white trim, the purple and blue flowers lining garden beds beneath the windows, and the wind chime with swirling silver musical notes hanging from the porch. He could imagine all the hard work she'd put in and the sacrifices she'd made to give Phoenix a nice, loving home to grow up in.

Mandy was still miles out of Zack's league, but hopefully, she still loved him anyway.

He'd thought Europe was his last shot at proving he could be the man she deserved, but no. This was it. Right now.

He was out of chances.

In between shows and other band duties, he'd spent their four weeks apart rearranging his life to prepare for this. But even if she didn't want him, he had to learn to be the father his son deserved. As nervous as he was about taking on that role and its responsibilities for the rest of his life, he refused to let Phoenix grow up thinking his dad didn't want him.

He'd rather try, make mistakes, and learn from them than quit.

Before he knew Phoenix existed, Zack never thought he'd want the life he was there to fight for. But now that he'd heard his son laugh, felt his tiny body relax in his arms while he fell asleep, and saw how happy he made Mandy, there was no going back. He wouldn't want to. And no matter what her thickheaded mother or anyone else thought about him, he wasn't going anywhere.

He hadn't reached out to Mandy since Paris because he didn't want to keep any more secrets and knew she'd try to talk him out of what he'd planned. Being minutes away from sharing those plans with her had him feeling nervous but determined. And so fucking excited by the possibility that it would all work out.

Finally, he released the steering wheel and marched to her front door, knocking softly in case Phoenix was asleep. He remembered that naptime came right after lunch, and it was twelve-thirty.

A shadow fell over the peephole, and the door flung open. Mandy's beautiful hazel eyes were wide as they met his. She clutched the doorknob in one hand and a small blue envelope in the other with his name written on the front.

"Zack." Her bottom lip trembled before she trapped it between her teeth. "What are you doing here?"

He pulled the stuffed green frog from his pocket and held it out. "I found this at the hotel. Phoenix must've dropped it. I thought he might miss it."

She released the doorknob and took the toy, their fingertips brushing. "You came all the way here to bring this?"

"I bought Rollin' Rockies." He had a lot of news to share, and that was the easiest to start with.

"You *what*?"

"I had my lawyer make the fuckwad an offer too good to pass up. He didn't deserve to own something only great because you made it that way." Her mouth fell open, but she said nothing, so he continued. "If you want to run it, it's yours. Or I can sell it back to Ted or his son. Whatever you think is best."

She touched her chest, a single tear slipping down her cheek. "I can't believe you did that. Is that why you're in Denver? To buy the club?"

He let out a stunted laugh, the full scope of his recent wave of major decisions sinking in. "No. I'm moving here."

Her eyes popped wider. "You're *what*?" Shock looked adorable on her.

"I'm staying at the Estes Suites for now, but I'll look for a house next week."

"A house? Are you serious? What about your band?"

"I quit."

Mandy gasped, horror overtaking her expression. "No! You can't!"

He shrugged. "Already did. I..." He paused, shaking off the echo of Jill's words. "I wondered if you were both better off without me, but that's bullshit. I want to watch Phoenix grow up, and he deserves to know his dad. That's not possible from a thousand miles away. As for us..." He shifted his feet, a rush of nerves tightening his belly over what he was about to say. "I don't expect you to trust me again until I can prove myself, but I hope you'll give me one last chance. I'd give you the cliché line that no one will ever love you this much, but look at you. Of course, they will. Who wouldn't love you? I just wanted us to be together so badly I fucked it all up. I'm sorry." His gaze slid inside the house to where Phoenix must be sleeping and back to her. "To both of you."

She held out the envelope. "I'm sorry, too. You hurt me, but shutting you out was a mistake."

He took it, tearing the seal. He pulled out a small card with a bright green frog on the front, hugging a big number one. Inside were the details for Phoenix's first birthday party in five weeks. He smiled, knowing it was a good sign she'd planned to invite him.

"Zack, you can't move to Denver."

His gaze dropped to his feet as her words kicked him in the chest. He slipped the card into his pocket. "I'm sorry I hurt you, Mandy. Please let me prove that I—"

"Stop." She set the toy on a table by the front door and grabbed his shoulders, their gazes colliding. "You can't move here because we're moving to Portland."

"You're *what*?" It was his turn to look shocked, but there was probably nothing adorable about his stupid mouth hanging open. Was she serious? If so, what did it mean for their relationship?

She laughed, her eyes glittering in the sunlight. "There's nothing left for us here. I'm selling my house. And I offered to manage Toxic Shade, but they're moving to Seattle. That's perfect since it's only a three-hour commute from Portland. I had a contract drawn up, and I'm officially their manager."

A massive smile overtook his face as it sank in.

She did it.

"Mandy, that's fucking incredible. I'm so proud of you."

"I appreciate that you've always believed in me. And you're right—Phoenix deserves to know you. So, we're moving to make that happen."

"You're moving to Portland." Even saying the words out loud didn't make them feel real. But was she only moving for Phoenix?

"I'll have to drive up to Seattle for meetings and their gigs, but I'll talk to Charlotte about swapping babysitting duties. Since we make our own hours most of the time, it'll be great for both of us."

"Are you serious? This isn't some joke or dream or fucked-up acid flash-back?"

She laughed as her hand rose to touch his face. His knees nearly buckled as he leaned into the comforting warmth of her soft skin that he'd spent four long weeks aching for.

"Yes, I'm serious. Phoenix and I are moving to Portland. Is it safe to say you still want us?"

Us. She said "us." The move wasn't just for Phoenix.

His smile grew as he hitched an eyebrow. "Have I not made that clear enough by showing up on your porch?"

"Good point," she said with a sweet, melodic laugh that he felt in every cell, a glowing warmth that chased away the last of the darkness he'd lived in since their last kiss. "But let *me* make something clear. It might be tempting to pull strings for me when I live in your town, but no more messing with my career. When I make it, I make it on my own. Understood?"

"I promise. From now on, the only strings I touch will be on my bass guitars."

"And you can't quit your band." She stepped closer and took his hand, her gaze dipping to his mouth and back up again. "I appreciate why you did it, but I never meant for you to choose between us and them. You can have both. Call Tyler and fix it."

He tucked a lock of hair behind her ear, still in disbelief that he was here, touching her. "Can I kiss you first?"

Her pretty pink mouth curled up at the corners. "Have I not made that clear enough by eye-fucking you on my porch?"

Unable to wait another second, Zack wrapped his arms around her waist and pressed his grinning lips to hers, kissing her as the disbelief morphed into warm, glittery bliss. Her hands slipped to the back of his neck, pulling him closer as she tipped her head and deepened the kiss. Their tongues tangled as their bodies pressed together, his cock already hard and begging to be inside her.

Someone across the street wolf-whistled, and he broke the kiss.

"We're giving the neighbors a free show." Zack looked in the direction of the sound to find an elderly couple giving them the thumbs-up before returning to trimming their hedges.

Zack and Mandy waved as they laughed.

"I'd rather give you one." She turned to him, the hunger in her eyes shooting straight to his aching cock. "You're going to call Tyler and un-quit," she said, pressing a quick kiss to his lips, "right after I show you my bedroom."

Hell. Yes.

"Phoenix is asleep, so we have to be quiet." Her hand fisted in his shirt, tugging him close as she walked backward inside the house. "No easy feat with your skills."

She shut and locked the door before grabbing his hand and leading him towards the rear of the house and into her bedroom. It was bright and cozy, like her old apartment, and his gaze caught on a photo on the wall of the two of them in Dallas, kissing under an awning in the rain. The laminate from that night's show hung beside it.

"I always wondered if you kept these," he said, touching the photo. "This one's my favorite."

All this time, she'd held on to him in her own ways—the photos, the laminate, his music. They'd never truly let each other go. And it felt like they'd finally reached the point where they never would.

"Mine too."

He moved to face her, grabbing the hem of his shirt and dragging it up and over his head. She gasped, her eyes snapping wide as she studied the tattoo of a red and black phoenix etched over the broken center of the heart on his chest.

"It's beautiful." She reached out and ran her fingertips over the ink. "You got this for him?"

Zack nodded, covering her hand with his and holding it to his chest. "I love you. And I love our son. Now that I know how it feels to be a part of a family with you... I'm ready to buy the ticket and take the ride."

She took his smiling face into her hands as she laughed. "I love you too, you crazy, impulsive weirdo. And I appreciate the Hunter quote. Now fuck me before *I* go crazy."

"I've got news for you, baby. If you're with me, you're already there."

42

Zack

Six Weeks Later

Everything at Mandy's house sat in boxes in the living room, waiting for the moving truck to arrive in a few days. The only things left out were the diaper bag, a few clothes, and whatever else they'd need before the flight to Portland in a week. Zack was eager to return home so his band could get cracking on the new album. Tyler and Adam were thrilled when he told them he was back in and signed the contract, but they vowed to kick his ass for quitting.

He set a box of photographs on the kitchen table. Mandy didn't want them getting damaged in the truck, so they'd be going on the plane. Her laughter echoed through the house, followed by another of his favorite sounds—Phoenix was laughing, too.

Zack headed into the nursery to find her sitting in the rocking chair by the window with Phoenix lying in her lap, facing her. She was expanding her cheeks with air and letting them shrink, something Phoenix found hilarious.

"Having fun?" Zack bent over, pressing a quick kiss to her lips. Then, he bent further to kiss the center of Phoenix's forehead. "I'm glad you appreciate this lady so much, little dude."

"It's weird seeing this place empty. We've been here so long."

"Portland will feel like home before you know it."

Phoenix craned his neck to look up at him, little hands reaching out. "Dack!"

Zack smiled at the request, scooping him up from his armpits and holding him close. It felt more natural every day to carry Phoenix around and figure out what he needed. It helped that he was sturdier, better at communicating, and less intimidating than tiny Anna Jude. He'd even started saying more words like "Mama," "bye," and "frog," although that one sounded more like Zack's favorite curse word than the animal.

"You'll love it there, too, bud," Zack said. "I'll show you the ducks at Waterfront Park, the rides at Enchanted Forest, and I can show your mom our killer music scene. And your other grandparents can't wait to meet you."

His phone buzzed in his pocket. He peeked at the message, biting back a grin as he pulled out his keys. "I'll grab us lunch. Any requests?"

"I'd love one last Tsunami Burger."

"You got it, gorgeous."

He kissed her cheek, still in disbelief that this was his life. Waking up beside Mandy, coming home to her beautiful face. And their son. He had a son. That still blew his mind, but she was always patient as he learned to be a dad. He still hadn't mastered changing a diaper without getting pissed on, but he'd figured out how to snap complicated onesies, pick out the organic baby food without the weird chunks in it, and navigate playgroups full of normies without offending anyone. In fact, a couple of the moms got a little flirty with him one day at the park. Of course, Mandy had nothing to worry about, but it was hot as fuck watching her stake her claim by shooting death glares at the ladies with her hand on his knee.

As they headed to the kitchen, he blew raspberries on Phoenix's neck, making them both laugh. Fart noises were funny no matter how old you were.

"You're getting your first milkshake today, kid. Since you wore more ice cream at your party than you ate, I think sucking it through a straw is more your speed."

Phoenix's first birthday party was a week ago. Mandy wasn't sure if her parents would show up and was almost as shocked as Zack when Jill walked up to him and apologized for being so awful. Then, she apologized to Mandy and promised to do better. Whether she only did it to stay in Phoenix's life or was truly remorseful was anyone's guess, but peace was better for everyone.

"Grab a strawberry one for me, please." Mandy took Phoenix and buckled him into his highchair.

"You got it." Zack pinched her chin and kissed her again, savoring her soft lips, knowing it could be their last one for a while. "See you soon, gorgeous."

Once in the car, he gripped the steering wheel so hard he thought it might crack. A surge of white-hot rage simmered his blood on the drive to Rollin' Rockies. As the private investigator he'd hired assured him in the text message, the BMW with the scratched driver's side sat alone in the parking lot.

He knocked on the front door of the club, willing the universe to make that fucking asshole answer even though it was hours before the place opened.

In four more days, it would officially be Zack's.

The door cracked a few inches, and half of James Sutter's douchey blond head peeked out. Zack recognized him from the photos the P.I. had faxed last week.

"Can I help you?"

Zack shoved open the door, the force knocking James off balance. He grabbed the doorframe to right himself, but Zack shoved him backward, and James fell hard on his ass.

"Who the hell are you?" His petrified shouts echoed in the empty room as he tried to scramble off the scuffed, black vinyl floor. With a steel-toe boot on the asshole's chest, Zack shoved him back down. "There's no cash here!"

Zack laughed, the sound as dark and menacing as he felt. "I have a shit ton more money than you do, fuckhead. I'm not here to rob you."

"Hey." His eyebrows furrowed as he focused on Zack's face. "I recognize you. You're in that band. The one Mandy toured with."

Zack's jaw clenched, his molars grinding so hard a muscle popped in his jaw. "You will *not* say her name. Keeping tabs on my girl just earned you an extra black eye."

James's soon-to-be-blackened eyes rounded with panic as he rose to his feet. This time, Zack let him stand. He wanted a fair fight, but there was no way this fucker was landing a punch.

"You don't have to hit me." James's voice trembled like the hands he held in the air. Maybe he'd piss himself. "I'll never contact her, never bother her."

"You're right." Zack cracked his knuckles, every muscle taut and aching to make this bastard suffer. "I don't have to hit you." He stepped forward, his fist slamming into the shithead's nose with the swift jab his dad taught him. Bones cracked against his knuckles with a resounding snap. "I fucking *need* to."

James cried out, his hands flying to his busted face. He turned and tried to run, but Zack was on him before he reached the bar, grabbing his shoulders and spinning him around. Blood trickled from his nose, flowing over his lips and onto the front of his perfect, tailored douchebag suit.

"Put up your fucking hands," Zack demanded. "You think you can talk to a woman like you did and not have to face the fucking consequences?"

James's hands remained at his sides, violently shaking and coated in blood. "I'm sorry. I shouldn't have—"

Zack drove his fist into the shithead's left eye, and James shouted a curse before crumpling in half. He rushed forward, his shoulder slamming into Zack's stomach. It hurt and stole his breath for a second, but he laughed, stepping back and jamming his knee into James's right eye to make it match its twin.

"Goddamn it!" James staggered to his feet, covering his battered face with his hands. "What do you want from me?!"

"Drop your hands." Zack's tone was as cold as his limbs, the adrenaline of the fight draining and satisfaction setting in. He watched as James lowered his hands and stepped backward, putting a few feet between them. "That's what I want. To see you bloody and ugly. You made my girl feel ugly, but she's so fucking beautiful you didn't deserve to breathe the same air." Zack spat at James's feet, his knuckles throbbing. "By the way, she got you on tape. If you try to sue me, I have people who'll make it really fucking public what a shitwad you are."

"I won't do that." James grimaced, his eyes glassy and wide. "I'm sorry."

Zack scoffed. "Fuck your 'sorry.' Next time you try talking to or treating a woman like that, think about this. Today. Think about someone who loves her hunting you down and beating the shit out of you, and ask yourself if it's worth it." He turned to leave but stopped, turning back to face the man with the red, bloody face that'd be purple in a few hours. "It probably goes without saying, but if you call her, look for her, or even fucking *breathe her name*, I'll find you. And I'll put you in the fucking ground."

Zack returned to his car with a mile-wide shit-eating grin. Relief from weeks of pent-up rage washed over him. He'd split a few knuckles, streaked with the bastard's blood, but they'd heal.

He hit the drive-thru at Mandy's favorite burger place and returned to her house feeling like a ten-ton weight had lifted off his chest—his last piece of unfinished business, finished.

Now, they could go to Portland, settle in, and start their life together.

When he walked inside the house, carrying food and milkshakes, Mandy was in the kitchen.

"Hey, handsome." She took the food, dug into the bag, and set the burgers and fries on the table. "You took so long I had to put Phoenix down for his nap. Was there a line?"

He walked to the kitchen sink and turned on the tap, washing the blood off his knuckles. "Yeah, must be the lunch rush." He dried off and sat beside her, picking up his burger. "All ready to go?"

Her gaze dropped to his hands as he brought his burger to his mouth. "Oh, my god. What happened to your hand?" Her words came out in a rush as she gently touched a sore knuckle.

"Don't worry, I'm fine." He bit down on a fry and chased it with a long sip of strawberry shake. "Did the movers call?"

Her eyes skittered over his face. "Yeah, they'll be here Thursday."

Three hard knocks startled her. Her gaze darted between Zack and the door before she got up to look through the peephole. She gasped, but he already knew what was waiting on the other side.

He hated to make her worry, but if he'd told her what he'd planned to do, she would've tried talking him out of giving James the beatdown he deserved.

"It's the *cops*!" she hissed in a whisper. "What the hell did you do?"

He stood, taking her face into his hands. "I'm sorry to make you worry. I couldn't let him get away with hurting you. I fucking needed to hurt him back."

She drew in a sharp breath. "James? You hit him? Is he okay?"

Zack chuckled, lifting a shoulder. "Sort of. I didn't kill or permanently injure him if that's what you're asking. A few black eyes and probably a broken nose." Although he wanted to do more damage, he'd purposely held back. He couldn't risk serious jail time, and the line between assault and attempted murder was narrow and not one he intended to cross. Especially now that he had so much to lose.

"You can't just..." She stepped back. "How could you..."

He waited for her to finish a sentence, but she lunged forward, her lips crashing against his. She pushed him until his back hit the kitchen wall.

"That's the sweetest, most fucked-up thing anyone's ever done for me," she said against his mouth. "Are you going to jail?"

"Don't worry, baby." He stroked her cheek, locking away every detail of her face to get him through the next few shitty hours. "I have an amazing lawyer. I'll be out before dinnertime. I'll have to fly back for court, pay a fine, and it's over. Not my first rodeo."

"I love you." Mandy shook her head. "When I bail your crazy, sexy ass out of jail, I'll show you how much." Her hands slid up the back of his shirt, and he groaned as her fingernails dragged along his skin. "Then, we're going to have a long talk about how violence isn't the answer."

"I love you too, gorgeous." He smiled at the warm affection in her eyes as she picked up his hand, kissing each of his sore knuckles.

Three more hard knocks shook the door. "Denver Police. Open up."

She took a deep breath and opened it. "Hi, officers. My baby's asleep, so please keep the noise down."

"Sorry, ma'am." The officer was short but built, and it was hard not to laugh at his mutton chop sideburns that resembled glued-on pubes. "We have a warrant for the arrest of Zachary Maine. We were told he might be at this residence. Is he here?"

"Yeah." Zack stepped forward. "I'm here."

"Put your hands behind your back," Side Burns said. Zack did as instructed, and the cop's partner slapped on the handcuffs. "You're under arrest for the assault of James Sutter. You have the right to remain silent."

The cop rambled on, but Zack's eyes stayed locked with Mandy's. She mouthed *I love you*, and he felt that love as her soft gaze stayed on him.

"Take the bail money from my account," he said. "If you need anything, call Ty or Adam."

The officers walked him to their patrol car and put him in the back seat. At least they were nice about it and didn't shove him around.

Mandy blew him a kiss through the car window, hugging herself with tears in her eyes before the car pulled out of the driveway and headed down the street.

"So," Side Burns began, "want to tell us why you beat the guy's face into ground beef?"

Zack shifted in his seat so the handcuffs wouldn't pinch his skin. "He hurt my girl. Trust me, he deserved it."

Side Burns met his eye in the rearview mirror. "Yeah, the officer who took the report said he was a dick. Kind of wanted to punch him himself." He laughed. "I know the circumstances aren't ideal, but I'm a fan. Your last album was epic."

Now, it made sense. Guys who looked like Zack didn't get gentle treatment from cops, especially after kicking someone's ass. He grinned to himself, appreciating yet another surprise perk of his job.

"Thanks. Wait until you hear the next one."

Epilogue

ZACK

Four Months Later

Mandy left the bedroom of their Denver suite with a phone to her ear and a silky red dress hugging every luscious curve of her body. Her long legs were on full display and begging to be wrapped around Zack's hips as he fucked her until she screamed his name. Unfortunately, the fucking and screaming would have to wait. There was no way she'd go to Ted's retirement party with smeared makeup and sex-ruffled hair. And whoever was at the other end of the line might not appreciate the audio porn.

She smiled, probably recognizing the lust in his expression. "Thank you so much for this opportunity. I look forward to working with you." Her smile grew. "You too. Have a fabulous weekend." She closed her mobile phone and slipped it into her purse.

"You're killing me with that dress, baby." He grabbed her wrist below the bracelet he'd given her, tugging her to his chest. Three diamonds sparkled where the silver was engraved with the words: *Don't think, just feel*. Her overthinking still sometimes led to unnecessary stress, but she was better at shutting it down and letting go to savor the moment. He pressed a kiss to her lips, not giving the slightest fuck if he came away stained with her sexy red lipstick. "I hope you're not too attached because I'll be tearing it off you the second we're back in this room."

Phoenix was spending the night with her parents. Despite their lingering issues with Zack and Mandy being together and moving to Portland, it had nothing to do with Phoenix. He loved his grandparents and deserved to spend time with them whenever possible.

"Turn it into confetti for all I care." She kissed him back before wiping her lipstick off his mouth with her thumb. "Wait until you see what's hiding underneath. I treated myself to some fancy lingerie, and after the party, we'll make the most of our rare kid-free night."

"Oh, yeah?" He slowly slid the hem of her dress up her thigh. "How are we going to do that?"

"You're going to fuck me on that table wearing nothing but your leather jacket."

He growled at the mental image, his cock already half-hard as the room phone rang. She answered, saying nothing but "Hello" and "Thank you" before hanging up.

"The driver's downstairs. I'm looking forward to tossing back a few cocktails and dancing with the hottest guy in the room."

He still wasn't drinking much, but it felt like a champagne kind of night. "Who were you talking to when you walked in?"

"I was going to wait to tell you when we returned to the room, but I can't help it." Her hands slipped around his waist. "It was Cassie Rose. I'm hired."

A shout of joy escaped Zack's lips as he grabbed her hips and lifted her into the air while she laughed. "That's amazing, baby! I'm so fucking proud of you!"

"Me too. My third and biggest client." The glow of pride in her eyes flared as he set her back on her feet and kissed her.

"It's all up from here," he murmured against her lips.

"Damn right." Her eyes flicked to the clock on the wall. "We need to go."

His hand snaked up the inside of her thigh, his fingertips stroking the bare skin above the black lace trim of her stocking. "Or we could stay here and do the leather jacket table thing."

Pink colored her cheeks as she grinned, swatting his hand away. "Later. I wouldn't miss Ted's sendoff for anything, even that."

Zack was excited to finally meet him in person. Ted was visiting his wife's family in Maine when Zack was in Denver, so they'd never had an opportunity to get together. He owed a lot to the man, including the second and third chances with the gorgeous woman he'd never be foolish enough to let go of again.

The party was in full swing when they walked into Rollin' Rockies. Blue and green streamers trailed from the ceiling, and a disco ball sent shimmering bursts of color around the room. At least three hundred people filled the space—some faces he recognized from bands he'd seen perform, read about, or toured with. The Who blared from the speakers, Roger Daltrey's powerful, legendary pipes demanding that the squares who don't understand their music fade away.

Mandy took his hand, leading him toward a man with black hair peppered with gray and a wide, warm smile that made the corners of his eyes crinkle. He clutched a bottle of beer, surrounded by a dozen people listening to him talk, his hands gesturing wildly as he spoke.

The man's head turned, his smile growing when he spotted them. "Mandy Marie Reid! Get over here and give this old man a hug."

She wrapped her arms around him and squeezed. "Old, my ass. Retirement looks good on you, boss." She let him go, aiming a thumb at Zack. "I'm sure you need no introduction to your co-conspirator."

Ted laughed, offering his hand before Zack shook it. "Glad to finally meet you, son. I hope you're treating her right. You've got a real gem here."

"Trust me..." Zack laced his fingers with hers. "I know."

"Thanks again for selling the club to my son. He's got all the old staff back, and the place is doing better than ever. We're all grateful James didn't have enough time to run it into the ground." Ted leaned close to Zack's ear. "And good job rearranging that asshole's face."

Zack laughed as Ted patted him on the back. "My pleasure. Worth every penny of the fines and court fees."

After a few hours of mingling, drinks, and dancing, the crowd had thinned. The music's volume lowered, and the song, "This Magic Moment," was perfect for what Zack had planned. In the seven months since Mandy returned to his life with Phoenix in tow, he woke up every day feeling grateful and lucky for everything he had.

Hopefully, that luck didn't change in the next few minutes.

He slipped his hands into his pockets as his palms began to sweat. When Mandy was done catching up with an old coworker who looked like an alternate for Metallica, Zack slid a hand around her waist and led her toward the hallway. Fortunately, no one was hanging around that area of the club, so they'd have some privacy.

"We are not having sex in the bathroom," she whispered in his ear.

He chuckled and kept walking. "Tempting, but that's not what I have in mind."

When they reached the spot where they first collided, he stopped. She burst out laughing, taking in the sight of two dozen CD cases scattered across the floor. He'd slipped a caterer fifty bucks to make the mess and clean it up after it'd served its purpose. The guy was understandably confused but came through anyway.

"What is all this?"

Zack took her hand and sank to one knee. "Mandy, I love you."

Her breath caught as her free hand clamped over her mouth. "Oh. My. God."

"Crashing into you, right at this spot, was the best fucking thing that ever happened to me." He pulled the small box from his pocket and opened it, holding it out with a trembling hand. "There's nothing I won't do to make you and Phoenix happy. And any other cool, sock-chucking kids that come along. Will you marry me?"

She swiped a knuckle beneath her eyes as she laughed. "Crashing into you made my neat little life loud, messy, and complicated. And so much better in every possible fucking way. Of course, I'll marry you."

He slipped the ring on her shaking finger before pulling her into his arms and kissing her, surrounded by the scattered CDs.

"Another one bites the fucking dust," he murmured against her lips.

Her head cocked. "Huh?"

"Nothing, baby." He kissed her again.

Every messy, loud, and beautiful moment they'd shared since they met played through his mind like a movie—every touch, every fight, every smile she ever gave him. At the end came the happily ever after he didn't even know he wanted until she came along.

Mandy showed him what love was, and he woke up the fun, adventurous rebel inside her who had gone into hiding as she struggled to do too much on her own. Now, they were partners, balancing each other's extremes while working together to give their son the life he deserved.

It took a lot of heartbreak and struggle to get to that moment, but Zack would've done it all over again. Now, their future would be filled with friends, family, loud rock music, and the love that held it all together.

And no more regrets.

Acknowledgements

First, I'd like to thank my amazing husband, Jason, who's always been my first reader (and listener). Again, your musician-related advice saved me from a lot of googling and frustration, and I appreciated the high-fives and hugs when I needed them. I adore all my books, but our love story is still my favorite.

Thanks to my beloved long-time bestie, Melanie, for taking the time to read anything I sent despite your crazy schedule and kid-wrangling duties. Your thoughts have always been absolute gold to me, from what vacuum to buy to whether I should swap one filthy word for another.

And thank you to my other beautiful BFF, Tracy, my most enthusiastic cheerleader on this book journey. You helped me achieve the massive dream of getting on bookstore shelves and were always ready to listen to me vent when my characters went on a rampage in my brain.

Thanks to my boys for all the tech help, TikTok knowledge, encouraging words, and for always supporting me even though I don't write horror like you wish I did. Maybe someday.

Special thanks to my incredible editor, Misha Carlstedt. You challenged me to dig deeper into my characters' minds and hearts, and your guidance has made me grow as an author in ways I never imagined. I'm grateful for your insight and expertise, which helped me to shape this story into one I'm incredibly proud of.

Thank you to my brilliant team of critique partners, Ellie, Bella, Sara, and Theresa, for all the priceless feedback and support that have made this journey so much sweeter. It's been a joy working with such talented women who understand the exhilarating and sometimes maddening rollercoaster of being an indie author. May we continue lifting each other up and cheering each other on for many books to come.

Thank you to Newsboy Books, Grand Gesture Books, and Literary Leftovers for carrying my series, creating blissful spaces for us bookworms, and making so many authors' dreams come true.

Last, but certainly not least, a HUGE thank you to my readers! If this is your first Bridge City Beats book, I'm grateful you decided to take the ride. If you've been with me since the beginning, thanks for staying buckled in. I hope you love these characters as much as I do, and I can't wait to show you what's coming up next!

About the author

Stephanie Louise has been obsessed with books since *Charlotte's Web* broke her heart when she was seven. She wrote short stories and poetry growing up, and now writes love stories set in the Pacific Northwest that contain angsty elements tempered with sweetness, humor, and spice.

Stephanie lives in beautiful Washington State with her husband, two sons, and a gaggle of adorable pets. She has a B.A. in English from Washington State University. When she's not writing, she's hiking in the rain, going to rock concerts, eating chocolate, or cooking something loaded with garlic.

Website and Newsletter Sign-Up: www.stephanie-louise.com

Email: stephanielouisebooks@gmail.com

Instagram: instagram.com/authorstephanielouise

Goodreads: http://www.goodreads.com/user/show/171231652

Facebook: facebook.com/authorstephanielouise